SILVERCREST ACADEMY
DESTINED SHADOWS

KC KEAN

Destined Shadows
Silvercrest Academy #2
Copyright © 2023 KC Kean

www.authorkckean.com
Published by Featherstone Publishing Ltd

KC Kean has asserted her right under the Copyright, Designs and Patents Act 1988, to be identified as Author of this work.
All rights reserved. No part of this publication may be reproduced or transmitted in any form or by any means, electronic or mechanical, including photocopying, record, or any information storage or retrieval system, without prior permission in writing from the publisher.
Thank you for respecting the hard work of this author.
This is a work of fiction. Names, characters, places, brands, media, and incidents are either the product of the authors imagination or are used fictitiously. The author acknowledges the trademark status and trademark owners of various products referred to in this work of fiction, which have been used without permission. The publication/ use of these trademarks is not authorised, associated with, or sponsored by the trademark owners.

Cover Design: DARK IMAGINARIUM Art & Design
Editing: Encompass Editing
Proofreader: Sassi's Editing Services
Interior Formatting & Design: Wild Elegance Formatting

Destined Shadows/KC Kean– 1st ed.
ISBN-13 -

To Nan,

I love you, from now until the end of time.
No one is stronger than you, no one fights harder than you,
no one loves as fiercely as you.
You are my idol, my queen, my everything.
To know you and to love you is a gift, to be loved by you is
more than words can say.
Keep fighting our queen, we're right here at your side.

Your Princess

ELIVEN REALM

AMBERGLEN

SHADOWMOOR

Haven Court

Crest
emy

Pinebrook

dale

Wastelands

lica Realm

KC KEAN

I might not have known then what secrets you were keeping, but I knew the fear in your eyes was real. If I ever saw that in the eyes of one of my own children, I would tear this world to pieces.

ONE
Raven

Darkness consumes me, threading around my veins, piercing my heart, and labeling me something I don't dare to believe. Twisted, torn, and in denial is how I sit, arms banded tightly around my bent legs as I rock slightly in the corner of the room.

My vision is blurred, a black, white, and gray hue to everything I see.

Everything but *him*.

I can't look, it's blinding.

He's blinding.

Latching my gaze on to my filthy hands, I stare at the grime etched into every crease and ridge of my fingerprints. My throat burns from screaming and my chest aches from the sobs that wracked my entire body, leaving me silent and cocooned in a room filled with people.

Dead bodies remain scattered across the floor, medics entering and taking them away one at a time. Finn. Gone. The enemies. Gone.

Smoke marks tarnish every inch of the office I woke in earlier, and I still can't recall how I ended up here. My head throbs as a reminder that something knocked me out. My last memory before this room was the tower collapsing. Everything else after that was black until I woke up here. Drenched in carnage.

I tighten my hold around my knees and my nails cut into my legs, grounding me a little.

Everything is fuzzy. I remember waking in the chaos, watching in horror as Creed, Zane, Eldon, and Brax all fought off some crazy faceless fuckers, who only seemed to gain more strength as they pushed, until Ari, my griffin familiar, came and…saved us? It feels like that's what happened, but I don't feel confident enough in my own breath right now to trust in my thoughts and emotions too.

Not when I saw him—Brax—injured, hurt, unresponsive. By the time I dropped to my knees beside him, his sword was gone. *He* was gone. It was too late.

Until it wasn't.

One brown. One green.

One fucking brown. One fucking green.

Those two colors flicker at the back of my eyelids as I slam my eyes shut. The pain that consumed me still flutters through my veins in waves of aftershock. The only reminder that I felt that level of torture because now he's…

I pry my eyes open, instantly finding him across the room where a medic tends to his blood-soaked wound. All of the gray shadows fall away and an amber aura shimmers around him. I shake my head and it fades away, my eyes zoning in on his eyes.

One brown. One green.

I choke on my breath, unable to process any of it, and quickly cast my gaze elsewhere to distract from the reality threatening to be acknowledged in my mind.

I lock eyes with Creed, who is leaning back against the large desk where I woke earlier. The medic before him is trying to look into his onyx eyes, but they're settled on me instead. He knows what I know, what I can't say or admit. I can't read him, though. I can't tell if disgust fills his thoughts, whether he's calculating his next move to use me to his advantage, or…

No, Raven. Not him, not them. They wouldn't…would they?

Slowly blinking, I shift my glance to Zane, who is by the door, helping one of the medics cover Finn's lifeless body. The muscles in his neck and shoulders are bunched tight, revealing the tension beneath his otherwise casual demeanor. He's not looking my way like Creed, and I can't decide whether I prefer it or hate it.

Swiping a hand down my face, likely smearing more grime over me, I find Eldon shuffling to lean beside Brax. He grips his friend's shoulder, confirming he is, indeed, standing before him, and another pang of pain and confusion swarms through my body.

As if sensing my stare, Eldon glances over his shoulder at me while still holding on to Brax. His jaw works from side to side, his mind in overdrive, and uncertainty claws at me again. He knows what I did, what I didn't mean to do… it wasn't intentional, I don't think.

Would I change it? Not when Brax is here and breathing right now, but I'm not delusional. Life won't ever be the same. Not when people learn of what I've done, what I can do.

Say it, Raven.

My teeth sink into my bottom lip, the taste of copper lacing my tongue as I drop my gaze.

Necromancy.

Resurrection is against The Monarchy's law. And the one subject not encouraged at Silvercrest…necromancy.

The reminder of Creed's words flickers in my mind. Tilting my hands up, I stare at them in wonder. It's not possible. There's no way I did that with my hands, my touch, whatever the fuck it was. But the proof is standing mere inches away from me.

"Miss, are you ready for someone to take a look at you?"

I flinch when a hand lands on my shoulder. Startled, I blink up at a man with a soft smile on his face. The concern is evident in his stare, but I take no solace in his closeness.

"She's good for now, man. She just needs some space." Zane reaches for the guy's hand while placing himself between the medic and me. I exhale when the medic steps back, nodding as he moves around the room, leaving me to look up at Zane like he hung the damn moon.

He crouches beside me, not touching me, despite the twitch in his fingers. I hate that I feel like I'm being difficult right now, as if he doesn't know how to handle me. Or maybe he does. I just don't like that he has to.

"Hey, Dove," he breathes, his words warming my chest as his eyes soften. Hazel orbs peering into my soul whether I like it or not.

"Hey," I croak, a bubble of emotion sitting on the tip of my tongue, sweeping my throat as I bite it all back. He notices it all, though. I can see it in the crinkle of his eyes.

Tilting my head, I swallow back the sob I'm sure was trying to escape, taking time to gather myself before I look at him again. I try to summon some humor to break the tension in the air between us, but my lips have barely parted when the clang of metal echoes around the room.

"Whose sword is this?"

My gaze locks on the silver, disbelief washing over me as another piece of the puzzle appears. It's identical to mine, similar in every way, but my sword isn't here.

"It's mine." Everyone whips around to look at Brax, who now stands with a frown on his face. He rubs the back of his neck, exhaustion clinging to his features as he bites back a yawn.

He looks dead on his feet. *Literally.*

My heartbeat quickens. It was gone. And now it's not. Just like him.

He can't even look at me, and I can't even process what the fuck is happening. Does he know? Does he remember? Does he feel any different?

I could sink beneath the questions swirling in my head, but I refuse to lower my defenses in a room full of strangers. Now isn't the time. That doesn't stop the deeper thoughts from rearing their ugly heads, making a tremble run through my bones from head to toe.

I should have stayed hidden. I should have stayed tucked away in Shadowmoor for all of eternity. The ward on my body was a blessing, not a curse.

My heart clenches with the thought, knowing full well that if I weren't here or attending Silvercrest Academy, then I wouldn't know the Bishops. I wouldn't know Ari. At the flicker of his name in my thoughts, a noise sounds out in the distance.

He's still here. He stayed for me. His call gets louder, as if he can sense my distress and he's hunting me down.

Tilting my head back again, the gaping hole in the ceiling remains cast in darkness from the skies above until a flash of gold streaks across the open air.

Ari.

"Let me take you to him," Zane breathes, offering me his hand. I stare down at it for a beat before slipping my palm against his. He squeezes gently, tugging me to my feet before plastering me to his chest. "I'm going to make sure no one can see us, okay?"

I frown, confused, until he starts walking us through the room. "Hey, where did the other two go?" The medic from earlier asks, and I catch a glimpse of Eldon's smirk before Zane carries me down what remains of the demolished stairs.

He used his magic on me. Made me invisible, like him.

I tighten my arms around his neck, my feet just off the floor with the full length of my body pinned against him as he steps over the rubble, only releasing me when we step out into the open. Crimson stains the black and gray hues as people rush around, aiding those who are injured while others gather the lifeless remains of those less fortunate.

Zane runs the back of his hand over my cheek and I whimper at his gentleness. There's so much to understand, so much to discuss, so many questions, but none of that matters in this moment. He's here, silently showing me the support he's never wavered on.

My Zane.

He lowers his forehead to mine, breathing me in despite the state of me, and I run my hands down his arms, squeezing his wrists in a silent thank you.

"I think he needs you as much as you need him, Dove. Go." He leans back, dropping his hands from my waist as he nods over my shoulder.

I turn to see golden feathers gracefully float through the air, despite the size of the griffin landing before me. Ari hits the ground, making it shake beneath my feet, and a few people around us startle. But it all fades to darkness as I take a step toward him. Then another, and another, until my head is cranked back to look up at him. His head dips down, his eyes peering at me over his beak. To anyone else, he might look scary. Understandably, there's a reason the griffins were in the Gauntlet: they're feared.

Yet, to me, Ari feels like... home.

I launch myself at him, burying my face in his soft feathers as I cling to him. A harsh breath morphs into a sob as I bleed my soul into him. The world around us drifts away, my body craving his comfort, and I feel his beak nuzzle against my shoulder as he consoles me in a way I can't even begin to acknowledge or explain.

His comfort lets the world and time seep away. I'm not sure how long we stand there, but it feels like an eternity before I lift my tear-stained face from his coat. I don't care that I'm raw, exposed, and vulnerable. I know he will protect me to the ends of the realm.

I am him, and he is me.

Testing the softness of his fur on his legs, I look back up at him to find his expectant gaze already taking me in. "Happy official first meeting," I breathe, a dry chuckle following while I shake my head in disbelief. I'm talking to a griffin. A fucking griffin. It sounds bizarre, but I've never needed someone or something to hear me as much as I do at this moment. "Thank you. For being here, for saving my life, for saving *everyone's* lives," I correct, waving a hand around us.

He doesn't reply, of course, but he leans down, nuzzling his beak against me from my shoulder to my stomach as he lowers until he's kneeling on the ground in front of me. My heart soars. I don't know what it means, what this feeling is inside of me, but it feels like love, like family, an unbreakable bond, like everything I've ever craved and needed. He feels like my mother's touch, but more. Different.

My fingers find their way to his head, stroking softly, and he mews, leaning into my touch, refilling the hope inside of me despite the carnage around us. I don't know what an attack would look like, but this isn't it. It's worse. Darker, deeper, etched in pain and sorrow.

I don't know what the purpose of any of this was, but I

get the feeling I'm going to find out whether I like it or not. Never have I wanted to be alive more than I do now. Even with all of the uncertainty and the unknown twists of my magic, I belong. I know it. But the priorities are quickly shifting around me. Everything is changing, and I'll never feel the same. For better or worse, one thing is for certain.

Fuck following the sun. Fuck destroying the shadows. Fuck everything but my next breath.

DESTINED SHADOWS

TWO
Brax

I'm confused, disoriented, and just...

Fuck.

Despite the healer's efforts, an ache consumes every inch of my body, making every move continue to throb. Something isn't right. I can sense it in the air. Like there's an elephant in the room, and I'm oblivious to what it is.

Eldon is hanging closer than usual, repeatedly touching my arm or shoulder for reassurance that I'm here or something. I don't know. He's always handsy, but never like this, not when he knows it irritates me. Creed is staring at me like I grew a second head, but a quick sweep of my hand over the back of my neck confirms it's still just me. Zane is busying around, helping the medics with shit that doesn't need our attention, but for some reason he needs the distraction. While Raven is...wilting.

I can't look at her right now, seeing the distress oozing from her while it's impossible for me to fix. I need this fucking healer to finish checking me over so I can bundle her into my arms and make it all go away. She's always so strong, so brave, so resilient, and it's not the battle remains around us that have broken her, but there's a switch I can't quite put my finger on.

I'm missing a piece of the puzzle and I can't find it with everything still happening.

A dead green guy is carried from the room, a reminder of what we were fighting against, and the pain from the wound on my back burns despite being healed. I don't know who the fuck sent them, but the ones responsible will meet them in Hell when I find out. Fuckers.

Everything feels foggy and I don't like it. I was turning to stone, defending myself, when the searing pain of the blade at my back seemed to make the world go dark. Nothing made sense as I floated in an inky-black pool of dread. The liquid in my mind was getting thicker and restricting every breath I took until it consumed almost every inch of me.

I can't say my life flashed before my eyes, I was too focused on the fight to get out, but my efforts weren't enough. Until a pink glow broke through the never-ending pit of emptiness and Raven's angelic voice whispered in my ear. My Shadow, somehow chasing them all away and leading me back to her.

The healers arrived just in time as I clung to the sound of my name on Raven's lips.

"Where did the other two go?" The medic's question cuts through my thoughts and I clench my eyes shut for a second before I blink them back open and focus on the present. I look around the room to see what he means and instantly notice the absence of Raven and Zane.

"Where did he take her?" I ask, tilting my attention to Eldon at my side.

"Probably to the griffin," he replies, wiping a hand down his face as I frown.

"The griffin is here?"

Eldon nods at my question and I push the pads of my fingers into my temples. When did that happen? A quick glance up gives a hint that Raven's griffin has been here. That gaping hole wasn't made by any of us. I vaguely recall the distant sound of it screeching, but I can't be sure. I was really fucking out of it. "Is she okay?"

"Who?"

I glare at Eldon's bullshit. "Don't play dumb. You know I mean Raven."

He sighs, his eyebrows furrowing as he avoids my gaze. "Once we're away from all of...this, I think I'll be able to give you a better answer." *A better answer?* What the fuck does that mean? As if sensing the bewilderment in me, he reiterates. "Well, a more accurate one, at least."

There's something they're not saying and it's pissing me off. I hate not being in the loop, unaware of what's going on around me. Control is a power you wield without magic. I need it more than I need air to breathe and I have no patience to wait this bullshit out.

"Can we leave?" I blurt, rolling my shoulders back, trying to shake the stress off me. Eldon looks at the healer, who gulps as he tilts his head back to meet my gaze.

"Uhm…"

"I'm going," I grunt, shuffling him to the side so I can go around him without trampling the dead body on the floor.

Eldon calls my name, but I don't glance back. I'm done. Creed silently falls into step with me as I make my way over the rubble, heading outside to find Zane watching Raven with her griffin. It's a fucking sight to behold. Watching a huge beast like a griffin kneel before the pink-haired wonder who has consumed my every breath since she appeared only confirms just how special she is.

I stop beside Zane, desperate to reach for her but understanding the moment she's having. Creed stands on my other side, and a moment later, Eldon appears on his other side. The four of us watch in wonder as she mindlessly runs her fingers over the griffin's head like he's a kitten familiar and not the terrifying creature that he is.

It's not lost on me that the world is crumbling around us. The Shadowmoor outpost took a huge blow, there's no denying that, yet we're taking solace in watching the missing piece of our world bask in her familiar's presence.

Everything else can wait. There's no coming back from any of this. That's not going to change in the time it will take Raven to gather herself. There's something different about her, I can sense it, but until I get us out of here, I'm not going to understand it. And I think I need that information more than anything else right now.

Whether she'll offer it or not, I don't know, but I won't be asking; I'll be demanding. If she expects anything different, she's delusional. She glances back, her eyes instantly locking with mine, and she gulps.

"Let's go home, Shadow."

She nibbles on her bottom lip, nodding lightly as she continues to stroke the griffin. Her hand moves down to his beak as she turns to face him again. It looks as though she's whispering something to him before he stands tall, the ground moving beneath him. Huge eyes lock on mine, pinning me in place before he ruffles his wings.

"How are we going to get back?" Zane asks, breaking my stare so I can look around. There are a few gateways set up down at the left tower. It seems to be standing a little taller than the other, which is nothing more than a pile of rocks.

"My magic won't get us out of here, so we'll need to take a gateway." I point toward the small line of people moving through the iridescent ovals below and everyone follows my line of sight.

"Let's go," Creed agrees, moving toward Raven and lacing his fingers with hers.

Asshole. I wanted to do that. Begrudgingly, I keep my pout to myself and the five of us trudge through the wreckage. When we near the line, sobs and cries vibrate from the other students and professors. Sounds which only intensify when they first catch a glimpse of Raven's griffin walking a step behind us. Raven looks over her shoulder at him one final time before stepping through the gateway, and in a blink of an eye, we're at the entryway to the main academy building.

The noises get louder as we are surrounded by more students and professors in hysterics, and it instantly gives me a splitting headache. "I'm not dealing with all of this. Head home," I state to the others.

"I think they're taking inventory of who made it back," Zane murmurs, pointing to the professors holding boards and taking everyone's names. I really don't have the energy for that. "Let them sweat until morning or something, I couldn't give a shit."

"Where's Leila?" Raven suddenly gasps, eyes wide as panic washes over her.

"She was with her father when we last saw her," Creed states, which seems to wane some of the fear from her gaze, but not all of it.

"Do we know if she made it back?"

"Not unless you've seen her in the past five seconds since we stepped through the gateway," I grumble, earning myself a glare from her, but I brush it off. "Why don't one of you go and find out, drop our names, and I'll find you back at the house," I offer, already moving to the nearby tree stump just out of view of the main hoard of people.

I hear Eldon murmuring something to the rest of them before I open a portal, only to find Raven, Creed, and Zane right behind me. "Eldon's gone to check," the latter advises, and I shrug, stepping through the portal to reveal our lounge. I finally manage to exhale the breath caught in my throat.

This is my safe space. No one but the five of us in here, no one else to see my stress and worry, the metaphorical gargoyle mask dropping from my face.

Dropping onto the sofa, I brace my head in my hands with my elbows on my knees. Despite leaving the mess behind at the outpost, I still feel a tightness inside me that won't unwind. Peering up at Raven, who stands with her arms folded around her so tight I'm sure she's going to suffocate, I know what I need.

"Shadow, come."

I lean back, opening my lap to her, my arms at my sides as my eyes do the pleading my voice can't. A nervousness washes over her as she assesses me, irking the fuck out of me, but Eldon comes rushing through the front door in the next moment, interrupting whatever the hell that was.

"You could have left the portal open for me, fucker," he grunts, glaring at me as the door slams shut behind him. I shrug, having nothing to say, and his eyes squint even tighter, but he doesn't push further like he usually would.

He moves to stand between Raven and Creed, Zane hanging on her other side as they all stare at me. I've had enough.

"What the fuck am I missing?" I bite, nostrils flaring as I give each of them a withering glare, Raven included, and they all falter, which only confirms my suspicions. "Someone better spit it out. Now." Raven flinches, her hold on herself somehow worming its way tighter. "And what the fuck is this about?" I add, pointing at her, and she stiffens.

"Brax..." Creed starts, looking between Raven and me warily, which only pisses me off more.

"Cut the fuck to it. Whatever it is, just clue me in." I can't handle the itchy feeling beneath my skin, and I know it's stemming from this invisible elephant that everyone can see but me.

"It's a little more difficult than that," Eldon states,

instinctively taking a step toward Raven.

"It's not, though, is it," Raven murmurs, finally unraveling her arms from around her waist and shaking them off at her sides. It's funny how my glare is supposed to spark fear in people, yet with Raven, it somehow manages to fuel her.

"How about you be the one to explain it to me then, Shadow." I'd rather she was doing it from my lap, but that doesn't look too likely, and the glint in her eyes tells me she's doing that more for my sake than her own.

Why does she think I want distance between us?

"I don't think explaining it is going to be so easy because I don't really understand it myself, but you deserve to know." She takes a step toward me, keeping enough space between us that I want to evaporate.

"Get to it, Raven."

Her name on my tongue instead of her nickname seems to be the shove she needs. Her hands twitch at her sides as she gulps, steeling her spine as her eyes latch onto mine.

"I got my magic, Brax." My eyebrows furrow, not remembering that during the massacre, but her next words explain that to me. "You were gone, sword and all, and it hurt beyond words. The pain was…colossal. I didn't really know what I was doing until it had already happened."

"Raven," I warn when her words slope off. She went from speaking so fast I couldn't register a word to silent once more.

"My magic… is necromancy, Brax. I brought you back from the dead."

DESTINED SHADOWS

THREE
Raven

His eyes are wide and his jaw is slack as he gapes at me. I don't know if blurting it out like that was the right idea, but fuck, how else am I supposed to say it? Besides, Brax isn't really the kind to listen to me talk a load of bullshit in the lead-up to it, either. And as much as I want to lighten the mood, I don't think humor would be a good alternative for him.

Hey, honey, you're sucking on that air right now because I went crazy as fuck and used my necromancy abilities to kickstart your heart. You're welcome.

It might have made me chuckle, potentially even Zane at least, but it's not going to get me the desired effect from Brax, whose stare only seems to intensify as he leans forward again, bracing his arms on his thighs. "You did what?" The vein at his temple throbs like it's about to burst at the absurd crap coming from my mouth.

I roll my eyes. "Don't make me say it again." I sigh. Whether I did a good job of explaining it or not, he knows exactly what I just said. Repeating it would be for his benefit alone.

"Brax—" Eldon states from behind me, but the grumpy gargoyle is quick to shake his head, cutting off whatever his friend is about to say.

"No. I want to hear it from her." He doesn't even glance away from me as he scoffs. "I would fucking *know* if I died."

It's my turn to huff. This man. This. Fucking. Man. I should not have expected any different, but it doesn't mean I'm prepared for it.

Giving him a pointed look, I keep my mouth shut, continuing to say nothing as a frown slowly knits his brows together. His hooded gaze is still a turn-on, despite the circumstances, and I find myself shuffling from foot to foot as I try to tamp down the thought of a distraction.

Creed, Zane, and Eldon remain just as quiet, waiting for this mess to continue to unravel until Brax stretches, arching his back when a wince twists his lips. He lifts a hand to his side before running it over where he can touch his back, seeking out the wound we all know existed earlier.

He clears his throat, eyes dropping to the floor for a split second before they find mine again. "My back?" I nod, nibbling on my bottom lip as I watch the confusion continue to morph his face. "But…"

Zane takes a step forward, emotion swimming in his hazel pools. "You were gone, man. Like *gone* gone, sword and all. We would have likely all followed you too if Raven's griffin—"

"Ari."

"What?"

"My griffin, his name is Ari."

Zane nods in response, thankfully not getting pissed at my ridiculous interruption, but I couldn't help myself.

"We would have been just as dead, too, if Ari hadn't shown up. Everything was a blur until I saw Raven drop down to her knees beside you, sobs wracking her entire frame. It quickly turned into screams or gurgles, fuck, whatever that noise was, and then… *poof*, your eyes opened." The back of Zane's hand grazes against my own as he looks down at me and I offer a weak half-smile in response.

I'm almost tempted to get to the bottom of what this sound is that I made, but that's not what I should be focusing on right now. Brax is.

Another throat clearing from Brax draws my attention back to him and I'm startled to see worry in his eyes. "Are you okay?"

I glance around in confusion at first, but I quickly

confirm he's talking to me. "Am *I* okay?" He cocks a brow at me like I'm being dumb and I manage to refrain from rolling my eyes at him again. "Brax, I'm not the one who—"

He waves his hand, cutting me off. "I'm obviously fine. I'm right here in front of you, aren't I?"

"Yeah, but…"

"But what?"

Give me strength with this man.

"I'm more than aware that things can look fine on the surface, but that doesn't always mean the inside matches. I need to know that you're okay in there, too," I state, tapping my temple. His jaw ticks and I take a step toward him. "Complete honesty, please."

He swipes a hand down his face and relief instantly rushes through me at the fact that he's not trying to brush me off with a generic *I'm fine* statement, but this is still Brax, so I never know what I'm going to get. As much as I'm desperate for an answer and eager to push him along, I keep my mouth shut as he tries to process everything in front of us.

The second he starts rubbing at the back of his neck in irritation, I know it's not good.

"Fuck. I don't know, okay?" he bites, nostrils flaring as he pushes up on his knees to stand, immediately taking a step away from me. Followed by another and another until he's standing in front of his bedroom door. "You all just need to give me a fucking minute."

His door slamming shut behind him efficiently puts an end to the conversation.

Eldon moves first, but he barely gets two steps before Creed's hand on his shoulder halts him in place. "No, let him have a minute. It's not every day someone tells you that you just died."

My heart clenches at his statement. "Or that someone brought you back to life," I add, the words feeling foreign on my tongue.

"Shutting us out isn't going to help," Eldon says with a sigh as Zane cuts the remaining distance between us and comfortingly drapes his arm around my shoulders.

"And forcing him to communicate will only make it worse," Creed protests, and as much as the truth has my insides tightening in knots, we have to give him a chance to handle this his way. To begin with, at least.

"So what do we do now?" Eldon looks at each of us for an answer, but we don't have one that will make all our troubles and worries go away. We've got some things to think about.

When none of the others reply, I reach for Zane's hand, squeezing for silent support. "We control what we can."

"Which is what?" Creed asks, finally dropping his hand from his friend's shoulder.

"Getting this grime off our skin. Fresh bodies, fresh minds, fresh everything, then we can start addressing all of the fucking elephants in the room."

Water beats down on me, every droplet discarding the reminder of what we just lived through, yet the scars are already burrowing themselves deep beneath the surface. This is exactly what I meant when I tried to explain everything to Brax.

On the surface, am I alive? Yes. Will I get through this? Yes. Will I stand tall, take on any challenge, and fight with every ounce of effort I have to survive? Yes. But will every image live rent-free in my mind? Yes. Will the reminder of the pain I felt at seeing Brax's lifeless body live inside of me forever? Yes.

It's a mind fuck. All of it. A mind fuck I could quite easily wallow in, or I can choose to focus on the one thing that's kept me going in life so far: survival.

The latter will always be my first instinct, and that's no different today. That doesn't stop the dull ache in my bones or the tiredness that lingers in my every breath from consuming me. I'm exhausted.

I need to sleep, then I can actually focus on the revelations of my magic and let reality set in before I attempt to broach the subject with the guys. There are a lot of questions that I'm not ready to dive into until I've slept so hard I won't remember my name when I wake.

Running my fingers through the length of my hair, I shut off the water and reach for the fluffy cream towel on the vanity. I hum in appreciation for the comfort the softness gives me as I wrap it around my body before re-entering my room.

I squeal, jumping back a step when I find Leila sprawled out on my bed. Her blond hair is splayed out around her as she lies on her back, throwing a ball up in the air and catching it.

"What the fuck, Leila?" I blurt, hand on my flushed chest as I gape at her, but she simply rolls over to look at me with a smile on her face.

"I'm glad to see you're okay too." She lifts herself so her legs dangle off the side of the bed, relief flashing in her eyes as she takes me in from head to toe.

The surprise quickly evaporates and I rush to her, tightly draping my arms around her shoulders. "I was so worried," I murmur, reluctantly leaning back and grabbing onto the edge of the towel so I don't lose it.

"I'm so sorry, Raven. My father dragged me out of there to safety despite my best efforts and pleas to find you." She looks down at her lap, embarrassment staining her cheeks, and I quickly shake my head.

"Good."

Her eyebrows pinch together as she stares at me. "No, not good, Raven. You were—"

"I'm fine, Leila. See, it's all okay. Your father did the right thing," I insist, interrupting her, and she gives me a glare.

A huff falls from her mouth as she twists her lips, trying to find a suitable retort, but she knows I'm right and eventually shakes her head, giving up.

"How bad was it?" she asks instead, my shoulders tensing as I fail to hide the wince on my face. There's no point lying, though. She knows it couldn't have ended well.

"It was bad. Like, really bad." Keeping hold of the towel, I take a seat beside her. "Finn's dead," I add, recalling his lifeless body in the room. He wasn't a close friend or even an ally, but he was one of the few people I didn't completely despise outside of the Bishops and Leila. Leila's eyes widen as she gasps, her hand lifting to her mouth with shock. "I don't know about anyone else, but there was so much destruction everywhere, I can't even begin to imagine," I admit, and she nods in understanding.

"My father insisted things weren't okay the moment they declared that the first years would also take part in the Gauntlet. It was too extreme, too fast, but he still doesn't seem to understand what the threat is. Or if he does, he's not willing to share it yet."

If Leila's father, Professor Fitch, is seemingly unaware of the bigger picture, what hope do we have? "Surely, after everything that just went down at Shadowmoor's outpost, they have to give us something. A reason why lives have been lost."

Leila runs her hand over the checkered school skirt she's wearing and it slowly dawns on me that she's still wearing her uniform. *What time is it?*

"Well, let's hope that's what they want us for." I frown at Leila's statement as she rises from the bed. "I'll wait for you outside while you get dressed."

"Get dressed? You say that like I have somewhere to be." I'm wiped. I don't have the energy for anything but sleep.

"You do." She opens my bedroom door and offers me a weak smile.

"Please tell me you're pranking me or something because I swear, all I want to do is collapse in this damn bed." Her smile spreads but doesn't actually get any stronger and I know I'm screwed. "Fine, hit me with it. What am I getting dressed for?"

"A gathering has been called. They're going to officially confirm the casualties."

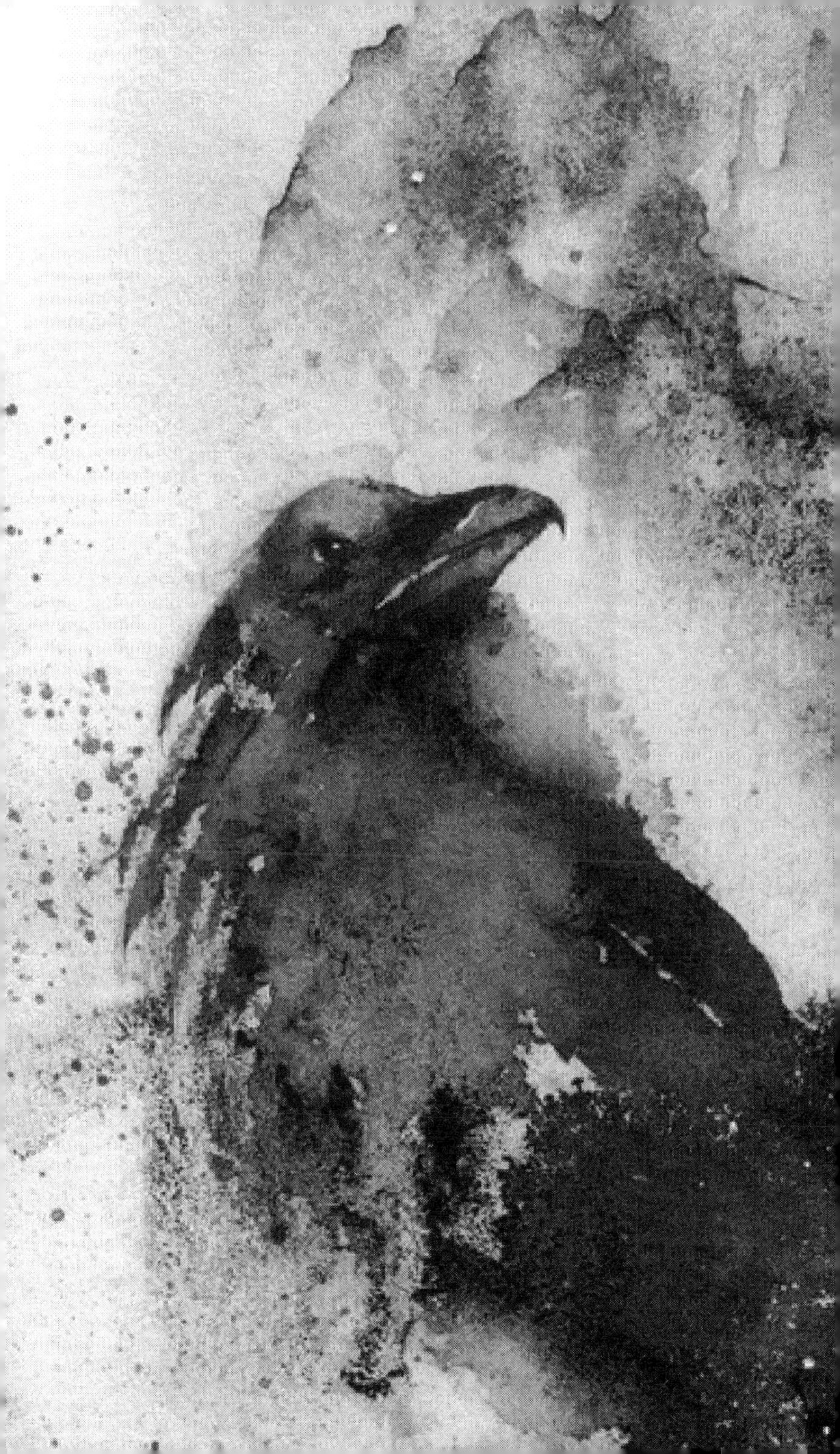

FOUR
Raven

It's not a surprise to find Zane, Eldon, and Creed waiting with Leila, all dressed in their uniforms and ready to go. But it is a surprise to see Brax there too. He's standing closer to the kitchen while everyone else is by the main door, so the distance he's trying to keep is clear, but the fact that he's still with us is a relief.

My pink hair is braided, the ends falling between my shoulder blades, but I've left my face makeup free. The night looms dark outside the back windows, I have no idea what time it is, and I'm ready to face-plant into my mattress as soon as I get back.

No sooner do I close my bedroom door behind me does Zane rush to my side, clasping my hand with his and heading for the exit without a backward glance at the others. I shiver at the chill in the night air as we step outside, but with the pace Zane has us walking at, I quickly shake it off. Leila appears to my right a moment later, and a swift glance over my shoulder confirms the others are right behind us as we follow the thin crowd of students sullenly heading toward the main academy building.

Zane's thumb softly strokes over my knuckles, grounding me, but I still have a niggling feeling in my gut because we haven't had a conversation about what happened and how they feel about it. It's like a barrier between me and them, and I can't deny that I want it gone. Yet the fear of rejection claws at my insides, despite my best efforts of exuding the "badass bitch" vibe I've wrapped myself in for most of my life.

I try to compartmentalize the irritation, but it still lingers at the edge of my thoughts as we step through the marbled halls and out into the courtyard where they hold all of the gatherings. I manage to cast a glance over my shoulder at Brax as we come to a stop at the back of the crowd, but he's gazing off into the distance, making it impossible to get a read on him. Eldon catches my attention, and the smile he offers fills me with hope, which only intensifies when the corner of Creed's mouth tips up too.

The murmurs that fill the air aren't the usual bubbly type. There's no giggling, no joking, nothing. Just a whole swarm of worry and fear, and it's so thick it feels like it's going to crackle through the air at any moment and zap everyone in the vicinity.

Through the sea of people, my eyes lock on the blue pools that match my own and my back stiffens. His eyebrows furrow as he blinks, almost as if he's seeing things, and a knot forms in my stomach, but before I can decipher any more of it, Genie appears at his side and steals his attention.

"Are you okay?" Zane murmurs against the shell of my ear, and I nod. The movement is more sluggish than usual, the tiredness seeping through my bones too hard to conceal at this point.

"Students." One word in greeting from Professor Burton, who appears as a projection in the sky as usual. It's odd seeing him with the dark background and the stars flickering instead of the light-blue sky we're used to. "I believe we have everyone in attendance?" His voice continues to echo around us, but the question is aimed at Lyra, who appears on the projection beside him. I haven't seen her since the first day I arrived, the memory instantly coming back to me.

The last time I saw her, she was in her office with her nose high in the air, a snarl to every word she spoke, fueled by a level of sass that could rival my own. Until she learned who my father was, that is. Then everything changed. Now, she stands to Professor Burton's right, her hair a little more unruly, chewing on her bottom lip, and a flash of fear in her eyes as she nods back at him.

With that confirmation, Professor Burton turns to look back out over the crowd, all gathered and ready. "Thank you so much for coming together after a devastating turn of events unraveled at Shadowmoor's outpost this afternoon. I'm sure many of you want to get a good night's sleep, but it felt imperative that we address the situation as swiftly as possible."

"It definitely could have waited until morning. I'm exhausted," Leila whispers, and I chuckle in agreement, thinking the exact same thing.

"For the second and third years that haven't been caught up to speed yet, the first years were able to take part in an outpost visit to Shadowmoor this afternoon. An attack ensued not long after their arrival. An attack that involved trolls, fireballs, and the faceless Amayans." *Amayans, that's what they're called?* Putting a name to their not-so-existent faces makes a shiver run down my spine. Gasps ring out around us from the older years clustered in the courtyard, but the first years continue to remain silent, still dwelling on the events that unfolded.

"Where did they come from?" someone asks, but I don't see who over the throng of students.

"We're unsure at this time," Professor Burton advises, and Zane scoffs, mouthing the exact same word that's floating around in my head too.

Bullshit.

These attacks have been going on at least since I got here, who knows how long prior to that? The entire reason we are here is to train to fight against the enemy in the Great War and protect our realm, yet we don't seem to know who the enemy is? Definite bullshit. Since I've been here, every attack has gotten worse. They can't really say this was a complete surprise or think we're dumb enough to accept that.

"Why are they attacking? What's the purpose behind it all?" Another question comes from the crowd, and the irritation is obvious on Professor Burton's face.

Fucker.

"As I said, we're unsure at this time. We will keep everyone updated as needed, but for tonight we are gathered to confirm the lives lost."

A solemn silence falls over the courtyard. It wasn't lost on me that he said we'll be updated when necessary, and not with every little piece of information, as I'm sure others paid close attention to. But he has an uncanny ability to handle the crowd, which includes distracting us with other news, like the death toll from the outpost.

He holds up a scroll of parchment and starts to read names. I almost consider tuning him out, but my frustration with him shouldn't affect the moment of recognition those lost deserve. So I suck back my own emotions and absorb every name he speaks. My gut clenches when he mentions Finn, but my ears pulse with relief at the fact that he's not calling out any of our names, especially Brax's.

By the time he reaches the end, he's called out twelve names in total. I'm going to assume that doesn't include any of the people who were stationed there, just the first years caught in the crossfire.

I might not have known any of them personally, except Finn, but it has more of an impact on me in comparison to when I used to watch people fight it out and die in the pits. The grander scale of all this is unfathomable.

"That's it for tonight. Get some rest. Classes will resume as normal in the morning." Within a blink of an eye, he's gone.

It's official. We've been completely strung along and dismissed. I shouldn't be surprised.

Zane's hand tightens around mine as Professor Fitch calls out for Leila. She rolls her eyes dramatically, mouthing her apology as she rushes after him through the crowd. Eldon takes the now vacant spot at my side, draping his arm over my shoulders before ushering me with the moving mob of students toward the exit.

The solace I hoped I would feel from finally being able to go to bed is completely tarnished by the sheer lack of information offered. Although, I keep putting one foot in front of the other, accepting that it's all we'll get for tonight as we make our way home.

I half expect Sebastian or Genie to make an appearance on our walk back, but it's a surprisingly uneventful trip and we're soon closing the front door to the house. The sound of the latch locking allows my body to sag, tiredness weighing heavier on me, but any hope of giving in to my needs is quickly diminished when Creed whirls to a stop in front of me with his finger poised in my direction.

"You need to eat before you pass out."

I pout, unimpressed with his statement, but my stomach doesn't get the message because it chooses that exact moment to rumble with need.

"He's right, Little Bird. Today has been a long day. We all need something, especially if we're diving straight back into classes in the morning like nothing happened," Eldon adds, dropping his arm from my shoulders before placing his palm against the small of my back, directing me toward the kitchen.

Zane reluctantly releases my hand and I let Eldon take the lead. My mind is blank as far as what I could have to eat goes, so I decide to open the fridge in hopes of inspiration. Nibbling at my bottom lip, I'm completely aware I'm staring aimlessly at nothing in particular when Brax clears his throat, gaining my attention.

"If your magic is running through your veins now, why aren't you using it? There's more to it than just casting your bigger abilities." He folds his arms over his chest, eyeing me like I must have been lying earlier about what I did, but for the first time since I thought I lost him, realization washes over me.

I'm not a Void. Magic is inside of me.

"I didn't even think to. Everything has been so crazy. The reality of not having to do such mundane things didn't register," I admit, meeting Brax's stare, which remains just as inquisitive as he assesses me.

"Give it a try," he urges, but the challenge is clear.

Wetting my bottom lip, I glance around at the others. Zane and Eldon nod eagerly for me to give it a go while Creed continues to glance between Brax and me. Nerves twist in my stomach as vulnerability worms its way up my spine.

I'm out of my element, and as much as I don't want anyone in the world to see me exposed, the only people I can trust to help me is them.

"I don't know how."

"I've got you, Dove." Zane instantly steps up, a reassuring grin on his face as he grabs both of my hands and pulls me over to the dining table. He doesn't stop until I'm standing behind my chair, where he releases his hold on me. "I'm sure everyone is different, but for me, my magic flows from my core. When I close my eyes and envision it inside of me, there's like a little amber orb waiting to be explored."

"You just have to reach in and connect with it, then anything is possible," Creed adds, and I gulp nervously.

"So I just, what? Connect with my magic, envision what I want to eat, and it will appear?" I've lived this life aware of magic around me, but now it feels dubious. I'm sure it's my nerves that are getting the better of me, but I spent so long hoping for this moment that it still doesn't feel possible, even now.

"Pretty much," Eldon encourages, standing beside me in his usual spot. "Watch me."

He closes his eyes, his tongue peeking out to swipe along his bottom lip for a beat before a pizza appears on the table before him. His gaze is back on mine a moment later and I nod, hesitantly closing my eyes too.

Exhaling slowly, I nervously shake my hands, delving deep into an abyss of the unknown as I try to connect with myself in a way I never have before. At first, I have no fucking clue what I'm doing, but as I try to slow my breathing, a new sense of warmth flickers through me. I can't sense where it's coming from or why, but the heat seems to start to coil in my chest and I know I've found my way to the hub, or the ball as Zane called it.

Once I acknowledge it, it blossoms even more through every fiber of my being, making my skin tingle as I think of what I want to eat.

Chicken Alfredo.

A chuckle vibrates around me, bringing me back to the present as I blink my eyes open to find pasta, chicken, and alfredo sauce on the table in front of me.

"Maybe next time I'll remind you that you need to think of the dinnerware for it to go on too," Eldon muses, and I realize the food is *literally* on the table with no plate or bowl. *Fuck.*

"It takes everyone a minute, Raven. You should be proud. Not just because you did your first piece of mundane magic, but you put that look on Brax's face," Creed murmurs with a grin.

I follow his line of sight to where Brax stands at the end of the table. The color has gone from his face, his jaw is slack, and the truth flickers in his gaze.

I wasn't lying, I have magic, and as scary as it is to say, I'm a necromancer.

DESTINED SHADOWS

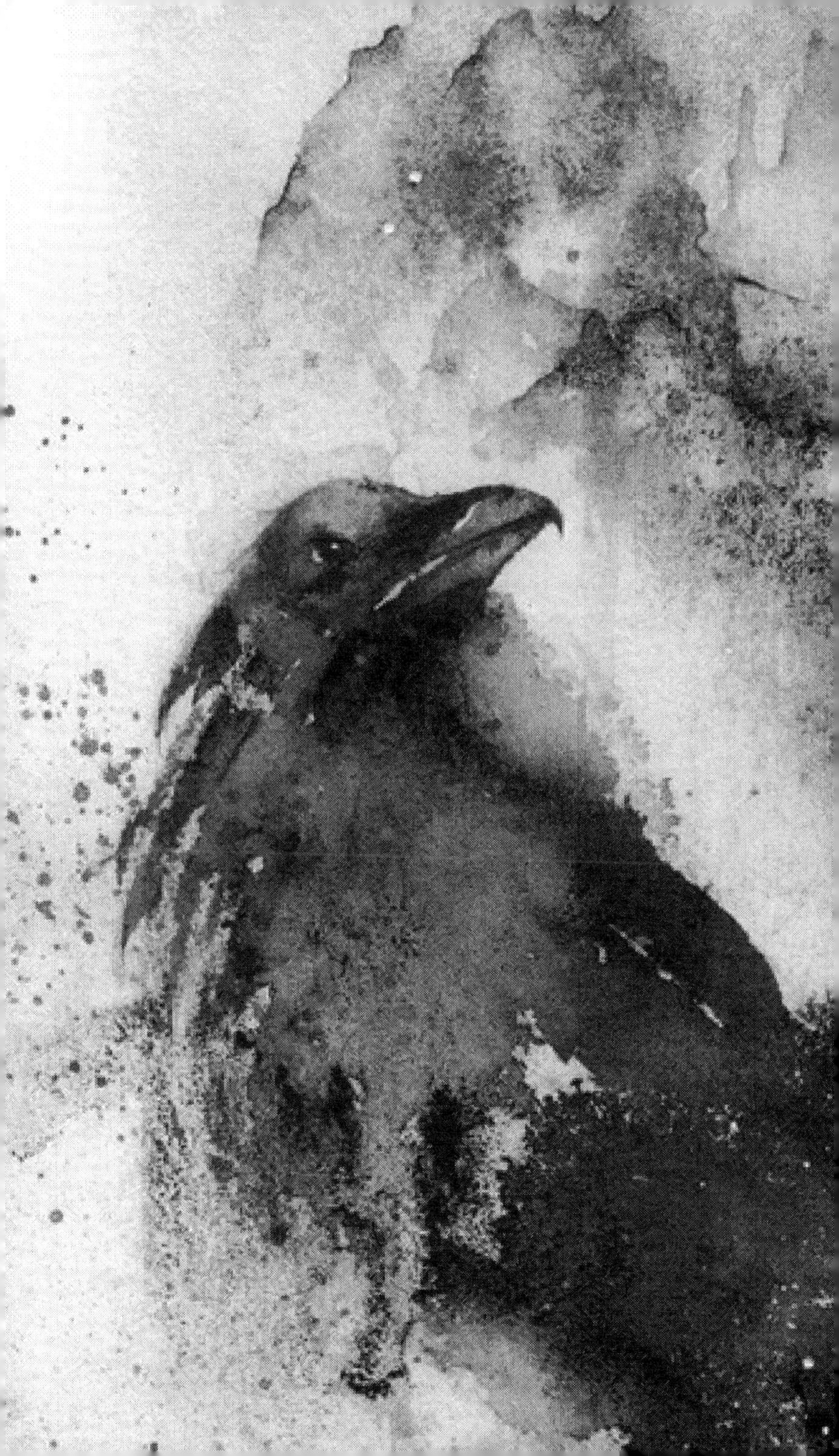

FIVE

Raven

Darkness seeps further into my dreams, deeper than usual, and I can't pinpoint why, but when my eyes spring open in the dead of night, I'm sure the room is drenched in it too. Not the usual twilight that comes at this time of the night; it's…darker.

A shiver runs down my spine, making my hands grip the edge of the sheet tighter to my chest. I quickly shake it off. The darkness has never scared me before, I'm not going to start letting it now. It must be the remnants of my dream, I'm sure of it.

Swiping a hand down my face, I move to roll onto my back, but I don't get far before I realize there's a presence behind me. I take a deep breath, relaxing deeper into myself as I take stock of the body beside me.

Legs sprawled alongside my own, an arm banded

around my waist, and now that I'm actually paying attention, I can feel their breath against my neck. The smell of sandalwood drifts in the air, confirming exactly which Bishop is with me.

Brax.

When will this man *not* surprise me?

Despite the uncertainty in the air between us due to our lack of common fucking communication skills, it's calming as hell to feel his body alongside mine. It doesn't stop the whirlwind of thoughts consuming my mind, though. I'm exhausted from all of the questions swirling around in my head, and I'm fed up with thinking that we need to decipher what's going on with me. Maybe morning me will attack shit better, because I can't continue repeating my thoughts and not doing anything about it.

"Go back to sleep, Shadow." The murmured words against my skin make my body tighten and my mind clear of everything but him.

Nervously rubbing my lips together, I consider doing just that, but intrigue has me wide awake. I know I'm going to be the cat that was killed by its own curiosity, but fuck it.

"Why are you here?"

His hand tightens around my waist at my question, shifting me a little more so my back is flush against his chest. "Go to sleep," he mutters after a second, his lips lingering on my skin like a whisper of a kiss.

"And if don't?" I push, wiggling my ass against his stiffening cock ever so slightly. Fingers dig into my hip, halting me in place, and the bite of pain swirls into a storm of bliss as he nuzzles at my neck.

"I came in here to sleep, but you're not making it easy, Shadow." I open my mouth, a smartass retort on the tip of my tongue, but he beats me to it. "Not that you ever make anything easy."

My body warms at his touch, heat coiling in my stomach, but despite my body's need for him, my mind wins out. "Why did you need to come in here to sleep, Brax?"

It feels like his face presses further into my neck and his grip on my hip tightens as silence stretches out between us. I'm certain I've crossed the invisible line he places between us whenever I ask too much, but as his hand slowly eases, his fingers slipping under my tee to splay out over my bare stomach, he lifts his mouth to my ear.

"I couldn't sleep knowing I was only breathing because of you. I couldn't sleep because you weren't close enough. I couldn't sleep…because despite how much I want to hate you, I can't."

I can't breathe. That was far more than I was expecting and likely the most raw and vulnerable thing I will ever hear this man say. His fingers trail over my skin, leaving goosebumps in their wake as he delicately strokes down the valley between my breasts. It's a far cry from the feral touches I usually get from him when the need takes over and he goes all primal.

Wetting my parched lips, I turn to face him. It's hard to make out his features in the darkness, but the flash of his eyes grounds me. "You don't hate me?"

The question leaves my lips before I can think better of it. I hate being vulnerable, but it's the least I can offer him in return when he's actually being open with me. His gaze drops to my mouth but he gives nothing away, slowly shifting so I'm lying flat on my back while he gets comfortable between my thighs, the sheets long forgotten.

"I want to," he admits, hooded eyes meeting mine as the press of his cock weighs down on my core, threatening to force my body to take over.

"But you don't." It's a statement this time, not a question, and my heart races in my chest. Twilight is my least favorite time of the twenty-four-hour cycle we call life, but right now, in this moment with him, it could just become my favorite.

He braces his arms on either side of my head, the tip of his nose brushing against mine. Every part of my body hums in approval at his closeness, yet weeps at the fact that he could be closer…deeper.

Running my hands up his arms, his muscles bulge

beneath my touch, and I keep going until my hands are around his neck, my thumb running over his pulse, reminding me that he's right here with me. The troubles of yesterday were a haunting nightmare that we miraculously avoided. I hitch my leg at his waist, my panty-covered core fluttering at the slight friction as he presses down a little more.

I want more. I *need* more. And it has to be *now*. Answer or not.

Nothing is going to make him more real to me than feeling him inside my pussy, taking what he wants and needs and leaving me spent, just as he has before.

His eyes storm as they pierce into my own, touching my soul and setting me on fire without a single word or action. It should be embarrassing how easily I melt beneath him, but I'm too wound up to give a shit.

Brax balances on one arm as he moves the other hand to my thigh, hoisting my leg up even higher before he shuffles down the length of my body, not stopping until his face is level with my pussy. The sound of my panties ripping echoes around the dark room with a snap. Brax's hot tongue swipes at my folds in the next second and the groan that parts my lips fills the room.

He starts off delicate and slow, running the pad of his tongue over every inch of me before he shifts to using the tip to tease my clit. Fisting the sheets beneath me, my back arches off the bed, but it doesn't alleviate the tension rising in me like I desperately need it to.

When he finally spears his tongue into my entrance, my whimpers turn into a cry as my toes curl and his fingers join in, trailing the path his mouth has taken.

"Brax," I plead, unsure exactly what it is I'm asking for, but that doesn't matter to him. It's like he has a sixth sense, knowing what my body needs before I do.

Two fingers thrust into my core next, scissoring and twisting inside of me, coiling my release even tighter before he sucks my clit into his mouth, and I'm a goner. My cries morph into a scream as my veins boil with the orgasm that rips through me, tossing me over the edge of ecstasy without a raft.

I blindly reach for him, attempting and failing to hold on to the short strands of his hair. I end up clawing at his scalp, too scared to look at the scratches I'm leaving behind as he wrings out every last drop of my climax.

"Brax," I repeat, my body spent as he removes his fingers and releases my clit.

He still doesn't utter a word in response as I make out the silhouette of him licking my essence off his fingers as he crawls back up the bed on his knees. He comes to a stop when his legs are braced on either side of my head, the outline of his cock beneath his boxers jutting out in my direction.

My arms are trapped beneath him, making it impossible for me to reach for his length, and a moment later, the layer of material separating us disappears. It takes me a second to process that he likely used his magic to do that, but the thought is brought to an abrupt halt when the tip of his dick runs against my lips.

I look up into his eyes, one brown, one green. Despite his words earlier, his silence confuses the fuck out of me. But there's no time for me to understand it before he presses his thumb against my bottom lip, drawing it down and allowing his cock to press past my lips.

His thick length quickly fills my mouth and I hum around his girth as he shifts, bracing his hands on the headboard for support so he can get deeper. I tilt my head back the best I can, relaxing my throat as I take another inch of him. Each one stretches my mouth wider, and the final inch renders me breathless as he nudges at the back of my throat.

Holy. Fuck.

It takes a second for me to adjust and begin breathing out of my nose, and the second I'm comfortable, he retreats, leaving me missing his invasion. Even if I could piece together any words to snap at him, I don't get a chance. The second the tip of his cock is resting against my lips, he's slamming back inside, filling my mouth. I splutter this time, my hands rendered useless as I swallow him down, my eyes watering, and it's the best sensation in the world.

He takes my mouth, he takes me, he takes everything, plundering his cock down my throat over and over, going deeper and deeper as I lay helpless to the onslaught. If anyone was going to bring out another kink in me, I should have known it would be him. This is on par with a hand around my throat, and I can't get enough. The only thing that would make this better is if we combined the climax he gave me at the same time.

I'm ready to swallow this man down, take every drop he has to offer, and claim every ounce for myself. But as soon as the thought enters my mind, he slips from my mouth altogether.

Gasping for breath, I glare at him in the dark, not caring that he probably can't tell how mad I am. "Brax," I grind out, acutely aware that it's the only word that's been uttered between us this entire time, just with a different emotion attached to the end of it.

He doesn't pay me any mind, though. He's already moving back down my body, grabbing the hem of my tee that's rolled up my stomach as he goes and yanking it off. The second the garment is discarded, I feel hands at my hips, and a breath later, I'm flipped onto my stomach.

Tingles trail up my spine, heat pooling in my core as I glance over my shoulder. His huge frame surrounds me as he lifts my hips into the air, bringing me to my knees while

I scramble to hold my weight on my hands.

The rustle of protection sounds out and I manage to catch a glimmer of him rolling it down his length before he positions himself at my entrance.

I want him to speak, say something, anything, but I need to feel him more. There's no denying the truth when it lingers so thick in the air between us. Not as he nudges my thighs even further apart. Not as he wraps his hand around my throat, flexing his fingers as he tightens his grip. And not as he thrusts so hard and fast inside of me, stars flicker at the corner of my vision.

His hips are punishing, unrelenting as he gives me no time to adjust to his cock, taking me again and again, chasing his own release. My whimpers are muffled by his hold on me, which only heightens everything I'm feeling under his rein.

I try to call out his name but it's too garbled for him to notice as he pistons in and out of me, drawing me closer to the edge once more. Tears prick the corners of my eyes again, my body accepting the punishing thrusts as my excitement coats his cock. The bed shakes beneath us, but that doesn't stop Brax or his efforts as his movements start to become jagged and he snarls. The guttural sound from the otherwise silent man is all I need to explode, my arms giving out as he continues to fuck me into the mattress.

I can't breathe, I can't see, I can't do anything but feel,

and it's euphoric.

The smallest sob parts my lips when he retreats from my core, his hand relaxing at my neck until it's completely gone, and the heat from his body disappears too. I'm a crumpled heap of limbs, succumbed to the pleasures that rippled through my veins.

The silence continues to expand over us as every second passes, and I expect him to get his shit together and leave. I'm counting down the seconds to it. But I should know better by now. Moments later, the sheets are draped over my bare skin as I'm enveloped in his muscular arms. He positions us in the exact same spot we were in when I first woke, his face nuzzling into my neck like no time has passed at all.

"Go back to sleep, Shadow." He finally speaks, only to repeat the words he murmured earlier, but I'm too exhausted to argue this time. My body lulled into a serene sense of calmness before the world becomes dark all over again.

DESTINED SHADOWS

SIX
Eldon

Sweat beads down my spine as I dig down deeper into my next push-up. The ache in my muscles is still relatively dull, so I keep going, letting the sounds of the waves crashing in the distance offer a sense of calmness that is much needed.

I slept enough to call it more than a nap, but I'm out here earlier than usual because it felt like my visions were trying to infiltrate my dreams. That's never happened before, and it didn't really succeed this time either, but it was enough to leave me restless. Remnants of ravens flutter in my mind, all black, bar one, but I can't recall anything else.

Shaking it off, I splay my fingers out in the grass beneath me, using nature to ground me, bringing me back to the present so I don't start digging too deep into my mind again. I'm expecting the guys to show up soon, which helps me focus better too. I don't want to consider Raven at this moment because she needs to rest, and if I manage to get my hands on her, that would be the last thing on my mind.

A creak pulls me from my thoughts and I tilt my head up just in time to see Brax through the floor-length glass doors. He's not stepping out of his room, though. No. He's tiptoeing out of Raven's.

Motherfucker.

He doesn't even bother to glance in this direction since he's usually the first one up, so I get the full view of watching him slip back into his room, leaving the shared living space untouched like he was never there at all. A tinge of jealousy passes over my skin, my face heating with irritation as I work faster and harder at these stupid fucking push-ups in hopes that I'll cool the fuck down before he gets out here.

Impossible.

My closed-off friend, practically my brother, casually saunters outside. To the untrained eye, it would appear he hasn't a care in the world. Except I know him and easily spot the crease between his eyebrows. The one that only shows when he's more stressed out than usual. He's wearing more than the black boxers he had on earlier, now in black jogger shorts matching my own as he moves over to the weights with a grunt as his offered greeting.

I try to keep my mouth shut, bite my tongue, and act unfazed, but my lips are already moving before I can stop. "Struggle to sleep?" I ask, my tone clipped as I push down once more.

"Yeah." He doesn't look in my direction, keeping his gaze tilted to the sky as he starts his weights routine.

"Is that because of all the fucking you were doing or because of everything that happened yesterday?"

I'm certain he almost drops the dumbbells as his gaze whips to mine and his eyes narrow. "What the fuck are you talking about?" His stumble is short-lived as he quickly continues his lifts.

Running my tongue over my teeth, I push down one last time before jumping to my feet, wiping my hands on my shorts as I turn to face him head-on. "Are we not going to acknowledge the fact that you slipped out of Raven's room just now?"

His jaw ticks but I don't put him off enough to stop lifting this time. "No, we're not."

He tilts away from me again and I reach for my water, gulping down half the bottle before wiping my mouth with the back of my hand. "It's not actually a question, you know. It's rhetorical."

"Still doesn't mean I'm having this conversation with you," he scoffs in response, which only irritates me more.

I like to be in control of everything, down to the last drop, and that includes the information I know. Especially when I know he's keeping his thoughts to himself and a lot of shit has happened in the past twenty-four hours. How has it only been that fucking long? I'm tripping out, so I can't imagine how he feels, but he's offering no sliver of hope that he's willing to share either.

Biting back my jealousy, I focus on my friend instead of my own needs. "I know you, man. If you don't talk about this shit, you're eventually going to explode, and I'd like to refrain from the hazards that come with that." My hand mindlessly moves to the scar on my hip from one of the previous times he's let his emotions build up inside of him. His eyes trail the motion but he continues to ignore me. Excellent. It looks like that's how we're playing it then.

I can play dirty if needed, and it seems he needs a reminder of that. "You can ignore me all you want, but you know I'll call in Mom for reinforcements." I cock a brow at him, silently pleading for him to challenge me, but all I get is a glare.

"You wouldn't."

I shake my head at him. He needs to see the bigger picture and fast. "It's more than just us now, Brax. It's Raven too, and I'll do whatever is necessary to keep her protected. Even from you."

I don't know who I want to get my hands on first; Brax for the shitty attitude he's been walking around with all day or Raven for bringing his grumpy ass back from the dead to begin with. Obviously, I'm more inclined to *not* want the latter, but damn, he's not making it easy.

Classes have continued all morning like nothing happened yesterday, and that's definitely rubbing me the wrong way too, but there are bigger things to address. Things that impact me on a more personal level. Like the fact that I'm growing attached to a damn necromancer.

A hot one at that.

I should have known this woman was more than any of us could imagine. I should have listened to what my vision was telling me, it was right there in front of me the whole time and I couldn't decipher it. As it plays in my mind now, while our history professor drones on, it all makes perfect sense.

Pink-feathered raven.

Black and white chess set.

A storm.

Everything shakes with the chaos, but only one piece falls.

A bishop.

The raven slowly moves toward it, rolling it around with its claw a few times before it finally manages to get a good grasp on it and stands it up again. The moment the base of the bishop reconnects to the chessboard, the raven's feathers turn black.

The only thing that hasn't technically happened is Raven's hair turning black. Even as I stare at the back of her head now, it still stands out with the array of pink strands.

As much as it all makes sense, it feels like it's stifling the air between us since there hasn't been a damn minute to go over everything. That's all going to change tonight, though. I'm done with waiting around. The second classes are finished for the day, we're hashing this out. She looks at each of us with trepidation in her eyes, like she's waiting for a witch hunt or something.

By the end of the day, this woman is going to know that if a witch hunt ever came, we'd all be shoulder to shoulder with her, ready to bring this whole fucking place to its knees. I'm not stupid, I'm aware she's spent a long time taking care of herself, but not on my watch. Not now. My little bird isn't facing the world alone anymore, nor is she withering away in a cage.

She's mine, ours, and she's going to learn what that actually means. Brax too. Whether he likes it or not.

Someone scraping their chair along the floor jars me

from my thoughts and I quickly realize the class is being dismissed. Rushing to my feet along with everyone else, I manage to sidestep Zane, beating him to Raven's side.

She blinks up at me knowingly, and I smirk. Leila takes her left side, knowing full well she's earning glares from the other guys, but I think Raven secretly loves that Leila doesn't back down from us. If I'm honest, it impresses me too. Most girls would be trying to befriend her just to get closer to us, whereas Leila couldn't seem to give a shit whether we're in the room or not. If anything, she'd like to steal Raven for herself to do whatever girly bullshit they get up to.

Not tonight, though. Tonight we're making waves with the new revelations of her magic.

Reaching for Raven's hand, I run my thumb over her knuckles as we head for the door, Zane leading the way with a grumble, Creed right behind him, while Brax keeps a step behind the rest of us. It should be weird that we instantly found the need to surround Raven and protect her, even when moving from class to class, but nothing else has ever felt as right as that.

Once we're through the door and heading toward lunch, I lean in close, the smell of her vanilla shampoo consuming my senses as I press a kiss to her temple. I want to convey how I feel about her without words, which is hard as hell for me since I'm better at expressing myself that way, but her clasp on my hand tightens at the touch and fills me with hope that she understands.

I'm here, and there's nowhere else I'd rather be.

The noise around us gets louder with all the chatter as we step into the dining hall. I expect Raven to try and direct me to the table she sat at with Leila on her first day here, but for the first time, she doesn't fight our pull as we gravitate toward our usual spot.

Leila pulls out her chair at the end and Raven grabs for the next one, but before she can take a seat, I lift her up in the air, her back to my front, before I take the spot and place her on my knee. The squeak that parts her lips makes me grin.

Zane snags the chair to my right, his hand instantly reaching for Raven's thigh as I breathe her in. Creed and Brax sit across from us, not uttering a word, but the disappointment that Raven is already occupied is evident. Creed's lips purse in distaste, while Brax's frown only deepens as his jaw repeatedly tics.

"How are you going to eat with me in your lap?"

I grin, my hand finding the bare skin at the hem of her skirt, and I trail delicate patterns over her thigh. "Little Bird, what if I want to be eating you?"

She shivers against me, a slight hum vibrating in her chest as she leans deeper into me. Her tongue sweeps across her bottom lip as she tilts her face to look me dead in my eyes. That should be my warning sign, but I'm too absorbed in her to notice.

"Do you want to spread my legs wide open and eat me out on the table for everyone to see, Eldon?" The purr from her lips stuns me, my eyes fixed on her mouth as I nod. "Do you want to feast on me? Make me yours in front of the whole academy?"

"Fuck yes."

I have no control. None.

Her hand cups my cheek, her thumb stroking over my lips as my cock stiffens in my pants and my heart pounds in my chest.

"Don't get his hopes up, Raven. That's not going to happen and you know it," Zane murmurs from my right, killing my fun. It startles me for a second that he can hear us and I chance a glance at Leila, but she's occupied ordering her food. If she can hear us, she's not letting on.

"Creed let me," Raven retorts, quirking a brow at Zane, and I frown for a second, trying to understand what she means. Then I remember when I found the pair of them out in the woods, putting on a little show, but still, it was only me who watched.

"I can make everyone see nothing but darkness if that's what you need right now, Raven," Creed chirps in from across the table, a slow smirk lifting the corner of his mouth, and my cock throbs.

I'm about to answer for her when a flickering blue flame appears to consume the ceiling for a moment, garnering everyone's attention and settling the room in silence. It disappears just as quickly and Professor Burton appears in its wake.

"Students, I apologize for interrupting your lunch, but I have news that cannot wait." *Fuck, what now?* I glance at Zane, then Brax and Creed, before settling on Raven. The uncertainty is clear. "Due to the unforeseen circumstances that took place yesterday, we had to advise The Monarchy who, in return, insisted that a parent and guardian visitation be organized." The disapproval is clear by the glare on his face, but we all know The Monarchy overrules everyone else, so he doesn't have a say in this any more than we do. "With that in mind, a family dinner has been arranged for tonight as a matter of urgency to put their minds at ease."

He disappears without another word, leaving everyone to gape at the now blank space. Our parents are coming. The worry on Raven's face has me on high alert and the knowledge that my plan to talk this shit out with her has been delayed irritates me. But there are some positives to the situation.

Although it might pause my Raven issue, I can defend her from her family and it, thankfully, aids my point with Brax. My reinforcements are coming, and the side-eye he gives me tells me he knows it, too.

DESTINED SHADOWS

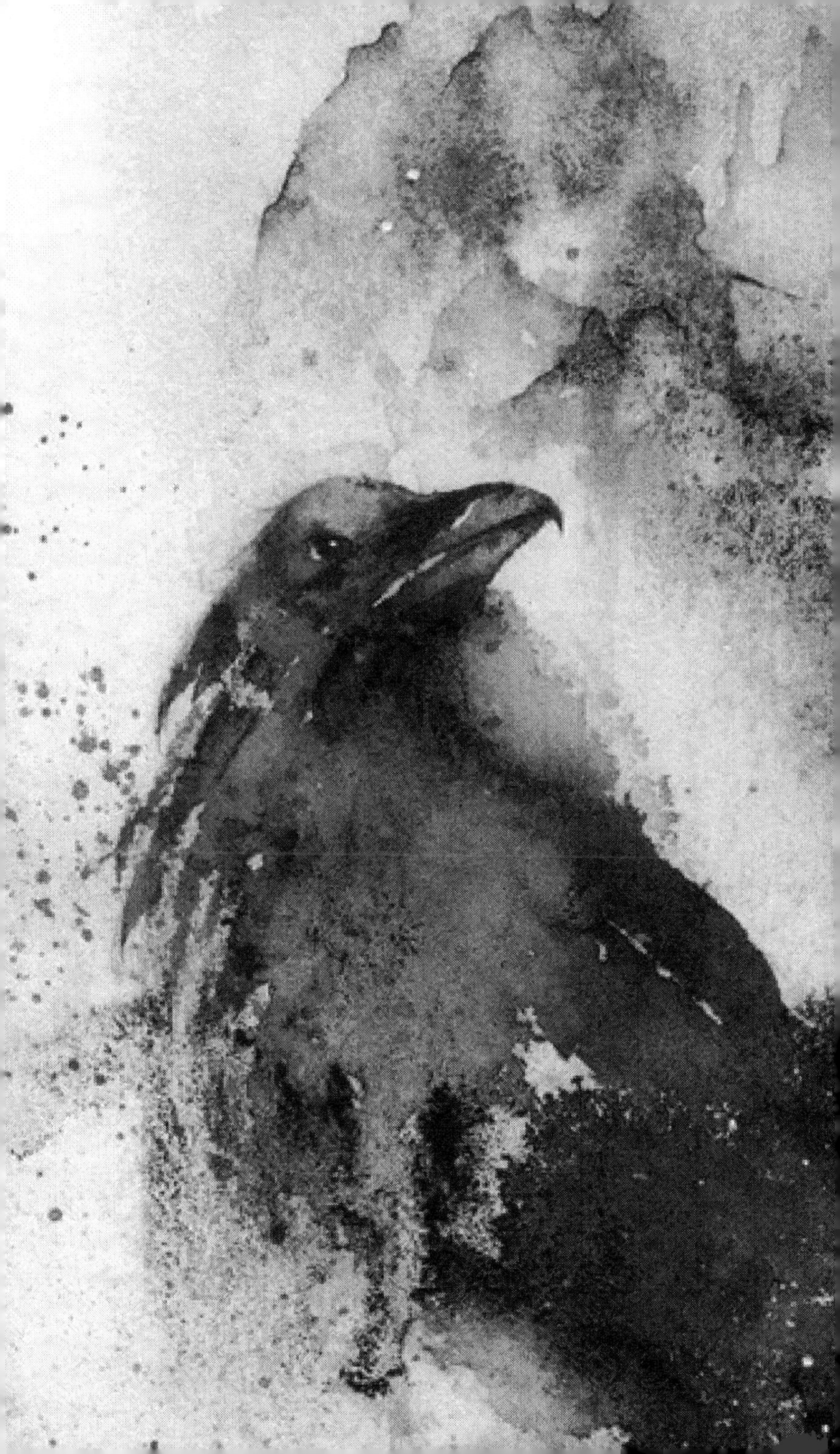

SEVEN

Raven

As if my life couldn't get any worse right now. I'm sinking in despair on the inside while the world keeps spinning around me, and to top it all off, my freaking parents are coming. I do *not* need the stress that comes with Abel, and my headache only increases at the thought of seeing Mama too.

She's going to take one look at me and know. She'll see the difference I'm feeling inside and there's going to be nothing I can do about it.

Swiping a hand down my face, I stare at my reflection. The natural light still streams in through my bedroom window, brightening up the room perfectly for me to touch up my makeup. I've kept it as natural as possible, wanting to have a layer of protection between me and the world, but I don't even feel like I look the same.

I've read of those times when women look in the mirror, assessing themselves, detailing every part of their appearance, and I realize that, until this very moment, it's not something I've ever done. Yeah, I've stared at my reflection, done my hair and makeup, but I've never looked deeper than the superficial, taking myself at face value.

It's typical my brain begs for me to do it now after so much has shifted inside of me. After I tried a little mundane magic last night, I've been addicted to trying other little bits, which has left a thrumming feeling in my veins all day. It's euphoric, and I'm obsessed. But now, when I look into my eyes, they seem deeper, bluer somehow.

Is that because of the secret I carry? The magic in my body? I don't know, but now that I've seen it, I can't unsee it.

Turning my palms up, I look down at my hands, fully aware of what I did with them yesterday, but now they look exactly as they always have. I think? Shit, I don't know. I don't think it helps that I woke in Brax's arms, the shadows disappearing with his touch, but as day came, his sweet words disappeared with them and his gruff attitude was back in place.

All I want to do is curl up in a ball and hide away from the world while I get my bearings, maybe visit Ari because the longing inside of me has already started. I don't want to have to people. I'm over it. But I'm also very aware that

I don't really get a say in the matter.

A knock on the door breaks through my musings and I sigh, looking at myself in the mirror once more. The smile I force to my lips falls flatter than my hair on wash day as the door creaks open a second later, and Creed appears in the gap. His own smile instantly drops when he takes me in and he kicks the door shut behind him without pause as he marches across the room.

"Whatever is wrong, tell me. I'll fix it," he murmurs, stopping behind me, leaning forward to nuzzle his nose at my neck, and my body instantly relaxes a little.

"Where do I even begin?"

His gaze meets mine in the mirror, a sense of understanding in his onyx pools. This time when my lips tip up, it's real. Pained, but real.

"Do you want me to go and slay your family so you don't have to see them tonight?" he offers, sincerity in the tension of his jaw, and I laugh.

"Please. That would at least take one thing off my plate." He stands tall as if to head for the door, but I grab his arm, holding his wrist and turning to face him. "I'm joking. For now, at least. I feel like there's enough blood on our hands for a few days, don't you think?"

"For you, I'd take more."

Hot. As. Fuck.

I don't think that was what he was going for, but it has

my core alive. Eldon was right; unhinged is definitely my thing.

He's not exactly saying I accept you and your crazy fucking magic, along with the unforgivable I did yesterday, but it almost sounds like it. *There goes my hope, getting ahead of me again.*

"If you're happy to see them, shall we get it over with so we can get back here and talk through whatever else is filling that pretty head of yours?"

I nod as his arm slips from my hold and he reaches for my hand. Lifting me from my seat, he pulls me into his chest, tightly wrapping his arms around me. It takes me a second to relax into the hug, not realizing how much I needed it until now.

One by one, my muscles ease, and it surprises me how tense I actually was, but I'm quickly reminded the second he steps back and I have to prepare for the family gathering. Steeling my spine, I roll my shoulders back, my jaw tensing along with it. Creed notices the shift in me but this time he doesn't try to ease my concerns.

Uniform is a requirement for the evening. Why? I don't know, but it feels like another barrier around me, so I'll take it. Creed's hand settles at the small of my back, guiding me toward the door, but before we reach it, it's opened from the other side.

Eldon.

"I thought you knew how to knock?" Creed grunts, making me smirk, but Eldon only grins in response.

"I know a lot of things, doesn't mean I give a shit." He winks like I'm supposed to know what that means, but he doesn't elaborate and I am too worked up to dig deeper.

"Let's get this shit over with," Brax states from the front door, Zane standing beside him, and I hum in agreement.

"Let's."

The air is thick as we step into the hall. The layout is the exact same as the night of the gala. Damn, that feels like an eternity ago. Everything was different then. I hadn't had the joy of my parents removing the hold on my magic or the feel of it running through my veins. It was also the night I got to experience three of the Bishops, a night I wouldn't give up for anything.

With that reminder in my thoughts, I put one foot in front of the other, heading toward where my parents are already seated with Sebastian cozied up to Abel. The other half of the table is empty, though, and I remember that's because it was Finn who was seated with us last time. There's a reason his parents aren't here tonight. A reason *he* isn't here tonight. A casualty of a war we have no idea about.

I feel eyes on me as I cut through the room and I know it's the Bishops, or at least some of them. The whole way here they were insisting on joining me, but I don't want my father to see their importance to me. Sebastian may have told him, but it's different than seeing it, and he doesn't deserve to see my growing weakness with his own eyes.

My father's back is to me, Sebastian murmuring in his ear while Mama glances around the room, looking everywhere but in my direction. I come to a stop next to Sebastian, hearing the slightest whisper as they seemingly don't realize I'm here.

"You told me to make sure something drastic happened to bring out her powers, but…"

"Raven, you're here," Mama exclaims, interrupting whatever the fuck I was overhearing. Sebastian's gaze tilts up with a glare and I want to press him on what he was talking about, my pulse ringing in my ears, but Abel stands, his chair scraping obnoxiously across the wood floor as he calls out my name.

"Raven, we're so pleased to see you. How are you feeling after… everything?" Abel moves to place his hand on my shoulder and I quickly sidestep him, recoiling at the thought of his touch on me. If he notices my distaste or even cares about it, he doesn't show it, which is far from a surprise. This man has the power to be oblivious to everything around him except what he deems important at the time.

He doesn't care if I'm loving and affectionate with him. He just wants to know if my magic has made an appearance. The glimmer in his eyes shows it.

"Abel," I offer in greeting, continuing to move around the table. Mama opens her arms for a hug, but my earlier worries resurface and I slip down into the seat beside her instead. Too scared that if she touches me, she'll know.

"I was so worried when I heard the news," Mama gushes, reaching her hand out, but I don't move to offer any kind of embrace and she eventually drops her hands into her lap. I don't miss the glance over her shoulder at my father and Sebastian's words from moments earlier repeat in my mind.

"You told me to make sure something drastic happened to bring out her powers."

Was he talking about me?

The way my gut swirls tells me he was. Did Sebastian and my father have a hand in what happened yesterday? I can't deal with this shit on top of everything else. Why can't things be more black and white?

"Raven..." Abel's voice sounds irritated, and when I bring my gaze to his, he nods toward Mama. A silent command to respond to her. What is it he expects me to say?

Clearing my throat, I run my hands over my pleated

skirt. "I'm fine, Mama. I'm here, aren't I?" There, how's that for some fake response?

Mama's eyebrows pinch, seeing straight through the façade while Abel leans back in his seat, assessing me with curious eyes.

"Any change since we last saw you?"

"You mean since you violated me?" I quirk a brow, my lips twisting at the vein that instantly throbs at his temple. If he wanted a good, obedient child, he should have remained focused on Sebastian and left me the fuck alone.

"Are you always this dramatic, Raven? As a child, I remember you being so sweet and innocent." His musing pisses me off, and I can't tell whether that's what he was aiming for or not.

Fucker.

"Do you always pull your children from class, pin them down, and let someone mess with their magic?" My blood boils as I snap at him. I hate that I'm giving him a reaction, but it's impossible not to.

"Raven, please lower your voice. We rushed here to make sure you were okay after the terrible attack. I don't want to waste what time we have with you arguing," Mama pleads with tired eyes.

My nostrils flare, my teeth sinking into my tongue to bite back another lashing they deserve. "I'm sorry I can't give you what you want, but it wasn't me who made decisions for our family all of those years ago. I'm just dealing with the aftermath of it." My gaze cuts between them both, not even bothering with Sebastian as I brace my hands on the table and rise. "Now, if all you wanted to see was me alive, you've had your fill. Unfortunately, whatever the fuck that was yesterday, I'm still as Void as I was the day before. And I can only assume your presence is to confirm whether I'm still a Void or not, so I'm sorry to disappoint, but I am what I am."

Before I can take a step away from the table, Mama grabs my arm, halting me in place. Her arms are around my neck in the next breath, a tighter embrace than I ever remember as she squeezes me close. "I love you, sweet Raven. Never forget that. You can lie to them, lie to my face, lie to whoever you want, but I see it, I feel it, I know it." Bile burns the back of my throat, my heart beating so hard in my chest I'm sure it's going to burst. "I can see the change in your eyes, a sense of distress like never before. Your secret is safe with me. Take a deep breath, gather yourself, and remember what I said. Follow the sun, destroy the shadows, and survive another dawn."

She releases me a second later, the truth flashing in her eyes; she definitely knows. I subtly nod in response before dashing from the table without a backward glance. I almost stumble over my own feet as I try to hurry away, but I'm quickly enveloped in strong arms a moment later.

"Where's my Dove flying off to?"

I sag against Zane, not caring that we're in a room full of people, as I let my heart calm and the tension ebb a little. "I was escaping my cage," I murmur back when I can finally focus.

"I've got you," he breathes against my hair, the words barely audible above the growing chatter. I'm not sure how much time passes before he leans back and drapes an arm around my shoulders. "Come and join us for a few minutes before we head out, okay? I've already spoken to my father about putting a word in with the administration over parent seating the next time they spring this on us."

I gape at him in surprise. "You definitely didn't have to do that."

"I know," he says with a shrug, guiding me through the crowd.

"I don't think I want to put them in anyone else's vicinity. They're a lot for me to handle, nevermind them tainting anyone else," I grumble, and he squeezes my shoulder in support.

"We've got you, Dove. Always. The good, the bad, and the ugly."

His words cause a stir inside of me, but I don't get long enough to accept them before he brings me to a stop at another table. Eldon sits across from the seat in front of me, his mother to his left and Creed to his right. I take the free chair beside Brax while Zane drops into the seat to my left.

"Your father had to rush out, Zane," Eldon's mother explains sympathetically, but Zane quickly waves her off.

"It's not a problem, Mrs. Rhodes. He warned me already that it might happen. You remember Raven, right?"

"Of course," she gushes, a wide smile on her face as she takes me in. I do my best to offer her one back, but my head is a mess. "It's so lovely to see you again, Raven. I spoke to your mother at the last event. She had wonderful things to say about you."

My smile grows tight at the mention of my mother, but I quickly shake it off. If what she murmured to me is true, I can trust her. I hope.

"She has to, right? She's my mama."

Eldon's mother chuckles at my response, her grin spreading from ear to ear like that's exactly the kind of response she was expecting. I don't add that if she had asked my father, he may have told her something else entirely, even though the words hang heavy on my tongue.

"I like your spark, Raven. Even when you were a young girl, you used to light up a room with your wit and presence." My eyes widen at her remark and my body freezes at the mention of me as a child.

"You knew me as a child?" My voice is softer than I would hope, but she doesn't seem to notice.

"Of course. Evangeline and I became fast friends when we attended Silvercrest Academy together. We lost contact when you two… went off the grid, but there are pieces of you both that are just as strong now as they were then. Shadowmoor can't take everything from us now, can it?"

Shaking my head, my shoulders relax as her words soothe me in a way I can't quite describe. "You're right. It can't." She winks at me, and I can feel the guys all staring in my direction, but I keep my gaze focused on her.

"Eldon tells me Brax is being quieter than usual and he's trying to bring me in as reinforcements to get our tough guy to break. Do you think it's necessary too?" She asks, changing the subject, and my gaze whips straight to Brax's.

I remember last night and how he whispered words into the darkness with no effort at all, only to fall into a pit of silence as he let his body do the talking. I'm certain my cheeks are reddening as I twist my lips.

Brax looks at me with hooded eyes, delving deep into my soul as the question plays on repeat in my head. The sound of someone clearing their throat jolts me and I quickly turn my attention back to Eldon's mother.

"He's been talking to me just fine."

Her gaze flickers from Brax to me a few times before she braces her arms on the table and inches closer. "Bottled up?"

I shrug. "Maybe a little, but he's a goddamn gargoyle. It's never going to be easy piercing through his tough exterior, right?"

She chuckles at me again, leaning back and giving Eldon a pointed look. "I think the reinforcements are already there, son. Give him time."

Eldon glares at that, pushing back at her like Brax isn't even present, but I don't hear a single word of it as Brax's huge hand grips my thigh. His thumb runs back and forth, making my body weep with anticipation as I refuse to look at him.

"Okay, you've seen us in the flesh now, you good?" Eldon grumbles, rising to his feet as he looks down at his mother, who continues to grin.

"I'm good."

"Awesome, because we've got other stuff to do," he states, making his way around the table until he's standing beside me and offering his hand. The others stand as well and I frown at him in confusion.

"Like what?"

He smirks at me as if it's obvious, but I clearly haven't caught on.

"Like you."

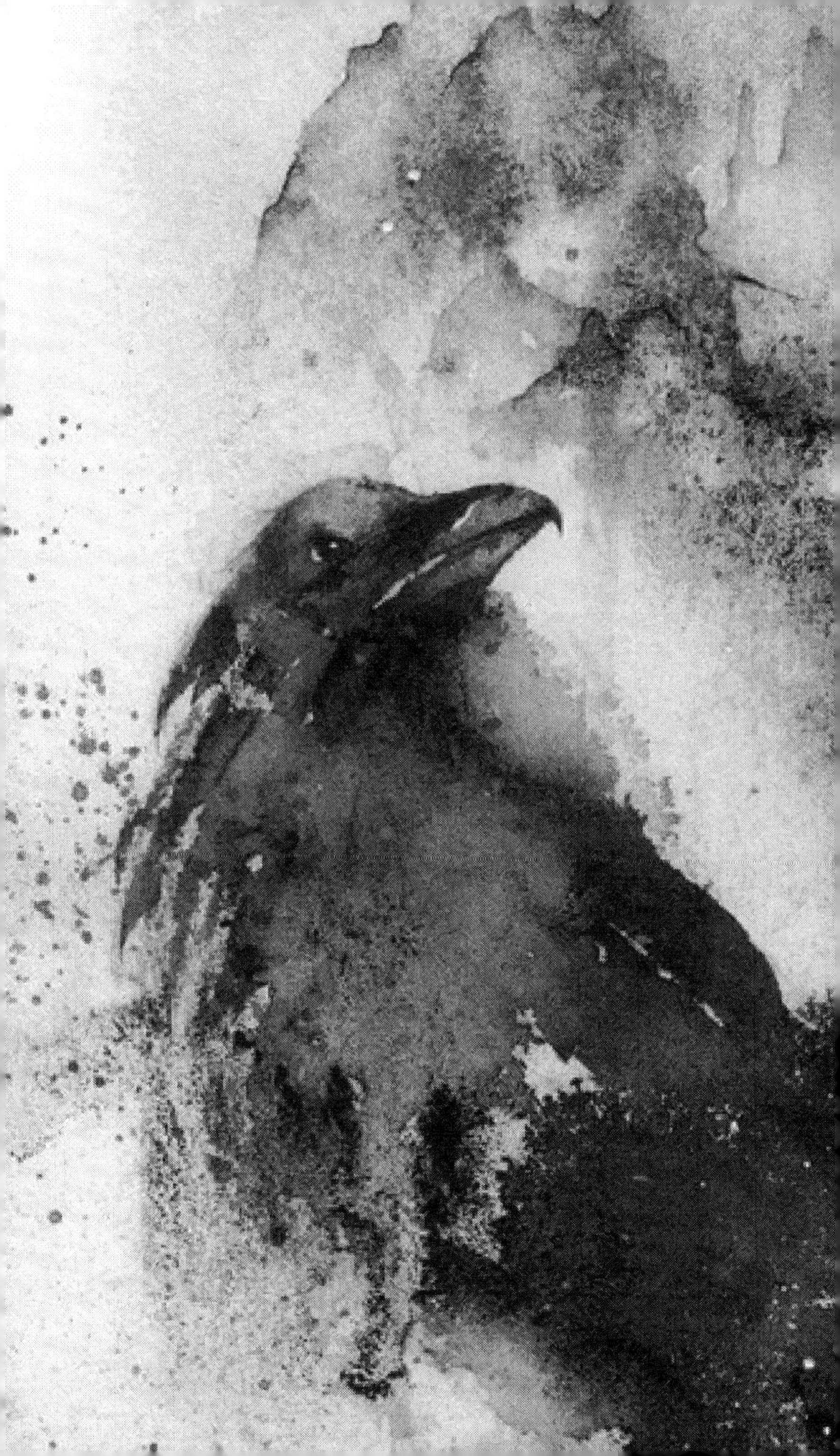

EIGHT
Raven

Eldon doesn't offer any more details as we make our way back to the house, leaving me just as tightly coiled as I was at the table. The way he holds my hand, shifting between squeezing tighter for a beat and running his thumb over my knuckles, reassures me but still gives me no preparation for what I'm walking into.

Creed's hand is solid at the small of my back, keeping him just as close, as Brax stomps in front, leading the way, and Zane hovers a step or two behind us.

It should be odd that there are four guys and only one of me, but I think it would break me if any of them demanded that I choose. All that matters is that it's working for us. They're not asking me to do anything like that. If anything, they like it even more. The housemate handbook flashes in my mind, combined with Zane's smart mouth, and I relax at the impending doom tempting to take over me.

Once Eldon has done whatever he needs, I can hopefully talk through everything running through my mind, so I'm not constantly triggered with a bout of worry over where I stand. Casual is usually fine with me, but I can't deny that this feels like more, and after what I did to Brax… there's no coming back from that.

We turn down the path that leads to our house and Brax unlocks the door, letting it swing open with a little more force than necessary before heading for the dining table. Everyone else follows him, so I keep in step, murmuring my thanks when Zane holds my chair out for me.

Eldon drags his chair out to my right, dropping down beside me with his usual smirk on his face. "Okay, what is it—"

"Food first," Creed interjects, and I glare at him. Pity my stomach doesn't get the memo that we're mad, though, because it rumbles in agreement a second later. He lifts his eyes, silently begging me to challenge him, but I know when to keep my mouth shut…

When I'm dead.

"I'm beyond stressed with this weird vibe between us. Food can—" Pizza appears in front of me, cutting off my train of thought as I gape down at the deliciousness, drool likely clinging to my chin. Deep dish, extra cheesy, topped high with pepperoni. Fuck. "Fine, food first," I relent, grabbing a slice. I sink back in my seat, groaning at the good stuff as my eyelids fall closed.

"Now my dick is hard," Zane grunts, and I peer out of the corner of my eye to find a grin on his face as he makes an exaggerated show of readjusting himself.

Food or dick?

Dick or food?

"You're distracting her. Let the fucking woman eat so we can go over everything. Then we can think about wet dicks and toe-curling orgasms, okay?" Eldon states, making my core clench at the idea. I can't find any words, so I hum my agreement and take another bite of pizza.

Thankfully, no one else speaks as we devour the pizzas. I have no control over my hunger and don't stop until I can't fit any more in my mouth. The others aren't far behind me when Zane makes a pile of napkins appear and I clean off my hands, the reminder of Eldon's announcement rearing its head again.

Turning to face him, I exhale nervously and brace myself. "What is it we need to deal with?"

"You." I can't decide whether he just enjoys causing me distress or doesn't realize that things aren't as simple as he says.

"Just because you know what you're thinking doesn't mean I do, Eldon, and it's not easy trying to play it cool all the time," I grumble, leaving myself more vulnerable than

I would have liked, but my walls come down so effortlessly in their proximity it's impossible to stop.

His eyes widen in surprise and he quickly adjusts how he's sitting so he's closer to me, our elbows almost touching. "I need to make sure we clear the air and we all know where we stand. We haven't really had a chance to do that since leaving the outpost, so I think it's more vital than ever that you understand what you mean to me. Powers or not."

Well then.

Gulping, I wet my bottom lip. *How the fuck am I supposed to be a badass, independent queen when he says shit like that and makes me all gooey on the inside?*

"That's a conversation I'm here for," Zane adds, while Creed nods and Brax simply stares at me, giving nothing away. Shocker.

"Maybe we need to start off with understanding how Raven's magic feels to her," Creed offers, a soft smile on his face as he eyes me across the table, and I nod numbly in response as I try to piece it all together.

"I don't really know. I just… Brax was just…" I swipe a hand down my face, trying to gather my words instead of rushing to answer. Sighing, I look at the gargoyle in question, his eyes burning into mine as I clear my throat. "I just know that I was petrified, heartbroken, and distraught beyond words. When you were unresponsive, when we couldn't find your sword, it was all too much. I couldn't bear to think about you not being here with us. And then my magic just..." I can't stop saying *just,* but it's just... indescribable.

"Can you remember what you did? How it felt?" Brax asks, leaning on the table slightly as he keeps his eyes fixed on me.

I frown, trying to remember, but it's all a blur, so I shake my head.

"Her hands were on you and she let out the most guttural cry I've ever heard. It was like the world stood still... and then your eyes opened," Eldon explains, my heart racing as he describes the scene, and I can't imagine how it makes Brax feel. His eyes still bore into mine, not even turning to his friend. Offering me the same reminder from that moment.

One brown. One green.

"You're a necromancer," Brax states, the words barely audible over the sudden pounding of my pulse in my ears, but I can't hide from it anymore.

"I am. I'm a necromancer." I've said it before, but it still feels foreign on my tongue. No matter what, I can't change this about myself. Whether any of us like it or not, it's not going to magically disappear.

"How does that make you feel?" Zane asks, running his palm over my thigh, and I turn to look at him.

"I don't know," I answer truthfully. "In Shadowmoor, there was no one with this level of magic, not even close. People could barely get by with mundane stuff, never mind…" I wave my hand around, trying to explain, and he nods in understanding. "It's not something I grew up around. Mama didn't really use her magic around me at home, and I don't really remember it from when I was a child. I've never met a necromancer. I know it's against the law to resurrect anyone, and I know I've already freaking done that," I ramble, my emotions clouding my thoughts. "I feel like I'm sinking and it's frustrating as hell and not who I am at all."

His hand tightens on my thigh, grounding me without words as he lifts his other hand to my cheek. "I'll never let you sink, Dove. Not alone, at least. And not because of something as incredible as this."

"Incredible?" My eyebrows pinch closer together, and he looks at me like I'm crazy.

"You heard me, Raven Hendrix. I wouldn't go all crazy over a girl, give her the housemate handbook and fall fucking hard for her if she wasn't incredible. Magic or not, you're everything. But I'm not shocked to learn that you're a badass fucking necromancer, just like you're a queen at everything else."

My cheeks feel like they're on fire, his words mirroring my own earlier, and the steel in his gaze shows me the truth I didn't realize I needed.

"He's right, Raven. I know necromancers are usually frowned upon, and what you were able to do, shit, we'll be eternally grateful for. If there's any doubt in your mind about our willingness to stay, I'll eradicate it right fucking now," Creed chimes in. Zane drops his hand from my face so I can look in his direction and the rawness in his gaze is just as strong as Zane's was.

"There shouldn't be any doubt at all," Eldon states, reaching for my shoulder. "That's not how this shit goes. We wanted you when you believed you were a Void, and that's not going to change now that you're at the complete opposite end of the scale. It also doesn't change how we feel inside either. I don't fucking love you more because of it. You're not a possession or a toy for me to wrangle and use at will. You're just Raven," he adds, making my chest squeeze tight and my breathing hollow out.

They're saying everything I hoped they would but was too scared to hear, and now I don't know how to process it. I've spent the past twenty-four hours lost in a vortex of doom, and they're tearing it to shreds with just a few words.

A whoosh of air swoops around me, flicking my hair, and I startle when I find myself sitting in Brax's lap, still nestled between Zane and Eldon. His strong grip on my chin tilts my head to meet his gaze, my heart hammering wildly.

The rest of the table fades away as his stare penetrates my soul. "I haven't forgotten what you told me on the lake,

Shadow. What your parents said to you about your magic. I know that will be playing on your mind." His words are softer than I've ever heard him speak before or I'll likely ever hear again. "We're not here to take from you, to use you for your powers, and that's never going to change, I promise you that. We're not going to run for the hills either. We're going to stay right by your side, protecting you just as strongly as you protect us." He reaches for my hand, lifting it to his chest, and I feel the soft thumping of his heart beating.

I feel what he's trying to portray without words and my mouth dries. It's beating because I breathed life into it. It's beating because I protected him just as they'll protect me. I nod, unable to find the right words, and he tucks a loose tendril of hair behind my ear as the rest of the guys come back into focus.

"We also need to consider the fact that with this being such a big gift, necromancers are known to struggle with darkness. The power you'll wield is on another level, and it's usually one of two, if not three, powers overall," Creed explains, making my spine stiffen. I gulp. "I know it's a lot, but if anyone can deal with this, Raven, it's you." The reassurance is clear, but I'm scared to take it.

"You have a lot of belief in me," I murmur, looking at Zane and Eldon, who nod in agreement.

"Why wouldn't we?" Zane retorts, leaving me

speechless. "We're going to have to work on trying to channel your emotions to help with your power so we can work out what makes you tick," he adds, and my eyes widen.

"Everybody operates differently. Anger, sadness, happiness, hope, and anything in between," Eldon states, reaching for my hand. "When you focus on your center, you will start to learn what emotion makes it burn brighter."

I'm going to need a lie down after all of this information. It's exactly what I need and overwhelming all at once.

"What is it for you?" I dare to ask.

"Brax is anger, not that you'll be shocked. Creed is kindness, Zane is happiness and laughter, while I'm connected more with love."

"How am I even supposed to figure that out?"

"I have a fun way we can figure it out if you trust me," Zane offers, a telling smirk on his lips as he caresses my cheek with the back of his hand.

"What's that?"

Brax grunts before anyone can speak and I know that's the only warning we're going to get that he's taking over.

"Outside. Now, Shadow."

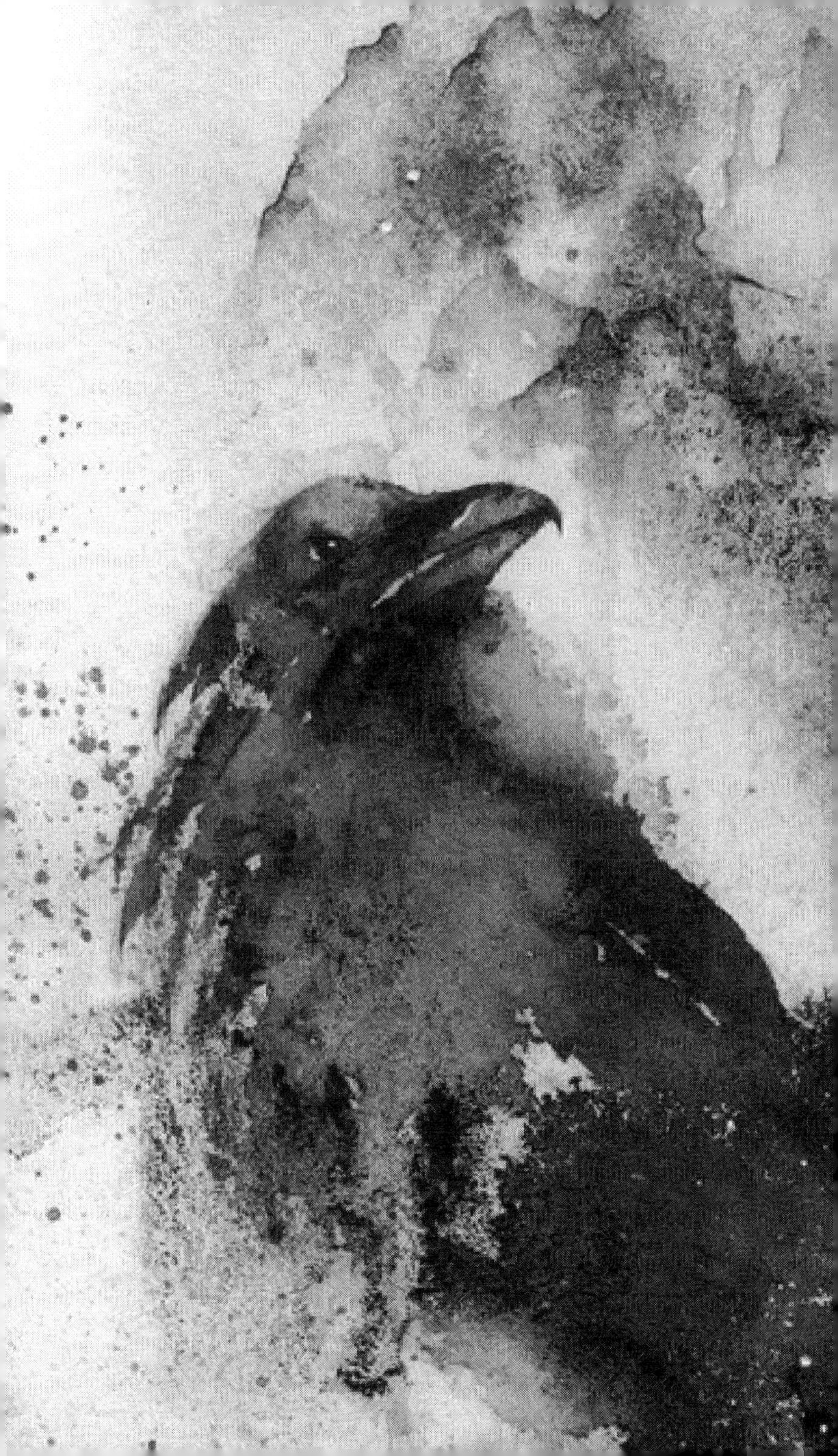

NINE
Raven

Intrigue and excitement coil in my stomach as Brax leads the way. Zane, Creed, and Eldon follow behind me, the tension heightening around us as we step out into the evening air. It's not cold, but a gentle breeze flutters across our skin, ruffling the leaves on the trees as the sound of the waves crashing in the distance echoes around us.

I wiggle my fingers, unsure what to do with myself, as Brax comes to a stop a few steps ahead, standing between two oak trees that are close to the cliff's edge. He lifts his hands out to the side of him for a moment, almost assessing the distance before turning to face me.

He crooks his finger, not offering me a word, and I'm moving despite wanting to give him a mouthful of attitude. Stopping toe to toe with him, I tilt my head back to keep my eyes locked on his. He doesn't utter a word. Instead, he reaches for my arms and extends them at my sides, just as he had done moments earlier.

Once he's satisfied that my arms are straight, he takes a step back, looking me over from head to toe. Retracing his steps, he's back in front of me a moment later, dragging my blazer off my arms before discarding it on the ground without care. A shiver runs down my spine, and it's not from the slight drop in temperature. If anything, I feel hotter now than I did earlier.

His fingers hover at the top button of my shirt, his thumb skimming over my skin, and my breath lodges in my throat. It's embarrassing how much of a goner I am after a single touch from these men, but it consumes me so much that I don't even care.

One button... two... three...

He stops, his chest rising and falling as rapidly as my own, and just when I think he's ready to eliminate the remaining distance between our lips, he fucking drops his hands as he backs up a step or two until he's in line with the other Bishops. Each of them are watching me with utter rapture, their gazes running from my face to the swell of my breasts at the opening of my shirt.

I don't feel intimidated under their stares, but it's impossible not to shift under their gaze. Yet, when I move to drop my arms, I find I'm locked in position.

"What the fuck did you do?" I blurt when I realize I

can't move at all. Not my arms, not my legs, not even the tips of my fingers.

"You lost your right to question my choices when you stepped outside, Shadow. Don't make me stop your lips from moving too. But, if you want to stop, I can—"

"No!" *Fuck.* "No, I'm good," I rush, quicker than I intend to, but he knows he has me exactly where he wants me and there's nothing I can do but succumb to his wishes.

That doesn't mean I have to like him for it, though.

Fucker.

"Eldon, I want you to touch her without actually touching her," Brax orders, and Eldon's eyes light up with mischief.

What does that even mean?

The question is on the tip of my tongue, but I'm quickly distracted by Eldon approaching me.

"Lift her in the air a little, Brax," Eldon murmurs, his grin spreading wider as I rise a few inches above the ground so we're at eye level with one another. "Yeah, just like that." He nibbles on his bottom lip, taking me in, and desire bubbles through my veins.

I'm going to self-combust and no one has even touched me yet.

As if hearing my thoughts, Eldon reaches out, stroking his fingers down my cheek and under my chin, making my breath shallow as I fix my stare on his gaze. His hand lowers, brushing over my collarbone, before teasing over the flimsy material of my bra, and a moan falls from my lips.

"I think that might be my favorite sound, Little Bird," he breathes, leaning in so close his breath flutters against my cheek, making goosebumps prickle on my skin.

"Make me come and I'll sound even better."

His chuckle against my ear is paired with his other hand finding the hem of my skirt at my thigh, caressing the skin so perfectly that I don't care which one of them it is, as long as one of them has their hands on me and makes me climax. I just want to feel it.

"I don't think that's what Brax has in mind, do you?"

I pout, hating the truth in his words, but that doesn't mean I can't try.

"I—"

"What are you feeling right now?"

His question stops me in my tracks, and even though I don't really understand *why* he needs to ask that right now, I answer honestly.

"Coiled tight with anticipation. Desperate for your next touch."

The next groan comes from him, not helping me out at all as my need builds even more. "Search in your soul, Raven. How does your magic feel about that anticipation?"

I frown, hating that he's pulling me away from the

sexual need twisting inside of me, but reluctantly do as he asks, only to come up blank.

"I don't really feel anything," I admit, earning me a sweet kiss on the corner of my lips before he takes a step back.

"It's not anticipation," he declares, winking at me before moving back to the others.

"You can't try and figure out the emotion behind my magic like…this!" I exclaim, my jaw tensing as uncertainty swells in me. This will surely be the death of me.

"You gave up your ability to challenge me, remember?" Brax retorts, cocking a brow at me, and I glare but keep my mouth shut. Whether we find out the emotion or not, I'm guaranteed an orgasm, right? "Good little Shadow," he adds, pissing me off and making my body thrum with even more need at the same time.

He knows exactly how to get under my skin in the most delicious way and I don't hate it.

Fucker.

He leans into Zane, murmuring in his ear for a moment before resuming his stance with his arms folded over his chest. Zane grins from ear to ear, his eyes dancing with desire as he steps toward me.

"Remember, Raven. Don't forget to channel inside of yourself, no matter what emotion you're feeling. That will help us," he states with a wink, and I nod, even though anticipation claws at me, making it impossible to truly process his words. "You trust me, right?" His nose is close to brushing mine, he's that close now, a surprisingly warm breeze fluttering around us.

"Yes," I breathe without question.

"Creed," he hollers, confusing me for a second, and I look to my quiet observer over Zane's shoulder. But no sooner do my eyes land on his does the world fade to darkness. I'm not scared, though. I know it's him, his powers, just like when we were in the woods, and it only makes me feel closer to him.

Taking a deep breath, I try to relax, but fingers trailing down the opening of my academy-issued blouse set me on fire. I assume it's still Zane, but I can't truly tell anymore. I just have to trust in them. One by one, each button is undone until I feel it hang loose at my sides, the breeze kissing even more of my exposed skin. A second later, I no longer feel the material draped over my skin at all and I shiver.

Fingers brush against the waistband of my skirt before the fabric is slowly dragged over my hips and down my thighs. Once again, the feeling lasts for only a moment before it's gone, and I swear my shoes have been removed with them because I can feel a slight breeze on the soles of my feet.

My skin heats, my need evident as I sink my teeth into

my bottom lip, ready to be completely exposed to them.

Excited for Zane's touch, my breaths start to come in shorter, sharper bursts, but an eternity passes and still nothing happens.

"What are you feeling, Dove?" Zane's words drift over me, breaking through the fog of desperation coiled up in my core, and I take a second to consider my answer, but it's hard to focus when hands run over the globes of my ass. "And I don't mean the sexual tension so thick I could cut it with a knife, I mean deeper than that."

Fuck, I don't have anything deeper to offer him, do I?

Running my tongue over my bottom lip, I inhale slowly through my nose before exhaling past my lips. The wind still gently whips around us, but I can't see anything in the darkness and I'm stripped down to my underwear, at their mercy.

Other than the sexual need, there's only one thing I feel. It's exactly what he asked of me earlier. "Trust... I trust you."

"That's it, Dove. And how does that feel in here?" he asks, his fingers trailing over my chest and down between the valley of my breasts.

Fuck.

"It's going to keep feeling hot as fuck if you keep touching me like that," I grumble, his chuckle ringing in my ears a moment later as I delve into my magic like I did before. Just as it was then, I come back with the same, shaking my head with a hint of defeat as my answer.

His lips press at the corner of my mouth a second later, leaving me just as needy as before, but any hope that he's going to continue is short-lived when my vision slowly comes back to me and I see him cutting back across the space to the other Bishops.

All of the anticipation and hope dwindles into irritation and I can't see past it. "This isn't fucking fun anymore," I bite, eager to cover my body and hide it from them, but my arms are still locked in place.

"Raven, you've got this. We just have to focus," Creed says, kindness and hope flashing in his eyes as he softly smiles at me, but I'm too annoyed for it to aid the insufferable feelings building inside of me.

"One more try?" Eldon offers, and my jaw tightens as I glance at him.

I don't know if I can survive another attempt under these circumstances. I'm worn out and exhausted already. Anything more and I might combust. If not with an orgasm, then with rage. The look in his eyes has the ability to work wonders on me because, despite the fury threatening to make me call this whole thing off and take care of myself, I find myself nodding anyway.

He grins with victory, but it's not him that steps forward. It's not Zane coming to rectify the misery he's left me in, or even Creed with his pending darkness.

No.

It's Brax.

The prowl in his every step quickens my heart, making it gallop in my chest. It's on the tip of my tongue to tell the asshole to fuck off and call it quits, but the second he's standing right in front of me, it's all forgotten. The lace covering my pussy is gone with a snap as he tears at it before plunging two fingers deep into my core, and I scream.

Relief and desire swirl inside of me, notable in my whimpers as he doesn't relent, swirling his fingers deep in my core. My muscles tense, excitement zapping through my limbs as the first note of my orgasm tingles in my toes.

It's gone the second I feel it, his fingers too, and my cries of pleasure quickly morph into frustration. "Don't fuck with me, Brax," I bite, my face dropping so my chin hits my chest. My eyes close as I try to calm my breathing, but it's not looking good.

"What do you feel, Shadow?"

I whimper at his question, my eyes squeezing even tighter. If I was ever curious if I was a submissive and into edging, this right here confirms I'm so far from it that my name will never be uttered in the same sentence.

I'm weak for their touch, desperate for their attention, and embarrassingly needy to let my body take control.

I know I'm not going to get anything without an answer, though. Digging deep, I only feel anger, fury, rage, frustration, and agitation, or whatever can describe the storm brewing inside me, and none of it elicits anything in my magic.

"Shadow."

"I feel like I hate you right now. I feel every version of torment, and none of it does anything. Is that what you want to hear?" I look at him through hooded eyes, my jaw tight, but he doesn't falter under my glare, likely because his magic continues to hold me in place.

"And how do you feel when my fingers are in your sweet pussy?" he asks, plunging his fingers back into my core. My anger doesn't ebb for a few seconds, but as the pad of his finger crazes my G-spot, it's impossible to cling to the emotion. "Tell me," he grunts, his motions getting harder and faster, and tears of ecstasy prick the back of my eyelids.

"I-I don't know," I chatter, my head tilting back as the need to press my thighs together becomes overwhelming but no longer possible in my current state. The tingles start in my toes and I try to hide my reaction to it, not wanting him to stop *again*, but something else gives me away because he retreats just as quickly as he did last time.

I'm done.

I'm *so* fucking done.

A cry parts my lips, like one I imagine at war, the brutal

end coming. That's what this feels like.

Clenching my eyes shut again, I can't look at him. "Let me down. Now."

"What are you feeling, Shadow?"

"Fuck. You." My chest rattles with every inhale. "Let. Me. Down. Now," I repeat, my insides trembling with the overwhelming disappointment and sadness colliding in my mind.

"Raven. Tell me what you're feeling," Brax pushes, but I'm done talking to this asshole.

My eyes collide with his, and I snarl. "Fuck—"

His hand grips my jaw tight, making me wince, but that doesn't make him falter as he looks deep into my eyes, piercing my soul like he always does.

"Feel it. Take a fucking minute and *feel* it."

My nostrils flare with annoyance. I don't want to listen to him. I don't want his guidance. I want nothing from this man. But I'm still a toy in the palm of his hand and the only way I'm going to get out of here is if I draw this shit to an end.

I close my eyes, my jaw still tight with irritation, and the second I enter the abyss that homes my magic, I feel it. More than that, I see the flickers of a purple flame. Whatever I'm feeling right now connects me to this very spot. Pinpointing what that is feels like a battle I'm not prepared for.

It's not the anger or anything else that wants me to rain

carnage down on Brax. I felt that earlier and it didn't give me this. No, this is something else, something deeper.

Blinking my eyes open, I feel the cool, wet stains of my tears along my cheeks, and it's a startling realization. One that has the purple flicker blossoming inside of me.

"Tell me what it is," Brax whispers, barely an inch between us.

I gulp, keeping my lips locked tight. Right now, he doesn't deserve the knowledge, and I can't bring myself to admit how I feel.

"Move out of the fucking way, Brax," Creed hisses, shoulder checking his friend so he can be the one standing face to face with me. I get the sense that Brax moved willingly, but I can't fixate on that fact while Creed cups my cheek, distracting me from everything but him. "It's sadness. Her magic is fueled by sadness."

"I didn't make her sad," Brax interjects, earning himself a deathly glare from the fierce onyx eyes in front of me.

"Don't bullshit me. That might not have been your intention, but look at her. She's fueled by it. Now drop the magic." His scathing gaze turns to a soft stare as he looks back at me and my arms drop to my sides as my feet dig into the grass beneath me.

"Sadness... fuck, that's hard. I don't want you to have to feel that every single time..." Zane murmurs, coming to stand beside Creed, and I sniffle, still at a loss for words.

"Fuck your sweet words at her discomfort, Zane," Eldon grunts a moment before he envelops me in his arms from behind. "Make her fucking scream." His hands splay out over my stomach, slowly stroking lower until he meets the apex of my thighs.

Creed drops to his knees in front of me as I stand in a daze, but before he can reach for me, he's shoved out of the way by Brax, who falls to his knees while swooping up my thighs and draping them over his shoulders.

I don't have time to deny him as his lips wrap around my clit, sucking like his life depends on it, and my back arches. Eldon holds me up, cupping my breasts and trailing kisses over my shoulder as I cry out.

The world goes black at Creed's doing at the same time two fingers consume my core. Hands are everywhere, lips brushing against every inch of my skin as the sadness ebbs and raw pleasure consumes me.

There's no stopping this time, no challenge, no ulterior motive as my climax peaks at the hands of my guys, twisting me into the tightest knot of my life before the weight gives out and my body sings for them.

The worry of what my magic means threatens to consume me as I come down from the elongated high, but the exhaustion clinging to my damp skin fades the world from Creed's magic into complete darkness.

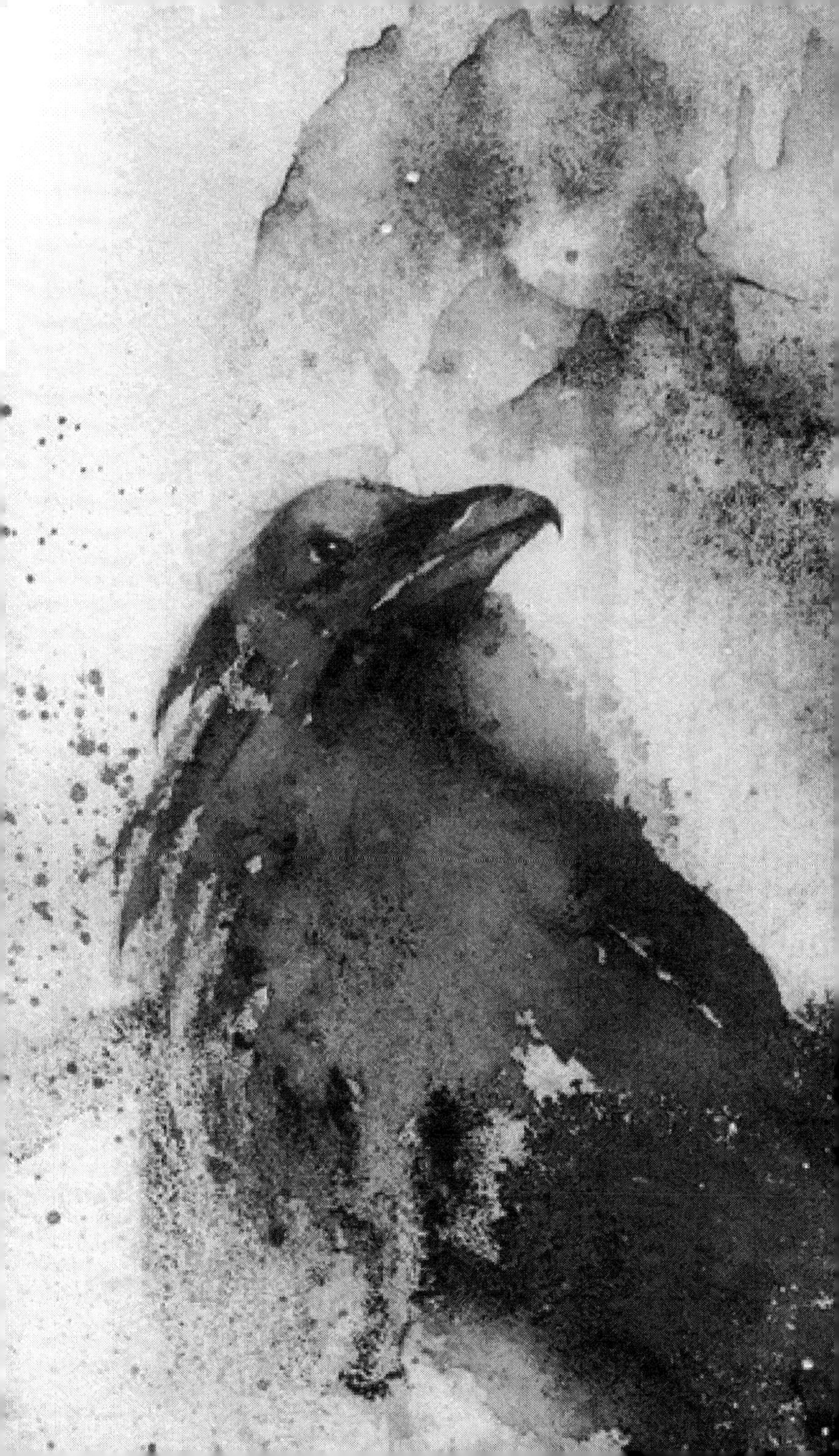

TEN
Raven

Darkness consumes me. Pressure weighs down my body, a tightness growing in my chest as I struggle to summon a single breath.

I'm trapped, lost, sinking.

My eyes ping open, my heart racing in my chest as I pant, struggling to take a deep breath, but even the knowledge that I'm safe in my bedroom doesn't quell the fear that threatens to consume me.

Shadows paint the walls and fill every available space, even the sheets covering me. They're moving, writhing around the room like I'm not lying here paralyzed, and it only leaves me feeling even more out of my depth.

Panic rises through me as the shadows grow, yet I can't see what's creating the darkness. It's just me and the shadows.

Finally, a gasp parts my lips as I gulp down a deep breath and the array of black and grays consuming my room seem to halt at the sound, slipping from the bedsheets and receding along the walls before disappearing into nothing.

I don't move an inch, my pulse ringing in my ears as I slowly gaze around the room. The silence and sudden drop in energy is startling and I'm ready for something to jump out, but after what feels like an eternity... nothing does.

Pressing my palms into the mattress, I lift myself up so I can lean back against the headboard. There's no gloom nor a single silhouette, not even when I blink a few times. Surely, it was in my head, a part of my dreams? I don't fucking know.

Maybe I'm going crazy.

Wiping a hand down my face, I sigh. Checking the time, a heavy weight settles on my chest again. The twilight hour. Perfect. Those two words always have such a negative impact on my mentality and I've never understood why.

I need some air, a moment to think, a second to feel the grass beneath my feet and know that I am truly grounded and tethered to the soil beneath it.

My bedsheets are rumpled at my waist from sleep, my oversized tee rising up my midriff, and I clamber from my bed in a rush. The second I've adjusted my tee so it falls mid-thigh again, I sneak through my door. The house is silent, not a single noise; not that I'd hear it over my heart anyway. And my magic. Every step I take, it seems to rattle inside of me, screaming for attention while tugging me toward the patio doors.

The lock on the door pauses me, but my magic thrums to the surface and before I even consider what I'm doing, I lift my thumb to the metal and watch as it quietly turns at my touch. I hear the latch and grab the handle, instantly feeling the chill of the night air wrap around me. Yet, at the same time, my heart warms. A feeling I have only experienced one other time.

Ari.

He's near, I'm sure of it.

Closing the door behind me, I wrap my arms around my waist as I step onto the lawn, my toes curling into the blades of grass as I take the deep breath I've been desperate for. The waves crashing into the cliffs in the distance lull me further, despite the wind picking up, but it all fades away a moment later when the thud of claws landing nearby catches my attention.

His golden feathers shimmer in the moonlight, his beak harsh but familiar. I don't know how I get to him—a run, a glide, a jump, I have no clue—but as quick as a breath, I'm standing in front of him.

A comfort I didn't know I needed, I launch myself at him, clinging to his front leg as my heart rate slowly lowers. An almost-purr echoes in my ears as he drops his head, a mixture of a hug and a nuzzle warming my soul before I take a step back and look up at him. There's a tension rippling from him that instantly raises my anxiety again.

"I can feel your panic," I murmur, stroking his chest. "I wish I knew what was causing it."

A beat passes as he blinks at me.

"*You.*"

I startle, jumping back a step as a yelp bursts from my lips. I was staring at his face, there's no way he said...

Glancing around for a moment, I double-check we're alone, and when nobody appears, I turn back to him just as confused as I was moments ago. "*My panic is coming from your panic, Raven.*"

The words consume my mind again but his face doesn't move at all.

"A-are you talking to me?" I tap my finger at my temple and he tilts his head.

"*Now that you have found the source of your magic, communicating will be much easier between us.*"

"So you're just... in my head?" My eyebrows furrow, a mixture of surprise and uncertainty swirling in my mind.

"*I'm not in your head, I can just project my thoughts so I can speak to you. You still have to talk out loud to me because I can't hear your thoughts. For now, at least. I'm sure we'll be able to work on it as you become more familiar with your powers."*

I blink up at him, overwhelmed by the startled awakening I had combined with the fact that I can now hear him. Folding my arms over my chest, I glance out over the cliff. I hear him move but I don't turn to check on him as I give myself the moment I need.

"Come sit, Raven. You're a ball of nervous energy."

Peeking out of the corner of my eye, I find him lying down, facing the shoreline. He's so calm, so at peace that it's almost irritating that his energy doesn't match my own. But despite that, I take the few steps toward him and settle into the grass to his left.

He waits a few breaths before he speaks into my mind again. *"What were you panicked about, Raven? I could feel it in every fiber of my body. I had to fly closer to make sure you were okay, so it's highly confusing considering you were lying in bed."*

I keep my gaze fixed ahead as I sigh. "I could feel... something. It was making me uneasy. Then I woke, but I still felt like I was in the midst of it." He adjusts his front leg so he's leaning in my direction and I find myself tilting into his side, seeking comfort in a way I haven't before. Which makes me delve further into it with him. "I don't know what it was, but there were shadows again."

"Again?"

I roll my eyes even though he can't see. I'm talking to

a fucking griffin, *my* griffin, and there are a million things I want to ask, but I don't even know where to begin. Talking about the creepy shadows and silhouettes taking over my room doesn't feel like the most fun topic out of all of my choices.

As the silence stretches and the first specks of dawn break across the horizon, he seems to accept my placidity as he changes the subject. *"Do you want to go back to sleep? You can lay here while I protect you if needed."*

I shake my head and stand. All of my questions for him are going to have to wait while I gather my thoughts. I'm too tired for the mental load right now. "No, the sun is starting to rise anyway, which means I'll need to get ready for classes soon."

Ari slowly rises, too, turning to face me as he lowers his beak to my stomach. *"As you wish."*

I smile, despite my inner turmoil, and turn for the door. My soul feels calmer now that I've seen my familiar, even though new revelations have come with it. Despite the overload, I pause when I reach the patio door.

Bracing my hand on the handle, I turn to face him, only to find him watching me already.

"Thank you, Ari," I breathe, and it's almost as though he stands taller somehow.

"Always."

My gaze is fixed on Professor Fitch, my ass is glued to the seat beneath me, but my mind is elsewhere. Thoughts of Ari this morning still linger, along with memories of the shadows cascading across my room. The second I stepped inside, Zane greeted me. He felt the floor vibrate, declaring Ari's arrival, but he didn't want to interrupt.

My brain was just freaking tired. There had been so much unsaid between the Bishops and me and the second the air was cleared, another hurdle was thrown my way with Ari and the shadows.

I need to start a list of things I have to accomplish because this is driving me insane. I feel so connected to the Bishops and Ari, yet so completely isolated that sometimes it's suffocating. Like now, I have no idea what Fitch has spent the entire lesson talking about, even with his daughter seated beside me. I feel like I'm in a sea full of people, yet alone.

One thing is for certain, though, Fitch's entire stance has shifted since the carnage at Shadowmoor's outpost. I can't put my finger on how, but there's a shift in him. I can sense it.

He's always been blunt, cut-throat, and straight to the point, but it feels even more intense. The way he scrubs at his jaw, constantly rolls his shoulders back, and casts a glance toward Leila when he thinks no one is watching confirms it.

Something has him tense and ready to leap into action. I don't want to say it has him scared, because he doesn't look the type to ever admit that fear is a feeling he's ever experienced, but he's spooked, at least. And if *he's* spooked, we're all doomed. The fact that Leila hasn't stopped frowning at him the entire time only adds to my theory.

My spine stiffens when the class is dismissed and I quickly shuffle to my feet with Leila. She's still staring at her father with concern, so I decide to cut my guessing and speak to her.

"Hey, is everything okay with your father? He seems… on edge," I murmur, careful to ensure no one can hear me. She nervously rubs her lips together as she tracks his every step.

"Honestly? I don't know. His protectiveness has increased, that's for sure, but not entirely a surprise after witnessing the attack on the outpost. But… I do think there's more," she admits, her worried glance turning to me, and I offer her a soft smile, hoping it conveys the empathy I'm feeling, but shit, it's not something I'm used to harnessing, never mind displaying to others.

"If I'm noticing it, Leila, I'm sure there'll be others

who are too." I hate to say it, but it's the truth, and the grimace that takes over her features tells me she knows it.

"You're right. I'll talk to him," she breathes, and I squeeze her arm in comfort as the man in question comes to a stop in front of us and the class disperses around him.

We both turn to look at him, only to find him assessing the both of us. Every time he turns to me, his mouth opens to speak, but nothing comes out, so he goes back to looking at Leila before repeating the same thing again. When I'm ready to step back from the awkwardness growing between us, he finally speaks. "You can join us if you wish, Raven."

"For what?"

"Training. We're focusing on Leila's strength and magic. Leila insists you're a good friend, so I can offer the same to you if you wish." He leans back on the heel of his boots, clearly still unsure whether he actually wants to extend the invite or not, but I'm still caught up on the reasoning.

"Why?"

He purses his lips, glancing at Leila again for a second before settling back on me. "Because it's easier than attempting to console my daughter if something happens to you."

I gulp. Wow. That's a bit fucking deep. It reminds me of the comment I got from Brax before the Gauntlet. I glance over my shoulder to find my gargoyle hovering by his table with Eldon, Creed, and Zane close by. They're clearly as intrigued as I am, but they're keeping their distance... for now.

Turning back to Fitch, I can't help but wonder why he's suddenly offering. My gut clenches and fear kicks in. Does he know about my magic? Is that why he's asking? Fuck. If I took him up on his offer, he would know what I could do then.

Instinctively, I step back. Plastering a polite smile on my face, I hike my backpack on my shoulder.

"Thank you for the offer, Professor Fitch, but she already accepted mine," Eldon interjects, declining for me as I still scramble to piece together the words. He drapes his arm over my shoulder, pulling me into his side as he winks at Fitch.

Fitch's gaze narrows, but Eldon is already spinning us around and heading for the door without a backward glance. I happily follow his lead, needing the space. Today has been a whirlwind and it's not even close to being over yet.

Maybe I should have stayed in bed with the shadows. At least I was too paralyzed to stress about everything around me.

"Are you okay?" Eldon asks, his lips brushing over the shell of my ear, and I nod.

"Thank you," I breathe, making him grin as he presses

a kiss to my forehead.

"Anytime, Little Bird."

ELEVEN
Creed

Green.
    Orange.
Red.
Black.
Green.
Orange.
Red.
Black.

We're all dealing with the aftermath of the destruction that unfolded at the Shadowmoor outpost. My coping mechanism, apparently, is to be haunted by those damn colors that play on repeat whether my eyes are open or shut.

Green faceless men flash in my mind, flickers of orange embers, which drastically deepen into crimson red as the blade pierces through Brax's skin before everything turns to black with Ari's chaotic arrival.

Black also represents the darkness I was consumed with when I tried to enter their minds. For the first time ever, there was nothing there for me to play with, to bend to my will. The powers I had been in complete awe of since the moment I got them were rendered useless.

Now, as the rest of the house sleeps, I repeat the same thoughts as I stare up at the ceiling. It's almost laughable that the guy with the ability to twist someone else's mind can't control the thoughts that consume his own. Tilting my head to glance at the time, I sigh when I notice it's a little after four in the morning.

It was the same last night and the night before that, but for the first time, I feel antsy. Lying here isn't helping. If anything, it's making matters worse because I now associate getting into bed with staring at the ceiling instead of falling asleep.

Swiping my hair back off my face, I get up, lethargically dragging my feet as I creep out of my room. My gaze instinctively drifts to Raven's room, but I don't want to disturb her with my troubles when I know she's dealing with her own. I want her to be able to rely on me rather than me be a burden.

I turn my attention to the floor-to-ceiling windows that line the back of the house and spot the silhouette of someone sitting outside on the grass. There's not a single light on, only the shimmer from the moon alerting me to them.

One step in their direction and I instantly catch a glimpse of the familiar pink hair I'm obsessed with.

Raven.

It seems I'm not the only one struggling to sleep.

I don't know if she's up for company, but she's going to get it. It's one thing to intrude in her space, but outside alone like that, I need her to know I'm here.

The cool air drifts around me as I step outside and quietly close the patio door behind me. She doesn't acknowledge my approach as she sits cross-legged, looking out over the cliffs and water in the distance.

"Is this a common occurrence for you?" I murmur, trying not to startle her, but she still whips her head around in surprise.

Her hand lifts to her chest as she shakes her head. "You made me jump." I cock my brow, waiting for her to answer my question, and she quickly catches on as she sighs. "Recently, yes."

Taking a seat beside her, I look out at the view and breathe it in too. "Do you want to share why?"

She wraps her arms around her bent knees. "I'm not sure if I even know myself," she admits, and I drape my arm around her shoulders, bringing her closer.

"Why don't you talk me through it," I breathe into her hair as she rests her head against my shoulder.

It feels like an eternity passes as she gathers her thoughts, but when she seems to process them, she lets me in.

"The shadows are waking me."

"The shadows?" I question, and she nods without looking up at me.

"I keep dreaming about the outpost, which then seems to be consumed by the shadows, and when I wake up in a panic, it's as if my room is filled with them." *What the fuck?* "My thoughts keep drifting back to Shadowmoor once they're gone. Like a niggling feeling that I'm missing something, I just don't have a single clue what it could be."

"Do you feel like you're in danger when you wake to the shadows in your room?" I ask, more to repeat her words and let them settle over me as I realize what my girl is going through.

She pauses a beat, taking a second to answer. "I don't think so. It's confusing because I wake up in a panic, and it does eventually drift away, but I can't differentiate between the dreams and the shadows to define what feeling actually aligns with which scenario." Her answer confirms she's been thinking about this too. Something I can't imagine is easy to process. Could this be linked to her magic? The necromancy that runs through her veins? Possibly, but I don't ask because I don't believe she has the answer either.

Focusing on what else she said, I rub my hand up and down her arm. "It doesn't help that we know absolutely nothing about what we're training and fighting for." She's completely valid in her feelings, and I need her to know that I'm with her no matter what.

"That's what scares me more than anything else," she admits, and I nod even though she can't see me.

"That makes total sense."

"At least when I was in Shadowmoor, I knew the battles I would face every day. This is something else entirely and there's no getting away from it. There's no off switch anymore, no stepping away." Fuck, I can't imagine the difference. But more so, I can't imagine how Shadowmoor looks more appealing with its polluted and toxic environment.

"We're putting our trust in the hands of those who offer us no reason to do so," I add, and she nods against my shoulder.

"Exactly."

Silence falls over us as the words of our reality linger in the air. My heart aches for her and the inability to magically make it all better. I want to take away her worries, but it's impossible. All I can do is vow to be at her side as we take on this fucked up world.

She's learning her magic, learning life beyond

Shadowmoor, and most of all, she's learning how to let her walls down and *us* in.

Shifting, I adjust us so she's nestled between my legs and leaning back against my chest as I hold her tight. Our heartbeats become one, our breaths syncing as the sun slowly starts to rise. She sighs, wistfully, like it's an all-too-familiar sight lately, but it still seems to fill her with a boost of positivity as she nestles further into me, a soft smile on her lips.

"We'll face this together, Raven. If that means we start digging into the bigger picture ourselves, then so be it. You're not alone anymore. It's the five of us to the very end. After what we've already been up against, nothing in this life seems to be what it is at face value, except us. Always us."

Her hand wraps around my arm, squeezing in acknowledgment, but before she can speak, Eldon's voice booms from behind us.

"What are you two whispering about out here?"

Glancing over my shoulder, I find him barefoot with only a pair of shorts on as he ruffles his fingers through his hair. He looks about as rested as we do, and I hate the effect the attack is having on us all.

"Getting some answers," Raven states, a glum expression washing over her face as she sits up to look at him too.

"Good," he says with a nod. "That's what woke me."

I frown at his statement as Raven quickly rises to her feet to get a better look at him.

"Woke you?" she asks, taking a tentative step forward, and he nods again.

"Yeah." His hand moves from his messy hair to drag down his face as he tries to wipe the exhaustion away. "My visions are all upside down," he admits.

"What does that mean?" I ask, rising to my feet beside Raven, but he quickly tries to wave us off. "Fuck that, man. We need to be a team here. We're all feeling shit, we're all awake in the dead of night, and we need to piece this together instead of isolating ourselves," I grumble, making Raven scoff.

"From what I recall, you came out here and we talked about me. You didn't delve into anything you're going through yourself." She gives me a pointed look, but the smirk on her lips lets me know she's teasing. I hope.

Shrugging, I look between them both. "The attack on the outpost keeps running through my mind when I'm trying to sleep. It's impossible." Pursing my lips, I consider how deep I should go before I decide to share everything, since that's exactly what I'm asking of them. "The green faceless men, the Amayans, were impossible for me to penetrate. I couldn't get into their minds at all. I was helpless."

Raven's hand finds mine without her eyes flicking away from me. The blue hues offer a glimmer of hope in my darkness.

"So what I'm hearing is the outpost is fucking us all over," Eldon murmurs, folding his arms over his chest as he pretty much sums it all up. "I think a trip to Shadowmoor is needed, don't you?"

Before either of us can answer, the latch on the patio doors draws our attention to Brax and Zane, both with tired eyes.

"I think that's exactly what we need," Brax declares, and I nod.

"I'm still startled by the fact that Fitch offered to train me. There's something we don't know, but by the look on his face, he doesn't seem so privy to the facts either," Raven adds, and my jaw clenches.

She's spot on. His offer caught us all by surprise, but the panic in Raven's eyes was clear. The fear of her magic being revealed to anyone else made it obvious that it is not an option for her. Goodwill gesture or not, Fitch needs to be kept at arm's length for the foreseeable future. Leila too.

"So what do we do then?" Zane asks, stepping outside and placing himself on the other side of Raven.

"There's something in my visions, a place I've never noticed before, but the darkness that it holds, I get the feeling it may be in Shadowmoor." Eldon's brows furrow as he speaks. Being unable to piece his vision together is clearly causing him some issues.

"Shadowmoor it is then."

TWELVE
Eldon

I looked at my brothers and my Little Bird with her noticeably pink hair and it was clear as day that we were all overwhelmed and exhausted. Two feelings we want to tamp down and pretend don't exist, but there's no avoiding them. There's no escape. Creed is right; we're a team. We need to eradicate the common denominator, and that's the unknown bullshit we're drowning in.

Fuck all of that to high Hell and back again.

I'm Eldon fucking Rhodes, I don't let shit get the better of me. Not even my own magic drifting into my dreams and hooking me up at its mercy. My visions may be demanding my attention, playing more frequently than usual, but the most persistent one is starting to drive me insane.

Darkness. A vortex of grays in every shade, the paler tones offering a small glimpse at my surroundings. There's no sun in sight, not even a glow from the moon as I slowly spin in a circle to see where I am. It's nowhere I've been before, which is what is hurting my brain the most. Black marble floor scattered with cracks and blemishes, stone walls with names carved into the surface, while burnt-out torches line the edge of the room. Nothing but a golden table stands in the center of the room, but the sound of scurrying feet echoes around me. I don't know where the fuck I am, but if I don't find out soon, I'm going to go crazy.

The location is key to understanding what my vision is trying to tell me. I don't know why I'm associating the vision with Shadowmoor, maybe it's the darkness, but since that's where everything started to go to shit, it's a viable place to begin.

Pacing the floor by the front door, I heave a sigh of relief when Zane, Creed, and Brax all filter in from their respective rooms. They all fade into the background when Raven steps from her room and my heart starts to race faster in my chest.

Her pink hair is scooped up into a high ponytail, two fine strands framing her face, which is makeup-free, offering me a glimpse at the beauty that is wholeheartedly her. She's wearing black combat pants, a fitted white tee, and a pair of boots that make her look so fucking hot it should be illegal.

I'm considering changing my decision to spend the first day of the weekend going to Shadowmoor, wanting to stay here tangled up in the sheets with her instead.

"Are we going or do you need a little longer to gawk at her?" Brax grumbles, but when I glance his way, he's sneaking another peek at her too.

Fucker.

"I don't know, I could gawk all day if she'd let me," I retort, winking at Raven as my gaze locks with hers.

She rolls her eyes at me, as usual, but the teasing smile beneath her attempt at acting indifferent tells another story.

"Open the gateway, Brax, before these two turn this into an orgy," Zane says with a chuckle, making Raven's cheeks heat. I'm expecting another sharp comment from that tongue of hers, but to my surprise, nothing comes.

"I could be down for an orgy," Brax states, making my jaw drop, along with Raven's, as she stares at him with wide eyes, clearly considering the offer. But the niggling feeling at the back of my mind forces me to put my body's desires aside to focus on the bigger picture.

"Zane's right. We need to go, but when we get back, it looks like we have a plan."

Nobody confirms or denies the offer now on the table as Brax grunts something under his breath, creating a gateway by the door behind me.

"Wait, have you been there before?" I blurt, gaping at

the gateway that's suddenly appeared.

His eyes meet mine as he gives me a single nod. "Once."

Why don't I like the sound of that? I roll my shoulders, trying to loosen the stress winding my muscles up tight, when Zane sidles up beside me with a concerned look on his face. "Wait, so we're going to Shadowmoor itself, right? Not the outpost."

"Right."

"Well..." He glances at Raven for a second, almost like he's considering his words, before he turns back to me. "We're not going to get some random ass tattoos on our temples the second we step foot there, are we?"

I stare at him like he's grown a second head, unsure how to even answer him, when Raven's giggle reaches my ears.

"Only you would think of that, Zane," she murmurs, shaking her head as she nears us. "But to answer your question, no. I don't think that's how it works. You're usually marked when your powers haven't come to fruition yet. That's why my mother never had it."

He nods a few times, taking in her words before a smile spreads across his face. "Good. Let's go then," he declares, not wasting a moment more as he steps through the gateway, leaving the rest of us to rush after him.

I don't know what I really expect to find on the other

side, but it's like stepping into the shadows of Hell. The sun that peered through the windows seconds ago is gone, only a dull sheen casting from the sky above, but there's no telling where the light is coming from.

It's hazy, a flicker of darkness on even blacker surfaces. Blinking, I take real stock of where we are and pinpoint the trees that rustle around us. Not a single green leaf sprouts from their branches, making the place look even more harrowing. Yet there are crisp leaves scattered along the ground.

This obviously isn't from my vision, but it's not like I was expecting to rock up in the middle of the exact room that has been overpowering my mind.

"What, exactly, is it we're looking for?" Brax asks as he closes the gateway, and everyone looks at me expectantly.

Scrubbing the back of my neck, I take a second to try and describe the kind of place I'm looking for. "It's dark, windowless, and I occasionally get the stench of blood wafting in my nose." Creed, Brax, and Zane all look at me with blank expressions while Raven taps at her lip in thought.

"I think I might know where you mean. Follow me," she breathes, taking off through the woods and leaving us to catch up. She's wearing a jacket I don't remember seeing earlier and she tightens it around her waist as she takes cautious steps. Like she knows exactly where to step in order to not cause a disturbance.

It's eerie, seeing her right now, like something has shifted and she's right back to being the girl who arrived at Silvercrest, not the one who was standing in our house moments ago.

"Is it like this all the time?" Zane asks as we all finally fall into step with her, and her brows crinkle.

"Like what?"

"So… dark?"

Raven shrugs, but there's a stiffness to her shoulders now. "Pretty much."

"I can barely see shit," I add, ducking just before I smack into a low-hanging branch.

"When you grow up in these surroundings, your ability to see in the dark naturally increases." Raven's words make me pause as I try to imagine what this was like for her. If this is how dark the days are, what are the nights like?

A break in the tree line comes into view but I can't see what stands beyond it. Not that it matters, though, because she turns at the last second and comes to a stop by a large tree. Her fingers skim over the bark, the hint of a memory flickering through her eyes, but I don't get to question her about it before the tree trunk transforms into a door.

She steps through the opening like she's done it a thousand times before and it makes my heart clench for her. Not with pity. Fuck, no. She doesn't deserve that. It is in awe of her and everything she has survived so far.

Following her inside, we come into a long, dark corridor. "I doubt anyone is here right now. The pits start later, but it's best we keep to the walls anyway."

I nod, keeping a step behind her as she presses her back against the stone walls.

"What are the pits?" Brax asks, not quite able to press into the sides with his wider shoulders and sheer lack of care.

Raven glances back over her shoulder with an almost solemn sigh. "The pits are where the strongest fight for bragging rights and a stack of cash."

My eyes widen in surprise; it's definitely not like the pits of the Gauntlet, but I don't get the impression it's any easier either.

"Is that why your knuckles were busted when you first came to Silvercrest Academy? Were you in the pits?" Creed asks, making my eyebrows shoot up into my hairline with surprise. I hadn't thought of that, but I do recall the broken skin on her knuckles.

We take a left turn and a huge room comes into view. Blood-stained pits line the floor with large spaces around them for spectators to stand and watch. It definitely has the same sort of smell we're looking for, but other than that, it's not the place from my vision.

"No, I didn't fight in the pits. I usually got attacked in

the woods," Raven casually replies like that's not fucked up.

"Who the fuck attacked you? I'll hunt every single one of those motherfuckers down right now," Zane bites, his teeth bared as the muscles in his neck bunch together, but Raven quickly waves him off.

"It was my knuckles that were busted, remember? Not my nose, not my face, nothing." I smirk, impressed with my girl. She turns to look at me as she waves her hand around, continuing on with the reason we're here. "Familiar?"

"No," I admit with a shake of my head. "It was windowless like this, and the stench of blood is the same, but the room doesn't look right." I close my eyes, letting the vision play more vibrantly in my mind for a second before I look at her again. "There are names carved into the walls and a gold table in the center of the room," I add, but the blank expression on her face tells me I'm not giving her anything else to actually go off.

"I can't think of anywhere else here that might resemble what you're trying to explain. Not unless it's someone's private quarters, but that almost feels too big and grand. A gold table? I can't even imagine there's one of those in the biggest houses around here."

"Then it must be somewhere else," I reply with a shrug, trying to hide the disappointment and irritation I'm battling.

"Let's get the fuck out of here then," Creed murmurs, nodding for Raven to lead the way back out. She takes the exact same route, hiding in the same shadows that led us down here, until we step back through the tree and into the woods.

"Do you want to head back to the same spot the gateway brought us to?" Raven asks, glancing at Brax, and he nods in response.

We take a handful of steps before voices echo around us and Raven's steps slow. As they become more clear, her instant frustration is visible as she sighs, her shoulders dropping for a second before she stiffens her spine and squares her shoulders.

"What…" My question drifts off as three guys appear a few trees away. They're laughing and joking among themselves, currently unaware that they're being watched. But when the second the guy in the middle looks up and locks eyes on Raven, I see the recognition on his face.

A sneer takes over his lips and his fingers flex at his sides as he turns to face her head on.

"Raven, my little Void, it's been a long time. Where have you been? I've been looking for you."

"You know this fucker?" Zane asks, louder than necessary, as he waves his hand in the asshole's direction.

My little Void? I'll kill this motherfucker myself.

"Wyatt, it hasn't been long enough," she grunts in response, answering Zane's question, and the guy laughs.

"Raven, don't be like that. You know I had to come pay

you a visit after our little encounter the last time I saw you. Make you repay me for your mistakes with your mouth on my dick, yeah? We can rectify it all now. I have time." He reaches for the zipper on his pants and chuckles.

Is this dude for fucking real?

"You're going to need to tell me real quick who this guy is, Dove," Zane snarls as my fists clench at my sides.

She takes a second to glance over her shoulder at each of us, trying to decide what to say, until she sighs. "He's the reason my knuckles were busted when I came to—"

A terror-riddled cry halts her next words, drawing all of our attention back to the weasely fucker who writhes on his knees where he stood moments ago. His hands are clasping his head, his screams getting louder until he rolls onto his back in pain, which is when the noise stops and silence cascades over us, hanging from the looming trees above.

"What the fuck?" one of his friends says with a grunt, glancing down at his friend.

I don't have the answer to what happened to him, but I know who does. "Creed?"

Everyone's attention drifts his way, including Raven's, who looks confused as fuck.

"What?"

"Don't *what* me like you didn't do that," I state, pointing at Wyatt with a chuckle.

"Wake him the fuck up," his friend shouts as Creed itches his cheek.

"Yeah, that's not going to happen."

It takes a second for his words to settle in my mind and understanding to wash over me.

"Did you just kill him before I even got a chance? That's not fair. She's my girl, too," Zane grumbles. Brax stares at Creed with wide eyes as Raven gapes at him.

"Was that necessary?" she asks, tilting back to see Wyatt's lifeless body on the floor.

"He touched you. He's lucky I didn't fucking torture him more, but we've got places to be and I really don't care to stay here any longer."

"He…"

"Isn't wrong," I interject, cutting the distance between Raven and me as I drape my arm over her shoulder. Turning to face the other two assholes still glancing between their dead friend and us, I smile. "Anybody else?"

Even with the dim lighting, I see the color drain from their faces, and it's almost comical as they take off through the trees without a backward glance at their friend. When they're completely out of sight, Raven scoffs.

"I'm not shocked they ran off like little fuck boys. That's exactly what they did last time, too," she admits, and anger quickly thrums through my body again.

"Don't remind us there was a last time, Little Bird, or

I'll have you resurrecting this motherfucker so we can kill him again and again and again," I breathe against her ear, and she shakes her head with a laugh.

"I can handle myself, you know." Her gaze is locked on Creed, who slowly steps toward her.

"I know."

How can one asshole be so smooth with such few words? Before I can ask him, Brax creates a gateway, hinting for us to leave.

"What about the body?" Zane asks, and without even thinking, I project my fire in his direction, incinerating his body in mere seconds before the flames die out and the embers flicker to nothing.

"It's official. It's not just Creed that's unhinged. You all are." Raven dips out of my hold and steps through the gateway without a backward glance, leaving the four of us to barge and shove each other to scramble after her.

I'm ready to wrap her in my arms and charge off to my bedroom with her, but when the other side of the gateway comes into view, it's not our house I find.

No.

Marble surfaces and stained-glass windows greet us. It takes a second for me to place where we are and when the realization comes, I know we're fucked.

"Excellent, you've all returned. Why don't you take a seat."

Professor Burton.
Shit.

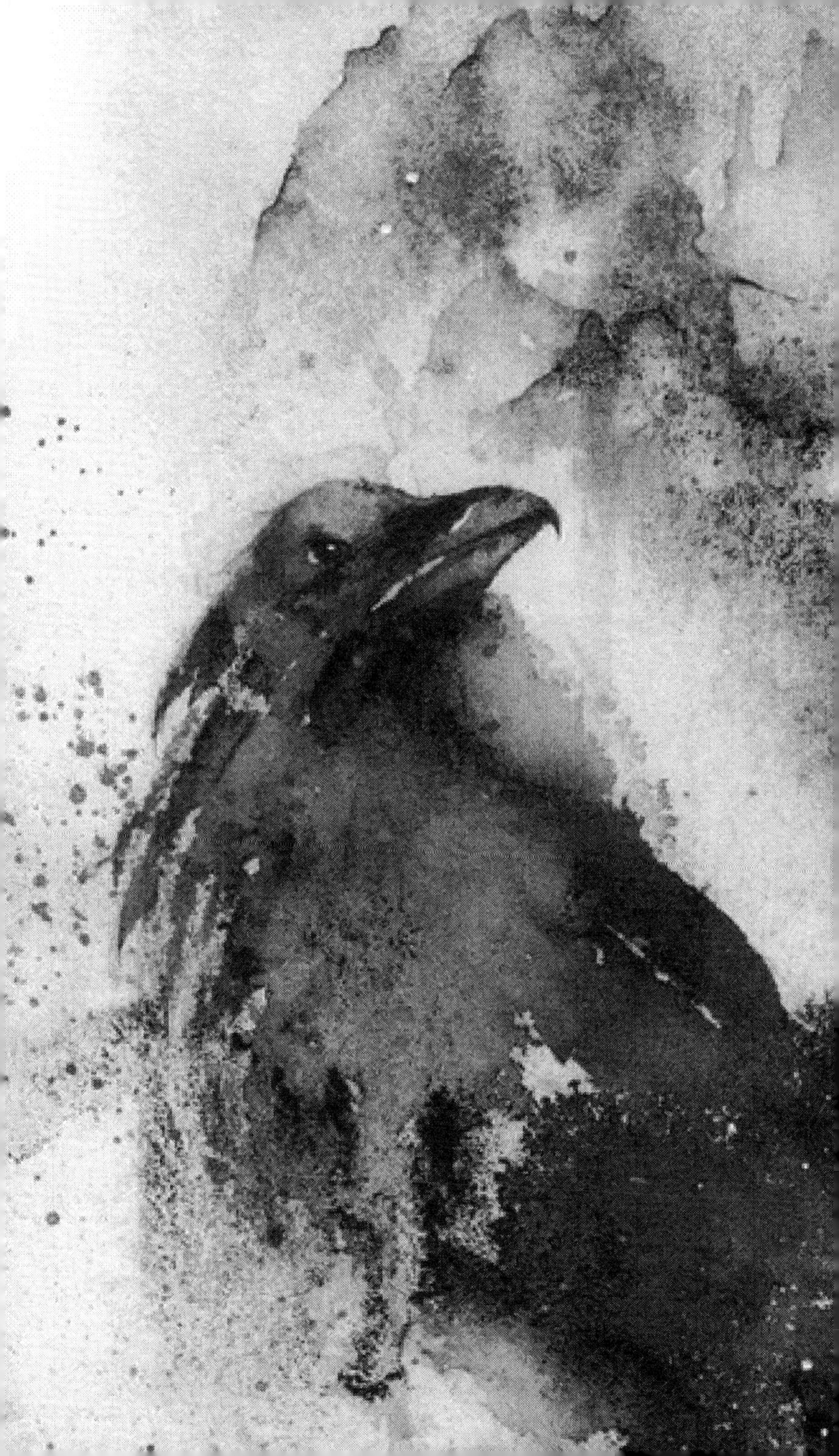

THIRTEEN
Raven

I need a fucking minute to process the fact that Creed just unalived Wyatt without batting an eyelid because he touched me before I even knew him, but instead, I'm standing face to face with Professor Burton in the flesh for a change.

That doesn't bode well for us. It feels like this is going to become an issue. He's dressed in his usual pristine suit, his piercing eyes assessing each of us. I falter under his intense stare, despite my irritation at the fact, but Brax doesn't.

He takes two strides to place himself at my side. "This isn't where I was heading." He's so matter-of-fact I almost laugh, but there's no amusement on Burton's face, that's for sure.

"No, it wouldn't be," he says with a sigh, taking a step

back to walk around the glass desk before slowly dropping down into his seat. He steeples his fingers together, eyes casting over each of us once more before he continues. "You triggered a barrier when you used your magic to leave, I redirected it for your return."

Fuck.

That's insane. We hadn't even considered the professors or administration knowing we were going, never mind awaiting our return.

"How nice of you," Brax grumbles, folding his arms over his chest. Anyone else would crumble under Brax's looming form, but Burton only leans back in his chair.

"Maybe the five of you should take a seat," he offers, waving to the high-backed velvet chairs behind us, but we don't move a step, happy to stand where we are as the unknown fire of his wrath beckons.

"We're good," Eldon says with a sigh, planting his hands on his hips as Burton purses his lips. When it's seemingly clear that we're not going to sit, he knocks his fist on the desk.

"Okay, I'll get right to it then. Do you realize how incredibly stupid you were today? Do you realize the unknown you were walking into? We have wards around the academy for this exact reason. I can't block your magic entirely, but I can guide it where necessary. Do you require a binding on your gateways so you can't leave the grounds,

Mr. Carlsen?"

"Isn't that against the Monarchy rulings?" Zane interjects, cocking a brow at Burton, who barely manages to bite back his sneer.

"Alternatives can be arranged, Mr. Denver. I'm sure if your father found out you took an unsupervised trip to Shadowmoor mere days after the outpost attack, I don't think he would be too happy about it, do you?"

"I think he would want us to have more information after such an attack. I think he would want us to be better prepared, and I certainly think he would not take too kindly to your threat to restrain our magical abilities with such great danger lurking. *Do you?*" I almost want to high-five the fuck out of Zane for his mightier-than-thou response. It's a huge difference from the mouthful he would have gotten from me, so I'm more than happy for Zane to lead.

"It's also against academy rules to leave campus in the manner you did "

"If you explained to us what the hell happened at the outpost, we wouldn't have to," Eldon counters, making Burton's nostrils flare with agitation.

He sighs deeply, shaking his head as he grips the arms of his chair. "Nothing I'm saying is being heard, is it?"

"No," Creed chirps in, making the professor sigh even heavier.

"I didn't think so." Burton's gaze settles on Zane, his

lips pursing as silence stretches between us to the point it's almost uncomfortable before he continues. "Your father resisted me extending the offer earlier, but it seems now may be a good time."

"For what?" Zane asks, his forehead crinkling as my eyebrows pinch in confusion.

Burton stands, bracing his hands on the glass desk for a second before he straightens, adjusting his tie as he circles around the desk. Only when he's sure he has all of our attention does he speak.

"To join the Nightmares Guild."

The what now?

"I'm sorry, you're going to have to say that again," Zane states, his head tilting as he assesses the professor.

"The Nightmares Guild, Mr. Denver. It's a secret society within the academy. Its purpose is to face the greater terrors that lurk beyond these walls."

I think I'm going to need that chair now. This just became very overwhelming really quickly. A secret society? Here? The confusion on each of the Bishops' faces only confirms I'm not the only one just hearing about this.

"Who else is a part of it?" Eldon asks, and Burton shrugs.

"That's the kind of information you would become privy to upon acceptance, not a moment sooner." He crosses his legs at the ankle, seemingly waiting for an answer right now.

"We'll have to think about it. Can we leave?" Creed replies, taking a step toward the door behind us with a blank expression on his face.

"You have five days." I take that as our dismissal and march for the door, but before I can follow Creed through the opening, Burton hollers my name. I spin to look at him and the inquisitive look on his face makes my stomach clench before he even speaks. "Your father advised your abilities could make an appearance at any time since he ensured the magical barrier was lifted from you. Has there been any change in that?" I gulp, bile burning the back of my throat as I shake my head, unable to speak. I hadn't considered my father telling Burton I was a Void, but I shouldn't underestimate his reach and want for power. Does he know what my magic is? "Very well. Should that change, Miss Hendrix, I expect to be one of the first to know."

One nod and I'm out of there, flying past Creed and racing down the hall until I burst through the doors at the end of the corridor, the fresh air filling my lungs.

"Are you okay?" The question comes from Zane as I slowly push up off my knees. I hadn't even realized I'd crouched over to heave in every breath, and I quickly glance around to make sure no one else saw my dramatics. Thankfully, we're alone.

"I'm good," I murmur, not truly feeling the words, and the gentle smile on his face tells me he knows it too.

He reaches for my hand without a word and pulls me toward the path to our house, the others falling in step with us.

"We have five days," Creed mutters when we're halfway home, and I nod in acknowledgment. "I think you're going to need to speak to your father, Zane," he adds, and Zane's grip on my hand tightens.

"I will." The determination in his voice is thick.

"None of this makes sense," I breathe, still at a loss, and Eldon rakes his fingers through his hair.

"How the fuck has there been a secret society operating here without us knowing? I feel stupid as fuck," he grunts. It seems clear to me that Zane's father may have had a hand in keeping them from the Guild, until now at least. But that fact only raises the question of why. What is he trying to protect his son from? Why hide this?

Not wanting the conversation to get too heavy as we pass a few students wandering along the path, I nudge Zane with my elbow. "Maybe you aren't as cool as you think you are."

He instantly scoffs, pulling me closer to his side. "Oh, please. I'm hot, and you know it."

I shrug, playing coy. "Maybe not everyone has my taste."

"Yeah, right," he says with a chuckle, and Brax, Creed, and Eldon join in, easing some of the tension that was building around us.

Turning down the path that leads to our house, I startle when I find Leila sitting cross-legged on the front doorstep. She perks up the second she sees us, with a wide smile spreading across her face.

"Oh, good. You're here."

"Is everything okay?" I ask, not really ready to deal with any issues she might have too. Everything is just getting more and more extreme with every breath I take.

"Everything is good. There's a party tonight. You in?" The short-lived relief at the fact that she's okay is quickly outweighed by the thought of having to act like everything is fine in front of a whole group of people I don't really care for.

Shaking my head, I offer her an apologetic smile. "I've actually got—"

"She's in... we're all in," Eldon interjects, stepping up to my other side so I'm sandwiched between him and Zane.

Leila claps her hands excitedly as I make a mental note to gut my favorite little firestarter later.

"Perfect. I'll leave you guys be for now, but I'll be back at eight. Wear something sexy," she hollers as she takes off down the path.

Yeah. Perfect.

Just perfect.

"Please remind me why you think this is such a good idea again. I'm really not feeling it," I say with a groan as I step into the lounge area to find all four Bishops ready and waiting. Usually, I would pride myself on not taking long to get ready, but this wasn't my idea and now I'm stuck with the ramifications of Eldon's decision.

"Because you look hot as fuck in that dress, Little Bird," he replies with a wink while readjusting the outline of his cock beneath his jeans.

"Don't try and flatter me with your hot mouth right now," I retort, cocking a brow at him before double-checking the contents of my clutch.

Black clutch, black heels, black dress, and dark, smokey eye makeup. It's the vibe I'm going with, matching my exterior to my interior mood. The dress barely covers my ass cheeks, which is what likely has Eldon's attention, and I've piled my hair into a pink messy bun on top of my head.

"Don't step out here looking so delectable, Little Bird, and I wouldn't have to." Eldon stands, prowling toward me with hooded eyes as my thighs press together.

Let's stay home and do that instead. I know he won't right now, though. They seem set on diving into the party tonight after the revelations of the Nightmares Guild.

He stops in front of me, hands clenching my waist as my eyes attempt to roll to the back of my head. "If you keep this up, I won't be going anywhere." My words are raspier than I expect and I hear Zane moan from his seat on the sofa.

"Fine, my Little Bird," Eldon whispers into my ear before sinking his teeth into my earlobe and making me groan. The second the sound parts my lips, he takes a step back, putting far too much distance between us. "We're going tonight so we can see the other students in a casual setting and attempt to feel out who might be a part of the Guild or not."

Zane appears at his side, clapping him on the shoulder as his eyes rake over the length of me from head to toe. "Besides, you should really have some downtime with your friend. I'm more than happy to fuck the tension out of you, but this also works. So, fun now, fucking later, okay, Dove?"

I glare at him, which only makes his smile spread further.

Today, on top of everything else, has been a total mind fuck. No one is sleeping well. Eldon's having visions that we thought might lead to Shadowmoor, but clearly don't, so after our brief visit to the dark smog that is Shadowmoor, where Creed fucking killed Wyatt and Eldon burned his remains like it was nothing, we then got back to Silvercrest to be lambasted by Professor Burton and invited to join a secret society. The Nightmares Guild.

Maybe I do need some downtime and a drink or two, or ten.

A knock sounds from the door and I know it's Leila. Right on time.

Eldon presses his lips to the corner of my mouth before waving for me to lead the way.

That settles it. They can investigate the students while I investigate the liquor. It's the only way I'm going to survive the night. Besides, it might just help knock me out tonight, so I can actually get some sleep.

Spinning, I plaster the biggest smile on my face without it feeling forced, before I march for the door and open it wide. Leila is wearing a sparkly deep-green v-neck dress and killer heels. There's only one thing to do.

"Bring on the shots."

FOURTEEN

Eldon

The idea of attending the party sounded good at first. On paper, it still makes total sense, but what I didn't consider was the distraction that is Raven fucking Hendrix swaying her damn hips on the dance floor like a vixen.

She's drinking, having fun, and making my cock impossibly hard with every second that ticks by. There's no smirk on her lips, no glimpse over her shoulder in our direction, nothing. She's having a good time for *her*. The show we're getting is just a bonus. The people naturally gravitating toward her and Leila, however, are pissing me off.

Nobody makes a move to touch her, though, not how they want to. I've seen a few glances in our direction from a couple of fourth years, but if my own glare hadn't turned them away, Brax's steely demeanor definitely did.

"If we're being real about all of this, who do we *think* we should be keeping an eye on?" Zane asks, spinning his half-empty glass on the high table we're all standing around. We've naturally opted to keep the drinking to a minimum so we can focus on the task at hand while also giving Raven free rein to go crazy, as we'll be here to protect her.

"Where do we even begin?" Creed mutters, tapping his fingers on the wood top as he tracks Raven's every move.

It's still crazy as fuck that he destroyed that fucker back in Shadowmoor without a second thought. I would have expected that behavior from Brax more than him, but they do say it's always the quiet ones you need to watch. His unhinged tendencies turned Raven on when he was in the Gauntlet and I'm sure her lady boner just got harder for him seeing him destroy that pissant. Shit, I was sure my own dick was going to twitch with awe.

"Sebastian." Brax's grunt interrupts my thoughts and I instantly seek out the other Hendrix. He's on the opposite side of the graveyard, his hands all over someone who is *not* Genie, and I almost barf at the drama that's going to unfold with those two. Especially when she catches wind of this. We were never really a thing, but even I know she quickly turns into a damn demon when she doesn't get her way.

My gaze travels back to Raven. The stark difference

between her and anyone else I've ever met in my life is staggering. I don't know what Leila's whispering in her ear, but she throws her head back a second later, laughing along like no one's watching.

She's a fucking goddess.

Our fucking goddess.

My little bird.

"Do you think we could get him to talk?" Zane asks, and my hands clench at the interruption again. This was my idea, I know that, but if I can't be over there with my woman, swaying to the beat blasting around us, then I at least want to fantasize about her without interruption. With these guys actually focusing on what we're here for, I've got no chance.

"I don't think so. Not when he's highly aware that he's on our shit list. I don't think we could trust a word out of his mouth. Do you?" I cock my brow at Zane and he grimaces, instantly agreeing.

"Maybe we need to consider what families people are from. The way he mentioned Zane's dad has me thinking this is some elite shit. They're not just going to invite anyone," Creed offers, and I purse my lips, considering his words as I cast my gaze over the space again.

"There are a few kids here with families in The Monarchy, my father mentions it sometimes, but I would have to find out who exactly. Not everyone exploits that fact like some." Zane rubs the back of his neck as he glances over everyone too, and I nod in agreement.

"Big-mouthed fools aren't going to be where we need to be looking. If they've managed to keep this a secret from us for so long already, then they've got to be tight-lipped," I summarize. I could be completely off track, but we only have five days to figure this shit out and make a decision, which doesn't give us much time to vet anyone.

"Who is the fourth year pressing up against Leila?" Brax asks, nodding in their direction, and I whip around to double-check that someone isn't trying to get close to Raven too. I should have known by Brax's calmness that there was nothing to worry about, but seeing her still dancing alone, hands raised in the air as she swings her hips, eases the tension that stiffened my spine.

"I think that's Grave Richardson. His grandfather is Monarch Richardson, head of Pinebrook if I recall correctly," Zane murmurs and my eyes widen. I didn't know that.

"Could he be someone for us to look into?" Hope rises inside of me and it only grows when Zane nods.

"He doesn't tend to have drama circulating around him and his grandfather is highly regarded. He could definitely be a member."

"Is there anything else we should know about him before we feel him out? We're going to need to know his abilities at a minimum so we know what we're up against," Brax states, making more sense than I want to give him credit for.

"Agreed. Let's focus on him and see what we can figure out," Creed declares, and my brows furrow.

"We can't rest all of our hopes on *one* guy."

"I'm not saying we should, but until we can gather a list of others to look into, he's our shot," he retorts, making me sigh.

"Fine, does that mean I'm off duty now?" I ask, already stepping around the table.

"This was *your* idea!" Zane exclaims, eyes wide as he gapes at me, and I shrug.

Turning my attention to Raven, I stalk toward her, my fingers itching to feel her bare skin. I don't try to sidestep any of the students standing between us. I'm completely locked in on her, and it's like they all know it, parting like the sea as I get closer until nothing stands between me and my little bird.

My fingers flex at her waist as I press my chest against her back. Her body melts into mine, her drunken gaze flicking over her shoulder at me as a slow smirk spreads across her lips.

"I knew it was you." Her arms lift over her head before reaching back to circle behind mine. The move makes her back arch and her hips sway perfectly over my stiff cock.

"How?"

"I've felt your eyes tracking my every move and about ten seconds ago, the hairs on my neck prickled. The sensation didn't stop until your scent wrapped around me."

Hot. As. Hell.

"Do you like that, Little Bird? My eyes on you, my fingers on you?" My fingers tighten on her hips. "My words in your ear?" I push, feeling her shiver in my hold. "I know you're a little exhibitionist. Is this your idea of foreplay? Teasing me with this ass while the rest of the world dances around you?"

She hums, her eyelashes dropping as she pushes her ass further back into me. Her sways quickly become a little sloppier, a telling sign of the liquor in her veins. As much as it puts a damper on all of the hot stuff I was hoping to do to her tonight, knowing that she's able to let loose like this in my presence, trust us more and more, fills me up in an entirely different way. Cementing even further that she is ours and we are hers.

"Are you ready to get out of here?" I ask, slightly rocking with her as she nods, but when she faces forward, I catch her frown as she takes in Leila with the fourth year from earlier.

"Who is that guy with Leila?"

The worry she has for her friend is so typical of Raven. She has a hard exterior, but the second you get past that barrier, her love is fierce.

Following her line of sight, my eyes lock on Grave's. He must sense the uncertainty because he leans down to whisper in Leila's ear, and a second later, her dazed eyes find Raven. She slips out of his hold, wrapping her arms around Raven's neck, forcing me to take a step back, but she's gone again a moment later.

"What was that?"

"Leila confirming she's happy and certain she's safe with him."

"If you're happy, then so am I, Raven. Let's get my little bird out of here to sleep off all the shots she's taken," I murmur with amusement against her ear, and she grins.

"I'm happy now I'm with you."

My heart warms and, for a second, I'm not sure if it's my magic warming my insides or my raw feelings for the pink-haired Raven that consumes me.

I'm such a goner for this woman, I make myself sick.

Sweat beads down my spine, panting breaths echoing in my ears as the sound of skin on skin slaps around the room. My dick is deep in the hot core of my little fucking bird as she cries out my name, and I never want to stop thrusting into her, claiming her, taking what's mine.

"Please, Eldon."

I grin, my hair clinging to my forehead with sweat as I lean forward, wrapping my hand around her pretty little throat. The dining table rattles louder with my next thrust, but I don't hear the scrape as Raven's raspy moan fills my ears. My fingers flex at her neck as I grab the back of her thigh with my free hand, angling her for even better access.

"That's it, Little Bird. Say. My. Name." I enunciate each word with another thrust, bringing us both closer to the edge.

Her eyes flutter for a second, unshed tears misting her eyes as she lifts her hand to my wrist at her neck. She doesn't try to loosen my grip, though. Instead, she surprises the hell out of me and grips me as tightly as she can, forcing my hand more tightly against her throat.

Fuck. Fuck. Fuck.

Lifting her thigh higher, I drape her leg over my shoulder and sink my teeth into the soft flesh of her calf. Her moan turns into a needy growl as her pussy clenches tight around my cock, milking me for all I'm worth as she comes on my dick.

It's impossible not to chase the tingles of my own climax as they zap through my body. I can feel my movements stagger, my thrusts deepen and elongate, and just as I'm about to plant my seed in my woman, breed the fuck out of her, everything goes black.

Blacker than black.

Pitch black.

What the fuck?

Looking down the length of me, my fingers tentatively run over the floor-length black fabric that covers my body. It drapes down my arms and I feel a hood over my head, but before I can lift up to confirm it, a dim candle flickers in the distance.

With a slow inhale and deep exhale, I take a step toward it, my cock no longer standing to attention as the room begins to lighten ever so slightly. Gray hues scatter throughout the circular room until a familiar sight comes into view.

Darkness. A vortex of grays in every shade. The paler tones offering a small glimpse at my surroundings. There's no sun in sight, not even a beam of light from the moon. I spin in a circle like always to see where I am. Black marble floor, which is scattered with cracks and blemishes, stone walls with names carved into the surface, while burnt-out torches line the edge of the room. Nothing but a golden table stands in the center of the room, but the sound of scurrying feet echoes around me.

I get ready for everything to fade away as it always does, only this time… reality doesn't come.

The room lightens a touch more to reveal long black cloaks with oversized hoods and gold masks shielding the faces of those surrounding me. There are maybe fifteen or twenty people staring at me, and as I shift, I notice it's the same black fabric I'm wearing.

Running my tongue over my lips, I lift my hand to my face, but before I can press a finger against my nose, I'm met with the touch of metal.

A mask.

One just like theirs.

I lurch upright in bed, a gasp burning my lungs as I try to gulp a calming breath, but it does not come easily. When I don't feel like my entire body is rattling with the remnants of the vision coating my skin, I push a hand through my hair and shift so my feet hang off the side of the bed.

What the fuck was that?

It's the same vision that's been haunting me for days, the same marbled floor, the same names etched into the stone walls, and the same fucking table in the center of the room. Resting my head in my hands, I try to replay the new addition to tonight's torment; the masked men.

I sit up straight, my spine stiffening as my foggy, tired brain slowly pieces it together a little more. The Guild. It's got to have something to do with the Nightmares Guild. I know it.

Scrambling to my feet, I rush for my bedroom door in just my boxers. My dick is stiff beneath the fabric, the real me still enjoying the sweet fucking dream about Raven I was having before I was so rudely interrupted.

I pause for a second when I step into the lounge, unsure of who to go to first, but a mere second after my door opens, so do Brax's and Creed's across the hall.

"What's going on?"

I don't have time to question how they know something is wrong or even heard me get up. I need everyone present so I can make sense of this while it's still fresh in my mind.

"Get the others," I rush out, my words far more breathless than I was expecting. To my surprise, they both move without further question.

Flopping down on the sofa, I stretch my arms up above my head as I try to ease the coiled tension stiffening my limbs.

"Please tell me this is something important because I was having the best wet dream of my life," Zane grunts, adjusting his dick as he flops down beside me with Creed right behind him. *You and me both, brother.*

Brax appears a second later with Raven draped in his arms bridal-style as she peers at me with concern.

"What's going on?" she murmurs, curling into Brax's lap once he sits to my left, and I heave a heavy sigh before I repeat the entire thing to them from start to finish. Well, I omit the part where I was balls deep in Raven first, but I make sure not to miss a single detail out of the actual vision.

"It sounds like the Guild," Creed surmises once I've spat every word out, the others nodding in agreement as my body slowly starts to come down from the adrenaline coursing through me.

"Have you heard from your father, Zane?" Raven breathes, her eyebrows pinched as she glances at him.

"Not yet, but the visions say it all, man. We always trust in them, and if they're practically leading us to it…" His words trail off. No need to finish a sentence we already know the answer to.

"Every time?" Raven asks, uncertainty still warring in her eyes, and I nod.

"They led us to you, didn't they?" Brax states, his lips at her temple, and I watch her softly shiver in his hold.

"Get a hold of him first thing. It makes sense. Then we can have all of the facts before we dive in," Creed says to Zane, solidifying the next step for us.

"Are we doing this?" Raven asks, sitting up properly in Brax's lap, and I sit tall, speaking the words I really wasn't sure we were going to settle on.

"We're accepting the invitation of the Nightmares Guild."

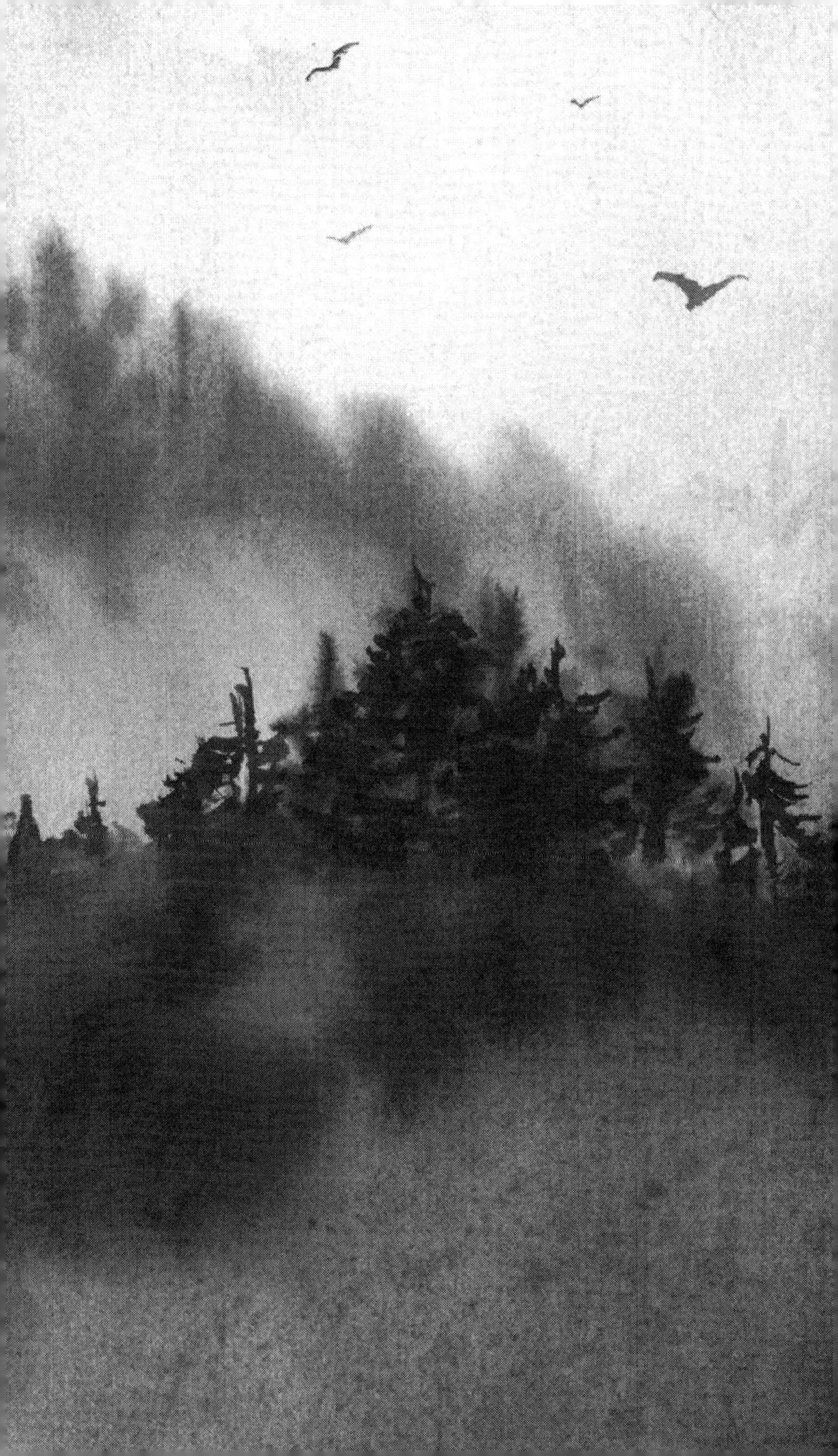

FIFTEEN

Zane

You would think that when your father is a member of The Monarchy, he would be easier to reach. Like, there would be a dedicated option to reach out, a family line of sorts, but if anything, it's the complete opposite.

Trudging toward the main office, my damp boots leave noticeable marks on the otherwise pristine marble floors. It might be the weekend for us, but I know for certain that there will be some form of academic or administrative staff on site somewhere. Because I need to reach someone off-property, the main office is the best place to start.

Since the sun is barely up, there are no students in sight as I push through the door, determined to find Lyra, the head of administration. Surprisingly, she's already at her desk in her usual white pantsuit with her hair twisted into a professional bun.

I don't slow my stride as I cut the distance between us, collapsing into the chair positioned across from her on the other side of her desk. But the second my ass hits the seat, I'm scooting it closer so I can brace my arms on the divider between us.

"I need to speak with my father."

She doesn't bristle at my tone or even shift her full attention my way, playing out some power game I'm sure she enjoys. Her lips twist and her eyebrow lifts as she finally turns my way.

"What seems to be the problem, Mr. Denver?"

"The problem is me having to repeat myself," I grumble, tapping my fingertips on the desk as I keep my gaze locked on hers. "Do I have to be a total douche and threaten to mention this to my father when I speak with him?" It's my turn to cock a brow at her while she gulps nervously.

"Am I correct in believing you're housemates with Miss Raven Hendrix?" I nod, confused about where she's going with this. "Before meeting that young woman, I would have faltered under that threat, given in, and bent over backward like a quivering idiot." Dear fucking God, what did Raven do?

"And now?" I ask, eager to know what mischief she's been causing without me knowing.

Lyra leans forward, bracing her forearms on the desk

as she levels her gaze with mine. "Now, I'm going to continue to give you hell because I'm cranky and in no mood for your pretentious bullshit so early in the weekend. So, if you think I'm going to help you with that attitude, you can think again."

I blink at the Lyra before me. She's not the same at all, it seems, and that just may be down to the woman who has flipped my life upside down. Lacing my fingers together, I lean back in my seat and grin. "She has a way of getting under your skin, doesn't she?" Lyra clears her throat, her eyebrows furrowing ever so slightly, so I clarify. "Raven, I mean. She comes across all harsh and rough around the edges, but I don't think I've ever met anyone else with that level of raw spark and energy. Have you?"

Her eyes soften, understanding twitching the corner of her mouth up, but she manages to bite back the smile before it transforms her face. "Something like that," she breathes before rolling her eyes and sighing heavily. "Fine, I'll set up a connection with Monarch Denver. It might take a few minutes at this time of day, so you'll have to bear with me. Would you rather have some privacy?" I nod, but she's already pointing to the door as if she knew that would be my answer. "Take the first left, I'll have it connect there for you."

"Thank you, Lyra."

She sits taller, the smirk on her face undeniable as she

waves me off while avoiding my gaze. That's pride dancing across her body, pride in herself, and I can't help but get the feeling that Raven has something to do with that.

I don't have the time to delve into that, though. Now, I need to speak to my father.

Following her instruction, I exit her office and take a left to find one of the small windowless rooms that I'm familiar with. This is how they connect us with the outside world. It's not the first time I've seen my father under this kind of circumstance, so I flop down on the sofa and kick my feet up on the coffee table in front of me. There's a water dispenser in the far corner, but otherwise, there's just a notepad and pen on the table, and that's it. Simple, yet functional.

Silence dances around me for a few more minutes until a gentle buzz zaps in the air, and a moment later, my father appears as a projection in front of me. He's on the family sofa at home, a linen shirt and chino shorts in place of his usual suit.

"Interrupting a casual day, Pops?" I ask, and he grins, swiping his hand over his hair as he relaxes in his seat.

This is the thing Lyra doesn't realize about my father. She said it might be hard at this time, but I know he's already been awake for at least two hours, putting in the weekend work while everybody sleeps so that when they do wake up, he's present and having fun.

"Your mother is insisting we have friends over. You know how she is. Is everything okay?"

Nervously rubbing the back of my neck, I instantly feel out of my depth and it takes me a few moments to piece together where I want to lead the conversation.

"I've been trying to get a hold of you. I used the shell you gave me to tap into your Monarchy office, but there was no response. That's why I'm reaching out like this now." Apparently, it's standard practice for Monarchy family members to have a shell. The most random-looking object ever, but it's a direct link to a system set up in The Monarchy to make them aware we need them. It just doesn't seem to want to work when I need it.

"Sorry, son. There's a lot of commotion at the minute." His brows dip ever so slightly, a move I don't see too often on him, and it immediately ignites my concern.

"Care to share?"

"Not really," he says with a shake of his head, and I sigh, frustrated while not actually expecting anything more from him. He loves us fiercely, he's a family man through and through, but that doesn't mean he doesn't love his job, his people, and this realm. That doesn't help me right now, though, when I need more information that I know he's been holding out on sharing.

"Just like you didn't want to share about the Nightmares Guild?"

He sits up straight, tension vibrating from him as his eyes narrow. "How do you know about that?" I raise a brow at him. There's absolutely no point in me answering that question when he already knows deep down. "Dammit. It was Burton, wasn't it? What did you do that made him offer it up?"

I gape at him. "Who says *I* did anything?" I challenge, but he rolls his eyes at me this time, pinching the bridge of his nose as he takes a few deep breaths before settling his gaze on mine again.

"That's how it works with him. That's how it has always worked."

If I want any chance of him sharing with me, I know I need to give him the truth. "We were trying to help interpret one of Eldon's visions and went to Shadowmoor yesterday."

"You went to Shadowmoor… yesterday? Of course you did, because you're insane."

Hoping to avoid a lecture from him, I push on to keep us on track. "When we realized that wasn't the location of his vision, we came back to find Burton waiting for us."

"Because you triggered one of his wards," he grumbles, swiping a hand down his face. I shrug, not wasting my breath in confirming or denying. "The Nightmares Guild is…" His words trail off as he tries to find the right ones to explain what he's been holding back from me, so I decide to add the next factor I know matters to him.

"We think that's what Eldon's vision is guiding him to. He mentioned names carved into stone walls, black marble flooring, no windows, and a golden table." My father starts to nod by the time I mention the flooring and doesn't stop for a few moments after I've finished.

"That's the Figment Lair."

It's my turn for my eyes to narrow as I stare my father down. My gut clenches, knowing the facts, but I want to hear him say it. "And you know that because…"

He leans forward, bracing his elbows on his knees as he sighs. "I was a member."

"Of course you were," I grumble, not liking the actual words now that they're spoken out loud. My father could have told me about this before I even got here, but instead, I had to learn about it from fucking Burton.

"Zane," he starts, but I wave him off. We've never held our feelings and emotions back and I'm not going to start now.

"How do you expect me to fight for all of this when I know nothing?" I throw my hands up in the air. "I want to defend our people and honor our family, but I deserve to know the reason behind it."

My father sighs so heavily that I'm sure I feel the rumble in my bones.

"Our land is under attack. It always has been and always

will be. Because we hold the greatest treasures in Gold Haven. The barrens that surround us, the realms around us, they're barbaric, Zane. So criminal that I thought I might be able to protect you from it if I kept you as far away from the Nightmares Guild as possible."

"Is that what has kept you so busy? Attacks?"

"No." He shakes his head with frustration and a hint of resignation. "One of the vision seekers on The Monarchy has seen a necromancer. Nothing more, nothing less. We don't know their strengths or intentions, but they must have cast magic to have registered on their radar."

Fuck.

My gut clenches so hard I think I might be sick, but I manage to hold the bile at bay as I nod in acknowledgment without saying a further word about it. Clearing my throat, I shift my stance so I'm sitting tall and alert. "So, about the Nightmares Guild?"

I can see the uncertainty in his eyes, and if this was just me coming to him because I had heard about it, I'm sure he would find a way to talk me away from it. But things are always different when Eldon's visions are involved. It's not just us being chaotic boys, it's the universe guiding us, and my father knows that. Whether he likes it or not is another subject entirely, but it's irrelevant. *That* part he knows.

"If that's where Eldon's visions lead you, then we both

know there's no stopping the inevitable. I must warn you, son. You have to be vigilant, be safe, and above all, do not trust a single soul outside of your close-knit group. Otherwise, the next contact request I'll be getting will be to confirm your death."

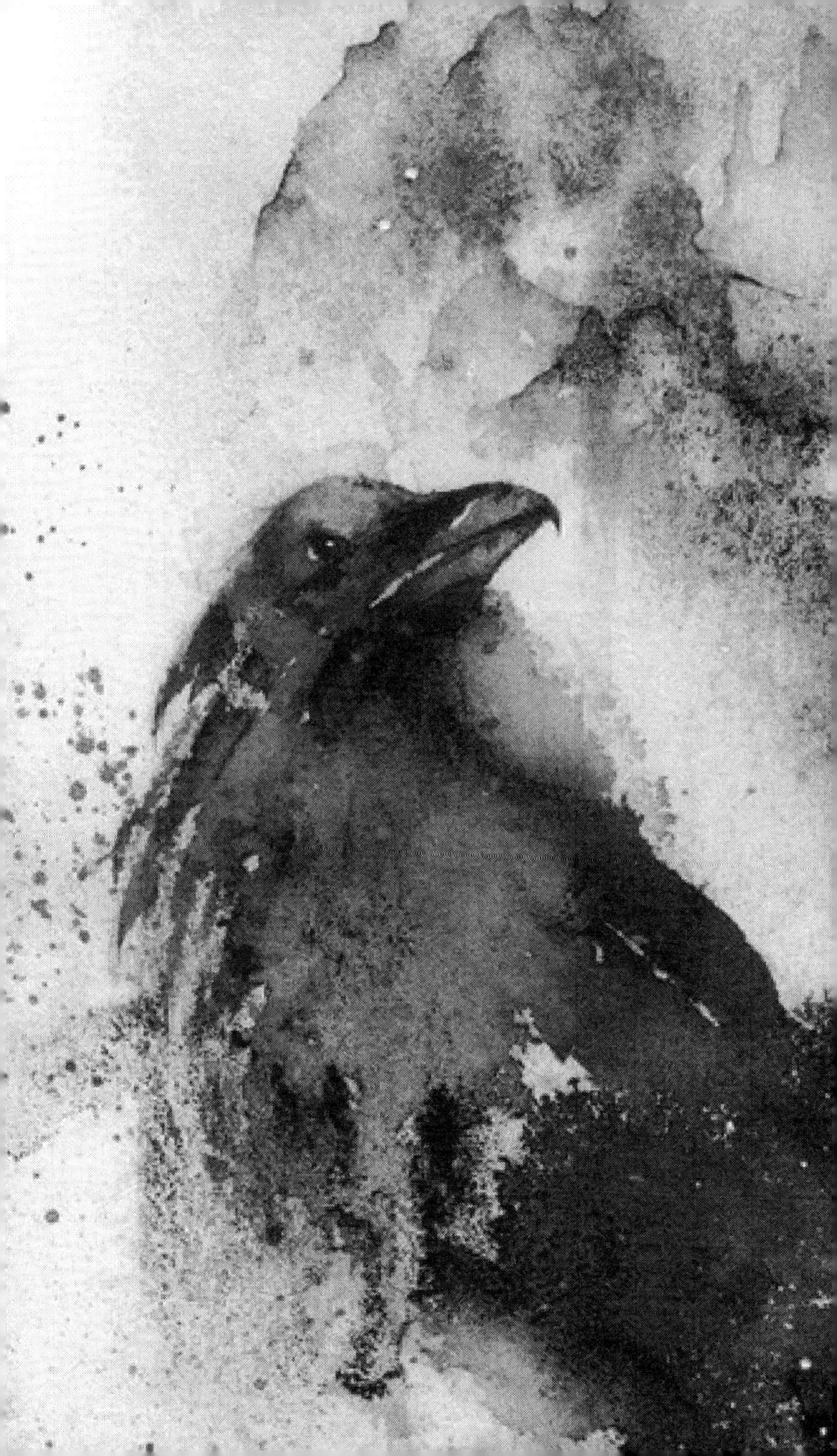

SIXTEEN

Raven

Water rains down on me like a gift from the realm, washing away some of my troubles as steam clouds my bathroom mirror. I know once I step out of here, reality will come crashing back down, but I can pretend for a little longer.

Zane left to speak to his father just over an hour ago, leaving Brax, Creed, and Eldon to dive into a workout outside. I joined them for a little while, but I'm not built for their level yet, so I soon bowed out and dived into the shower.

Thoughts of the Guild continue to flicker in my mind. Or, more specifically, the fact that Eldon's vision was pointing us in that direction to begin with. We just didn't know it. The uncertainty of what the Nightmares Guild stands for and means for us is gnawing at me.

There's only one way we're going to find out, though, and that means joining to discover the secrets hidden beyond the veil of the Guild.

A fucking guild. I never thought this would be where my life would be heading. Back in Shadowmoor, guilds were a thing of legends, a mythical society that would never find itself in the dark and rotten end of the world where we lived. Now I'm being invited. In-*fucking*-vited. That might just be by association with the Bishops, but it's an invite all the same.

Part of me wants to RSVP 'No thanks, motherfuckers,' but the intrigue outweighs anything else, as well as the potential it has to being the key to getting the answers we need. Especially with Eldon's vision playing a pinnacle part. Plus, the sheer wonder of who else is a member has me practically bouncing on the balls of my feet.

Rinsing the shampoo suds from my hair, I squeeze the ends. I almost considered trying to use my magic to do it, but the methodical action was needed. A hint of normalcy to help me make it through the day.

With one final deep breath, I turn off the stream of water and step out of the shower, grabbing the fluffy towel I placed on the vanity earlier. I wipe a hand over the steamed-up mirror, the reflection still blurred, and quickly tap into my core and generate a tingle of magic to clear the task for me.

A grin peers back at me, the smile on my face pure awe at the fact that I have the ability to do such a simple thing. Banding my towel around my waist, I continue to channel the magic as I dry every droplet of water from my body before doing the same to my hair. Once I'm completely dry from head to toe, I lean in closer to the mirror as I notice a black streak of hair just behind my ear.

When I run my fingers through the length, I don't see any other spots, but the growth at my roots is noticeable. Wetting my bottom lip, I think about what I want to happen. I think about the dark roots turning to the same shade of pink that covers the rest of my hair. It takes a second or two, but with my next breath, the dark hues transform into gloss pink...all except the full-length black strip behind my ear.

Focusing harder on that one section, my eyebrows furrow as I try to make my magic transform it, but no matter what I do, it stands dark against my skin. I give up when it's clearly not going to shift, hanging the towel on the hanger by the vanity before I head back into my room.

"Holy. Fuck."

I startle as I find Zane sitting at the foot of my bed. His eyes are fixed on my body and it takes me a second to realize I'm completely naked. The clothes I had pulled out for the day are folded beside him on top of the sheets, but I get the feeling that he's not going to make putting them on very easy.

My skin prickles under his intense gaze as his eyes slowly make their way up my body, burning into mine when I take a step toward him.

"The fact that you don't shield yourself or hide away is hot as fuck. I'm adding this as a rule in the handbook," he states, the corner of his mouth tugging up, and I shake my head at him.

"I didn't think it would be possible to add anything else to such a thick handbook," I breathe, taking another step toward him, and his gaze drops back down to my bare chest.

Zane clears his throat, swiping a hand over his mouth, and it takes a good few moments before his eyes find mine again. "I came in here to talk, but my brain can't function with you looking like this," he admits, and it sends an additional shiver of need down my spine.

Nibbling at my bottom lip, I slowly move toward him, eliminating the remaining distance between us until I'm standing between his open thighs. His hands instantly find my waist, tugging me an inch closer, and my palms settle on his shoulders.

"You're a fucking tease, Dove," he says with a groan, his fingers ghosting over my hips as he draws delicate circles. I need to be closer to him.

With my gaze locked on his, I shift to place my knees

on the bed on either side of his thighs so that I'm straddling him. His fingers tighten at my waist, pulling me down on top of his cock, making me groan this time.

"I don't know what you mean," I mumble, playing innocent, and he scoffs.

"Please," he rasps, stroking his thumbs to the apex of my thighs, teasing the sensitive flesh as my hips instinctively roll. "My dove wants her cunt stretching with my dick, doesn't she?"

My core clenches, my nipples pebbling as the air around us thickens with need, and I shiver. I'm a bundle of tension, a ripple of desire, and I want to watch this man play my body to perfection.

He tightens his hold on my left side as he grinds up against me. At the same time, his other hand pinches my nipple, making me gasp. "Tell me what you want, Raven."

I'm already putty in his hands and we've barely even started. I want him as breathless as me, as desperate as I am. Leaning closer, I bring my lips to his ear, swiping my tongue over the lobe first before sinking my teeth into his flesh. When he groans against my skin, I force myself to release my teeth so I can press my lips against his ear and whisper. "I want you to use me, bend me, break me."

"Fuck, Dove." His grip on my waist and nipple tighten, bringing me so close to pain, but the butterfly-soft kisses at my throat add the perfect sprinkle of pleasure. "I want your cum dripping down my dick."

Shit, I want that too. Now.

"What else do you want?" I push, my voice getting raspier as he leans back slightly to use his magic to remove his boots, pants, boxers, and t-shirt so he's as naked as me. Feeling his skin against my own heightens my senses and I'm ready to grind against his leg to get off, I'm that needy.

"I want you to be a good little dove and sit on my face," he orders, and before I can truly process his demand, he's shuffling up the bed with me in his grasp until his head nestles against my pillows.

Before I can place my hands down on either side of his head, he's grabbing my waist and lifting me around like a rag doll. I fucking love it. The room spins as I'm hoisted into the air before I'm unceremoniously draped over his face.

This motherfucker spun me around so my pussy is a breath away from his lips, but I now have the pleasure of taking in the length of his body. His hands on my thighs make my spine tingle, his glistening cock pleading for me to lean closer.

One sweep of his tongue through my folds and I'm dropping to my elbows, my mouth an inch away from his length. "Taste me, Dove." His lips drag over my clit as he speaks and my back arches with need.

Desperate to give him what he wants to satisfy us both,

I drag my tongue all the way from the base right to the very tip before slowly repeating the action in the opposite direction. As I work my way back from base to tip again, his tongue penetrates my core as his hands palm my ass, kneading my body perfectly as I blindly seek more friction.

"Fuck, Zane," I bite, pushing up onto my palms before I press the tip of his cock against my tongue and swallow him down.

The air thrums around us as our groans mingle together. "That's it, Dove. Take my dick. All the way," he demands, his hips lifting up off the bed to aim further down my throat. His tongue at my core is instantly replaced with his fingers as he nips at my clit with his teeth.

The heavy weight on my tongue and the fullness at the back of my throat combined with the stretch of my pussy has me on the cliff, ready to dive head first in a matter of seconds. Hollowing out my cheeks, I bob my head in time with his thrusts, eager to please. His moans turn to snarls as he thrusts up past my lips, harder and faster, and I start to gag. The second he relents, I slam my hand on his thigh, digging my nails into his skin as I continue to force him deeper into my mouth.

I fucking love it.

"Fuck, Raven. You like that, huh?" Zane asks, a fistful of my hair in his hand as he pries me from his cock, forcing me to glance back at him. "Fuck yeah, you do. Which birdie wants to be a good girl and choke on my cock?" I can't answer, I'm breathing so hard, but it's like my panting speaks to him directly. "Do you love the feel of unshed tears filling your eyes as my cock hits the back of your throat, Dove? Is that it?" I manage a nod and his grin spreads wider across his face. "Come for me as you do it."

His words are barely past his lips as he releases his hold on my hair and I collapse over his length again, eagerly sucking him down without further prompt. The second he's nudging the back of my throat, he plunges two fingers deep into my pussy as his tongue swirls around my clit. My hips are moving of their own accord, grinding and riding like my life depends on it. Only seconds pass before the telltale sign of an orgasm burns at the base of my spine.

A whoosh glides over my skin, offering the briefest of warnings before his hand claps down on my ass, and I'm coming. Wave after wave of ecstasy consumes every limb as my body spasms around his fingers, my release flooding his tongue. The slap to my ass is quickly soothed with a stroke of his hand and I somehow manage to swallow him down further, desperate to return the favor. He doesn't hit the back of my throat twice before he's tugging at my hair again and lifting me off his body.

This time, he pulls me off him completely so I'm kneeling beside him, staring down at his face, and my eyes widen at the sight of his lips glistening with my climax all over him.

Holy. Fuck.

He's watching me watch him and his hand relaxes on my hair ever so slightly, so I take that as my opportunity, eliminating the remaining distance between us as I crush my mouth to his. His hands grab at my waist, the hold close to bruising as his tongue delves past my lips. I taste sweet on his tongue, but I love the essence of him underneath it all.

It leaves me lightheaded.

"I need you to come for me too, Zane," I finally manage as his mouth on mine calms. "Tell me what you need," I push, desperate to see him chase it, feel it.

"Fuck, Dove. You've given it to me already," he murmurs, his hand lifting to cup my cheek. I lean into his touch, my eyelashes fluttering for a moment.

"Tell me," I repeat, refusing to give up, and his thumb stroking my cheek pauses.

"Ride me."

Another shiver down my spine, another clench to my core. I lift my leg to straddle him once again, pushing up off his chest as I look down at him with hooded eyes. "Like this… or this?" I turn, bracing my arms on his thighs instead as I look back over my shoulder at him.

His pupils are blown, his lips parted, and his chest slightly flushed. It's hot as fuck. I can't even begin to imagine what I look like.

"Just like this," he breathes, stroking his hands over the globes of my ass as I shift down a little more so I'm perfectly over his cock. "This ass is something else," he adds, digging his fingers into my flesh, and I instinctively drop down, grinding my core over his length. "I'm taking that next, Raven. Do you hear me?" His thumb glides over exactly where he's talking about, and my whole body stiffens with desire.

Needing to show him how in agreement I am, I push back slightly, the pad of his thumb teasing the tight muscles of my ass. "Fuck. You want that, don't you, Dove? You want me to claim every inch, every hole, every piece of you." My head falls back as I groan, his length between my thighs as he pushes a little further into my ass with his thumb. "Say it, Raven. Tell me what you want."

I take a deep breath, my voice lodged deep in my lungs as he stares at me, expectant. With his free hand, he maneuvers his cock so he's right at my entrance. When he cocks a brow, I know he's not moving until I say it, and fuck am I desperate to feel those words on my tongue.

"I want you to claim me, body, heart, and soul."

As the last word parts my lips, he slams into my pussy, stretching me inch by inch. Gone are the expectations of me riding him, taking what I want, and putting on a show. In its place remains a carnal man with carnal needs and a carnal woman desperate to take it all.

His hands on my waist direct my every move, working me up and down his length with precision. I feel weightless in his hold, my body alight with toe-curling pleasure. I'm not sure whether the room just blurs or my eyes can't stay open anymore, but all of my senses redirect to the feel of him claiming my core with every thrust.

"That's it, Dove. Come on my dick, make me yours," he rasps, his breath coming in short, sharp bursts before he quickly starts to become jagged with his movements, sloppy, yet pounding as my body works to his demand. My second orgasm comes out of nowhere, burning through every nerve ending as I scream at the top of my lungs.

I collapse in a heap on the bed, sobbing at the sudden loss of his cock at my core, before the warm shots of cum hit my stomach in ropes. Gaping up at him, I'm in awe of how fucking stunning he looks in this moment.

It was completely lost on me that there was no protection, and I'm silently thankful that he at least remembered, but that was too close. I need to get a grip on myself instead of letting my body do whatever it pleases.

Zane drops down beside me a second later, sweat clinging to every inch of him, and I sigh serenely. A soft chuckle parts my lips as I try to remember how we even ended up here. Peering at my handbook-wielding Bishop, I stroke a finger down his arm. "What did you even come in here to talk about?"

"Don't spoil a good thing," he grumbles, wiping a hand down his face, and my eyebrows pinch together in confusion.

"What are you talking about?"

He glances at me from the corner of his eye for a moment before he sighs, and I instantly know that what he's about to say isn't good at all.

"The Monarchy knows there's a new necromancer. They don't know who, what, where, why, or when, but they know. They know you exist."

DESTINED SHADOWS

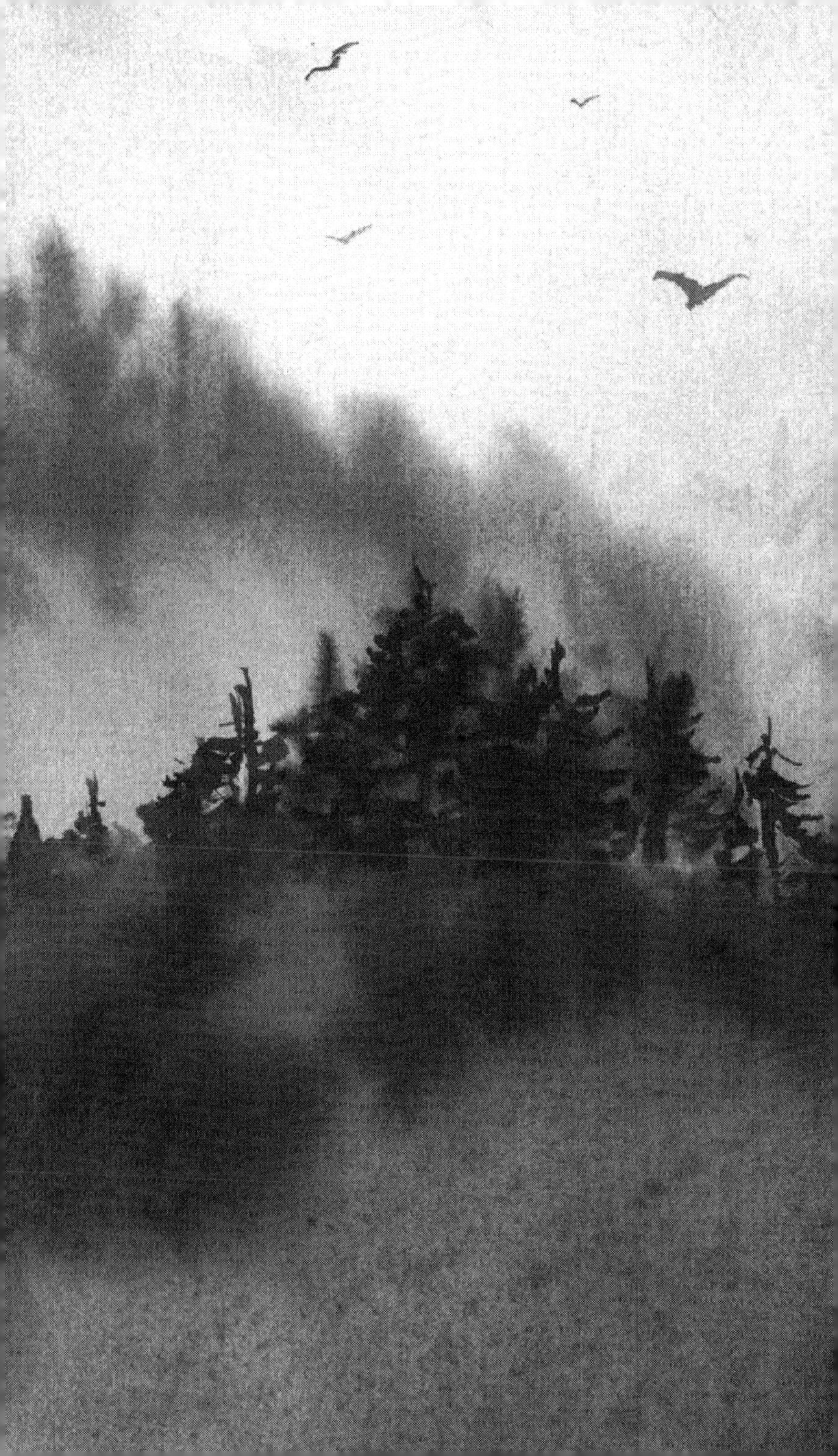

SEVENTEEN
Brax

It feels like ever since the attack on the Shadowmoor outpost, we've become nocturnal. No one's fucking sleeping, everyone's getting grouchy, and not a single one of us can put a finger on what's happening. It's driving me insane.

After Zane met with his father yesterday, we spent the majority of the day going over the revelation that The Monarchy has a whiff of a new necromancer. They've got a scent of Raven, my fucking shadow, and it infuriates me.

By the end of the day, we had decided that we need to keep her magic locked up even tighter. It's not for anyone to know or see. Not that she would really be able to put on a show with it, but what it does mean is that we need to see if she has a secondary ability to focus on. At least in public.

All necromancers ever reported have had at least one

other power, and we're hopeful that's the case for Raven as well. We've gone from one extreme to another, from protecting a Void to hiding a necromancer. What the fuck is my life right now?

Classes today were a huge fuck up. I was too tired to pay much attention, and as every minute ticked by, I could feel myself getting grouchier and colder. I get the sense Raven and the Bishops know it too because they've left me out here to work out alone while they do whatever the fuck it is they're doing inside.

Dropping the weights at my feet, I lean back, taking a deep breath as sweat beads at my temples. My muscles ache since I worked out early this morning too, but I need the distraction. With my hands on my hips, I turn my attention to the coastline, searching for an answer to a question I can't quite put my finger on, when I hear the patio door open behind me.

"Appreciating you working out when the sun is setting instead of when it's rising is an entirely different thing," Raven states, her voice wrapping around me like a fucking prayer, and all I can do is grunt.

Fucking grunt.

I keep my gaze focused forward, my back to her, hoping for… fuck knows what, when I sense her getting nearer.

"Are you doing okay? I know we're all kind of going through some shit right now, but everyone else seems more open to airing their troubles." She comes to a stop beside me, facing out over the cliff as I read between the lines. I'm in no mood to talk about my feelings, not even to Raven.

"You don't need to be privy to everything about me because you saved me," I bite, instantly hating the taste of the harsh words on my tongue. Peering out of the corner of my eye at her, it's impossible for me not to see the subtle sting on her face.

Fuck.

What's that I'm feeling? Clawing at my chest like a feral beast, burning a hole through my body as it tries to escape. Guilt?

Shit.

Pushing people away and keeping them at arm's length is all I know, all I used to want. After losing my parents, why let anyone close if you know what the inevitable loss feels like? But Raven... damn, she just keeps trying to worm her way under my skin and I have no control over it.

With a sigh, I dip my head and look down at my feet. My eyelids flutter closed for a second as I exhale, trying to summon the words of apology that feel foreign to even think about, nevermind express.

Just when I think I have something to ease the guilt in my chest and the pain I've caused in my shadow, a screech startles me from my thoughts. Turning to my left, I freeze up, tension coiling in my gut when I find three bodies draped in black cloaks wearing golden masks grappling with Raven, who now has a black bag secured over her head.

What. The. Actual. Fuck?

"You just signed your death warrant," I snarl, clenching my fists at my sides as two more fucking black-and-gold clad people charge me. My right arm is stone before they get within arm's reach and I smash my enlarged knuckles into their faces. They hurtle through the air, crashing into the glass at the back of the house with a bang.

That better get the attention of the others or I'm about to add them to my kill list.

"Fuck," one of them hisses, their head bouncing back and forth between me and the injured fucker still slumped against the glass. "How can we initiate you into the Guild if you fucking fight like this?" It sounds like a guy's voice, but it's not one I can place.

My chest heaves with every breath as I slowly turn my attention to each of them before settling on Raven, who remains still in their hold. She doesn't look harmed, just restrained, but that still doesn't sit well with me. Not one bit.

The urge to continue fighting is hard to overcome. It's what I'm good at. Despite that, I force my muscles to relax, release the magic from my arm, and drop my chin to my chest. They act quickly, pulling a black cloth over my head as they render me useless.

What the fuck have we gotten ourselves into?

Every second feels like an entire year. The air shifts around us and the cooling breeze of the distant sea is gone. It's almost stifling in comparison as I try to focus on what I can hear and sense around me. My body aches from the battle inside me, keeping my anger at bay.

Hands shove at my shoulders and I tumble backward, landing in a seat with a huff. A moment later, the cloth over my head is removed. Manically searching around me, my gaze crashes with Raven's a moment later and relief whooshes through me.

I track my gaze over her from head to toe, checking for anything and everything, and when my eyes land back on hers, she offers me a soft smile.

"I'm fine, big man," she mouths from her seat across from me, and I relax a little more.

Glancing around, I find Eldon and Zane to my left and Creed to my right, completing the somewhat circle we've been placed in. Their scowls match my own, their distaste for this shit competing with mine as I fold my arms over my chest and glare at the closest fucker in black and gold.

I hate that I can't see their expression beneath the mask more than I hate not knowing who it is.

Fuckers.

Taking stock of the room, I note the black marble flooring, the carvings in the stone windowless walls, and the ornate gold table sitting in the center of the five of us. I turn my head back around to Eldon. His gaze is locked on Raven's, but he must sense my stare because he turns my way a moment later.

I cock my brow at him, the silent question registers on his end and he nods at me.

This is the room from his vision.

At least that piece of the puzzle is arranged. Now we have to go through all of their bullshit to figure out why we need to be here to begin with.

"Eldon Rhodes, Brax Carlsen, Creed Wylder, Zane Denver, and Raven Hendrix." My gaze whips to the guild member stepping forward, our names hot on their lips. "You have been summoned forward to be inducted into the elite ranks of the Nightmares Guild." It's on the tip of my tongue to say, "I'll pass," but I manage to keep my mouth shut. "This is a Guild built on blood, fueled by the enemy, and shrouded with darkness in order to achieve what others cannot."

As they speak, more and more black suits and gold masks step forward, circling around us. One of them carries a large gold pot and places it on the table without a word before they rejoin the others. This is weird as shit.

"Do you agree to follow the values of the Nightmares Guild?"

I scoff as Eldon huffs. "You're going to have to be a bit more specific with what we're signing up to first, don't you think?" I grin, pleased with his retort since he beat me to it.

Silence descends around us, the torches around the edge of the room dimming as the member speaking steps into the smaller circle we've been placed in, walking the perimeter and making eye contact with each of us.

"The Nightmares Guild does what is necessary for the people of our realm. We believe in a truer future for everyone, even those from Ashdale and Shadowmoor. The Nightmares Guild began as a handful of vigilantes whose bloodlines now trickle through the generations, each with the same goal; to rid the realm of the darkness that continues to claw at our very center."

My brows rise, my intrigue piqued, and when I glance at Raven and my brothers, I see the same expression there too.

Why would Professor Burton, along with Zane's father, a member of The Monarchy, be a part of this? If there was ever a telling sign that there's more going on than we know, this is it. A startling reality comes to mind. We were caught coming back after sneaking off to Shadowmoor. Burton saw the determination in us to find answers, and this is seemingly the way we're going to get them.

Perfect.

"Do you believe in something along those lines?"

Blinking up at the person peering down at me, my jaw tightens with their need to call me out specifically, so I shrug, uncaring.

"I'm in," Raven blurts, and my eyes dart to hers. The second they mentioned that they wanted an equal realm for everyone, Shadowmoor included, I knew she would be fully committed. She will forever be attached to a place that treated her like shit, made her life Hell, and carved away at her every day. On the surface, she's strong, resilient, and unwavering. That remains the same underneath too, but she also cares, whole-fucking-heartedly, without a drop of need for anyone to care back.

She was made to be a vigilante.

"Anyone else?" the slightly distorted voice asks, glancing around at the others before settling back on me. Raven's acceptance triggers the rest of us, a resounding yes murmuring past each of our lips. "Excellent. Rites of passage and challenges will present themselves along the way, but for now, to begin your induction and acceptance into the Nightmares Guild, repeat after me. Follow your heart, find solace in the shadows, and take down the dawn."

Raven's eyes widen, making me pause, but her lips

move without pause and I quickly follow to keep up with her. "Follow your heart, find solace in the shadows, and take down the dawn."

As the last word echoes around us, the light completely evaporates, drenching us in darkness. Only the soft sound of steps can be heard around us until a small flickering reappears, and only one member stands before us.

Ignoring them for a moment, I fixate on Raven. "What was that look before you spoke?" I ask, and she gapes at me for a second, her gaze flicking to the member for a second before she shakes her head at me.

Reluctantly, I take the hint, wiping a hand down my face as I try to gather my thoughts.

"Are you here to guide us out or show your face?" Zane grunts, rising from his seat as the member stands by the table.

It's almost as though they're considering what to say, if anything at all. I'm ready to ignore them altogether and get the fuck out of here, but as I stand, the member turns to face Raven head-on.

One tentative step toward her and my spine stiffens.

Sebastian. If that's him, I'll fucking kill him before he can get within arm's length of her. My feet are already moving, refusing to fail at my own vow, but I stumble to a stop when the black hood is dropped and the mask is discarded.

It's not him, but the look on Raven's face has me unsure whether she would feel the same if it was.

"Hey, Raven."

Leila.

DESTINED SHADOWS

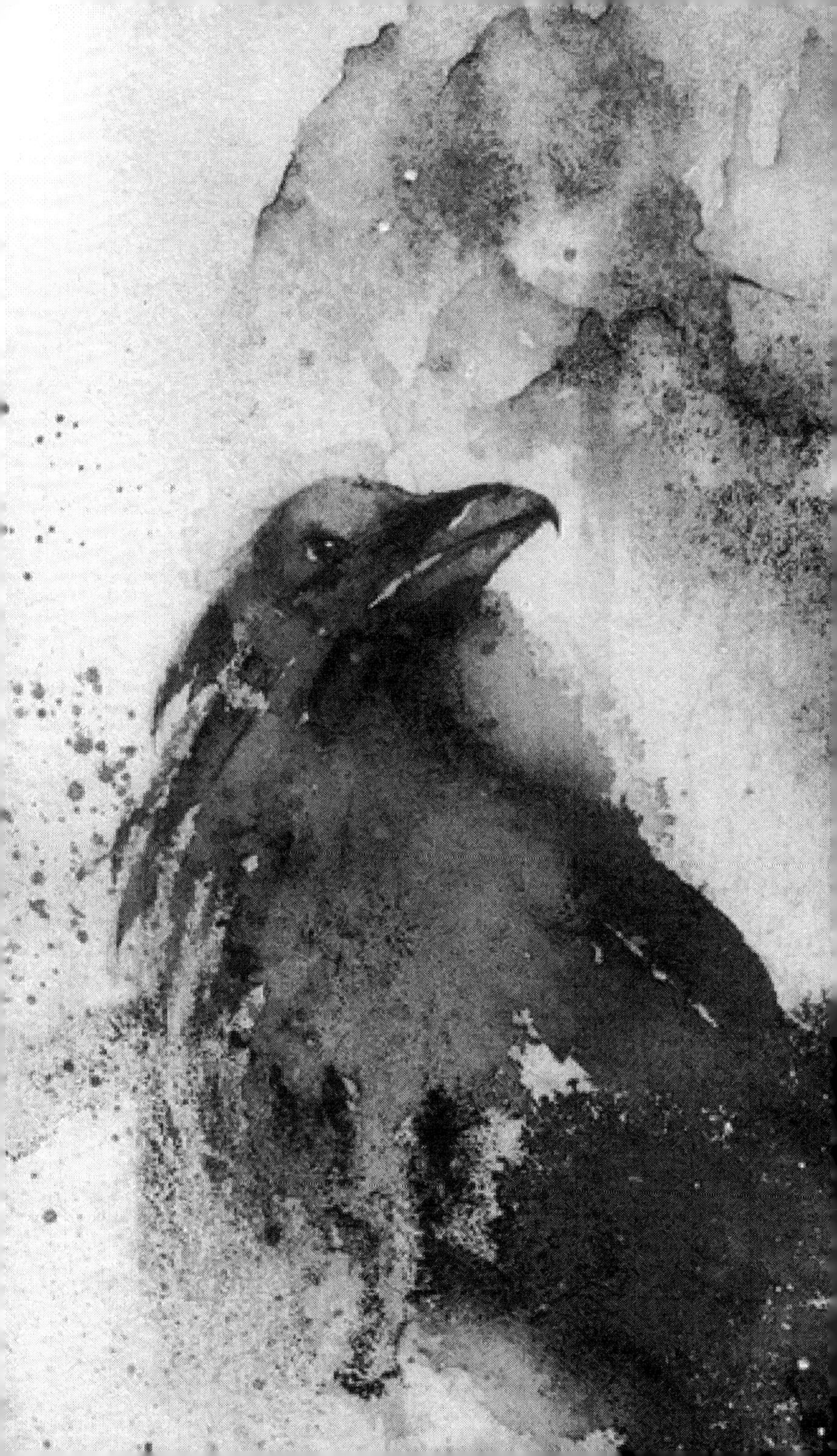

EIGHTEEN
Raven

Leila. *Fucking* Leila. I understand why she's standing before me, I just can't seem to process the betrayal I feel along with it. On top of that, I'm even more pissed that I've allowed myself to be swept into a position where I feel any kind of hurt from anyone at all.

The look in her eyes is a mixture of nerves and guilt, and I'm not surprised one bit. Composing myself, I stand, brushing my hands down my thighs.

"Talk to me, Raven," she murmurs, nervously shuffling from one foot to the other. All I can do is stare at her, my jaw locked tight as I bite back the hint of disappointment threatening my tongue.

"I don't know why you think she's going to talk to you after this little revelation," Brax grunts, not trying to hold back his thoughts like me. "Let's get the fuck out of here," he adds, nodding to the open archway at the far left of the room that seems to lead down a corridor.

"I didn't have to reveal myself, you know. Not yet at least. But the second you were inside of the Guild, I wanted to come forward," Leila states, answering Brax's question, but her gaze is fixed on me.

She wants me to respond, to give her some kind of hint of how I'm feeling, but my mind is shut down tight, allowing a familiar numbness to creep up my spine.

Still unsure about Leila, I make the decision to follow Brax's lead and get out of here, and she quickly falls into step beside me.

"No. Fucking. Way," Zane grinds out, rushing around me to block Leila's way. "You can stay here."

Leila's shaking her head before he's even finished talking. "I-I can't. I'm really not a fan of it down here," she breathes, eyes nervously scanning around the space. I can sense Zane's about to tell her just how much he doesn't give a fuck, and despite my own feelings being twisted into knots, I nod toward the exit for her to follow along with me.

She offers a soft smile in response, but I don't return it as I focus on keeping up with Brax, who is now halfway down the narrow hallway. Reaching the other end, steep stone steps greet us. It feels like an eternity before we reach the top, but when we do, I startle at the fact that we're at the back of the main academy building.

"That place is under the academy?" I clarify with Eldon, who nods, frowning at me as he comes to a stop at my side.

"It seems so. But what I think we need to consider more than anything, Raven, is the fact that my vision could have been more of a warning sign for who we were letting into our inner circle," he states, nodding toward Leila as she appears breathless at the top of the steep steps.

"Vision?" she asks, with her eyebrows crinkling, and Creed quickly wags a finger at everyone.

"Don't say another word in front of her."

Leila's jaw slackens as she gapes at him, hurt dancing in her eyes as the rest of the Bishops stare at her. She clears her throat, waving her hand in front of her, and the black cloak and gold mask disappear. She folds her arms over her chest and turns her full attention to Creed. "Why? What do you think I'll do?"

Creed shrugs, not indulging her with a response, but the same can't be said for Zane.

"I mean, the possibilities are endless. You could spy on us, feed information about us back to the Guild. Who the fuck knows what lies you've already spun to Raven," he lists off, moving to step in front of me a little, positioning himself perfectly between Leila and me.

Leila shakes her head at him in disbelief. I know I

should interject and piece this together for myself, but I'm still at a complete loss with it all and I can't find the words to get Zane to back off and walk away.

"I'm not a liar, Zane. I omitted a fact, yeah, but that's exactly what the five of you are now going to do, too. It's a part of being in the Nightmares Guild. People don't know about it because that's the very definition of a secret society."

Well, snap.

The two of them continue to stare each other down when Eldon throws his arm around my shoulder and turns me in the direction of the path that leads us home. My eyes widen in surprise when I see that Brax is already a good way down it, clearly not sticking around to deal with this shit. The sound of footsteps rushing behind us is the telltale sign that the others are following after us.

Hopeful to make it back to the house without anything else being said so I can actually think, I barely make it a dozen steps before Zane chimes in again, still not ready to stop pushing Leila for more. But she's choosing to follow us back, so she must be open to it.

"You've always acted like an outcast because of your father, but—"

"Wait, do you actually think me being one of the Nightmares gives me anything more than additional grief? I'm one of them *because* of my father, nothing more, nothing less. It doesn't mean they like me. As a matter of fact, it's probably another reason for them to hate me, but I believe in the cause of the Guild, so I withstand their bullshit in the hopes of making a difference," she snaps, rendering Zane silent as we all march back to the house.

Eldon's hand strokes patterns over my arm as I lean into him, taking silent strength and comfort as the house comes into view.

"She doesn't step foot inside," Brax hollers, not bothering to glance back at us.

"Raven," she pleads, and my steps slow. Eldon's arm drops from my shoulders as I turn to face her, but he doesn't completely step inside.

"I don't really know what I'm supposed to think right now, Leila," I admit. I know it's not what she wants to hear, but fuck if I can give her anything else.

Tucking a loose tendril of hair behind her ear, she sighs. "For real, Raven, is this something you would have plucked up the courage to tell me about tomorrow if I wasn't standing here already? Without prompt or reason to spill the truth? Would you have said, 'Hey, Leila, guess what I was initiated into last night?' Because I don't think you would have." Her words are heavily laced with defeat, while a twist of guilt and reality clenches my stomach. She does have a point there. That doesn't mean I have to like it, though. "Or how about the fact that you guys snuck off to Shadowmoor? Was that going to be an omitted fact between us as well?"

"How do you know about that?" Eldon interrupts, and Leila doesn't remove her gaze from mine as she answers.

"Burton." Pushing a heavy exhale past her lips, she looks down at her hands then back at me. "I get that I've caught you by surprise, but it doesn't change who I am. This is what my father was leaning toward when he invited you to train with us. He sees the fight in you too, but I need you to understand that guilds are secrets for a reason, and I wouldn't be following the code if I just told the first person I ever considered my friend."

My chest tightens at the sincerity in her voice. Through the fog in my brain, I can see and believe in her words, I just don't like how it left me feeling to begin with, and I can't shake it. If she asked me if I trusted her right now, I don't know if I could give an honest answer and the one she's hoping to hear at least.

"Are we just supposed to believe that?" Zane asks from behind me, and Leila shakes her head again.

"No, Raven is. I don't owe you guys shit, but I owe her something."

I can feel everyone's gaze on me, waiting for my response, but I'm still falling flat.

Creed clears his throat from the open doorway. "Are you going to answer any questions we might have?"

"That depends…"

"On what?"

"Who it is that is asking," she retorts, cocking her brow as she plants her hand on her hip.

A beat of silence settles around us before I roll my neck, trying to alleviate some of the tension riddling my limbs. "Let's take this around the back. I might be able to think better there."

I don't wait for anyone else as I head for the garden. Leila, Zane, Creed, and Eldon follow after me, and I find Brax already standing back there. The tension in his jaw seems worse than it was moments earlier, and when I catch a glimpse of his eyes, it's anger I see burning in them.

"Someone's been in here."

"What, who?" Panic ripples through me as Brax's gaze cuts to Leila.

"I don't fucking know, but maybe your little friend here might have an idea," he snarls.

"Why would I know?"

He steps around me to go toe to toe with Leila. "Was it your job to keep us busy or something while they snuck in? Tell me who it was and I'll opt to slaughter you instead of torturing you."

"What? No, of course not," she hastily replies.

"I don't believe you," Brax pushes, but she doesn't back down. Instead, she rolls her shoulders back and somehow stands taller.

"You don't have to believe me. I didn't take part in getting you guys to the Guild, but I wouldn't be shocked if whoever did snooped, Brax."

"Bullshit. You know."

"Read me."

"What?" I interject, confused with what the hell is going on now.

"Brax can read my mind. Do it."

He doesn't even glance in my direction as he lifts his hand to her head, happy to take the facts from her mind without taking her word.

"No, don't you dare," I interrupt, knocking his hand down before he can touch her. I don't care if it would clear things up. It's violating. Whether she's agreeing to it or not, I'm definitely not okay with it.

Shoulder checking Brax, he reluctantly moves aside so I can take his place in front of Leila. Pinching the bridge of my nose for a moment's reprieve, I drop my hands to my hips and stare her straight in the eyes.

"I'm fucking trusting you, Leila. One foot out of line and we're done, do you understand?"

"Of course," she agrees quickly.

"I wanted more time to process and fucking think, but the five of you make it impossible to do things at my own speed," I grind out, flicking my gaze to Brax, Creed, Zane, and Eldon too. "You're right, I had no intentions of telling you about Shadowmoor, and that's not the only thing I'm keeping guarded. The same goes for you, but that's going to take a certain level of trust out of our friendship whether we like it or not."

"When you first acted like my friend, I thought it wouldn't last, Raven. I expected you to realize what a loser I was like everyone else, so I didn't get into the deeper stuff. I would change that in a heartbeat if I could."

"I don't know if we can," I admit, heaving a sigh. She nods, my words disappointing her, but at least I'm not giving her false hope or lying. "There are things we're going to need to talk about, facts we're going to want to hear about the Guild, and I'm kind of expecting that to come from you."

"If I know it, I'll share."

Eldon steps to my side. "The fourth year, from the party, is he—"

"A member of the Guild? Yes. However, now I can't bear to show my face because he's been talking about me and... being with me, to... everyone." She winces, and my heart clenches for her.

Fuck. That's shitty, I wouldn't wish that upon anybody. Well, maybe Genie, but that's different. My fists curl at my sides. I want to punch someone in the face, the fourth year to be exact, and the stark reality that I want to defend her so fiercely is a reminder that as much as this sucks right now, I still care for my friend.

"Are there any other notable members we should be aware of?" Creed asks, pulling me from my thoughts.

Leila sighs *again*. "You know exactly who I'm going to say."

My breath stutters as my pulse starts to ring in my ears.

"Say it," Brax orders, and she offers me a soft smile as her eyes dip to the floor.

"Sebastian… and Genie."

Fuck. My. Life.

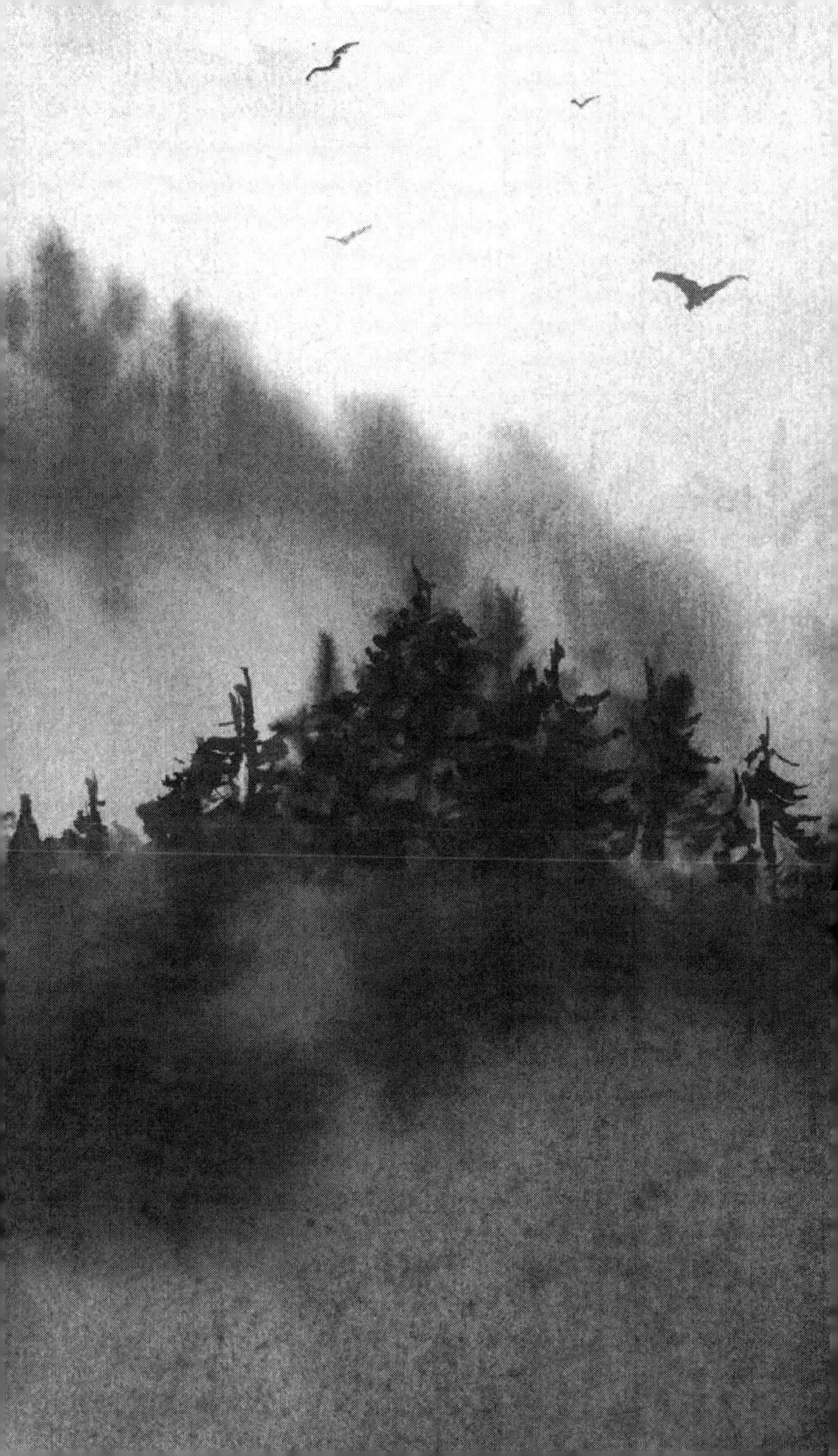

NINETEEN

Brax

Smoke billows around me in a vortex, my vision blurring as faceless men storm the room. Finn's lifeless body is a heap at the door as they clamber over him without an ounce of care. My blade feels heavy in my hand as I try to wield it, but it's impossible. I'm losing, they're winning, and there's nothing I can do about it.

I have to turn to stone if I have any hope of staving off their attack. Magic floods through my veins, starting at my toes before creeping up my spine, but the perfect shiver I get whenever I've completely transformed doesn't come. Instead, an unwavering slice of pain consumes me.

My back burns, my smoke-filled vision fading to black in an instant, but there's no reprieve for me. Blinking my eyes open, confusion grips me tight as the smoke disappears, the faceless men along with it, as the room morphs into another haunting sight.

Black marble flooring, carved stone walls, and the imposing gold table.

My attackers no longer come in the form of faceless men and my surroundings are no longer those of the Shadowmoor outpost. Instead, a flock of black-cloaked gold-masked motherfuckers swarm me in a circle that continues to get smaller and smaller. I can't find my blade; the handle gone from my grasp. It's only me and my fists now, but the uncertainty of shifting is overwhelming. The last time I transformed when in danger, I still wound up leaving myself vulnerable.

I can't just turn my back this time.

Clenching my fists, my magic swirls down my arms, turning them to stone, but as the nearest member of the Nightmares Guild gets even closer, my body refuses to move.

"You're helpless against us, you fool. You're dead." A cackle rings out, the lights diminishing as their gold masks begin to glow in the darkness.

I'm not dead. I'm fucking standing right here in front of you.

"I can hear your thoughts, you know. As adorable as it is that you think you're alive just because you're standing here, you're going to need the reality check you deserve. This is the realm of the Shadows, Brax Carlsen. Get comfortable. You're here for the rest of eternity."

"No!"

I refuse. I refuse. I refuse.

My back burns, the pain of death taking its hold on me once again as the room's blanketed in darkness. With a single blink, my surroundings shift before me; only this time, I'm familiar with where I am.

Home.

The pale-blue exterior glistens in the late evening sun. The sound of laughter echoes around me as I double-take on the people standing on the white wraparound porch.

"Mom? Dad?"

The words feel strange on my tongue, but the two sets of eyes that turn to greet me are not.

"Brax?" My mother's eyebrows pinch together as I race up the footpath, taking the steps up to the porch two at a time. My chest heaves with every breath as my mother's worry grows. "Brax, what are you doing here?"

"I... I don't know," I admit, swiping a stone hand down my face. I quickly bring in my magic and let my gargoyle rest.

"Son, you're not supposed to be here," my father states, clapping me on the shoulder as his green eyes take me in.

"I don't know where here is."

My mother wraps her arms around my waist, squeezing

me tight as she takes a deep breath. "Either way, I get a minute to drink you in," she murmurs with a happy smile.

Tentatively wrapping my arms around her, it's startling to notice that she now comes up to my shoulders. The last I remember of them, I barely came to her waist, but a lot of time has passed since then.

"I'm worried that you're here again so soon, son."

I blink at my father, confused by his worry and mention of it being so soon. It's been forever. "I don't know what you mean."

A look passes between them, one I don't recall or understand, but whatever it is, it isn't good.

"Son, you were here merely a week ago, hurt, bloody, injured. We thought the worst, but then you disappeared in the blink of an eye. Are you hurt again? Is that why you're back?"

Slipping out of my mother's hold, I look between them. They're so startlingly different it's almost sweet. My father is built like me, with blond floppy hair and piercing green eyes, while my mother has olive skin, brown hair, and matching brown eyes. A blond Viking warrior and a golden goddess. And then they have me.

"Why would I have to be hurt to be back? I don't remember being here."

As much as everything looks like home, the feeling in my chest tells me it's not the same, I just can't pinpoint how or why.

"Honey, this is the afterlife. We're in the—"

I jolt, my body stiffening as I bolt upright in bed. Sweat clings to every inch of me and my heart feels like it's about to burst from my chest. Lifting my hand, I place my palm against my chest, feeling the rhythm of my heartbeat slowly calm down.

What the fuck was that?

I've had nightmares of the night at the outpost ever since we got home, that part isn't new, but the Nightmares Guild and my parents? Fuck. Swiping a hand down my face, I flop back down in bed, staring up at the ceiling as confusion gets the better of me.

It felt so real, so vivid, yet… I was asleep? I've never felt anything like that in my life. Until now.

Glancing at the time, it's a little after two in the morning, even earlier than the past few nights. I'm not going to work out in the yard at this time. It was almost midnight before I finally passed out.

A soft knock slightly rattles my door, and a moment later, it pries open to reveal a sliver of Raven through the crack.

"What do you want?" I rasp, my defenses rising at her arrival. I don't want to be seen this vulnerable right now. I feel raw, like my emotions are completely exposed, and I think I might be sick.

"I heard a noise," she whispers, slipping through the door and clicking it shut behind her. Her hair is messy from sleep, her nightwear stopping midthigh against her soft skin. Despite how good she looks, though, I feel like I can't breathe.

"I'm fine," I grumble, clearing my throat, and she shrugs, cutting the remaining distance between us. Without a word, she crawls up the bed, nestling her head on the pillow beside me as she snuggles in.

"Well, I'm not."

"Make yourself comfortable, why don't you." The words snap from my tongue, but the harshness isn't there like it usually would be. Her cheek presses against my shoulder, her hair brushing against my throat as her palm flattens on my chest.

"I will, thanks."

I'm rendered speechless as she effortlessly snuggles into my side. Her breathing evens out quickly before she's fast asleep beside me.

I don't know what I'm supposed to do with her, but it's as if my body has been waiting to have her in my bed again, in my arms, for an eternity because I shuffle around so she won't strain her neck and band my arm around her waist.

Quicker than I care to admit, my breathing evens out too, and for the first time since the Shadowmoor outpost,

I simply sleep.

I don't know what it is with this woman and her ability to just... be her, but my soul fucking likes it. I slept like the dead, barely waking up with enough time to work out this morning after a fucked up night from Hell, and even though I don't want to admit it, I know it has something to do with her being in my bed.

It was a close call whether I was going to get my exercise in by fucking her hard and fast or actually going outside with the others. And despite how desperate I was to feel her, the night's revelations forced me to put a little bit of space between us so I could think.

Not that I've really done much thinking that hasn't revolved around her.

Even now, as we head toward the main academy building for today's classes, she doesn't stay a step behind me like usual. No, she clings to my arm. Her fingers flex around my biceps, sending a direct shot to my fucking dick. I'm seriously considering that something might be wrong with me.

"Are you okay? You feel tense," she states, looking up at me with those long fucking eyelashes that flutter like butterflies, luring me in and making me soft.

"I'm fine," I grunt, and I feel her hand begin to slip from my arm. Before she can release me completely, I press my tricep into my side, trapping her fingers between them. She takes the silent hint, holding onto me once again.

"Are we shocked Leila didn't show up this morning like usual?" Zane asks from behind, and Raven shakes her head.

"No. After she dropped the bomb on us about *the* asshole on campus, I told her I needed some breathing space. Which included leaving me to come to her. She can listen at least," she mutters.

I can see why she's able to see both sides of the coin with the Nightmares Guild and Leila's participation, but my brothers and I all saw the pain on Raven's face when she first saw her. If I can be a pillar of strength to ward off anything that may make her feel like that again, I will. Shady friends included.

I'm not trying to be a controlling fucker, even though it's definitely in my nature, so I'm trying to respect her wants, but if Leila rocks with Sebastian and Genie, then she's out. No questions asked. Possibly dead because that shit would be a betrayal.

"You know you're sitting beside her in most of the lessons today, though, right?" Creed appears at her other side, concern in his dark eyes, and she shrugs.

"That I can handle."

"Or, you could sit with one of us instead," Eldon offers, wagging his brows at her, and she rolls her eyes.

"No thanks, I actually need to focus," she retorts, like we would be some kind of distraction, but before I can call her out on it, a shadow falls over us and we instinctively stop.

"Raven."

The sound of Sebastian's voice saying her name is worse than dying, I'm sure of it.

Raven's hold on my arm drops, but I clutch her fingers before she can take a step back.

"What do you want, asshole?" Eldon bites before I get the chance, and the slimy fucker smirks.

"Just wanted to check in on the new... recruits. Wondering if you're ready to be put through your paces or if you'll even survive it," he says with a sneer. Even though Raven's glare doesn't budge on her face, I feel her fingers wrap slightly tighter around my own and I take that as my cue to make sure this fucker can't get any closer to her.

"Thanks, but fuck off," I grunt, pulling Raven a step behind me as I sense Creed, Zane, and Eldon all inch closer too.

"I'm talking to my sister."

"No. She stopped being your sister when you stopped protecting her," I snarl, feeling the eyes of other students on us as they slow down to watch the drama unravel. "Now, she's mine. And unless I fucking say so, you don't get to speak to her. At. All."

My pulse pounds in my ear, screaming one word over and over.

Mine.

I feel possessive as hell and I really couldn't care less.

"Yesterday's excitement changes all of that because I'm a faction leader. Which means I overrule every word that comes out of your mouth," he spits, inching closer to get in my face, as if I'm going to back down from him.

This guy has no damn clue who he's pushing at. But if he wants to get familiar, I'm more than happy to help him along. Shuffling Raven completely behind me and out of his view, I straighten my spine so I stand a few inches taller than him.

If he wants to play the intimidation game, I'm all in.

I get myself so close that my chest brushes against his. "Fuck you. Fuck your ranking. Fuck your last damn name. It means nothing. Not after you put hands on her and tried to play God with her life." His hand lifts to my shoulder, ready to push me away, but it's too late; my blood is already boiling.

Rearing my fist back, it's stone before it touches him, blasting him backward into the academy building with a grunt and a splattering of his blood coating my fingers. I hear the gasps ring out around us, but none of that matters. All that matters is him knowing the new fucking rules. Moving up beside him, I crouch, bringing my nose to his as I sneer.

"I'm done letting you think you can harm what's mine. Next time it won't just be your blood on my hands. Mark my words, it'll be your death."

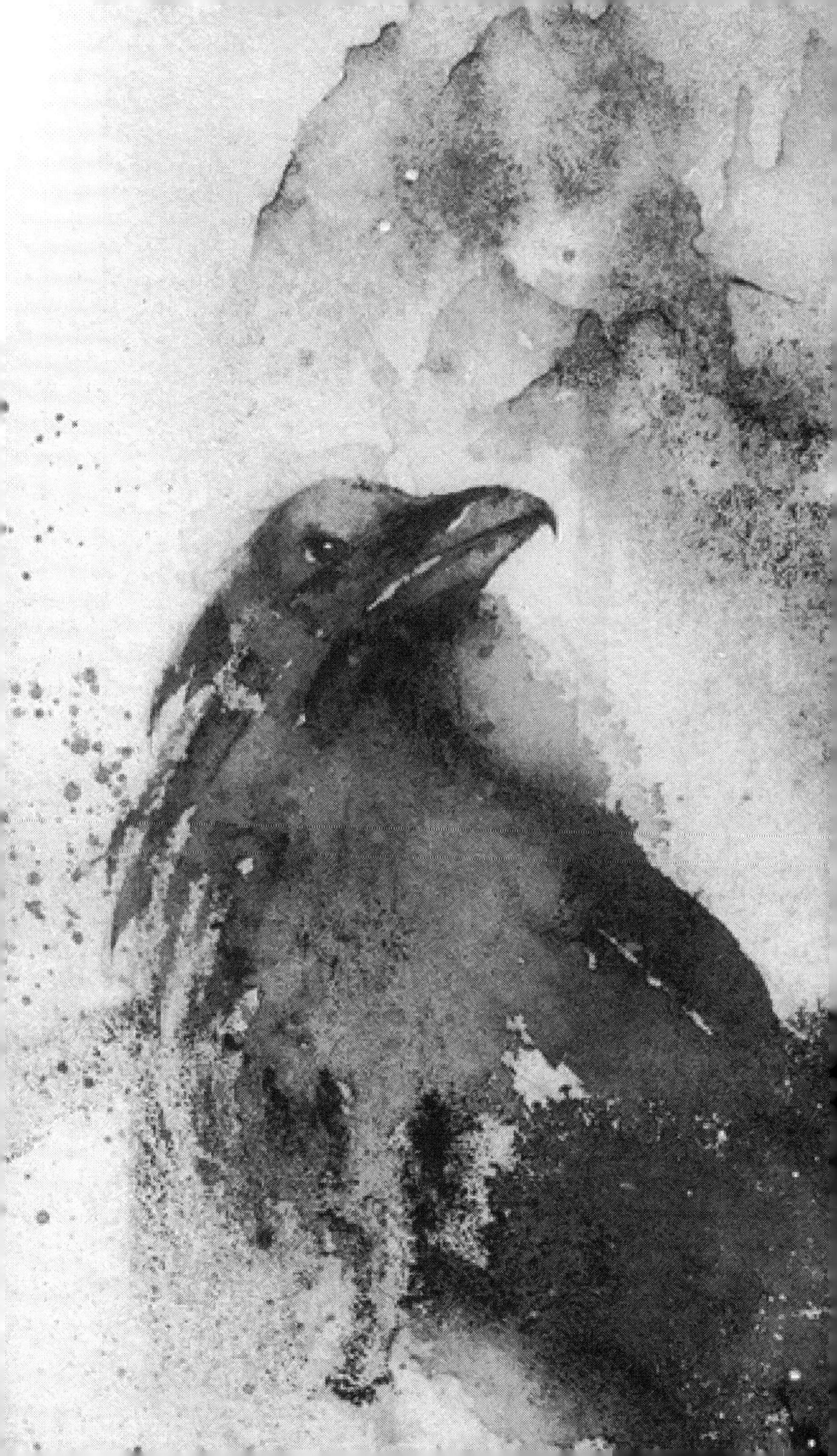

TWENTY

Raven

It really shouldn't be this hot watching Brax lash out at Sebastian, but fuck me, I can't deny the effect it has on me, and if I tried, the lies would be written clearly across my face.

Students watch our every move once Brax shakes himself off, and Zane pulls me into his side before guiding me toward the changing rooms for our first class of the day. I'm desperate to look back over my shoulder but I manage to hold it together. A quick glance in Brax's direction confirms he's eager to get ahead of me and pretend he didn't just do that in front of a crowd of spectators.

Eventually, this man is going to learn that his actions speak far louder than his words, or lack of them most of the time. That doesn't stop everyone looking, though, waiting for another outburst, but they're not going to get one.

Creed falls into step on my right as Eldon purposely keeps himself a step behind, the four of them effortlessly guiding me while I enjoy watching Brax's neck muscles clench, bundled tight as he moves.

All too quickly, we're in front of the changing rooms and Zane tightens his hold around me instead of releasing my shoulder, making me squeal when I almost trip over my own feet.

"Do you need me to escort you inside?" he whispers against my ear, and I shake my head at him.

"I can take myself into the changing rooms, Zane. I'm fine. I'll only be a minute," I insist, grabbing his hand on my shoulder as I purposely step out of his reach. I don't manage to make it two steps before he's pulling me back toward him, only this time, we're chest to chest.

His lips crush mine, a searing heat creeping up my spine as his hands cup my face, claiming me. I'm breathless when he releases me a moment later, leaving me needy for more as his hazel eyes burn into mine. "You're in my bed tonight." It's a statement, a promise, anything but a question. He winks, briefly squeezing my fingers as he passes, and like a gust of wind, he's gone.

Creed and Eldon stare at me knowingly, and I quickly tuck my hair behind my ear and rush inside the girls' changing room. The tips of my fingers graze over my puffy lips and a grin spreads across my face.

I see Leila in our usual spot and head in her direction. She smiles tightly at me as I press my thumb to the hook, producing my uniform. She's almost dressed in comparison to me, so I make quick work of catching up. Once my sneakers are secure, I look up to see her smirking down at me.

"I'm just saying that was the best start to the day I've had in ages," she nods toward the door, and it takes me a moment to understand she means Sebastian and Brax.

"I can agree with that." I stand and we follow the crowd of girls heading toward the door.

"I think we're going to need it because my father gave me a whole speech this morning about eating extra protein and stuff. Something to do with what he has planned for us today," she admits, and my eyebrows raise in surprise.

Keeping my voice low, I lean in while maintaining our pace. "Does it concern you when he says stuff like that? Completely out of the blue and with no real explanation," I ask, intrigued to know her answer.

She looks ahead as we approach the large, grass combat field, her father dominating the space without even lifting his head from the device in his hand.

"If I'm honest, yeah. I can always see in his eyes that he can't tell me what he wants to say, but he's desperate for me to read between the lines. I just suck at it. I'm a black and white kind of girl, and there's just so much…

gray space here." She waves her hand around us and I understand what she's saying.

"I feel like I've been drowning in the gray all my life." The truth parts my lips before I can consider saying it or not.

"Then it's about time we turned it around, huh?" she replies without missing a beat, making my heart warm at her casual offer. Not wanting to delve into it right now, I look around the crowd and find Zane and Brax in front of Fitch already. It takes me a second to find Creed and Eldon, but that's because they're behind me, and the way they're watching my every move has me guessing they waited at the changing rooms and I just didn't notice.

I'm wondering if they're going to call me out on not being alert enough as I come to a stop beside Zane, but to my surprise, they don't say a word.

Once I'm surrounded by the Bishops, Leila dips her head, taking a step away as if ready to leave, but before I can think better of it, I grab her wrist. She looks at me with wide, hopeful eyes, and I quickly drop her arm and shrug.

"It looks like he's setting up for pairs. We'll be odd if you leave," I murmur, waving my finger around the Bishops and me. Leila nods in understanding and shakes off whatever tension is clinging to her as she takes a step back to be beside me again.

"Good morning, class. I hope you're ready to focus

on your strengths today, and I don't mean your magical abilities." He clasps his hands together behind his back as he walks along the length of the students hanging off his every word. "I'm talking about actual strength, your body, your muscles, everything. If every fiber in your body isn't screaming by the time we're done today, then you weren't trying hard enough," he declares, piquing my interest. "First, we're going to work on agility and longevity in your legs, your strides, and your posture."

"You mean you're going to make us run our asses off," a guy I'm not quite familiar with hollers, making a few people laugh. I'm not sure if he used to be friends with Finn, and the thought of his lifeless body flashes in my mind, reminding me that it's not fun and games right now. Fitch is serious as hell and we'll do well to treat his words with respect.

When he orders everyone to start off with the outer path of the field, I take a deep breath and do just that. I keep my pace slow enough to jog beside Leila and the Bishops hang close by. Working on my breathing and strides, I quickly find a comfortable rhythm and a calmness washes over me.

One lap turns into two, and by the time we're ending, the last third of the students have given up. They are either catching their breath in front of Fitch at the starting point or slowly completing the path with no intention of pushing further. Sweat has my shorts and t-shirt clinging to me, and

I swipe at my hair to stop the wispy pieces from sticking to my face too.

The look on Fitch's face, however, tells me he's nowhere near done with us. "That was embarrassing. We're training here to defend Silvercrest Academy, to defend the realm, and half of you can't even make it around the field three times. Do I just fail you now?" Fitch barks once everyone is back in, and the silence that stretches out around us is almost deafening. As much as most of us won't want to do this, it's still vital to why we're here, and a startling reminder of it too.

After that, everyone remains pretty quiet as we follow one order after another. From building strength in our muscles, working through repetitions on our core, arms, and legs, to racing through an obstacle course he summons from thin air.

By the time we're close to being done, my body is definitely fucking screaming, and I'm not sure whether it's sweat clinging to the corner of my lashes or unshed tears of exhaustion. Those who couldn't withstand the pain called time earlier, and now the number of students sitting out the rest of the class is greater than those still participating. The Bishops, Leila, and I are hanging on, some better than others. More specifically, better than me.

I'm sure Fitch is about to shout another demand at the group when a thud sounds from behind me and a few screams ring out, making my heart race as I whip around to see what the commotion is.

A few students are up on their feet, running past me faster than they've done any part of the training today, but instead of fleeing with the rest of them, I smile.

Ari.

His golden feathers ripple with the light breeze, his claws digging into the grass as I hear Fitch call time on the class, but I don't turn around to look at anyone. Instead, I cut the distance between Ari and me.

"Is everything okay?" I murmur, worry instantly tingling through my veins at his sudden arrival.

"*As amusing as it is watching you be put through your paces, the exhaustion I could feel between us outweighed the joy. I had to make sure it was brought to an end,*" he grumbles into my mind, and I huff.

"Sorry about that." I place my hands on my hips, stretching from side to side as he tilts his head down slightly.

"*Don't be.*"

I don't really know what to say in response, so I lift my hand to stroke over his feathers and fur, in awe at where the two textures meet at his side. Touching him instantly brings a sense of serenity I'm not at all used to, but I cling to it desperately.

"What do you do all day when you're not checking on me?"

"I'm usually trying to figure out how to help take care of my pride."

"Your pride?" I ask, my eyebrows pinching in confusion as I tilt my head back to look up at him.

"Yes, the other griffins in my family," he explains, and I stare deeper at him.

"It's played on my mind a little, but I always forget to ask," I state, and he instantly bends his back legs to lower himself a bit more.

"Speak."

I roll my eyes at his bluntness. "When I met you, the Gauntlet was set up as a simulation, in the sense that we wouldn't die, so how on Earth are you even real? It doesn't make any sense for me to actually find a familiar under those circumstances."

Rustling sounds from behind me and I glance over my shoulder to find only the Bishops remain. Everyone else is long gone and it's almost embarrassing how much I let the world disappear for a minute as I focused on him instead.

"Raven, that was a simulation for the students, not for the griffins."

Horror burns up my spine as I take a step back, gaping at him. I want to call him a liar, but I know it to be true. The burning sensation in my veins, although it may cause an inferno in line with my own emotions, it stemmed from him first.

"They can't do that," I mumble, at a complete loss.

"*Why? They did it with the sirens and used them as targets for the Gauntlet for their own gain. It's been happening since long before now, and it's not going to change.*"

Shaking my head in disbelief, I can't figure out how to comfort him, but then what he said moments ago replays in my mind. "How is it, exactly, that you're trying to help your pride?" I already know the answer before he says it, but as the words slip from his mind, it only confirms the terror I didn't know existed but now requires my attention.

"*They're held captive. We all are.*"

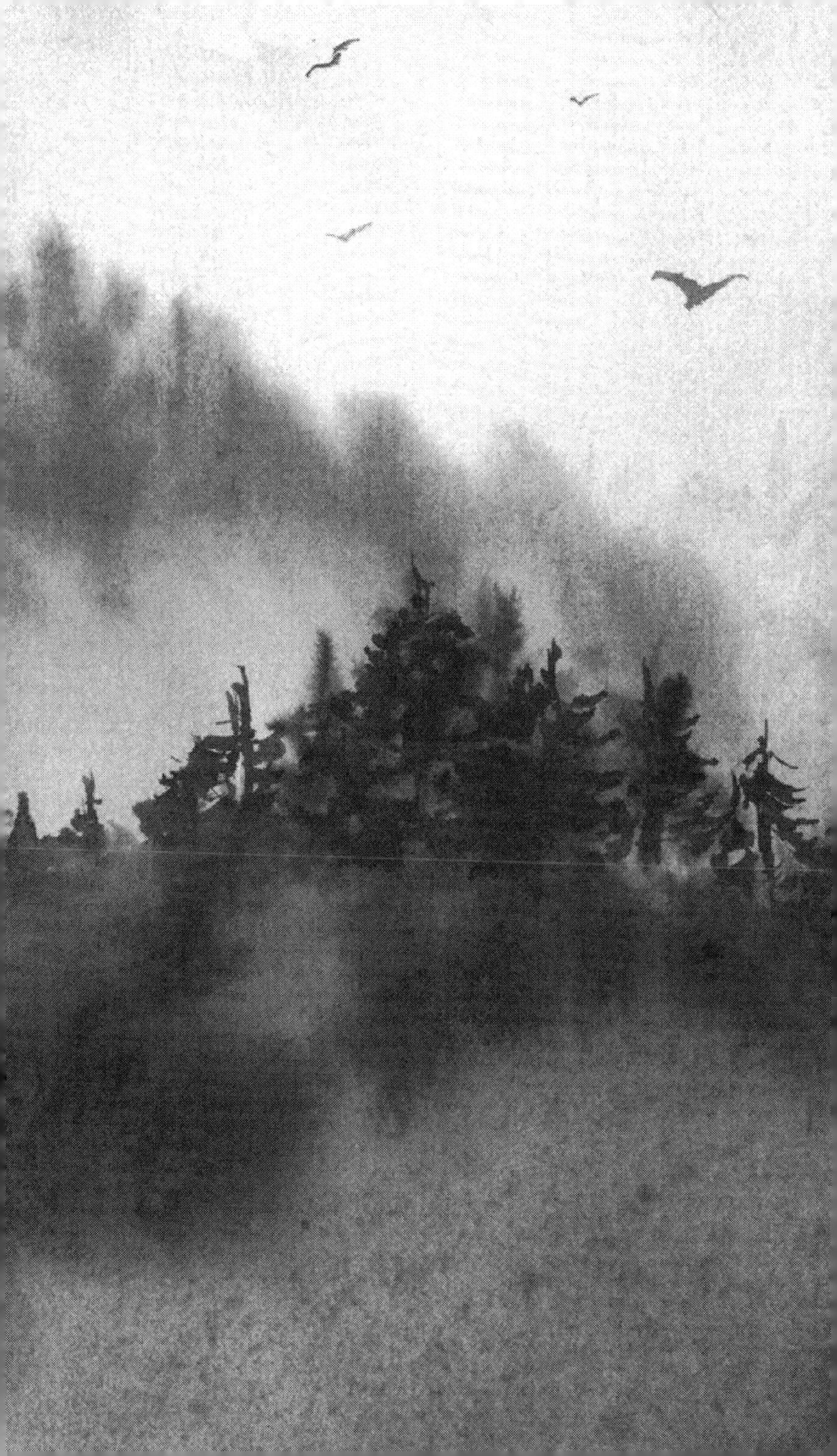

TWENTY ONE

Zane

A thud vibrates in my head, unsettling me from the depths of sleep and leaving me disoriented. Rolling over, my mind groggy, I pull Raven's sleeping form against my chest, hugging her tight as my nose nestles in her hair.

She spent the entire night worried about the captive griffins, another layer of stress to the already-building pile, and we were left none the wiser on how to solve the matter. I expected her to pull away and isolate herself in her own thoughts, but when I whispered some bullshit about the handbook, she smiled softly, placed her hand in mine, and let me usher her to my room.

As much as I wanted my fill of her luscious curves and stunning body, I kept my stiffening cock at bay and wrapped my arm beneath her, softly stroking her hair until she fell asleep. I wasn't far behind her, a rarity these days, and I wasn't taking it for granted.

Another rapid burst of thuds in the distance disturbs me even more and I blink into the dead of night, irritation curling in my bones.

"What the fuck is that noise?" Raven groggily asks, snuggling further back against me, and I press a kiss against her exposed shoulder.

"I don't know, but it's driving me insane," I admit, and she hums in agreement. "Go back to sleep, I'm sure it'll stop."

As if hearing my certainty, my bedroom door swings open, ricocheting off the wall and I blink at Eldon standing in the open space. "Someone's at the door," he grunts as I wince at the bright light coming from behind him and wipe at my tired eyes.

"Of course there is," I grumble, still quite set on digging deeper under the duvet, but Raven is already slipping out of my hold and shuffling across the floor.

Fuck.

I guess I'm going too.

Dramatically tossing the sheets off, I don't bother to throw on a t-shirt and just march into the lounge in only my black boxer shorts. Brax is leaning against his doorframe while Creed hovers by the door, ready to open it. Eldon stands by the sofa, Raven steps up beside him, and I slow to a stop next to her just as Creed opens the door.

The tension in the room is thick. I almost expect to see a haunting creek and for sinister music to start playing, but when the door is opened fully, it's Leila we find on the other side in her black cloak with a gold mask hanging in her right hand.

"What the fuck?" Brax grunts. "It's the middle of the night."

Seemingly not one to waver under his intense stare, Leila rolls her eyes and sighs. "I know, and I'm sorry about that, but well, we're about to go and I had a gut feeling that even though Sebastian was given the order to round you up, he wouldn't." She looks around at each of us and sighs again. "And by the looks on your faces and disappointment at the time, I'm going to assume I'm correct."

"Wait, what is it you're here to tell us?" I ask, wiping a hand down my face, the sleep that was still clinging to my limbs slowly disappearing as I become more alert with every breath.

"About the outing," she offers before snapping her fingers. A scattering of five golden masks appear in front of her with a neatly stacked pile of cloaks beside them.

"When?" Raven asks, frowning down at the unwanted outfits on the floor.

"Now. Let's go."

Black joggers. Black sweater. Black combat boots. And a weird as fuck black cloak topped off with a garishly gold mask. I feel ridiculous, nevermind how bad it might look on top of that.

"Is this really necessary?" Eldon grumbles from beneath his mask as we silently trudge through the academy grounds in the darkness.

"I don't personally think so," Leila admits, staying one step ahead of us as she leads the way. "But I also understand that if we want to remain anonymous, then it's what we have to do." She shrugs, not bothering to turn around, and as annoying as it is, that makes sense to me too.

"Where is it we're going, exactly?" Raven asks as we find ourselves at the top of the stone steps that lead down under the main academy building. The same ones it felt like we escaped from the last time we were in the presence of the Guild. It's weird that the cause seems to be for good, but there's a strange undertone that I can't put my finger on. Which inconveniently means that we'll only find out more by inserting ourselves further into the Guild.

"We're heading to the outpost," Leila explains as she leads us down the steps. When we reach the bottom, I clear my throat.

"Which outpost? You know there's more than one, right?"

I can envision her rolling her eyes behind the mask,

but to my surprise, she does manage to answer me calmly. "*The* outpost, at Shadowmoor. Where everything went to shit last time."

An open gateway awaits us as we step into the now-familiar room with the golden table. Uncertainty wars inside of me for a moment, but when Leila steps through without a backward glance, I find myself doing the same before Raven can consider going next.

If there's danger lurking, you better believe I'll face it first for her.

My surroundings shift in the blink of an eye and the gloomy landscape of Shadowmoor drapes over me once again. There are dozens of people in black and gold, confirming that the Guild is here, but I focus on the crumbled buildings in the distance. It's like I can still feel the smoke in my lungs, the fear in my veins, and the overwhelming sense of helplessness, just as I did at that moment.

A hand on my back pulls me from my thoughts, and when I turn around, I know it's Raven. "You okay?" she asks, and I shake my head. I'm supposed to be asking her that.

"Always with you by my side, Dove. Are you okay?"

"I will be when you stop with that sweet talk," she whispers, making me grin beneath my mask. Eventually, she'll learn that there's plenty more sweet talking where that came from because I mean every fucking word of it.

"Nightmares, gather around."

"Come on, quick," Leila mutters, waving us to follow her to where the large group has already formed.

It's hard to know who the hell is who under these damn masks, but I make sure to keep beside Raven.

"Why are we even here?" Eldon asks, nudging Leila, but before she can respond, the figure at the front of everyone, the one with a copper mask on, speaks.

"We're at Shadowmoor's outpost in the early hours of the morning so we can try and retrace the steps of that tragic day and see if there is something we can piece together. I apologize that meant pulling you from your beds, but if we want an uninterrupted visit, now is the best time."

Silently, everyone around us takes their masks off and I slowly follow suit, along with Raven, Leila, and my brothers. It's unbelievably stuffy under there. I take a deep breath, filling my lungs with fresh air, but I swear it tastes like charcoal.

I look down at Raven to see her staring across the group with a frown. Following her line of sight, I grumble when I spot Genie and Sebastian standing side by side.

Fuckers.

Distracting myself from their presence for a second, I look around at everyone else. There are a lot of fourth years, including the one Leila isn't too happy with, along with a few other students in the higher years. But there are also five or six first-year students that I recognize, I'm just not familiar with them.

"What I can't seem to wrap my head around," Raven murmurs, jutting her chin in Sebastian's direction. "Is why Sebastian is here. Like, he's not here to do good, and he definitely doesn't care that there's a hierarchy in our realm as long as he's not at the bottom of it."

"That's very fucking true. Genie as well. They're too happy with their heads wedged firmly up their own asses to see anything else. It doesn't make sense," I agree.

The sound of someone clearing their throat stops our conversation and we turn to see that the speaker behind the copper mask is Professor Barton himself. How did we not recognize his voice?

"I know some of you were here that fateful day, and I'm truly sorry if this causes any distress," he announces, and I discreetly glance at Brax out of the corner of my eye, but he's glaring straight ahead with his usual sharp jaw and no-bullshit expression. "It's been with heartfelt anguish that I have announced death after death so far this year already. The only difference has been that the previous deaths were those of Guild members fighting for a cause. Whereas here, in Shadowmoor, there was no purpose, no warning… nothing but the deaths of unnecessary victims."

Holy shit. I hadn't considered piecing those facts

together. As I glance at Raven and the others, I see the same realization on their faces too. There's so much going on around us, and my father played a part in keeping us in the dark.

It's frustrating, but I understand it, too, especially when they're constantly reeling off deaths. We're here now, and this is exactly what we have to be focused on. Silvercrest wants us to put our lives on the line when we graduate, even while we're training, so doing this is no different.

"I've had some of the fourth years scour the buildings toward the back of the outpost and you'll be pleased to know that even though they continue to look crumbled and derelict, they are, in fact, back in working order. A veil has been draped over them to make it seem like it's as bad as it was left, to hopefully stop any further attacks."

"Do we know who attacked?" Raven asks, but not out loud to Barton. She turns to Leila instead.

"They haven't announced it," she whispers back, her eyebrows pinching together at the fact, but Barton continues before I can press her further.

"We know the fireballs were being controlled with magical abilities, which is a first from our enemies. We had always believed their magic was weak, if it even existed at all, which is why we insist on combat training. That leaves us at a loss for what the focus of the attack was."

"How long have we been so misinformed? How long

have we believed this to be, that they are so weak in their magical abilities?" I ask before I can think better of it, and I sense a few members of the Guild frowning in my direction.

"Excellent question. I believe it's not quite as simple as being misinformed. I believe it's a fact that we've never been privy to," he explains, but the fact still confuses me. "Come, follow me," he insists, waving for everyone to follow his direction as he takes off toward the giant wall that still stands at the edge of the outpost.

Looking up at it as we get closer, it's startling how tall it is. We didn't really get close to it last time, so to see it from this angle is overwhelming. How the hell did they get fireballs over this? How the hell did they get *anything* over this?

"Are those steps?" Raven murmurs, lacing her fingers with mine as she sidles up beside me. I follow her pointed finger to see a very narrow and steep set of steps that lead up to the top of the wall.

"Holy fuck," I mumble, eyes wide in the darkness as the moon offers a glimmer of an outline. "Are we..." My words trail off as the answer to my question becomes apparent. We're taking the fucking steps.

It's single-file width, with no handrail for support. Searching for one of my brothers, I spot Creed and nod for him to go first. I usher Raven forward then trail right behind her so she's safely sandwiched between us.

With every step, it becomes colder, darker, and more unsettling. It feels like it takes forever to even get close to the top, and with one small look down, it's like we're miles away.

"Are you okay, Dove?" I ask, and she gives me a quick *uh-huh* without glancing back over her shoulder.

The top of the wall comes into view and I'm thankful to see a piped fence protecting the edge of the platform as Barton continues along the great width of it so there's room for everyone. We're high enough for the wall to come up to my shoulders, so I can see over it, and what greets me is nothing short of chaos.

Black and red. Red and black. Molten rock, lava, embers. That's where the scent of charcoal is coming from. It's as if nothing has ever lived there, been able to grow, or survive. It's what you envision when you picture Hell itself. There were trolls here that day too. I never quite considered where they would come from, but this is… indescribable. Amidst the madness, I can see the outline of what looks like men in the far-off distance.

"What is this?" Raven asks, eyes wide as she gapes at me, but it's Leila who manages to answer since I don't have a clue either.

"That… is the Basilica Realm."

"What the fuck is the Basilica Realm?" I grumble,

swiping a hand down my face.

"The enemy."

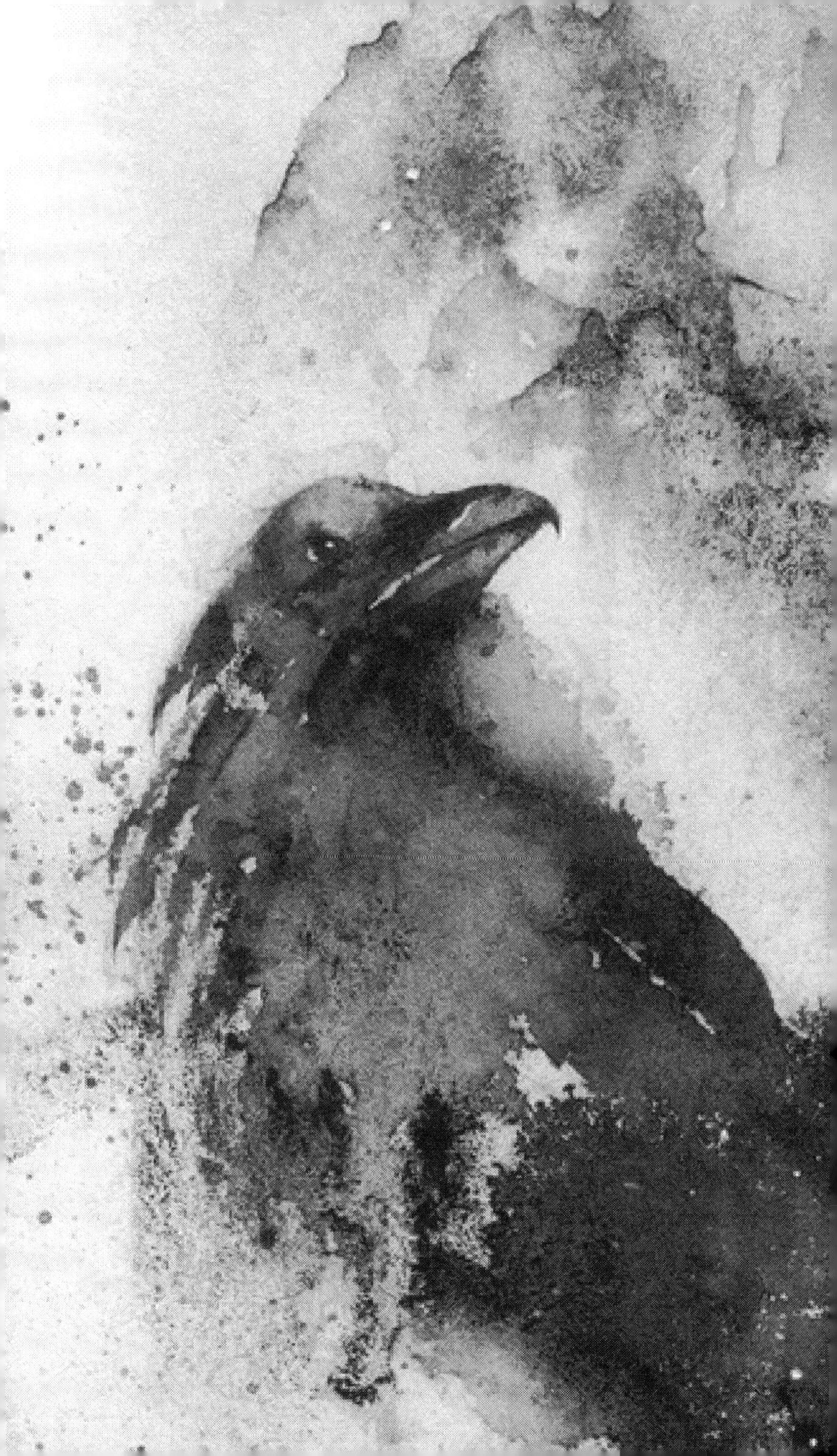

TWENTY TWO

Raven

Exhaustion clings to me like an unwanted parasite. Rubbing at my eyes for the hundredth time today does nothing to ease the tiredness, leaving my body depleted. I see the same weight on Creed, Eldon, Brax, and Zane's shoulders, but Leila seems surprisingly at ease. She's definitely more used to it than we are. Which leaves me wondering how often they actually go out in the dead of night like that.

I get the feeling it's going to be too often for my liking when the alternative is being wrapped up in bed fast asleep.

The information we gained last night made it all worthwhile, though.

The Basilica Realm.

I knew places existed beyond our borders, but I didn't expect them to be so close, so different. It was like looking at the remnants of a battlefield, a layer of fog cast over them as molten lava bubbled around the already burnt lands.

Being a part of the Guild is going to be a huge adjustment, but if it means we get to learn these things, facts that are otherwise concealed from everyone else, then it'll be worth the strain. I think I'm more disappointed with the fact that I thought I almost had my sleep back to normal, but other adventures await.

My main issue now is the fact that I have no brain power to focus on this class. Even as the professor speaks, I can't pinpoint which lesson we're in, never mind the topic. I knew it was all futile the second I stepped foot in here. We have lunch next, so maybe the energy boost will wake me up a little more.

Thankfully, when I took my usual spot beside Leila, I focused on my magic and managed to get the paper and pen working of their own accord. Creed had mentioned how to make it capture the professor's words so it would take notes for me and I've never been more grateful for the new magic running through my body. Except when it came to shaving my legs the other night. That's high on the list, too.

A knock rattles the classroom door, jolting me from my thoughts, and I'm surprised to find Professor Barton in the doorway.

"I'm sorry to interrupt your class, Professor. I just need

Miss Hendrix." His attention shifts from the professor to me and my chest tightens. "Please, get your belongings. Your presence is required elsewhere."

My entire body stiffens and I instantly start to shake my head. "Uh, no thanks. The last time someone came to escort me from a class, it didn't end well for me," I ramble, unnecessarily oversharing, but I can't control it.

He frowns down at me as my hands ball into fists. "Well, I can assure you, Raven, I'll escort you to your parents myself."

I scoff as my eyes widen. "You see, that's still not filling me with the confidence you're hoping for. I'll stay put, thanks."

"Is everything okay?" Leila whispers from beside me, but my gaze is locked on Barton's and I can sense that he's not going to take no for an answer.

"Unfortunately, it's not a request," he replies, unknowingly confirming my thoughts.

Raking my eyes over him in his navy suit, perfectly pressed white shirt, and copper tie, he looks nothing like the man from last night. It's crazy. Despite the two sides to the coin before me, he still has absolutely no clue what he's leading me to. It's his funeral if I get pissy.

My chair scrapes behind me as I stand, reaching for my backpack as the entire class watches me, but as I wrap my hand around the strap, a hand falls over my own.

"There's no chance in Hell she's going alone. You heard her. If her safety is a concern, we'll come too," Creed states, taking my backpack from my grasp as he stares Barton down.

"That's not an option. Academy policy states parents can call a meeting with their children whenever they choose. They've requested this one to be private. Whether you like it or not, Miss Hendrix *will* attend. Alone."

Fuck.

This is escalating quickly.

Taking a deep breath, I turn to face Creed, only to find Zane, Brax, and Eldon on their feet too. Anger dances in each of their eyes, the colors swirling like vortexes. I reach to take my backpack from Creed, gaining his attention.

"It's fine."

"No, it's not," he grunts, refusing to let go of my bag.

"No, really. I'm good. The quicker I leave, the quicker I'll be back, right?" I don't know who I'm trying to convince more, myself or him, but I can tell it isn't really working. Rolling my shoulders back, irritation burns through me. Before I came here, I was a badass bitch. Now, I'm constantly second-guessing myself and I hate it.

"Raven." My name feels like a warning on Creed's tongue but I shake it off, snatching my backpack from his grip.

"Creed," I hiss, hating the feel of everyone's eyes on us.

He steps closer, towering over me, so I have to crane my neck back to see him. It feels like he stares deep into my eyes for an eternity before he sighs. "You can't be a lone ranger forever, you know?"

My heart clenches at the desperation in his tone. "I'm not trying to be, but I'm a big girl."

"I couldn't give a shit if you were deemed the golden warrior of Elevin. You're still mine to protect." The memory of what he did to Wyatt back in Shadowmoor flashes through my mind.

He means every word.

"Miss Hendrix," Professor Barton interrupts, and despite wanting to soothe Creed, I step around him and head for the door. Burton steps out into the hall and I glance back over my shoulder to see every student looking at me, but my gaze is locked on the Bishops and the twisted expressions on their faces.

Is that... hurt? Fuck, I don't know, but I need to deal with one thing at a time. And since this seems to be such a pressing matter with my parents, I'm going to need to tick that off my list first.

Burton keeps one step ahead of me with no interest in inquiring about what I meant earlier, no desire to discuss what we all saw last night. Nothing. It's this kind of behavior that has left me unable to trust people and now that issue is slowly driving a wedge between the Bishops and me.

I know I'm going to fuck it up if I don't stop acting like I can face the world on my own, but after doing it all of my life, it's a hard shift to make. I just have to hope that they can be patient with me and all of the messed up drama I come with.

My footsteps echo off the marble floor as we approach Lyra's office and I'm at least thankful that we're not heading anywhere near the medical center this time. He opens the door, not glancing back at me before he leads me to what I can't help but feel will be my impending doom.

I thought I was prepared, but seeing both Mama and Abel sitting on a cream sofa to the left of the room, which I don't recall from the last time I was here, makes my spine stiffen and my heart start to race.

A quick peek around confirms that Lyra herself isn't here, not that I'm sure she would have done anything to interject, but standing in a room with three people who all seem to hold some kind of power over you is intimidating as fuck.

Professor Burton waves me into the room and my gaze instantly latches onto the open gateway in the corner of the room. I hope that's what they came through and not…

"Mr. and Mrs. Hendrix, thank you for being patient. Please keep your visit as short as possible. We don't want to interrupt Raven's education too much now, do we?" The smile on his face seems fake but I can't say I know him enough to confirm it.

"Of course, Professor. This won't take long," Abel states, rising from his seat to shake hands with Burton before he slips from the room, closing the door behind him.

Fucker.

"Raven, how are you?" Mama asks, and I tilt my head at her.

I don't know what I'm missing between these two, but I'm guessing it's not simple. Once upon a time, they clearly loved each other. Was it because of me, my magic, that it all fell apart? My brain wants to feel guilt over that, but really, it's not like I chose any of this. They both made their decisions. But why, after so many years, is Mama suddenly giving in to Abel's demands? That's what I'm struggling with.

"I'm doing as well as can be. Why are you here?" I ask, folding my arms over my chest as I remain in place.

"We've got to make a little trip, Raven. You'll be back in no time. Who knows? You might even ignite your magic by then, too," Abel says with a smile running from ear to ear, and my pulse quickens.

Wetting my lips, I glance between my parents, noting the apprehension on my mother's face. "Where is it we're supposedly going?"

"To Haven Court."

My eyebrows pinch at my father's excitement. "I'd rather not," I grumble, shaking my head, but he waves me off, just as I expect.

"Raven," Mama starts, rising from her seat with concern knitting her eyebrows together tighter than my own. This obviously has something to do with giving me my magic, which she already knows *I have*, so why the hell is this happening? It surely can't be something crazy on the other side if, deep down, she knows that... can it? Still, I'd rather stay exactly where I am.

"Raven, that's unfortunately not a choice you get to make," Abel announces, pointing to the gateway. Refusal is on the tip of my tongue, but it never comes as I'm cast off my feet and begin drifting through the air.

A little shove from the wind swarming around me has me tumbling backward through the gateway, a scream tearing from my lips before I land with a thud on a white porcelain floor.

"What the fuck?" I mumble in shock, staring down the length of myself as I try to piece together what the hell just happened.

Polished shoes appear next to me and I tilt my head back, ready to give my father a piece of my mind, but the first word is paused on my lips when it's not Abel I find. Cropped brown hair is styled back from the man's face, inquisitive eyes peering down at me as he, too, tries to place where we've met before.

"Are you okay?" he asks, offering me his hand. I take it, letting him pull me up as my backpack stays on the floor. "Have we met before?"

I run my hands over my skirt, completely overwhelmed, and the reminder triggers that I've felt overwhelmed and under pressure in his presence before. "I think… are you Zane's father?"

A warm smile spreads across his face at the mention of Zane's name and he eagerly nods. "Raven, correct?"

I nod too, but the smile doesn't come. I'm too on edge from wondering over where my parents are.

He releases my hand, taking a step back as he frowns. "I must say, Raven, you're a fair distance away from the academy. What's going on?"

Looking around at where I am, I try to gather my thoughts. White porcelain tiles cover every inch of the floor as the sun brightly shines down from above, but when I peer up, a glass roof confirms we are, indeed, inside. People move around us, the large open space seemingly like some kind of entryway as gateways open and shut in every direction. The startling confirmation that I am, indeed, in Haven Court is that every piece of furniture in here is gold; the scattered tables and chairs, photos on the wall, physical doorways leading off in different directions, and the grand staircase off to the left are all dripping in it.

With the sun glaring through the glass, it only seems to shine brighter.

Turning my attention back to Zane's father, I gape at him, my mouth opening and closing a few times as I try to explain, but I don't really know how to answer his question.

"Ah, Monarch Denver, I see you have met our daughter, Raven." Abel's voice sends a tremor down my spine.

Zane's father looks over my shoulder, his frown deepening for a second before easing. "Evangeline, it's fabulous to see you. Abel." I take great pleasure in the fact he addresses Mama first, which will surely get under Abel's skin. "What brings you here today?"

I reluctantly turn to face them, not appreciating my father at my back. He's clearly even more unpredictable than I expected. To my surprise, Abel doesn't seem thrown off by Monarch Denver's tone.

"We're just here for an assessment of Raven's magic. We're all booked to see Monarch Perkins," he explains, and I take an instinctive step back, unable to stop the panic from building inside of me.

I spot Zane's father curiously looking at me out of the corner of his eye. "What seems to be the problem? Is everything okay, Raven?" he asks, turning to me for an answer, but once again, I'm standing with a slack jaw and no words for the man. If I somehow manage to get back to the academy after all of this, I'm sure he'll be kicking me out of his son's house and banishing me from all of existence.

"We don't want to bore you with it, Monarch Denver. I'm sure you're a busy man, and this isn't anything for you to worry over," Abel replies, far too smoothly, while Mama continues to stand with her lips tightly sealed shut.

"I can assure you, bored is far from what I'm feeling, Abel," Zane's father retorts, straightening the lapels of his suit jacket.

Mama's eyes widen at Monarch Denver's reaction and she clears her throat. "Her magic was blocked when I took her to Shadowmoor, Rhys. We recently lifted the barrier and—"

"You lifted the barrier?" he growls, surprise and a hint of anger in his tone. "That would have meant…" His words trail off as he turns back to me, his lips twisting in disgust, and I gulp. Yup. Definitely fucking hates me, and I can't even pinpoint the reason why. "My apologies. I understand when things must be done; there isn't always an easier alternative," he murmurs, frowning at me a moment longer before looking back at my parents. "How does that bring us back to now?"

Abel plants his hands on his hips, glaring in my direction before turning to Rhys with a sigh. As if it's my fault that he's having to explain himself. We wouldn't be here right now if he hadn't thrown me through the damn gateway.

"After she experienced the attack at Shadowmoor, we thought that may have helped trigger its... blossoming, but alas, she still doesn't show any signs, and for her to excel at Silvercrest and for the betterment of the realm going forward, it's paramount she's at her full potential."

Holy fuck.

What an absolute load of bullshit.

I definitely hate how slimy he is, almost as much as I hate that he's my goddamn father. How I share DNA with this man, I'll never know.

"Mr. and Mrs. Hendrix, is that you? I'm ready when you are." A woman in a brown pantsuit approaches, adjusting her glasses up her nose as she politely smiles at the four of us.

A hand on my back ushers me in her direction and my feet instantly start trying to create some kind of traction beneath me to stop the momentum, but it's the hand on my wrist that halts me. I look from the white knuckles at my arm up to the face it belongs to, to find Rhys frowning at the person behind me. A glance in the same direction confirms my suspicions when I find Abel doing the pushing.

"I don't think this is suitable. Does our Silvercrest Academy student consent to this?" Rhys grits out, and my chest clenches so tight I think I'm going to pass out.

Is he… helping me? Or trying to? Fuck, I don't know.

"It doesn't matter if she does or doesn't. She's my child. I have rights," Abel snarls, the cover of his high-society mask slipping and allowing his true colors to shine through the cracks as someone pushes back at him.

"You believe your rights outweigh hers?" The hand on my wrist somehow tightens.

"Yes," my father replies without missing a beat, and I glance to find Mama standing with her head in her hands, allowing it all to unfold while watching someone else put a stop to it.

Turning my attention back to Rhys, hoping for fuck knows what, I watch his nostrils flare as he straightens his spine. "I will do the reading."

My heart drops to my feet. Fuck. I thought he was going to help me, be on my side, but this… I don't even know what the hell any of this is.

"What? No!" Monarch Perkins yelps in sync with Abel, but Rhys doesn't pay either of them any mind.

"Yes, you're dismissed, Perkins." She rapidly blinks at him for a solid thirty seconds before nodding once and rushing to get lost in the crowd, which is still moving around us like we're not causing a scene. "Come," Rhys orders, yanking on my arm, but once I fall into step with him, his hold loosens.

My parents are right behind us, Abel's angered breaths

burning against my neck as Rhys steps through a door and down a long corridor. Everything passes by in a blur as we take two more turns and two more doors before he finally comes to an abrupt stop.

"The door to the right," he says, nodding at my parents. Mama moves instantly while Abel stares Rhys down a beat before reluctantly following the order.

Once the door clicks shut behind them, he steps through the door in front of us, and I gape in horror at the glass cage waiting inside. Movement to my right catches my attention and I spot my parents through a pane of glass, watching.

"What is that?" I ask, but Rhys doesn't bother to answer as he pulls me toward the cage and opens the door. He spins us slightly with his back to my parents, shielding me from their view.

"What don't I know here, Raven?" Fuck. I gape at him, my heart stammering in my chest. "Whatever it is, it had your mother reaching out to my wife to make sure I was available to intercept you in some way. What's that about?" I still don't have a goddamn answer for him. He swipes a hand down his face, his voice getting more urgent. "Whatever it is, does my son know?" Despite the secret that weighs heavy on my shoulders, I nod. "And your father?"

"No," I whisper with a slight shake of my head.

"Is that on purpose?" he pushes, stress lines forming

on his forehead.

"Yes," I admit, my words barely audible to my own ears over my pulse ringing like crazy.

"Why?" I gulp. I can't tell him that. I can't. My gut tells me I can trust him, but I just can't. "I'm not asking you to tell me the details, Raven. I'm asking for the way it makes you feel inside."

I pause at that, swallowing down the lump forming in my throat. I can answer that. As much as it pains me, I can give him that. "Fear. I feel raw fear for the safety of my life."

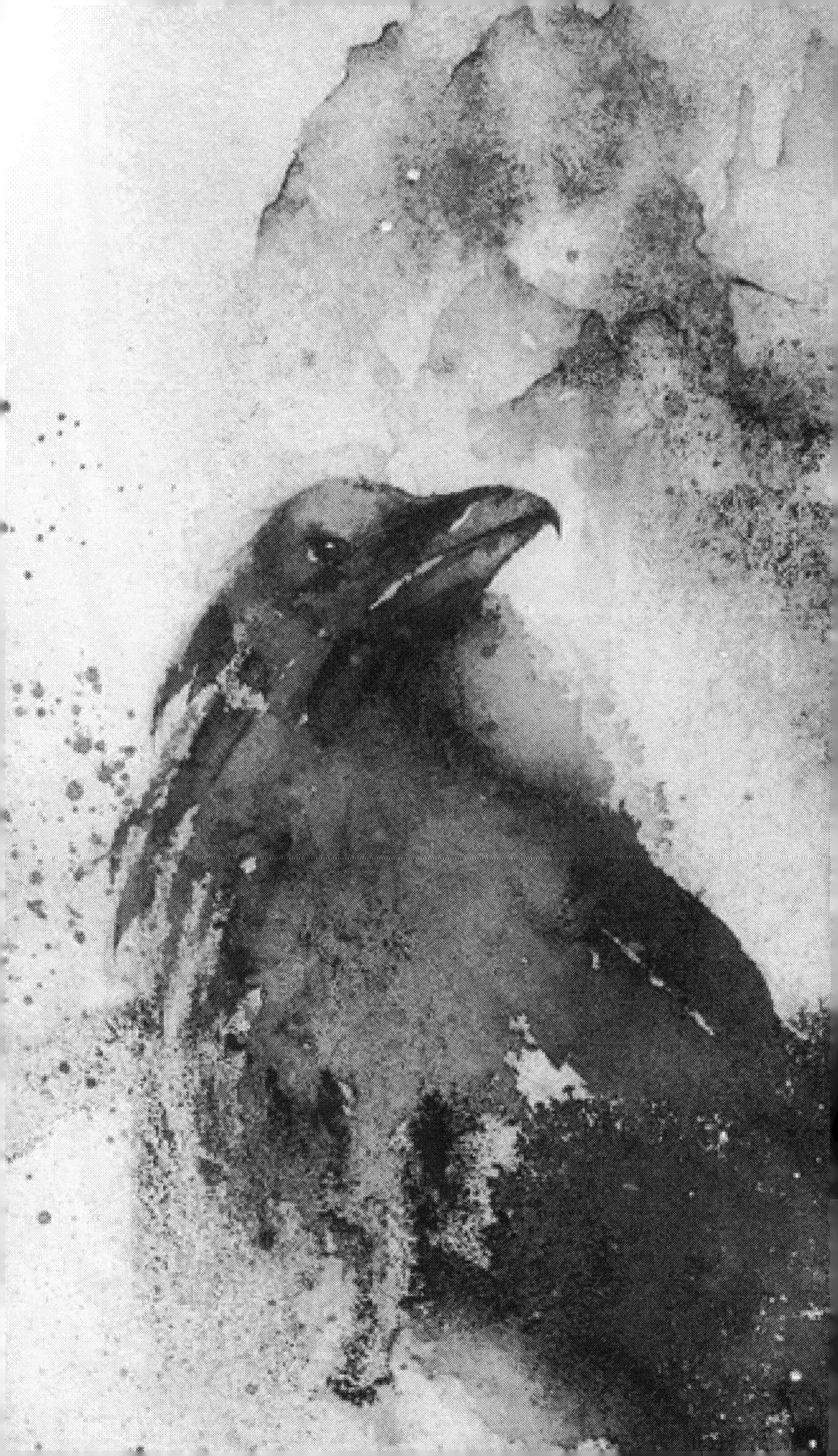

TWENTY THREE
Raven

The sense of falling sinks into my gut and I hit a hard surface, my breath lodging in my throat. Gasping in breath after breath, I feel dazed as I blink up at the ceiling. I think I might be sick. I don't think I've ever felt this disoriented in my life. The room is spinning like I've enjoyed one-too-many moon rocks. I would prefer that kind of haze instead of this.

"What on Earth? Raven, are you okay?" Following the familiar voice, I tilt my head to find Lyra staring down at me with a confused look on her face. I can't imagine what I look like, but seeing her can only mean one thing: I'm back at the academy. Relief floods me as I slowly shake my head at her. I'm unsure how to explain what I'm feeling.

"No, I don't think I am," I manage, surprised I'm that honest about it. Talking discomforts me further and bile rises up my throat. My hand lifts to my stomach like that will make the nausea pass, but it does nothing at all.

"Let me help you up," she mutters, offering me her hand, but she wobbles on her heels when I clutch it and I instantly take my hand back. She grimaces, but I don't mind, opting to push up off the floor instead. What did Creed call me? A lone ranger. Yeah, that's me. I can get myself up off the floor, thank you very much. Especially since the whirlwind I've just been through practically began with me being helped up off a floor.

Once I'm steady on my feet, I plant my hands on my hips and take a deep breath, the nausea slowly ebbing. Lyra seems to take this as a sign that all is good and carries on prodding me for more information.

"How did you fall through the gateway like that?"

Frowning, I look at where she's pointing just as the last flash of a gateway disappears. It's not in the same spot as the one I left through, though, and I'm sure it has a more golden hue to it, but it's no longer there for me to clarify. I'm intrigued to know exactly how I fell through it, but the thought of reliving that sensation again is enough to stop the question on the tip of my tongue.

"I don't even know, one minute I was…" I press my fingers against my temple, silently pleading for the facts to resurface, when I'm bombarded with them all at once. "Zane's dad. Rhys. Monarch Denver, whatever the fuck we're calling him. It had to be him. I admitted my inner fear surrounding my parents, or more specifically, my father, to him, and a breath later, here I am." I clap a hand over my mouth, desperate to shut the fuck up, but Lyra takes a step closer.

"What did he do?" I glare at her, my lips twisting as I try to bite back the truth, but I can't seem to stop myself.

"I don't fucking know, but he saved me from whatever the hell they were going to do to me," I admit with my hand still over my mouth.

What. The. Fuck, Raven. Shut. Up.

"What are you doing to me?"

"Sorry?"

"Why are you making me tell you things?" I bite, my hand dropping from my face to curl into a fist at my side.

A guilty look widens her eyes and her jaw falls slack as she shakes her hands.

"I'm so sorry. I..." She glances back at her desk, like the answer is there, but I don't see anything. She turns back to me with an uncertain glimmer in her eyes before she sighs. "Fine, but I'm only explaining myself to a student because I inadvertently made you do that."

"Do. What?" I grumble, frowning at her.

"I... I've been working on my second magic. When I was a student here, I was told to suppress it, hold it in, conceal it, don't feel, and all that," she states, like that makes any sense at all.

"Why would you be made to suppress it?"

"Well, not suppress, but hide it, I guess. It's frowned upon."

My chest lurches. "What is?"

She nervously rubs her lips together, glancing around the room as if someone could jump out and hear her at any point. "I can emit my magic into my surroundings and it turns into a truth serum of sorts. So people talk honestly, are unable to lie, and speak more freely than they may usually do."

Wow. That's... wow.

"That's..."

"Awful, I know, but—"

"No, no. If anything, that's cool as fuck. Useful as hell in a place like this, but I say all of that when it's not actually being used on *me*."

She grimaces again, but I wave her off. If we're talking about her, we're not talking about me, and if anything, this is a handy piece of information for future reference.

"Raven, what happened?"

Dammit. I thought I had completely distracted her from my mess, but it seems I can't get away from it that easily. Real concern is thick in her voice but I need to get the hell out of here and process all of this myself before I start sharing with anyone else. Besides, the people I need to talk to aren't her. I need the Bishops. *My* Bishops. I was prepared to deal with bullshit when Burton pulled me from class, but this? This is a whole other level of crazy.

"Sorry, I'm good," I finally manage, relieved when I don't continue to spill my truth to her without my consent. Although, I'm sure she would prefer it if I did. Staring at my feet, I frown down at my backpack on the floor. I thought that had been left on the porcelain floor where I first landed in Haven Court. I don't know. Reaching for it regardless, I hike it over my shoulder and plaster a fake smile on my lips. "Can I head back to class now?"

"Class? Raven, they've finished for the day."

My steps toward the door pause as I slowly spin to stare at her. How is that possible? I wasn't gone that long, was I? It wasn't even lunchtime when I left. I need to find the Bishops, and quickly; otherwise, I'm in for the world's worst headache for being gone so long when they knew I was likely being lead into danger.

"They have? Oh, well, I'll head back to my house instead then," I reply, far too chirpy as I all but run for the door. My hand has wrapped around the door knob when I flinch at her hand on my shoulder.

She quickly removes it and I force myself to bite back the grimace as I turn to face her again.

"Are you sure you're okay, Raven? I can arrange a

gateway to your house if that would be easier," she offers, concern marring her forehead as she purses her lips, and I frown.

"You can do that? You didn't the day I got here." I don't know why I'm even bringing that up right now and extending this unnecessary conversation.

Lyra shrugs. "I wasn't so keen on you then."

Oh. "And now?"

"Now, your words of wisdom give me life. I can make an exception or two for someone with that kind of impact." My eyes widen at her admission as I try to remember what bullshit I gave her to begin with, but it feels like forever ago. "So, the gateway?" she offers when I just stare at her, but I shake my head.

"Thanks, but I think I could do with the fresh air and a second to think after all of... that." I wave my hand toward the corner where the gateway was, as if that makes sense, before tugging the door open.

I can tell there's more she wants to say and do, but she must sense that I'm at my limit because she nods. "That's fine, Raven. But if you need anything, anything at all, let me know. I can try and help." I mumble my thanks, ready to slip through the door, but she stops me again. "Is that your magic, by the way?"

"What?" Confusion clouds my thoughts as she waves between us.

"Not one person has noticed me using my magic since I've been trying to unleash it more, but you saw right through it without missing a beat."

My eyebrows pinch together. "I would never talk to someone I barely know so openly like that," I state, but she shakes her head.

"Usually, people don't notice how loose-lipped they're being, even if they're normally locked down like a fortress. It's like you could sense it in the air or something. I've heard of that kind of magic before, but I've never actually met anyone with it."

Stumped for words, I plaster a tight smile on my face and nod before finally slipping through the door and closing it behind me. I'm certain it's going to slam, but I'm far quieter than I expect with the current frenzy running through me.

Fuck.

I slump back against the wood, giving myself a second to catch my breath. Thankfully, it's dead in the hallways since classes are somehow over, and I use that to my advantage while I still feel so vulnerable.

My eyelids drift shut and the glass cage or chamber or whatever the fuck it was flashes on the back of them. What was that torture chamber about? I have so many questions about that room, about Abel and his craziness, Mama and her... help? Rhys and his questioning...

A snarl echoes off the walls around me but it seems distant, and when I open my eyes, I don't see anyone around. Intrigue gets the better of me as I hear another, and another, and before I can think better of it, I'm tiptoeing down the hallway to the right to listen better.

"You've got some explaining to do, Sebastian."

I stop, pressing my back against the wall behind me as the sound of Professor Burton's voice comes from around the corner.

"About what?" Sebastian sounds bored and inconvenienced rather than worried like I would expect anyone else to be. He's way too cocky for his own good and that's going to kick him in the ass someday.

"Who authorized your parents to come onto campus a few weeks ago?"

"How should I know?"

"Because it was you who pulled Raven from class to meet with them. Don't play foolish with me, Sebastian. I want answers."

Holy shit. Is he talking about when I was taken to the medical center? I press myself further into the wall like it will allow me a chance to get closer.

"I don't know."

"Why did they visit your sister?"

"I don't know."

"What did they want, Sebastian? Think harder."

"I. Don't. Know."

Burton sighs. "Of course you do. Otherwise, you wouldn't have taken her from class. How was I kept in the dark about this?" The latter question is more to himself than to Sebastian, but that's what he responds to.

"No idea, Professor. You probably need to keep a better eye on the staff you have here if you ask me." I roll my eyes at his stupid answer, and it seems to piss Professor Burton off too.

"My trust in you is wavering, Sebastian. You'll be long gone if I find out you have been aiding and abetting unlawful magic on my grounds. Guild and all. That's not what we stand for or believe in. Do you hear me?" Like earlier, the snarl echoes around me as Burton's distress and anger get the better of him.

"Loud and clear," Sebastian grunts in response, and a moment later, footsteps retreat into the distance. I can't tell if I'm shielded from them or if someone else could walk my way, so I don't move, holding my breath as I wait for the second set of footsteps, but they don't come.

Instead, I hear Sebastian speaking, but he's quieter now. "Yeah... No... He's not a threat, not like he hopes to be anyway... No, we continue on as planned."

Footsteps move farther away from me and I slump against the wall. What the hell is my brother up to? Something isn't right, but I can't put my finger on it.

But I've known Sebastian was trouble all along, and whatever he's tangled up in isn't good.

Not one bit.

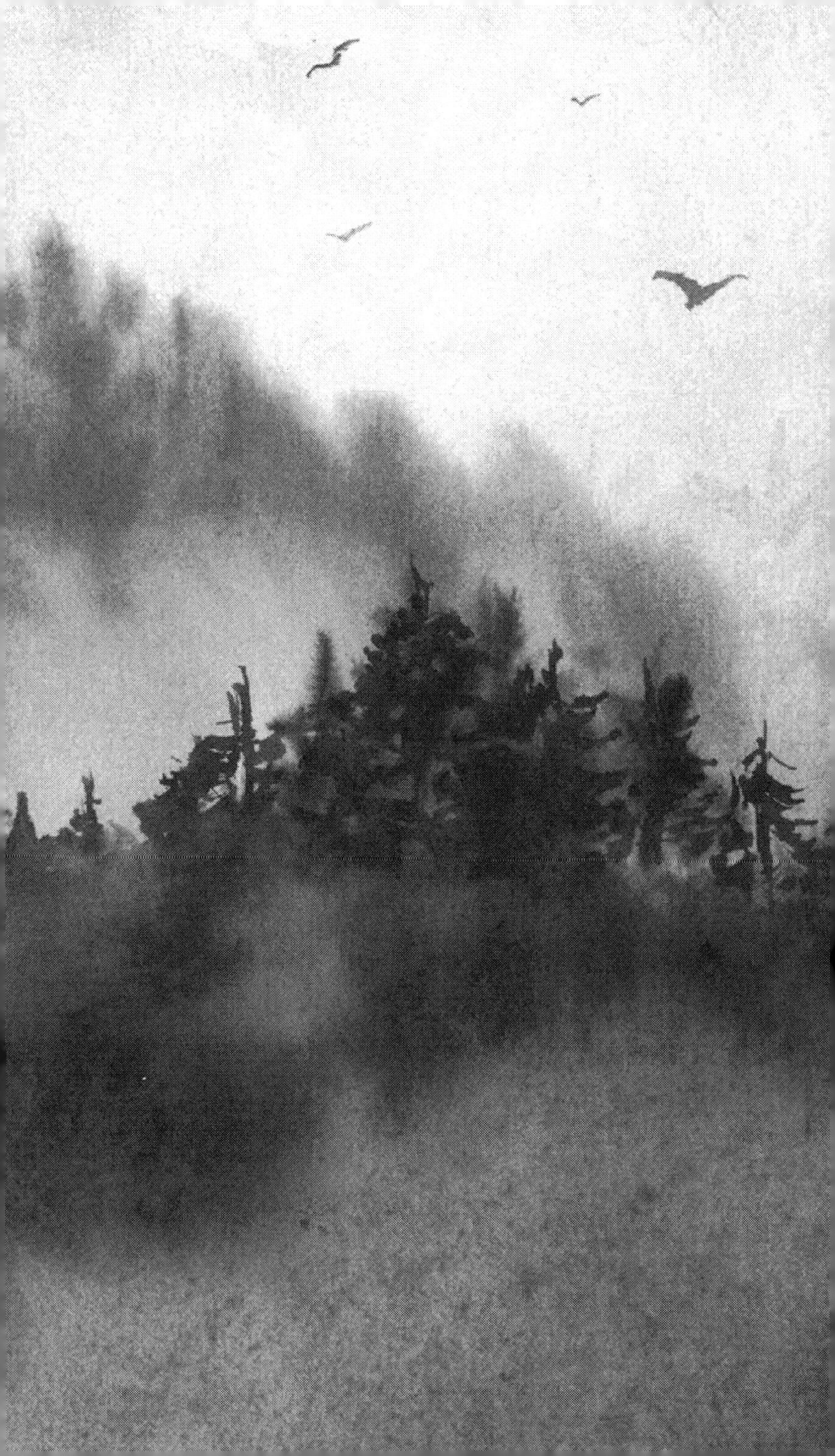

TWENTY FOUR
Creed

It's been hours. Fucking *hours*. I shouldn't have let her out of my sight. Now we're simply uselessly waiting and it's driving me insane. We searched the academy grounds three times, pestered Professor Burton for answers, and waited outside Lyra's office until we were forced to leave.

All we know is her parents took her off campus. *Off fucking campus*. Who in their right mind allowed this? Not me. Far from it.

I can't sit still any longer, I've been pacing back and forth by the front door for at least the past thirty minutes. I feel antsy as hell. I've never worried for someone else's safety quite like Raven's, but that's no surprise with everything life keeps throwing at her.

"I say we find Burton again and demand some answers because this is getting ridiculous," Eldon grunts, swiping a hand down his face.

"Lyra already told us he left the academy a while ago. We don't even know if he's back yet," Zane grumbles, not liking his answer any more than the rest of us. His leg won't stop bouncing, even as he braces his arms on his knees, leaning forward on the sofa.

"We have to be able to do something," Eldon continues, his face reddening with stress and frustration as he starts to pace behind Zane. While Brax… he's too busy getting lost in his own mind outside in the drizzle. It's the first time we've had any rain for ages and it feels almost too coincidental that it should be tonight when it finally comes.

"We shouldn't have let her go off on her own to begin with," I grind out, my hands clenching at my sides as I spin and pace back to where I just was.

"We can't just wade in all of the time. We've talked about this," Zane states, adding more irritation to the already overwhelming sensation that's creeping up my spine.

"But if we had stayed with her, she would be safe with us right now. Instead, we have no clue where she fucking is and what danger she might be facing," I snarl, my worry and frustration twisting into anger as the door slams shut right beside me, echoing as the floor practically vibrates with the force.

I whirl around to gape at the woman in question.

My heart races in my chest with relief at the sight of her while my eyes take her in from head to toe. She's wet, her clothes soaked through and droplets of rain clinging to her lashes. On top of that, she looks worn down, exhausted, and completely ready to drop. Despite that, I can't stop the words from breaking past my lips.

"Where the hell have you been?"

She looks at me like she knew someone would ask that exact question as her backpack drops with a thud on the floor at her feet. She just hadn't decided which one of us it would be. "Before you start blasting me, can I at least get a drink? Despite how sopping wet I am, I'm thirsty."

"Use your magic," Brax grunts, shutting the patio door behind him as he stalks toward us.

Raven shivers. "No thanks, my magic and I are… taking a minute."

My brows furrow in confusion as I assess her.

"Is that why you also didn't use it to protect you from the rain?" Zane asks, still sitting on the sofa. At least his leg is no longer bouncing.

"Wait, I could have done that?" Raven gasps, instantly reconsidering the sudden hiatus with her magic.

"You forget your abilities, Raven. You're the strongest person I know," Eldon soothes, producing a glass of water out of thin air and bringing it to her. She softly smiles at him and I'm instantly pissy with his brown-nosing.

Asshole.

I wait a few moments for her to down the water before I push on. "You're going to need to explain, Raven."

She hangs her head for a beat, exhaling slowly, as if she's trying to gather the words. "I know, let's sit."

Eldon sweeps her up off her feet and moves to the sofa, dropping her into his lap as he gets comfortable beside Zane. The second she's in his lap, she's dry to the bone and she instantly nestles into him. Brax sits on the other side of them while I opt for the sofa across from them.

Raven looks down at her hands as she speaks. "My parents took me to Haven Court to have my magic tested."

"What the fuck?" Brax growls as my chest clenches.

What the fuck, indeed.

"Right? What's with these people?" Raven says with a sigh, swiping a hand down her face.

"What did they do to you, Dove?"

"It doesn't matter. I'm gonna kill them anyway." The snarl bursts from my lips without a care as my knuckles turn white in my lap.

"Maybe," Raven breathes, casting a soft smile in my direction. "But not right now. They didn't manage to do anything." I can't decide if she's just saying that to appease us or whether she means it, but the longer I stare into her eyes, the more clearly I see the truth in her words. Why do I get the feeling it was damn close, though?

"How?" Zane asks, like he's as disbelieving as me.

Raven turns her attention his way, eyes fixed on his as she speaks. "Your father."

"My... how?"

She tucks a loose strand of hair behind her ear as she softly shakes her head. "I don't know, he was just there and he refused to let them do anything. He must have sensed the panic in me or something. He mentioned something about my mama reaching out to yours to be there to interject, but I don't truly understand anything right now."

Why is everything always a mindfuck? Nothing is as simple as I wish it could be.

"What did he say?" Brax asks, breaking his silence as he leans forward to look at our girl.

Her eyebrows pinch as she tries to retrace everything that happened. "He asked if you knew about whatever made me worried, Zane, and I said yes." She winces as if bracing for a negative response, but Zane places his hand on her thigh.

"Good, go on."

"Then he asked if my parents knew and I said no. He wanted to know why, not the details, just how I felt inside. Which is the most bizarre thing I've ever heard, if I'm honest. People always want every detail, but that didn't matter to him in that moment at all."

Zane's father isn't like many, and he's definitely not

as cutthroat as other members of the Monarchy. Which makes it very easy to forget who he is sometimes.

"And what did you tell him?" Eldon asks, his lips close to her ear, and I'm instantly jealous of his proximity. I'm half lost in my head over the entire thing and half desperate to press every inch of myself against her so she knows where I am.

"I told him I was fearful for my life."

"Good girl," Eldon praises, and she smiles, her eyelashes fluttering closed for a second.

"What happened then?" Brax pushes, and she blinks at him with a frown.

"I don't really know. One second, I'm standing there with him, and the next, I'm falling through the gateway into Lyra's office."

Yeah, that doesn't make any sense at all. "At least you're back now," I offer, tension still coiling my muscles as she grimaces.

"Well, I wish that's where the drama ended."

"How is there more?" Zane grumbles.

"Because it follows me around, apparently," Raven admits with a sigh, and there's no denying that fact.

"You're telling me," Eldon says with a smirk, making her fake glare at him.

"Hit us with it." Brax shuffles, bracing his elbows on his knees like he's getting ready for it.

"I heard Sebastian and Burton talking."

"About what?" I ask, already not liking where this is going.

"About me." Thankfully, before I start storming for the door to get my hands on the fuckers, Raven continues explaining. "Sebastian is up to something shady, I can sense it, but so is Burton. He threatened to pull him from the academy and the Guild if he was aiding anybody in any unlawful way." Her eyebrows practically touch her hairline as she explains.

"Fuck. My head is spinning," Zane murmurs.

"Tell me about it," she retorts, her body going lax in Eldon's hold as exhaustion continues to take over her.

Rising to my feet, I cut the distance between us and offer her my hand. "Come on, I'll take care of you." There's so much more I want to say, so many things I'm feeling, but she needs someone right now, and holy fuck, it's going to be me.

Eldon's hands flex at her waist but I pull her from his grasp the second she places her palm against mine. Without a backward glance, I lead her across the room to my bedroom and kick the door shut behind us with a finality that tells those other fuckers to back off.

I'm all for her being our girl. I crave it. But right now, she's mine.

She remains quiet as I guide her toward my bed,

stopping short as she scans the room with wide, inquisitive eyes. I can't imagine what she sees when she looks at my space. When she continues to spin on the spot, releasing my hand to do so, I quickly realize that this is the first time she's been in here.

How?

Shaking my head, I glance from the navy sheets on my bed to the white desk and nightstands, then follow her gaze to the bathroom and closet. Other than that, there are plain white walls and a gray carpet. Nothing more, nothing less. We're given creative reign over our personal spaces, but I have nothing to give.

I actually don't know if the others have put their stamp on their rooms and I don't care. If I'm not going to be here forever, or might even die in the process, what's the point? I'm sure I have a dumb way of thinking, but ever since my father died, it's how I've seen the world.

It's difficult to come back from a loss of that magnitude. It's even harder to wonder how your death could impact somebody else in that way. But it does. Whether we like it or not, whether I decorate this room or not, we all leave a legacy. We all touch the world in some way like no other has or ever will.

My gaze shifts back to Raven. None of my internal thoughts are plastered across the wall, explaining why they're blank and void of presence, but she doesn't push.

Another quality about her that draws me in even closer.

You know if you've been in her presence, the fact will never leave you, right up until the moment death claims you and you're left craving one more second of her. One more taste.

Her eyes land on mine, an uncertain lift to the corner of her mouth as she tries to assess me. Without lifting my gaze from hers, I reach for the lapels of her blazer and slowly drag the material down her arms.

"Thank you," she whispers, her shoulders relaxing as she speaks. I don't utter a word in response, even though I don't truly know what she's thanking me for. My brain is overloaded by my thoughts and feelings, so I reach for the top button of her blouse instead.

As one gives way, I move on to the next, dragging my fingers down her chest as I go until I'm untucking the tail of her blouse from her skirt, repeating the motion again. Satisfied with my efforts, I let the material hang loose at her sides, revealing the perfect hint of her pale-pink bra underneath.

Her chest heaves with each breath, making my heart race faster as I lift the tip of my finger to her jaw and draw an even slower trail down her soft skin. I avoid her tie as I trail through the valley between her breasts, not stopping until I'm back at the waistband of her skirt.

Teasing my way around to her back, I easily find the

button and a moment later, the material is pooled at her feet. Finally, I opt to sweep my magic over her shoes and socks so she's standing before me in just her lingerie and tie.

It's one thing to use magic to be rid of clothes that are in the way, but it's something else entirely when you strip one piece at a time. Slowly taking each layer until nothing more stands between you.

Her bra is nothing more than a thin layer of lace covering her pebbled nipples, the deep pink shade of the taut flesh teasing through the light, contrasting material. My gaze meets hers after I've drank in every inch of her on offer, and the moment our eyes connect, she shivers.

"Say yes, Raven." She nods immediately, but no words follow. "You have to say it or I'll go and turn the tap on now and run you a hot bath. Your choice."

"Yes," she breathes without wasting a second, and I take that as control falling straight into my lap.

Reaching for the length of tie around her neck, I yank her forward, eliminating the remaining distance between us as she stumbles forward.

"Why do I get the feeling you're mad at me?" Her chest brushes against mine as she peers up at me with want and desire still swirling in her gaze, despite the statement on her tongue.

I take a step forward, fist still wrapped in her tie as

she stumbles backward, step by step, until the back of her knees hit my bed. Snapping at the lace covering her core, it flutters to the floor far more delicately than it should before I grab the front of her bra and do the same.

She gasps, her chest harshly rising and falling with every breath as I release the tie still around her neck and grab her thighs, hoisting her into the air and throwing her unceremoniously down onto the bed.

Her legs spread as she peers up at me, watching as I crawl up the bed on my hands and knees until my face is centered above her core.

"Raven…"

"Creed…"

"Mad doesn't even cover it," I bite before feasting on the pretty pink folds between her thighs.

Nipping, biting, lapping, I take from her pussy like a man starved. Her back remains arched up off the bed as one cry turns into a moan before the tempo picks up, and she's close to screaming when I stop.

"Fuck, Creed," she gasps, panting for breath as she tries to settle her dazed eyes on mine.

Pushing her thighs up, I spread her wider before getting my fill once more. This time, I tease two fingers at her entrance, biting back my own groan when I feel just how wet she is. As I take her pussy with my fingers, I lap at her clit as she tries to clench her thighs around my head.

It takes no time at all to have her trembling beneath me again at my touch, and I stop. Once her gaze is locked on mine, I move to crawl above her so she's looking up at me. I wave a hand over my body, removing my shorts and tee so that not a single stitch of fabric stands between us.

"If you ever deny me the right to protect and defend you again, the consequences will be at your own risk. Do you understand me?" I snarl, letting my true feelings out, and she frowns.

"But I—"

I grab the length of her tie and tighten the fabric so it sits flush against her throat and she gasps.

"Do. You. Understand. Me?" I growl before sinking my teeth into her left breast until she cries out from the pain. I relish the sound, my eyes rolling to the back of my head as I softly drag my tongue over the spot. "Answer me, Raven."

"I thought I would be fine," she rasps, her fingers wrapping around mine that cling to her tie.

"But you weren't. You weren't *fine*. Since you've gotten here, not once have you been just fine. When will you see that?" The desperation is clear in my voice, my vulnerability on full display, and for the first time, I don't care.

"Please, Creed," she whispers, running her tongue over her bottom lip.

"Say it."

"Say what?"

My throbbing cock nestles against her core as I lean in closer so our noses brush. "Tell me that you won't defy me like that again."

"I wasn't defying you," she snaps back, her usual fire bursting to the surface as her blue eyes widen, and I grin.

There she is. My Raven. My warrior. My pitch-black silhouette in the fake gold realm we find ourselves in.

I need to feel her. Now.

Envisioning the protection in my nightstand, I sheath my cock without moving a finger from her body, line myself at her entrance, and slam all the way home. Her cry echoes around us as ecstasy clings to me at the feel of her heat.

My fingers flex around the tie in my grip and her eyes roll with pleasure. "It won't ever happen again, Raven. I swear it," I promise, whether she wants to hear it or not.

Letting the weight of the situation leave my body, I focus on the here and now, but more importantly, I focus on her. Every thrust of my hips is not enough. Every swirl of desire that feasts on my very being trembles with the carnal need to claim her over and over again.

"Come for me, Raven, come on my cock and make me yours," I growl, my own orgasm already burning at the base of my spine. Her hands dig deeper into my sheets, her knuckles white with her grip, and my eyes catch on her tits bouncing with every slam of my hips.

"Creed," she cries, her voice raspy from the tightness of the tie around her throat as she climaxes, drenching me in her release, and I topple over the cliff with her. I don't stop thrusting until every last drop has been rung out between us.

I magically discard the condom, and the tie from her throat before collapsing on the bed beside her. She rolls onto her side, gently placing her hand over my heart as she hums against my shoulder, planting little kisses in her wake.

When I can finally see straight again, I peer down at her and instantly panic over the red marks around her neck. With the way she's lying, I can see the finger-sized bruises along her thigh forming, too.

Fuck.

She's calm, relaxed, and pliant in my arms, and I'm feeling my cock come alive again at the sight of my marks on her skin. Marks she might fucking hate and I didn't even think to consider that.

Pressing a kiss to her forehead, I slip from beneath her, not missing the pout on her lips as I head to the bathroom. I hurry to fill the bath, making sure to fill it with some girly-smelling shit that I saw when I took her dress shopping a few weeks ago.

I stride back into the bedroom to find her exactly where I left her. Swooping her up in my arms, she giggles as she tightens her arms around my neck, letting me lead her toward the steam that's starting to billow out of the bathroom.

She gasps when I step into the bath and slowly place her between my thighs in the water, but she quickly lies back against me with a sigh. It's like she's floating in the water, delicate and calm, a rarity in these four walls at the moment.

Trailing water over her exposed chest, I band my other arm around her waist and breathe her in, dragging my nose over the shell of her ear as I finally speak. "Are you mad at *me* now?"

A beat passes, then another, and another, until she tilts her head to look back at me with a grin on her lips. "Never. I knew you were unhinged, remember? It was deliriously fucking hot and everything I didn't know I needed," she admits, nipping at her bottom lip.

I press a kiss to her shoulder, concealing my own smile.

How is this my life?

How is she mine?

I don't fucking know, but I'm never letting go.

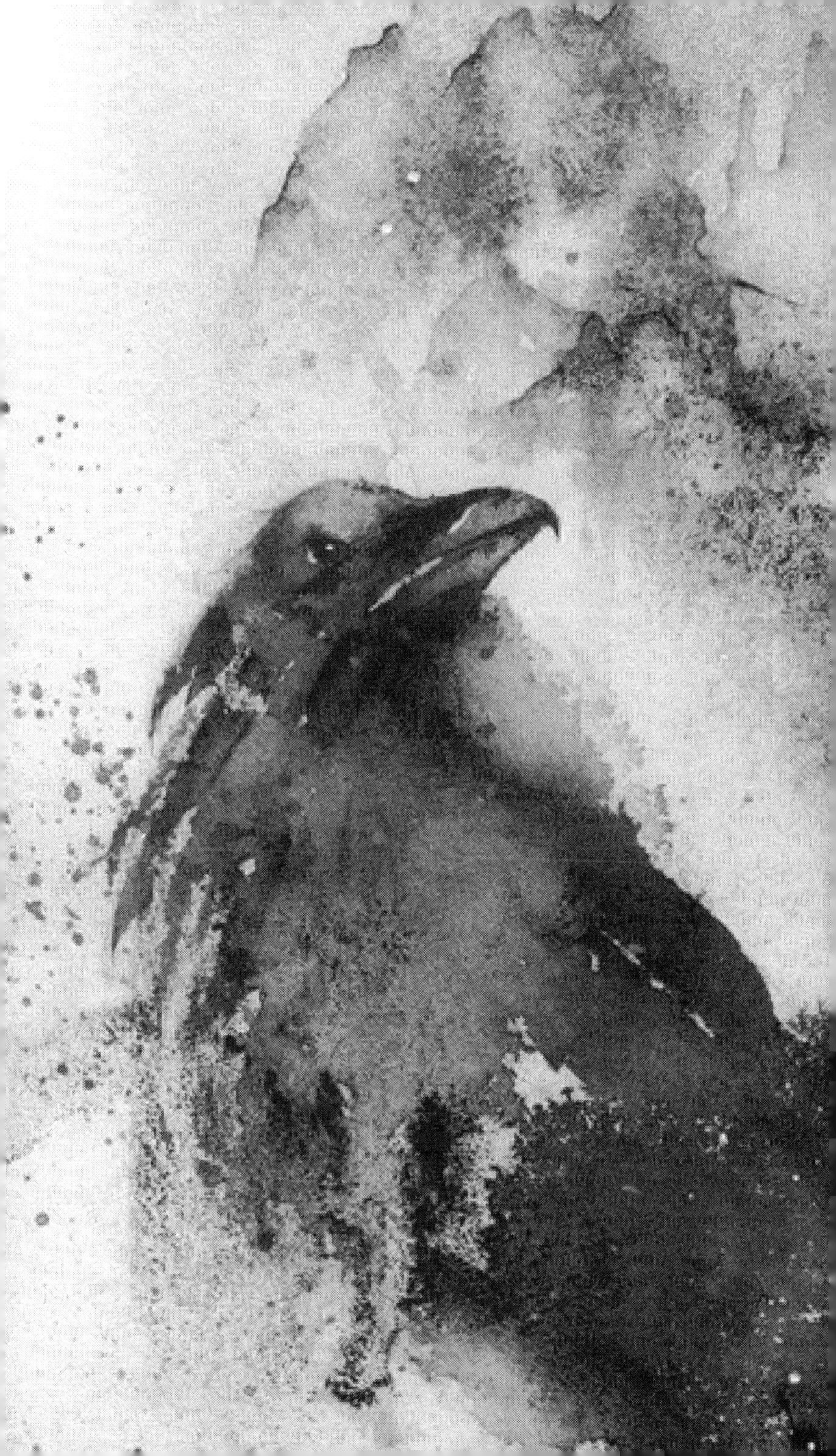

TWENTY FIVE
Raven

It's too quiet. Not in the way you would hear a pin drop from five hundred miles away. No. This is worse. It's the type of silence that makes everything feel fine, okay, good—*too* good—and you're waiting for the other shoe to drop. I'm always alert and mainly on edge most of the time as it is, but even this is a new level for me.

There hasn't been another peep out of Sebastian today, not even after Brax threatened him in front of everyone. Genie hasn't reared her ugly head to have her say either, and I think that might be the more startling part. I also haven't been pulled from classes again, which is a relief. I have no idea what my parents are doing or expecting of me, but I was certain after yesterday they would be back sooner rather than later.

Leila wasn't in our last class today; her father called

her out, but otherwise, we're semi-normal again. I hope. Maybe. For now, at least.

Having a friend is harder than handling the Bishops, and that's saying something.

I know it won't continue like this, but it's giving me a damn headache waiting for the ax to fall. Classes are finished for the day, and as we make our way through the marbled hallways of the academy, I almost let myself relax into Zane's hold.

His arm is firmly around my shoulders while Eldon holds my left hand. Creed is so close behind me that I'm sure he's going to walk with his hands on my ass in a minute, and even Brax walks a step closer today as he leads the way.

The crowd heads toward the double-arched doors that stand wide open. Rain pours from the sky in a deluge, spoiling the atmosphere as gray clouds loom overhead. It was exactly like this when we left the house this morning as well. I'm already bored of it. It reminds me too much of Shadowmoor.

None of the guys move to ready their magic so they don't get wet, while I get nervous, wanting to be sure how to do it before I actually step outside. But just as the doors get within reach, the sound of my name echoing off the walls around us makes me pause.

Spinning to look behind me, the guys remain frozen in

place, with Eldon on my right and Zane on my left, while Brax hovers at my back and Creed stands front and center.

It's Lyra.

Her eyes meet mine through the crowd and she waves for me to come closer. It's like she heard my thoughts from a moment ago and waited until I was sure peace and quiet were guaranteed before perking my weariness back up again.

It's surprisingly easy to get through the crowd, which parts like the sea for the Bishops that surround me.

"How are you today? You had me worried yesterday," she states, folding her arms over her deep-navy suit jacket, her red lips twisting as she assesses me.

"Uh, I'm fine," I mumble, noting that I can't sense her magic around me, and I make a mental reminder to bring it up to the guys as soon as we're done here.

"Good. I also have Monarch Denver in one of the communication rooms." Her gaze shifts to Zane, whose eyes widen, but I almost feel like it's surprising it's taken this long. Then again, I don't know the man well enough to make that call. I purposely hadn't thought about him reaching out in hopes I didn't jinx it, but it seems it was meant to creep up on me nonetheless. "He's waiting in booth one," she adds, and Zane sighs.

"You guys go ahead, I—"

"No, no," Lyra interrupts as she takes a backward step

toward her office. "He requested *all* of you."

"*All* of us?" Eldon clarifies, and she nods.

She disappears back into her office after that and Zane waves for us to follow him toward the booths. Fuck. Fuck. Fuck. Now I'm panicking. "Have I fucked up with him?" I murmur, glancing at Zane from the corner of my eye, and he grabs my chin and grinds us to a stop as he looks deep into my gaze.

"No, never." He sounds so certain that hope fills me with the chance of those words being true.

"The quicker we get in there, the quicker we can get out," Brax grunts, stepping around everyone else to grab the door handle and push it open.

With no more time to prepare, I follow after him and find a projection of Monarch Denver sitting on a sofa to my right while Brax drops down onto the empty one facing him. I take the seat beside him and Zane presses into my other side, sandwiching me between the two of them.

"Zane, boys, all okay?" Rhys asks, accepting the nods as a reasonable response before settling his eyes on me. "Raven, how are you today?"

Gulping, I nod. "I'm okay." I think. What else am I supposed to say?

"Good."

"What's this about, Pops?" Zane asks, leaning forward to rest one elbow on his right knee and the other on mine.

"Don't make me come there for real and get you in a headlock, son," Rhys grumbles, catching me by surprise. My back stiffens as I stare between the two of them, but Zane smothers a laugh, which eases the rising tension flooding my veins a little. "Quit your bullshit. I did some digging around after I got Evangeline and Abel out of Haven Court and I understand exactly why they've been pushing for Raven's magic to come to light."

I can't breathe. I can't move. I can't be a weapon.

Panic burns up my spine. I can sense it by the mere look in his eyes; he's not lying. He knows. I fucking know it.

"Pops, what—"

"Test me on the headlock, Zane. I dare you." He stares his son down and Zane slouches back in his seat. I immediately feel exposed without his hand on me. Brax must sense it, though, because his hand clamps down on my other thigh, pinning me to him.

"Maybe what Zane should be trying to ask is if you could be more specific with what you believe you know," Creed interjects, but Rhys's gaze is fixed on mine.

"It's okay, Raven. It's all going to be okay. I'm extremely sorry I didn't know about their intentions this entire time." Is he trying to bullshit me to make me fall for some false sense of security? My fight or flight instincts are kicking in, and although I'm currently stuck on freeze, my arms are going to be swinging as I run for the hills. I'm sure of it.

"I still don't know what you're talking about, Pops," Zane insists, and I grimace.

"I said, quit your bullshit. I told you a necromancer had been sensed, and when I mentioned it the other day, you didn't think to mention you knew who." He cocks a brow, glaring at his son, while all I can do is gape at him.

Fuck. Fuck. Fuck.

The silence extends between them, consuming the room for what feels like an eternity until Zane sighs. "It's not my story to tell."

He's not doing this right now, right? Handing me over so effortlessly. I'm fucked.

"You're right, it's not, and you better keep your mouth shut. This information in the wrong hands would… fuck." Rhys runs a hand through his hair, the stress as clear on him as it is on us. "Luckily, Monarch Perkins, who your parents were in contact with, isn't aware of the information I have, nor will they be in the future since I've sent them on a field mission this morning. Return date set to indefinitely."

I blink at him, his words slowly processing through my mind. Is that… relief I feel? Trust? But I still don't know him well enough for any of that. Turning to Zane, he nods, his lips in a thin line in comparison to the usual smirk that sits there, and I take the trust I feel from him and channel it myself too.

Clearing my throat, I place my hand on top of Brax's at my thigh. "What does this mean for us now?" He takes a moment to glance over each of us, like he's assessing us as individuals and as a whole, his son included.

"Who did you save, Raven? To activate the magic?" he asks, not answering my question, and I gulp, but the knot in my throat doesn't budge.

"It was me, Monarch Denver," Brax states, and I grip his hand even tighter as I tilt my head to look at him. His face is as void of emotion as it usually is, but there was a hint of something in his voice that I haven't heard before and likely never will be able to figure out where to place it.

When Rhys doesn't respond straight away, I turn back to him to see his eyes wide as his throat bobs with a large gulp of his own. I guess asking the question and actually getting an answer to it are two entirely different things.

"I'm glad you're okay, Brax," he states with a sniff.

"Me too, Sir," he grumbles in response. This man will speak the same way to anyone and everyone, Monarchy included, and it makes me love his natural ruthlessness.

Rhys clears his throat and turns back to me again. "Have you pieced together your other magic along with it yet?"

"No," I admit, but then a sudden thought comes to mind. "Although someone mentioned I might have something."

"What?" Eldon blurts, staring at me expectantly.

Tucking a loose piece of hair behind my ear, I shrug nervously. "Wait, first, I have some questions," I insist, and Rhys nods for me to proceed. "Did you help me get back here? Are my parents likely to try that again? And why did so much time pass between me leaving and returning?" I don't even pause to breathe as each question quickly flows into the next.

"Yes, I helped you. When you admitted your fears in the chamber, I knew I had to protect you. There's clearly something bigger at play, which is why your mother had someone else intercept you instead of protecting you herself, and as much as I don't understand why, it also means I can't guarantee there won't be another attempt like this," he admits, making my heart clench. "Thirdly, more time passed than you likely expected because I kept you in a comatose state in my private gateway." My eyes widen in surprise and he quickly lifts his hands in surrender as Brax rushes to his feet. "If I had sent you straight back there, your father would have been right behind you. I needed it to look realistic."

"What does realistic look like, *Pops*," Zane snarls, speaking my exact thought.

"I made it look like there was an issue with the chamber when I tried to place you in it. You weren't in the gateway alone, though. My wife was with you the entire time. Just in case."

"Just in case what?" I breathe, my brain overwhelmed with the facts I'm not sure I was prepared for.

"Just in case anyone came after you. I might not have known then what secrets you were keeping, but I knew the fear in your eyes was real. If I ever saw that in the eyes of one of my own children, I would tear this world to pieces. Added to the fact that I've *seen* the way my son looks at you, I knew protecting you at all costs was the right thing to do. Am I correct?" His gaze shifts to Zane beside me, but it's Eldon who speaks first.

"You're the coolest fucking man in The Monarchy, you know that, right?" Zane rolls his eyes at his friend's declaration while his father smirks, pleased with himself.

"As true as that may be, what's the magic you mentioned?" Rhys asks, not steering completely off track as he turns back to me.

Despite being a lone ranger, I lean into my Bishops and take the single nod from Zane to proceed. "When I got back here, I was speaking with someone and instantly knew they were doing something to me against my will."

"Explain," Creed grunts, his onyx eyes silently pleading with me after spending last night together.

"Lyra was practicing her magic, or... her second magic, I think, which is a sort of truth serum, and I called her out on it. She insisted no one had done that before and that even those who are usually tight-lipped don't realize when they're oversharing, but I did."

"That sounds like you could be able to taste magic, as they call it, but if you're a necromancer as well, hell, you could sense it to manipulate it. Mirror it. It's been known that a necromancer can sense magic, feel energy in the air, and contort it to their own desires." I have no words to say back to that and he must sense it, too, because he pats his thighs and smiles. "Either way, they'll come through when they're ready, right?"

"Yeah," I whisper, still bewildered.

He rises from his seat and I expect the hologram to stutter, but it doesn't. His arm comes out swinging and I flinch as a slap hits Zane on the head.

What the fuck?

"Don't fuck with me again, son. You little shit," he says with a chuckle, and Zane jumps to his feet, wrapping his arms around his father in a loving embrace as I stay frozen in place, fear licking at my nerve endings. A moment later, Rhys's attention turns my way once more. "With your abilities, Raven, the world is going to be in the palm of your hand, and it's going to be our job to make sure you don't become anyone's weapon."

DESTINED SHADOWS

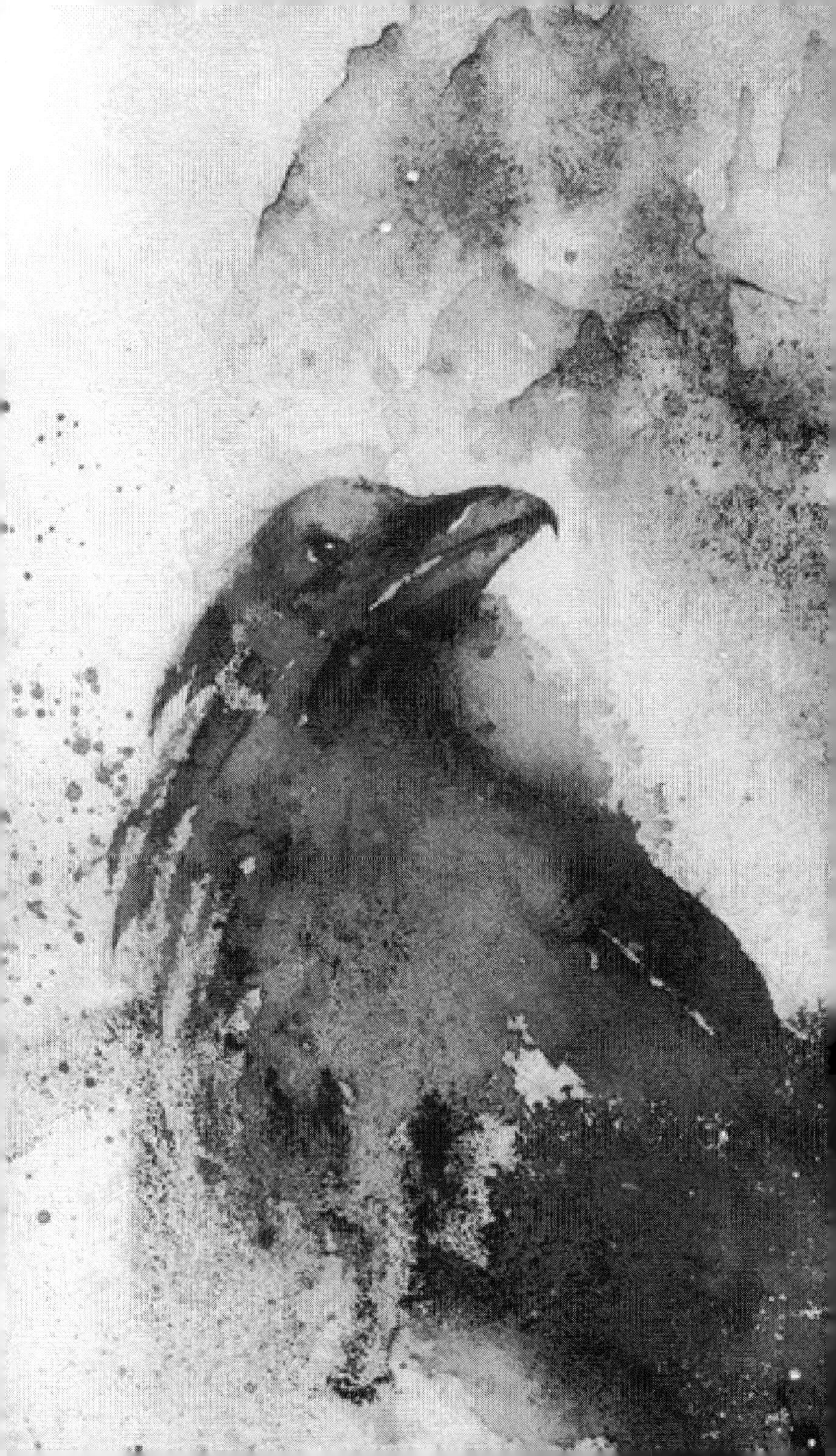

TWENTY SIX
Raven

I let the front door click shut behind me as I exhale. Fresh day, fresh start. That's the vibe I'm working with this morning after the talk we had with Rhys yesterday evening. I'm sure if I got the chance to actually process everything that's happened that positivity might be possible. But instead, I'm drenched in impending doom vibes because there's always more bullshit heading my way.

I'm not going to jinx myself today and think about what the day might bring, I'm just going to focus on putting one foot in front of the other and hope for the best.

It's still strange that Leila isn't waiting like she usually would be, and I'm almost wondering if I miss her presence. I need to pull my head out of the sand with that entire situation, too, and either get over myself or stick to my guns.

Eldon's hand wraps around mine, distracting me from my thoughts as Brax heads down the path without a backward glance. Fucker knows we'll follow. This time, Creed swoops into my right side while Zane grumbles behind me about how unfair it is that he doesn't get to touch me this morning.

His pouting and complaining always make me grin, lifting a little of the weight weighing heavy on my shoulders by just being him.

The throng of other students on the main path gives us a wide berth as we join them, but I can't help but get the sense they're looking at us extra hard today. Usually, the girls all focus on the Bishops, *my* Bishops, but when I look at them now, they're staring at me too. I can't decide if it's a snarl or a smirk on their lips, but I opt to focus on myself and my guys rather than their issues.

"Tonight, we're going to try out the theory of sensing other magic around you, yeah?" Eldon murmurs, nudging his arm against mine, and I nod.

"Sounds like a plan." It'll be good to try and figure out what other abilities I might have, despite the craziness of how real this all is. If I've thought it once, I've thought it a thousand times. Never in my life did I expect to go from a Void to a necromancer in the blink of an eye. Regardless, we're here now, and I'm a bundle of nerves and excitement at the thought of delving further into it all. "I'm ready to explore the possibilities, but more than that, I'm ready for a day of doing absolutely nothing. A day where I'm just Raven. At the moment, I can't fucking blink without something causing a stir and the constant drama is driving me insane," I admit, and Creed hums in agreement.

"Your wish is my command, Little Bird," Eldon declares, brushing his lips over my knuckles in a quick kiss before he winks at me, continuing on like nothing happened.

As the crowd grows bigger and we get closer to the academy building, the underlying feeling I got from the other students increases with the density of the crowd.

"Does it seem like people are staring more than usual?" I mumble, hating how ridiculous I sound, and Brax stops dead in front of us, despite not hearing what I even said.

"They do seem more... observant this morning," Creed states as we slow to a stop behind Brax.

"What the fuck is going on now?" Zane grumbles, his hand falling to the small of my back at the exact moment I lock eyes with Genie. Her hand is covering her mouth as she makes an exaggerated giggle ring out around us.

What the fuck am I missing?

"Hey." Leila appears in front of Brax, blocking Genie from my view for a second, and the grimace on her face doesn't ease the tension building inside of me.

"Hit me with it."

"She's being a bitch."

"Who?"

"Who do you think?" she retorts, glancing over her shoulder to where Genie stands.

Of course she is.

"What has she done now?"

Leila sighs and I notice the piece of paper she's clutching in her hands. She slowly spins it around so I can see the other side and understanding washes over me.

Picture after picture, frame after frame, my heart races in my chest. They're all of me. Not alone, though. With one of my men. In every single photo. It's not a montage of cute pictures where we're staring at the screen offering a peace sign as we live our best lives.

No.

It's basically a compilation of my *O* face in compromising positions with each and everyone one of the Bishops. There are multiple pictures with Brax with the patio glass smashed from when he chased me from class. There are a few that are hazy at best, but I'm still pinned to a tree with Creed between my legs. While others show my lips pressed against Zane and Eldon's.

I'm still committing every inch of the paper to memory when it's snatched from my hands, but the bright red marker that is scrawled over the front is imprinted in my mind.

Whore.

"What the fuck is this?" Brax snarls, but I don't stick around to give him the answer, I'm already cutting through the crowd and their watchful stares as I storm toward my target.

"What the fuck is your problem?" I bite, and Genie smirks at me like I'm giving her the exact reaction she wanted, but I don't give a fuck.

"Problem? I don't have one. Maybe you do, though, if it's taking four men to..." Her words trail off as she looks down the length of me. If she's going to point fingers at me, I want to hear the words from her lips.

"To what, Genie? Give me things you always wanted?" I push, watching as the grin drops from her lips and her eyebrows pinch together.

"So you're not denying it then," she hollers, gaining everyone's attention. If they weren't already paying attention, they are now. "You're sleeping with *all* of them."

"You're damn fucking straight I am." I don't know if she was trying to make me feel embarrassed or expecting me to deny it, but the Bishops are mine and I want everyone to know it.

"You're a whore," she snaps, rearing back like I've got the Lulum Plague from eight hundred years ago. Fool.

"A whore having the best fucking time of her life. But what I'm more concerned with is the little fucking creep that seems intent on watching me orgasm again and again and again. How did it feel when you took those photos, Genie? Were you hot for what you saw, or were you angry that you weren't the one on the end of their dicks?" Whispers pick up around us as she vigorously shakes her head, failing to deny it. "I might be in some compromising positions, but I'm not embarrassed by a single one of them. They're my fucking men. *Mine.*" I glance around the crowd, which is completely enraptured, making sure they know the warning goes to them too. "I would, however, be beyond fucking embarrassed at being caught taking pictures of someone like a total creeper. Wouldn't you?"

I can feel my face heating with anger, but hearing the murmurs from the crowd twist in my favor fills me with an extra boost of confidence I've never really had the privilege of before.

"I never."

"They didn't just magically appear, Genie. You're fucked up. Now, do you have anything else to say before…" I play her at her own game, letting my words trail off. My pulse rings in my ears as every second rolls by and my muscles clench.

"Before what?"

Rearing my hand back, I slam my fist into her throat, relishing the sound of her choking and gagging as she keels forward, struggling to breathe.

Fuck, that feels good. My fist throbs, and I'm sure it won't leave as good of a lasting impression as Brax's stone hand smashing into Sebastian's face the other day, but those two deserve each other and their matching bruises.

Laughter echoes around me as I feel hands land on either side of my waist from behind.

"You're a savage," Eldon murmurs against my ear, and I grin.

"I didn't realize we were throwing compliments around today."

His chuckle sends a shiver down my spine as one of Genie's friends steps forward, wagging a finger in my face.

"You disgust me," she says with a gasp of horror, and I join in with the laughter that continues to rumble through the crowd.

"You're welcome," I offer with a wink, turning to see Leila laughing with her hand over her face and awe dancing in her eyes.

"You're the coolest fucking person I know."

I roll my eyes at her while Genie continues to splutter. I'd love to have caused her that much discomfort, but surely she's exaggerating now.

"What in the realm is going on out here?"

Laughter quickly dissolves into silence as everyone's attention shifts to Professor Fitch, who is frowning at all of us. When Genie continues to hack like an idiot, he settles his stare on her. I'm expecting some bullshit to come my way any moment, but to my surprise, he sighs, pointing over his shoulder.

"Everybody get to the changing rooms. Now."

There are a few grumbles around us as everyone follows his command, and I take two steps with Leila at my side before I'm halted.

"Not you, Raven."

"Like fuck is she staying out here alone," Brax bites, hands fisted at his sides as he squares off with Fitch like he's not a professor.

"I don't expect her to with fools like that around. She's going to want to retaliate, you know," Fitch states, turning to me with a tired expression, confusing me even more than usual.

I shrug. "It seems to be her hobby."

He nods like that makes sense to him before clearing his throat. "We need to talk after class."

"Why?" Creed answers for me, his onyx eyes staring holes into the side of Fitch's head.

"About your extracurricular activities," he breathes in response, glancing around at the guys as well as me. I'm assuming he means the Guild, but I also don't want to say it out loud to clarify. I frown at him, unsure how to respond as he swipes a hand down his face with a sigh. "The five of you stay behind. It won't take long."

Every single limb aches from head to toe, but surprisingly, it doesn't feel as rough as the last time he put us through our paces. I'm relieved to be getting the stamina boost I need, but the pain it comes with outweighs the pros right now.

Genie glared in my direction the entire class, exclaiming that, in her current condition, she wasn't able to participate. Her friends tossed death glares along with her, and I fought back the eye roll threatening to burn my eyes. I couldn't give a shit how they look at me. They don't scare me. Even with the knowledge that Genie will attempt to get her revenge. It's just another reason for me to be on alert, but fuck, it was worth it.

Getting changed into my uniform, I'm taking extra precautions to avoid putting my back completely to her when Leila clears her throat.

"Hey, I know we're all up in the air and stuff at the moment, but I just wondered if you wanted to go to the party tonight?"

My eyebrows knit together in confusion. "Wait, is it Friday already?" I ask, completely lost.

"Yeah, are you okay?" she replies, concern thick in her tone as she frowns at me.

"Yeah," I murmur with a sigh. "My brain is just a mess with everything. I think I'm going to pass, though. Not because of how things are between us. That has nothing to do with it. I need to decompress and I'm not in the mood to put on a fake smile and pretend like everything is great to people I don't care about."

She nods with understanding, the smile on her face showing no strain. "Of course, if you decide you need some girl time, let me know."

"I will." It's true. I will. I have to give her the benefit of the doubt. She revealed she was in the Guild pretty much straight away, explained who the other members were without pause, came to get us when she knew other members wouldn't, and today, with Genie, she showed up as a friend should.

Heading outside with Leila, we find the Bishops standing beside Professor Fitch. I expect Leila to stay too, but she waves me off as she follows the rest of the students heading to their next class. Once everyone is completely out of sight, Zane turns to Fitch with his arms folded over his chest.

"What's the issue, Professor?"

"There isn't one."

"So why are we here?" Eldon interjects, and Fitch takes a step back.

"Follow me." He heads toward the academy building

and, as instructed, we stay a step behind him as he leads us inside, down a few hallways, then through a door with a gold plaque displaying his name on the front.

He waves us inside and we shuffle into the surprisingly large space with a desk sitting in the center of the room. There's a high-back leather chair on the other side and a bookcase taking up the entire wall behind it, while the view out of the window to my right looks over the main entrance. That probably explains how he knew something was happening earlier with Genie and me.

At the sound of the lock latching, I turn my attention back to Fitch, who trudges around the desk to take a seat, leaving the five of us to stand.

"I believe you've been initiated into the Nightmares Guild."

The five of us remain silent, expecting to wait him out, but it seems he's better at it than us, and Eldon eventually relents. "It's possible."

"I'm still an active member. It's not a secret to me. I just haven't had a chance to speak with you until now."

"Oh," I mumble. I knew Leila was a member because of who her father was, but I hadn't considered if *he* was still active himself.

"Why do we need to speak with you about it?" Creed asks with his head tilted to the side as he assesses the professor.

"You don't, but I thought there might be some questions you were eager to get answers to," Fitch offers, leaning back in his seat as he glances us over.

"At what cost?" Eldon asks, making my eyebrows rise in surprise. When he doesn't instantly get a response, he continues. "You're a calculating man, Fitch. Nothing is without a cost."

Fitch laces his fingers together in his lap as his eyes narrow at Eldon, but he doesn't budge or soften the words he just spoke.

"I believe an attack is getting closer and closer to the academy with every passing day. If we're not prepared, we'll be destroyed in the blink of an eye," Fitch finally admits, making my gut clench. That is something to worry about for sure.

"How?" Brax asks, stepping closer to brace his hands on the table as he stares the professor down.

"Well, the Basilica Realm is where our enemies lie, but it's not the only realm we're up against. Since we cut ourselves off from them a long time ago, we have no idea what they're now capable of or who they are allied with." I'm trying to read between the lines because I know there's a hell of a lot more to that statement than the impactful words already spoken, but I can't decipher what.

"What does any of that mean for us?" I ask, folding my arms over my chest as I give him an expectant look.

"It means everything is balanced on a ticking time bomb. As a realm, as a nation, we should have been keeping our friends close and our enemies closer. Instead, we've turned a blind eye to anything and everything beyond our borders, choosing defense instead of offense, and I sense a storm is coming."

"A storm?"

"A war."

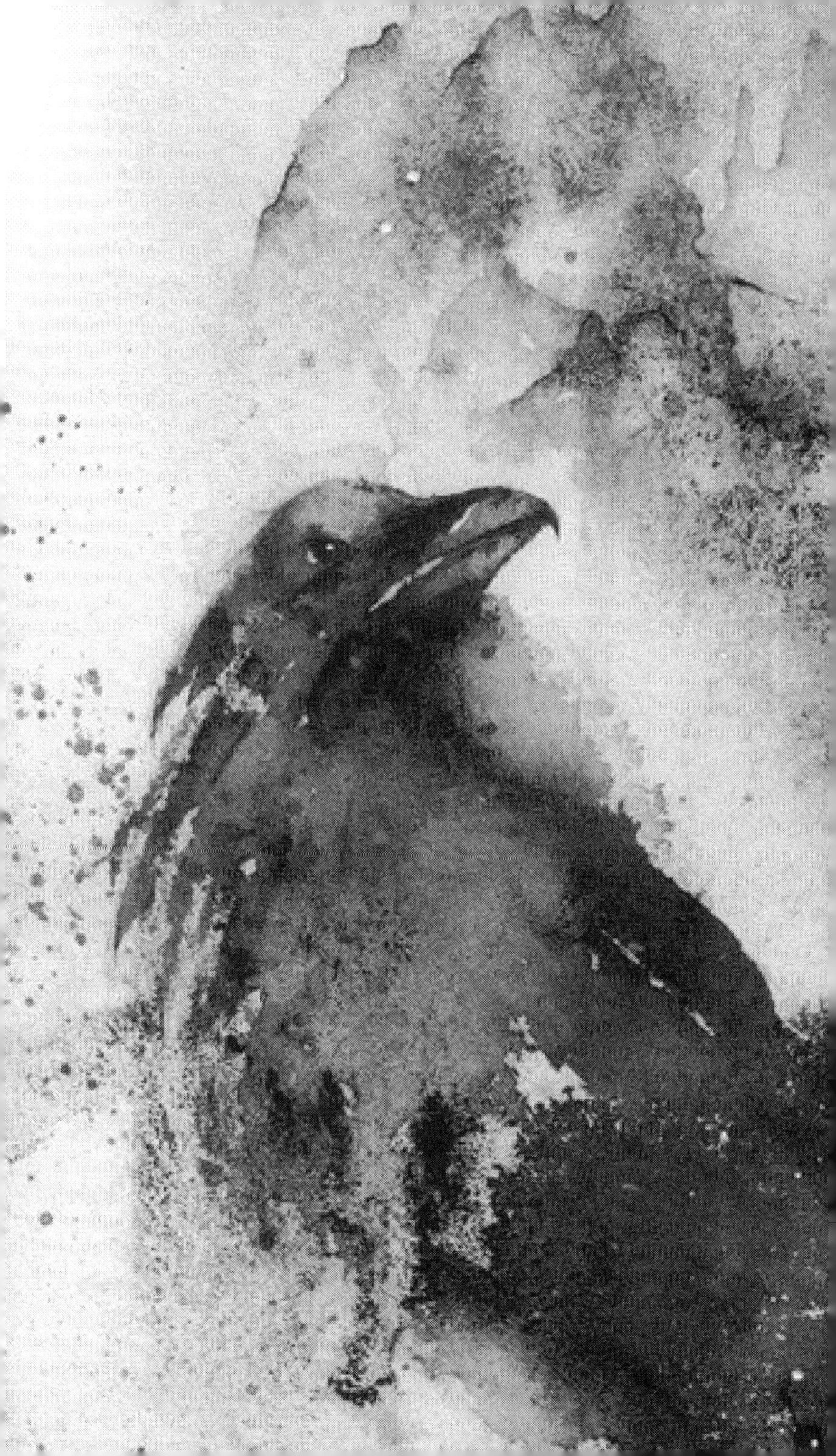

TWENTY SEVEN
Raven

I run my fingers through the blades of grass beneath me as I stare up at the sky, hoping for the answers to come to me. A storm is coming. A *war* is coming. Those were his words and they've been rattling around in my head ever since.

What is it Eldon said to me not long after I got here?

"In my vision, a war was coming, a war across realms, threatening all of existence. And the raven… she saved us all."

I don't like the startling resemblance one bit. Every day, I wake up free of the life I was living in Shadowmoor, yet the noose around my neck only seems to get tighter.

The clouds gently float across the sky, set on their destination, while I lie here, fumbling to understand which way is up. The mention of the word war has my gut twisting. I feel it in my bones, the truth behind those words, and I don't understand why.

I'm sure the truth will happily come along and smack me in the face eventually. That's how it's been going recently, at least.

Fingertips ghost over mine as someone lies down beside me in the grass and I tilt my head to find Eldon getting comfortable on my left. He's not looking at me, though, he's staring up at the sky with a sense of wonder that feels far more hopeful than my own.

Turning back to the blue background and smattering of white clouds that have now replaced the gray and gloomy weather we had earlier, I lace my fingers with his.

"What are you thinking about, Little Bird?" he asks after a while, and I smile at the nickname.

"Nothing. I'm pretending there is nothing crazy going on in my life right now and my life is as simple as this," I explain, glancing at him out of the corner of my eye to see a smile tipping the corner of his mouth up.

"You deserve nothing less," he breathes, warming my soul.

"Yet it's an uphill battle like everything else," I say with a sigh, dampening the moment with reality.

"It's a good reminder that we're living." He lifts my hand to his mouth, peppering kisses over my knuckles as another deep sigh passes my lips.

"That's true. I know I'm doing more than just surviving now, which is overwhelming sometimes, but the hurdles we're facing aren't getting any easier and I can't help but question whether I've got the strength for it." I don't even know where that truth came from but the second it parts my lips, I know I mean it.

"I know, but if there's anyone who can handle this life, it's you. All of these trials are here to remind you how strong you are, Raven. That might sound shitty, but I promise I'll be with you every step of the way." His words don't take away the uncertainty in my veins, I wouldn't want them to anyway, but they don't mask or downplay how I'm feeling either. They're exactly what I need when I don't even know what it is I'm searching for.

"Are we ready to trial some magic for my dove?" Zane asks, his shadow casting over us a moment later as he stands with his hands on his hips, a hint of concern in his eyes.

Eldon looks at me expectantly and I nod, still uncertain about it. "As ready as I'll ever be."

That's all they need to take over my serene space from moments ago, helping me up to sit cross-legged in the grass, and they drop down with me to create a kind of circle between the five of us.

Zane is to my right, Eldon to my left, while Creed and Brax face me. The sun breaks through the clouds at that exact moment, a soft glow shimmering over us, and it warms my heart.

"Let's start off small, shall we?" Creed offers, and I nod. "If I do some mundane magic, can you try to see if you can feel it in the air?"

I nod, not bothering with words. He goes through the motions of making a platter of cheese and crackers appear in between us all before I manage to let my hair out of my hair tie and twist it into a bun on top of my head. "What's this black strand here?" Zane asks, making me frown for a second before I realize he's pointing at my hair.

"Oh, I don't know. I used my magic to refresh my hair color the other day but that strand just won't change," I reply with a shrug. He purses his lips in thought but eventually shrugs and focuses on the task at hand.

When the general magic doesn't seem to connect or register with me, Eldon opts to shift to the bigger stuff. "My visions aren't controllable, so I can't bring one on, and my fire magic is a literal energy source you can feel from the heat, so I don't think that will work any better. What about you guys?"

At the offer, Zane instantly goes invisible beside me and my breath lodges in my throat. It was phenomenal seeing him do it in the Gauntlet, but right beside me, and so casually, is something else entirely.

A shiver runs down my spine as I close my eyes,

focusing on the purple orb inside of me and the energy in the air around us. "I feel like there's a disturbance in the air," I murmur, a sort of static-like feeling flickering against my nerve endings.

"Is that because Zane's probably moved closer to you, though? I wouldn't be shocked if he had," Creed states, and a moment later, legs appear on either side of mine. He's shuffled around to sit so I'm between his open legs.

"Fucker," he grumbles at Creed, dramatically moving back into position with a huff, and I grin.

"If Brax goes gargoyle, it's a physical shift and not so much a danger to Raven, so that may not help," Eldon continues, working down the list of magic they can sprinkle in front of me to see if I can sense it.

"Creed?" Brax grunts, nodding in his direction to encourage him to help, but my quiet and observant Bishop scrubs the back of his neck with uncertainty.

"I've controlled her sight recently and there didn't seem to be anything that she noticed. Besides, it's probably not helping that she's fully aware of what we're doing instead of catching her by surprise with it."

"That's because she's as unhinged as you, and you're right," Eldon points out, and my teeth instantly sink into my bottom lip at the memory before coiling into irritation at the fact that Genie had somehow managed to sneak into the woods and take advantage of a moment between Creed and me. She deserves another punch, this time to the face.

"How about you try something on someone else and Raven can see if she senses it," Zane offers. Creed glances my way, waiting for a nod of approval before turning his attention to Brax beside him.

"Fucker," my gargoyle grumbles under his breath, his hands clenching in his lap as he slowly blinks.

The hairs on the back of my neck stand on end and everything but the two of them fades into the background. Tingles ripple down my arms and I'm up on my knees and shuffling toward them with the next skip of my heart.

Stopping dead center between them both, the hairs on my arms are as sharp as those on my neck as I look at them. "I can feel… something," I whisper, unsure how to label it, but I know it's there. I'm certain of it.

Slowly, I lift my hand in the air and reach between them. Not *at* either of them, specifically, more at the energy I can feel zapping between them. My eyes close of their own accord as I inch closer and closer and when I softly blink them back open again, I notice the faintest blue line of what can only be described as magical particles seeping from Creed into Brax's mind.

Holy fuck.

"It's there," I breathe, and everyone else remains silent as I start to eliminate the remaining inch between my fingertips and the blue glow. Just as my finger is about to sweep over the delicate strands, a thud vibrates the ground.

My heart races in my chest as my hand drops to my lap and I turn to find the culprit of the interruption.

Ari.

He looks exhausted, and the second I acknowledge it, I feel the weight of that tiredness in my bones.

I'm instantly on my feet and rushing toward him.

"*Where have you been?*" he asks, making my eyebrows pinch in confusion.

"What do you mean?"

"*I knew you were in danger, I could sense your panic, but it was weak, like you were far away and I couldn't get to you...*" Does he mean the other day? Possibly.

"I'm fine. Is everything okay with you?" It's clear that it's not but I need him to acknowledge that. He dropped in here concerned about me when I'm clearly not the only one handling crap.

"Do I need to be concerned about another man here or..."

"What?" My head whips around to Eldon, who looks between Ari and me with a tense jaw and a frown.

"*Tell him not to be a fool. Just because that one is a shifter doesn't mean I am too,*" Ari says into my mind, making me smirk.

"He told me to tell you that he's a griffin through and through. No shifting involved. Is that okay?" I cock a brow at Eldon, who relents with a shrug.

"You can hear him?" Zane asks, and I nod, tapping my temple.

"In here, but currently, he can't hear me the same way, so it's a one-sided spoken conversation," I explain, and a hint of guilt creeps up my spine with the fact that I didn't mention that to them, but I quickly reason with myself. I haven't done anything wrong and I'm learning what it means to have a familiar. Besides, I don't need to lay out every inch of my life, right? When none of them speak up again, I turn back to Ari. "Are you okay? You seem strained."

"That's why I couldn't get to you. I was recaptured with the other griffins until one of the professors recognized me as your familiar. I came straight here when I was released."

"Released? From where?" I snap, anger coiling inside of me as Ari hangs his head.

"The compound."

The compound? What fucking compound?

"Show me."

"Show you?"

"Show. Me."

He takes a heavy step toward me, nuzzling his beak at my neck before standing tall. *"Come."*

His right wing dips, as if to offer me aid, and I move toward him without a second thought.

"What are you doing, Shadow?" Brax asks as I pull myself onto Ari's back.

"The griffins are being held against their will, I want to see what the situation is," I state, clutching Ari's feathers a little tighter than necessary, but I feel completely disoriented up here.

Creed steps forward, glancing between Ari and me before he takes two steps toward us and points a finger in my griffin's face. "You bring her back here in one piece with a fucking beating heart or I'll destroy you all by myself, do you hear me? And do not let her get off because she'll start waging some kind of fucking war and we already seem to have one of those looming over us as it is."

I blink at him with wide eyes as Ari slowly tips his head.

"*I like him,*" he says into my mind, and I grin, my teeth sinking into my bottom lip in a failed attempt to conceal it.

"I like him too," I murmur, just loud enough for Creed to hear before Ari takes a step back.

"*Are you ready?*"

"No."

It's like my answer doesn't register, or he simply doesn't care for my uncertainty, because in the next breath, his feet push up off the ground and we're up in the air.

Holy. Fuck.

I hold tighter somehow, plastering my face against his

feathers as my thighs hold on for dear life.

My stomach somersaults as the air whooshes around us and I'm unsure if I'm going to be sick or not. Loose tendrils of my hair sweep around my face as I realize my eyelids are slammed shut.

"*Are you not going to enjoy the view?*" Ari asks, a sense of amusement in his tone, and I scowl, even though he can't see me.

"I wasn't aware there was anything to enjoy," I snap, attempting to pry an eye open but faltering at the last second.

"*If you would just open your eyes, then you would know,*" he grunts back as we soar through the skies at an unreal speed, confirming that I'm good where I am.

A few minutes pass and it almost feels like we're holding a steadier speed and a level height. Confidence gets the better of me and I manage to ping one eye open as my hold on him turns deadly. Not that he seems to notice as I focus on the sky first.

The clouds look just as they did when I was lying in the grass, offering me a sense of familiar comfort and a hint of courage. My jaw falls slack as I look around us. Mountain tops, the ocean, and an array of trees in a variety of colors cascade around us.

"It's beautiful."

"*It is. It's just a pity it's only superficial and if you look below the surface, it's not as sweet at its core,"* he replies, and sadness floods me.

I don't know what to say, so I don't say anything, appreciating the view despite his words as Ari guides us to the compound. Glancing over my shoulder, I see the academy in the distance, standing tall and dark among the otherwise vivid scenery.

"Hold on, we're going down."

It's impossible for me to hold on any tighter, but I don't tell him that as he dips toward the ground. A squeal lodges in my throat, but I at least manage to keep my eyes open as he lands with a thud at the edge of a forest.

He tilts his wing as he did earlier and I shuffle down, slightly relieved when my feet touch the ground.

"Where is it?" I ask, glancing around, and he nods toward the forest. "I don't understand, it's just a…" My words trail off as I see a griffin, just like Ari, on the other side of the tree line. "Do you know them?"

"Yes."

"Why don't they come closer," I ask when the other griffin remains exactly where they are and Ari doesn't take a step closer.

"Because she can't."

"Why can't she?"

Ari lifts a claw, pointing one talon forward as a ripple dances through the air in front of us.

A force field. Why is there a force field surrounding the forest? "Is that the compound?"

"*Yes.*"

The longer I stand beside him, the more I see. The griffin closest to us isn't the only one and I'm sure I can see a group of minotaurs in the distance behind a fallen log as well.

The sadness coming from Ari, combined with the sight of the trapped magical creatures before me, has my heart lurching so hard I'm sure it's going to leap from my chest.

"We have to change this. Hearing about it and seeing it are two very different things," I breathe, looking up at Ari with sorrow shining in his eyes. Something has to be done. It's diabolical. Does it look comfortable enough from the outside looking in? Sure, but it is still taking away the simple rights of these living creatures. If we worked together with the other beings instead of caging them like animals, then we would have allies instead of more enemies.

"*That's my love. My Gia.*"

I look back at the closest griffin and understanding consumes me. If this was me and my men, how would I feel? My gargoyle, my firestarter, my invisible laughter machine, or my onyx observer? My heart would be torn from my chest. I know it.

Standing tall, I place my hand on his side and run my

fingers through his mane, the feeling a stark contrast to his feathers.

"What are you thinking, Raven?"

I take a deep breath, resting my head against him as I speak the words true to my heart.

"A change is coming and we're going to be at the forefront of it."

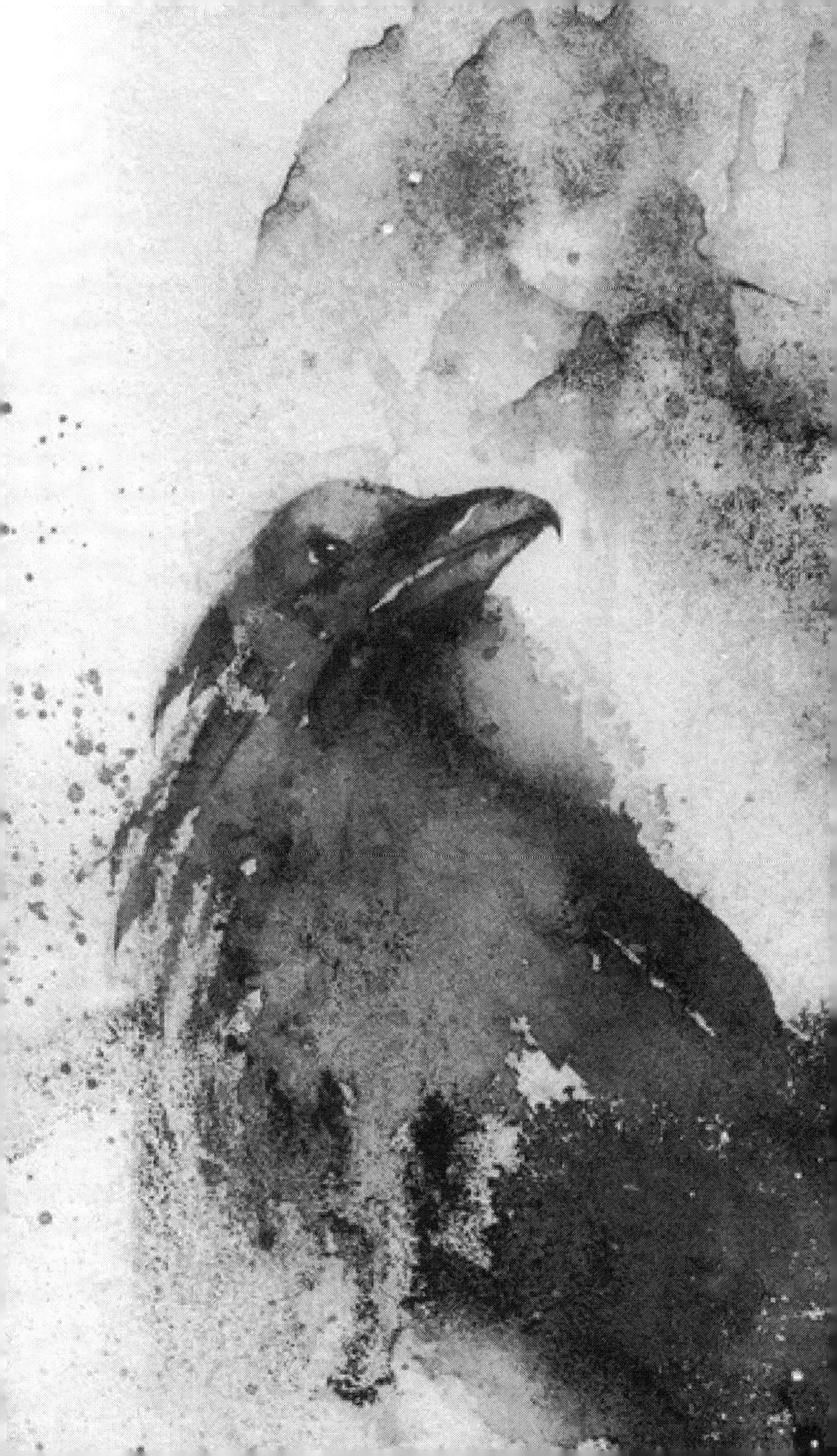

TWENTY EIGHT
Raven

Two days have passed and I'm still in a trance. I can't shake the feeling that rattled me so deeply at the compound; the fact that the view of the academy and its surrounding landscape is so beautiful, yet every day that passes, something else seems darker and more tainted than before.

The weekend passed in a blur and I'm still locked on the ache I felt in my chest when Ari looked at Gia. The pain of seeing your loved one in that situation and not being able to do anything about it is gut-wrenching.

I have to help them, I have to help *all* of them. I just haven't figured out how, and that's exactly what has me completely locked away in my head. I'm sure the Bishops can sense it, but they can't ease my worries.

One thing after another has piled on top of me and now

I'm struggling to withstand the strain. Maybe I wasn't the raven from Eldon's vision. Maybe that had nothing to do with me at all. Would that change how he felt about me? Would that change how they *all* felt about me?

Fuck.

I don't know where this sudden urge to doubt myself so harshly is coming from, but it's impossible to avoid it. Just as it's impossible to focus in any of my classes so far today. Another lesson, another shitload of information going straight over my head.

I'm letting my thoughts and surroundings affect me too much, and as much as it's a slippery slope, I'm not really fighting all that much to get out of it to begin with.

Chairs scrape across the floor around me as students rise from their seats, pulling me from my swirling thoughts. Thank goodness for my magic copying down whatever the professor was talking about. I can glance over it later. Maybe.

Stuffing everything into my backpack, I hitch it over my shoulder and turn to find Leila frowning at me.

"Is everything okay? I know you have a lot going on that I'm not aware of, but you seem really distant today."

"More distant than usual?" I remark with half a smile, and she rolls her eyes at me.

"Standoffish? Maybe. Distant? No. You're always focused and alert, but I don't think you would have even noticed if a fireball exploded in the room," she states, falling into step with me as I head for the door.

I can sense the Bishops around me, and knowing they're there, I let myself focus on my conversation with Leila. "Did you know that when we entered the Gauntlet for the simulator exercise, it was only a simulator for us and not the griffins?" It's not a trick question, and I'm not going to be mad if she did, but I want to understand if it's common knowledge or not. The instant her eyebrows knit together is all the answer I need.

"How is that even possible?"

"I don't know." I shrug, my emotions coiling in my stomach and leaving me queasy. "But there's a compound on academy grounds where the magical creatures are held until they're brought into the Gauntlet or whatever else they might want them for. But it's no wonder they're taking out students without care if they're being kept against their will." I know I'm rambling, but if there's a fresh set of ears to hear me out, I'm going to take it.

A soft smile glosses Leila's lips, despite my upset, and I frown, but she quickly explains. "You're passionate about this, aren't you?"

"Yes. Ari was kept there, and he's only out because he's my familiar, but that doesn't help his love, Gia. But more than that, if there's so much at stake around us, why don't we have allies in these creatures instead of using them as tools?"

She purses her lips as we take a left turn down one of the corridors, approaching our next class.

"Do you want me to try and find out from my father if I can?" she offers, and my eyes widen. That's not what this was about. I hadn't even considered it, but if it's available, who am I to deny a source?

"I mean, I wouldn't say no, but that was not my intention here."

"I know, that's why I'm offering," she replies with another genuine smile. "I'll speak to him later and see what he can tell me."

A burst of hope sweeps through me but I tamp it down, not wanting to get my hopes up too much. "Thank you, Leila."

"Yeah, thanks, Leila," Zane adds, stepping into my side as we walk through the doorway of our next class. Her smile widens, but before I can consider anything more, a gust of wind smacks into me at full force and I'm whipped off my feet and pinned to a wall before I can even understand what's happening.

What the fuck?

Laughter bubbles around me and my gaze darts around the room until my eyes land on my new victim.

Genie.

I can't move a muscle but that doesn't stop my men

charging at her. Brax looks like a charging bull, but when he gets within arms reach of her, something stops him. Her friends chuckle louder and I realize there are three girls just a step behind her. Their magic must be at play, too.

My insides burn as I try to fight against the hold on me. What's weirder is I can practically feel every inch of it touching me. If I could just move my hand, I might be able to help myself.

Keeping my gaze locked on Genie as Zane and Creed also fail to reach her, I take a deep breath and try to calm my rising frustration.

Eldon stops short of the others, tilting his head as he assesses Genie, who pulls her stare from me to look at him. "Come closer, Eldon," she purrs, seductively sweeping her tongue along her bottom lip, and my whole body stiffens even tighter when he doesn't miss a beat, edging closer to her, just as she wants.

He sidesteps Creed, Zane, and Brax, no magic holding him back as he stops beside the table Genie is sitting on. Leaning in close to whisper in her ear, I think I'm going to be sick as fury burns the back of my throat. His hand grips her chin and she smirks as she blinks up at me.

My body aches from trying to fight against the magic, but it's useless. I'm not going anywhere. My lungs burn with every breath I take as I try to understand why the fucking hell Eldon would even be entertaining her right now.

Then a scream rips from her lungs, her face heating, and her focus on me shifts as she recoils from Eldon's touch. I slump to the floor with a thud, unable to ready myself to land solidly on my feet.

"I'm going to fucking kill you," I bite, scrambling to my feet and racing between the chairs and desks to hunt this bitch down.

By the time I get there, Eldon has released her and she's sobbing into her hands uncontrollably.

"I'm sorry, are you a little hot?" Leila sings, stepping up to her side as Genie's friends simply gape in surprise at the fact that their plan failed. "Let me cool you down," she says with a smirk before squeezing Genie's hands that are cupping her face. She screams even louder as icicles erupt across her features.

"Enough!" Professor Figgins screeches from the top of her lungs, and the whole room goes still. My chest heaves with every breath as I continue to stare at Genie. I don't care if Eldon and Leila have already caused her pain; I'm ready to let her have a taste of my anger, too.

Professor or not.

"Find your seats. Now."

I hear people shuffling around me but I don't budge until Zane moves to my side and places his hands on my shoulders. "Come on, Dove," he murmurs against my ear, and I release the breath I didn't realize was lodged between my lips.

This isn't over. Far from it. And when Genie looks at me, I know she feels the exact same.

I drop down into my seat and Leila goes to take her usual spot beside me, but before she gets a chance, Eldon is moving her out of his way. "Take my seat," he grumbles, pointing over his shoulder to his usual spot beside Brax.

Leila looks nervously between me and the seat and decides against arguing. Although, in my current mindset, I think that would have been fun to watch.

"Raven," Eldon starts, brushing his hand over my knuckles, but I'm already shaking my head at him.

"Don't."

I don't know what I'm asking for; my mind is a whirlwind. Seeing him with Genie, I went to the worst-case scenario in my head and now I can't shake it. I need a minute.

With a sigh, he seems to accept that for the time being as he slouches back in the chair and Figgins begins talking. I instantly drown her out, acutely aware of just how close Eldon is, but more so, how fucking mad I am.

Now that the moment has passed, I can see and almost understand that he did as she asked, moved in close, to lead her into a false sense of security. Or I assume so, at least. But the jealousy that zings through me is unrelenting and I can't fucking shake it.

My hands clench in my lap. I haven't even pulled out my things so I can keep track of what the professor is talking about, but I don't care enough to rectify it.

Minute after minute ticks by but the tension doesn't ease up and I feel like my brain is going to explode if I don't find some kind of release for it. I want to kick, punch, scream, and tear this damn place to the ground. With or without people in it.

Squeezing my eyes closed, I try to take a calming breath, but it's futile. I know I'm overreacting, but that doesn't make the feelings any less real. I need an outlet, something to channel, but fuck, if I open my mouth now, I feel like I'm going to burst into flames.

With every beat of my heart, the same word repeats.

Mine.

Jealously can't look good on me. It certainly doesn't feel it, that's for sure. It's turning me into a raging lunatic.

I need to get out of here.

I ping my eyes open as I sit up straight in my seat, ready to push away from the table and do just that when Eldon's arm stretches across my chest, holding me in place.

"I need to go," I bite under my breath, not really caring if anyone hears, and Eldon shakes his head at me. Which only makes me madder.

"You're not going anywhere."

"You don't get to—"

He ignores me, glancing behind us and making me frown at the dismissal. "Creed. I want no movement, no eyes, and no hearing. All senses gone except one," he nods, but I don't understand what's going on. I'm too fucking mad.

Spinning to face Creed, I glare at him. "Don't you *dare* leave me helpless like that," I grind out, earning my name as a snarl on Professor Figgins's lips, but when I turn to tell her to go fuck herself, I find her in her seat with her head down and eyes closed.

"Who said anything about you, Little Bird?"

I turn to face Eldon, confused as hell, as he cocks a knowing brow at me. Glancing around the room, I notice that every student in the room has the exact same posture except the Bishops. Everyone else is… under Creed's magic?

"I don't understand," I reluctantly grumble, my temper unwavering as he slowly removes his arm from across me.

"I'm not going to lie, Raven, jealousy looks hot as fuck on you."

My eyes narrow.

"I'm not jealous," I lie, and he has the audacity to chuckle at me.

"If you say so. Want me to go and sit beside Genie for the rest of the class?" he offers, and I snarl.

"You wouldn't fucking dare."

"I didn't think so."

Sighing, I fold my arms over my chest. "I need to go."

"Why?"

"Because I said so." Why do I have to explain myself to him right now?

"I can feel the tension and anger coming off you in waves, Raven. Tell me what you need."

"I already did," I reply, rolling my eyes. "And you're not listening. I need to get the fuck out of here before I combust with all of the anger rolling around inside of me."

He leans back in his seat, a smile spreading across his face. "That sounds more like it."

"More like what?" This man is driving me insane.

"What I wanted to hear," he states before rising to his feet and planting his palms flat against the table.

"What—"

My words are cut off as he suddenly yanks my chair back and grabs my waist, effortlessly lifting me onto the table before resuming the position he was in moments ago.

"What are you doing?" I grumble, confusion getting the better of me as my annoyance falters for a second.

"Giving you what you want."

"Which is what?" I fold my arms over my chest and cock a brow at him.

The devilish smile on his face should be my first hint, but I'm too focused on my racing heart to fully pay attention. His hands shift to my thighs, skimming under the hem of my skirt as he grazes higher and higher.

I glance around the room, surprised, but everyone is exactly as they were when I last looked. "Eldon, what the fuck are you doing?"

"You want to get out of here so you don't combust, right?" His finger teases the trim of my panties, making my core clench as I nod. "Well, I think you'll feel a hell of a lot better if you *did.*"

I blink at him, his words slow to process in my head as he snags at the material covering my pussy in one move before plunging his fingers deep into my core. "Oh my... Fuck," I groan, my hands slamming down on the table to either side of me so I don't fall.

"That's it, Little Bird, let it all out," he murmurs with a grin as his fingers fuck me on the classroom table.

This can't be happening, but it fucking is.

I should tell him to stop but the words feel like a lie in my thoughts, nevermind on my tongue. Besides, with the way he's making my pussy clench, my tension is quickly morphing into sexual need, having the exact effect he wanted.

"Eldon," I gasp, wrapping my fingers around the edge of the table as I scoot back a few inches, exposing even more of myself.

"That's it, Raven. Say my name as you come on my

hand," he growls as he leans down, flipping my skirt higher up my waist so he can latch his mouth around my clit.

Fuck.

Every drop of anger and jealousy, every ounce of tension coiled through my body, dissolves in rippling waves of ecstasy as I climax, chanting his name like a prayer. When I'm completely spent, I collapse back onto my elbows, looking up at him in a daze.

"I'm not done with you yet, Little Bird."

I gape at him as he reaches for the zipper on his pants, revealing his thick length that's pleading for attention. He sheaths his cock with protection and lines up the tip at my entrance without looking away from me.

"I told you the first time I tasted your sweet pussy who I belonged to. Have you forgotten?" he asks, barely slipping an inch into me as I desperately move to take him deeper, but he holds all of the power right now. "Answer me, Raven."

"No. I haven't forgotten."

"Then tell me, who do I belong to?"

"Me."

That's the magic word. He thrusts deep into my core, stretching me around his cock as the rest of the class sits, seemingly unaware, around us. That shouldn't get me hot. But it does.

"Don't ever fucking doubt that again. Do you

understand me?" he grinds out with every slam of his hips, and I see the frustration and disappointment in me flash in his eyes. I blink at him, unable to find the words as I nod, but that's not good enough for him. "Never. Again. Raven. Tell. Me." Every word is punctuated with another thrust of his hips and I'm sure the table is going to start screeching across the floor beneath us.

"Never again," I manage, between gasps and groans, ready to fall apart in his grasp once more.

"Good. Now, only one other person in this room, aside from the Bishops, can hear everything we're fucking saying right now. Who do you think that is?" I can't fucking think when he's pounding me so hard and fast. I manage to glance behind him to where the Bishops are, but that doesn't make sense with what he's saying.

"I-I don't know."

He snickers. "Think harder, Raven. I'm yours, you're mine. Tell me who you want to hear that fact more than anyone else in this room?" My eyes widen as a knowing grin spreads across his face. "Tell her, Raven. Tell her who I belong to."

His hips don't falter as he claims me over and over again while I gape at him in a mixture of surprise and… shock? I'm not fucking sure, but either way, I can't stop myself from letting the words flow from my tongue.

"You belong to me."

"Louder, Little Bird," he shouts, his hips relentlessly pistoning in and out of me.

"You belong to me," I yell, my chest burning as my toes curl and another orgasm rips through my body, making me combust at his touch.

His hips falter, jutting with need as he follows me over the cliff. His lips claim mine, capturing my moans for himself as the world spins around us.

Panting together, we take a moment to catch our breath before he retreats from my core with his hand on my chin and his nose brushing mine as he peers into my eyes.

"I love you, Raven. Everything I do is for you," he whispers so only I can hear, and my heart pounds like crazy in my chest. He adjusts my skirt, straightens my blazer, and smooths a hand over my hair before sorting himself out and pointing down at my seat.

"I don't have any panties on."

"Good," he retorts with a wink, dropping down into his seat.

Fucker.

"That was hot as hell, Dove," Zane muses from behind me, and I stare at him with wide eyes as he grins.

"He's not even exaggerating," Brax adds, making my thighs clench as Creed smirks.

"Are you ready for the world to return?" His onyx eyes are set on mine, and as much as I want to say no, I nod and turn forward.

All of the anger, all of the fury, all of the rage is gone. From me, at least.

In the blink of an eye, movement takes over the room and Figgins is quick to her feet.

"Who did that?" she snarls, eyes wide and panicked as she glances around the room.

Genie whirls around in her seat, disgust on her face as she points a finger in my direction, but before she can say a word, Creed rises from his seat.

"Me."

"You?" The surprise is evident in her tone, but she still points toward the door with narrowed eyes. "Get the hell out of my classroom. Now."

He winks at me, a smirk on his face as he tucks his hands into his pockets and saunters from the room without a backward glance as chaos spirals around us. I could almost get swept up in it, too, if it wasn't for the warm palm against my thigh and the soft brush of lips against my cheek.

Maybe combusting isn't always a bad thing anymore.

TWENTY NINE
Zane

It's not hard to find Creed after he sauntered out of Professor Figgins's classroom like it had been him who was balls deep inside Raven. He's waiting in the main entryway of the building, back pressed against the wall and his foot kicked up against it.

The entire show between Raven and Eldon was fucking spectacular. There's no other word for it. Watching her go from a ticking time bomb to a writhing bundle of need was something special.

The entire start of the class was a complete clusterfuck. Who even plans an ambush like that? Genie, of course. But what was she actually trying to achieve? I don't understand. I don't think I ever will, either. She's a fucking fool.

"Did I miss anything fun?" Creed muses as he falls

into step with us as we approach, and my eyebrows rise in surprise.

"Who died and made you funny?"

Eldon chuckles beside me and Raven smirks as her cheeks redden under Creed's gaze.

"I can be funny," he grumbles, shouldering past me to place himself next to Raven, and I glare at him.

Motherfucker.

"No, you can't. Don't bullshit the bullshitter." I nudge him with my shoulder as Raven giggles, making me relent.

Stepping out into the mid-afternoon sun, I'm ready to kick back, relax, and spend some much-needed downtime with my girl.

"Hey, I have to go and find my father, but I already know that a meeting has been confirmed for tonight. Ten o'clock. Do you want me to come get you guys or meet you at the steps again?" Leila casually asks like she didn't just spoil my nighttime plans. I may be able to spend some time with Raven, but now this will be hanging over our heads.

"Come get us. Or we can come to you? Don't go out there on your own. It's not safe," Raven answers, and Leila shrugs.

"I've done just fine so far," she muses. "But sure, I'll stop by your house twenty minutes before ten so we're not late. And don't worry, I'll mention the compound to my father too," she adds before heading off without a backward glance.

The five of us continue toward our house, but instead of our usual formation around Raven, we hunch together a little closer. The fact that Brax doesn't take off in front like usual instantly tells me there's something on his mind.

"Spit it out, big man," Raven sings, giving the gargoyle a pointed look.

"Are we trusting her now?"

Raven rubs her lips together in thought. "Honestly, I don't know. I'm not declaring myself a good person, and I definitely don't have all of the answers. I'm just taking her at face value right now. She hasn't done anything shady since revealing herself in the Guild and I can use all of the allies I can get. Especially when I have Sebastian and Genie making plays at me." I nod in understanding while Brax doesn't reply.

He's far more black and white and definitely more cutthroat. If it were his friend, Leila would have been cut off by now, potentially even dead. I'm surprised he hasn't invaded her mind, despite what Raven said.

"It sounds like a plan to me," Eldon states, and tension eases in Raven's shoulders.

"I hope so."

Silence blankets the five of us as we continue down the path, the crowd thinning out the further we go. The second the front door clicks shut behind us, I sigh in relief that we're cut off from the rest of the world. Even if it is just for a little while.

"What's the plan for the next couple of hours?" Raven asks, stepping further into the room before turning to face us.

"Seeing if my dick fits in your pussy as snug as a glove?" I offer, and she smirks, but Creed clears his throat, ruining my chances as he points toward the patio doors at the back of the house.

"I have a feeling the griffin out there has other ideas."

Following his line of sight, there is, indeed, a griffin staring expectantly at the house. Without missing a beat, Raven drops her backpack and rushes toward him. The rest of us slowly follow.

Having a familiar is a rarity that is to be cherished, and we're trying to give her the space to learn and grow with hers, but that doesn't mean I can't be pissed off that I have to share her with someone else.

When she came back on Friday, she was heartbroken, revealing a softness to her I hadn't seen before, and now she's determined to take on the weight of that burden. I get it, I do, but she's wearing herself thin.

Stepping outside with the others, I hold back, watching and listening to their one-sided conversation. I can't imagine what it's like to have Ari in her head like that, but watching her interact with him melts me. She's soft, gentle, and caring. Her walls are completely down since she can sense his emotions and I long for that level of connection with her.

A few moments pass before Ari takes off to the sky as Raven turns back to us.

"Is everything okay?" I ask, my brows furrowing as she folds her arms over her chest, almost hiding behind them.

"No. Apparently, the third years had Gauntlet practice today and they lost six of the minotaurs."

Until three days ago, that wouldn't have mattered to me, if I'm honest, but now, seeing the pain on her face angers me to no end.

"Maybe you and Ari could show us the compound this week? And if we don't really get any information from Fitch, we could always try Lyra or something," I offer, thinking out loud and hoping something will stick.

"Thank you," she whispers, stepping into my outstretched arms and burying her head into my chest.

If I hadn't vowed it before, I vow it now.

I will protect this woman at all costs. Always and forever.

Dressed in my favorite black cloak and golden mask, we trudge through the shadows of the academy grounds with Leila as our guide again. Even though we haven't seen so much as a glimpse of anyone, she still keeps us off the main pathways, just in case.

As much as we need to be a part of this damn Guild, I need some rest. The academy building grows closer and we're heading down the narrow steps in no time. The hum of chatter echoes around us as we make our way into the Lair, where everyone is waiting in black-on-black combat gear.

Leila guides us to a table in the far corner, where a neatly folded pile of clothes awaits each of us. Using our magic, we transition from our casual clothing to the black combat pants, long-sleeved black top, and lace-up black boots provided. To finish it all off, we're each provided with a black knitted hat.

"What's tonight about?" Raven asks, glancing at Leila, who shrugs in response.

"No clue. Nothing is ever really explained in advance. It's all about trust and being blindly guided through the craziness," she replies, waving her hand around.

"Fantastic." Raven sighs as she resecures her hair tie.

"I did manage to learn from my father that it's Professor Figgins who tends to the compound of magical beings. I know it's not much, but it's a positive, right?"

Raven smiles tightly. "Thank you. At least we know who to be looking out for." She doesn't mention that we're going to speak to Lyra as well, as we discussed earlier, but she accepts the help. I guess this is what keeping someone at arm's length looks like.

"Everyone, gather around." We follow Burton's voice to the center of the room where everyone else is waiting. Genie and Sebastian are whispering together on the other side of the group while the rest of the members focus on Burton. "If everyone can summon your swords, please."

His request surprises me, but I do it, just like everyone else. I frown down at the metal in my hands and it takes me a second to realize that the last time I had hold of this was the night of the Shadowmoor attack. It feels like a lifetime ago, yet as if no time has passed at all. It's bizarre.

"Do any of you guys find it weird that we haven't had these out in any of Figgins's classes since the night at the outpost?" Raven murmurs, frowning down at her blade, and my eyes widen at the realization.

"I think everything is weird these days," Eldon grumbles, making me smirk despite the circumstances.

"We could be reading too much into it," Creed offers, and Raven hums in agreement, but it doesn't ease the crease between her eyes.

"If you would like to follow me, we'll be combat training tonight," Burton orders as a gateway appears beside him. He steps through it first, leading the way.

"The mottos are confusing me as well," Raven murmurs as she stays close to my side.

"Which mottos?"

"What does Burton say after every gathering within the school?"

"Follow the sun, destroy the shadows, and survive another dawn."

"And what does the same man make us say when we enter the Nightmares Guild?" she pushes, and I take a second to recall what I said as we step through the gateway.

"Follow your heart, find solace in the shadows, and take down the dawn."

She nods in approval. "My mother whispered those exact words to me the day they forced me into the medical center and removed the magical barrier from me. I didn't understand it when she did, and if I'm honest, I don't understand them now, but it's odd to me that Burton leads the school with one motto while swearing us into the Guild with similar words that feel so different at the same time."

She has a point. I don't know the answer, and she knows that. She's just venting to me, but it still causes a stir in my chest.

Looking around at where we are, there's nothing but perfectly cut green grass for what feels like miles. Not a tree, shrub, house, or anything else in sight except for the moonlight glowing down upon us.

"Tonight, I want the fourth years to ensure they pair off with a younger member of the Guild. We're going to be doing the battle sequences that we discussed earlier," Burton states as the nearby fourth years nod in agreement.

"You, come with me," a girl murmurs to Raven, and my back instantly stiffens. Is this a ploy to get her away from us? I'm not the only one to think it, either. Brax, Creed, and Eldon all step forward as well.

"Hey, are you the girl who works at the uniform store?" Raven asks, completely oblivious to the concern rippling around her, and the girl nods.

"I remember you too. Raven, right?"

"Yeah. How long ago did you graduate?"

"Two years ago. I took the mundane job so I could commit myself to the Guild."

"Nice, what's your name again?"

"I don't usually give that out, for obvious reasons," the girl states, waving her arm around. "But it seems you're in the Guild now. So, I'm Florentine."

"Nice to officially meet you, Florentine. Are you about to whip my ass?"

"You better believe it."

Raven strolls off with her new-found friend while the four of us gape at her in confusion.

"If you fuckers are going to actually get some work

done tonight, I'll take one of you. Let's go."

I frown as I glance around to find the source behind the backhanded comment, only to see the guy who was dancing that night with Leila. Searching for the girl in question, she's already slipped off with a fourth-year girl, so I take the asshole's offer.

Spinning the handle of my blade, I follow after him as the others pair off, too. Once we've given ourselves a good amount of space, he spins to face me with his blade aimed in my direction.

"How are your blade skills?"

"Good," I confidently reply, and he smirks.

"We'll see about that, shall we?" He charges toward me without wasting another second, barely giving me a chance to defend myself, but I do, much to his disappointment.

Taking a step back, I plant my feet shoulder-width apart and tighten my grasp on my blade. This time, when he comes toward me, I'm ready and poised. The clang of metal on metal echoes around us as our swords clash over and over again. He's fast, but I'm faster, and as his face gets redder, his moves get sloppier.

I let him lead the movement, footwork and all, until he takes a bit too long lifting his blade and I thrust mine toward him instead. He deflects with a startled look in his eyes, his emotions clearly getting the better of him as he defends each blow. It doesn't take long for the tip of my sword to be pressed against his exposed neck, and he gulps, his Adam's apple working overtime as he glares at me.

"I thought you said you were good," he grunts, knocking my blade away with the side of his hand, and I let it drop to my side as we both take a couple of deep breaths.

"I am," I grunt, beads of sweat already dancing down my spine, and I can't deny that a zing of excitement goes along with it.

"No, that was phenomenal. I'm the best swordsman in the Guild. What's your name again?"

A hint of surprise touches the corner of my lips as I stare at him. "Zane, Zane Denver."

It's his turn to look shocked this time. "As in Monarch Denver?"

"That would be my father," I reply with a nod, which he mimics.

"I'm Grave. I have a family member who is a part of The Monarchy as well. Please tell me they put a blade in your hands from a young age, too, and it's not just some weird rite of passage for my family alone," he grumbles, making me smirk.

"That would be a correct assessment. It's your grandfather, right? Monarch Richardson."

His brows furrow. "How do you know that? I don't make it public knowledge."

"Which is exactly why I make it *my* knowledge," I retort. "No one who goes around bragging about their lineage to The Monarchy is worth shit, in my opinion. Although, someone who beds a girl and goes around bragging about *that* is also low on the totem pole." I don't care if we're besties with Leila or not. I don't want this guy thinking he's similar to me if he pulls stunts like that.

"Wait, what? When did I do that?" He scrubs the back of his neck, genuinely confused. At least he gets the hint that I'm referring to him.

"Leila Fitch."

"Wait, what? No, I didn't. How does anyone even know about that?"

My gaze narrows. "Maybe I misheard, but that's what it sounded like when she spoke of you after the party the other weekend. It seemed like everyone knew about it afterward."

"But all I did was dance with her. See? This is why I keep myself to myself and don't deal with other people's bullshit, man." The truth is in his eyes. He's completely bewildered with the drama spilling from my lips and now I feel like a fool.

"Ignore me, I clearly have no idea what I'm talking about." He takes the offer and we jump into another bout of attacks, taking turns on offense and defense. We push harder and longer with every pass, and it's true: I've met my match with him.

When we take another break, gulping down as much water as possible, I decide to ask a question that's been playing on my mind since we learned the Guild existed. "Can I ask you something?"

"Sure."

"Why is it called the Nightmares Guild? Like, why Nightmares?"

A dark smile grows across his face. "Because we're the Guild that gives the nightmare creatures of our realm and beyond *their* nightmares."

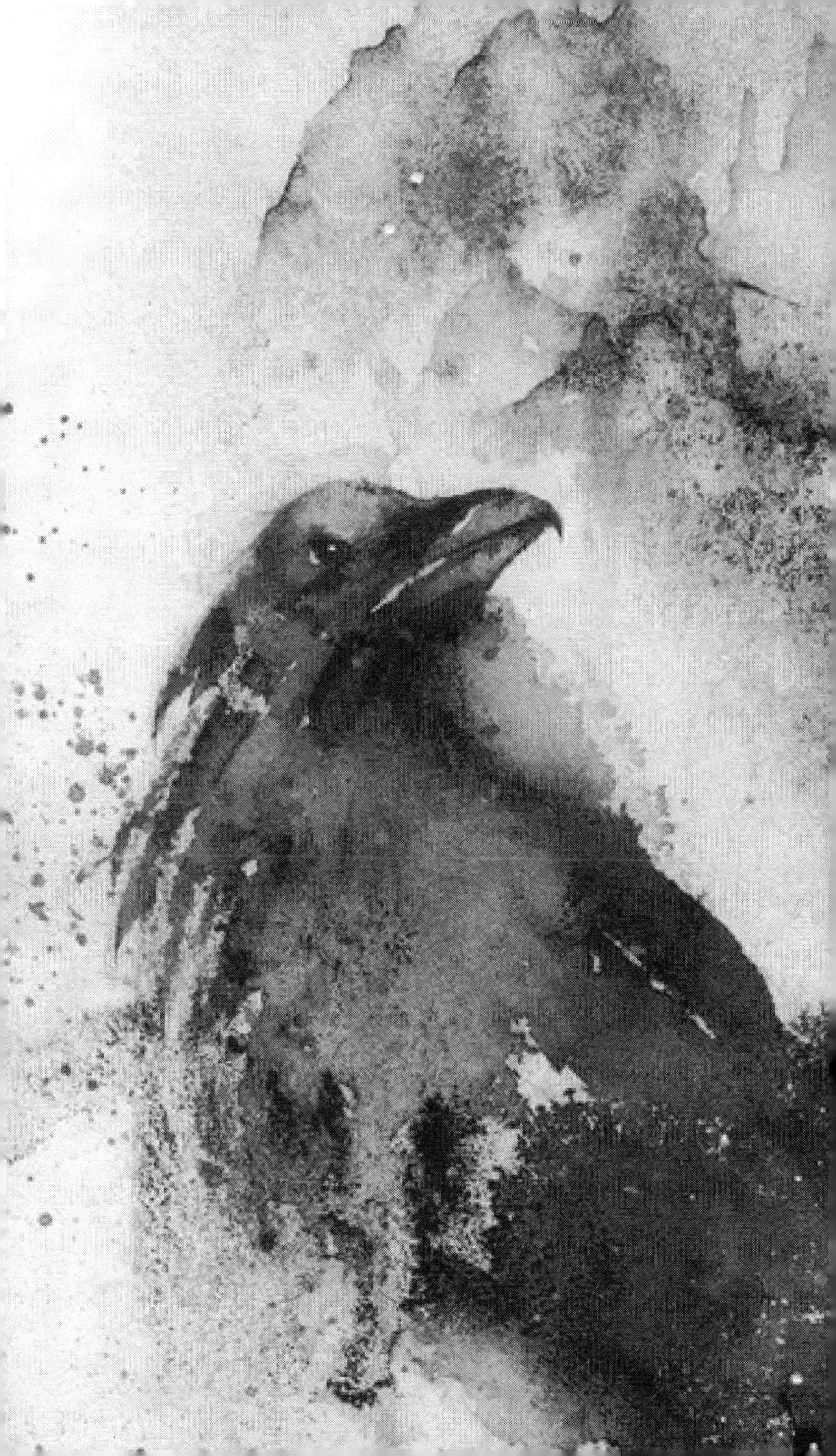

THIRTY

Raven

How, in this realm, is there no ability to magically make me feel any less tired? It's like that's all I am lately: tired, drained, exhausted. They all amount to the same thing and they're all completely unsolvable unless you're actually able to get uninterrupted sleep, which feels like a distant memory at this point.

The shadows occupying my room seem to have calmed, but now our nights are disrupted by the Nightmares Guild instead.

After last night's training, there was a promise of another session tonight and most nights going forward. One thing is clear, something is brewing on the horizon. If it's not, then they're scared of something, which is why the training seems to have been kicked up a notch or two for the foreseeable future.

Whatever has them shaking things up is lost on us. We're never privy to that information, but we're training for it regardless. At least I made a connection last night with Florentine. She's now the closest thing I have to an ally in the Guild, other than the Bishops and Leila, of course.

The fact that she gave up any further future within the realm to dedicate herself to the Guild is a telling sign that she truly believes in the cause. I wasn't the only one to gain another friend in there either. Grave, Zane's partner, was all handshakes and high-fives when we were done, and Zane seemed to like him well enough.

Brax didn't mention the guy he worked with, but that's not a surprise. Neither did Creed, but Eldon said the fourth year he paired off with was focused and determined yet easy-going when they broke off.

I never thought I would be actively seeking allies, but it's clear we really don't know what is around the corner, and the more people we have on our side instead of against us is vital.

With my hair braided down my back, I've changed out of my uniform and into a pair of leggings with an emerald-green sweater and my newly-acquired combat boots issued by the Guild. Stepping out into the lounge, I pause when my gaze settles on my men who are waiting for me.

Brax is sitting the farthest away, wearing gray sweats

and a plain white tee all casual, with his usual brooding face on. Eldon is beside him, leaning back in his seat in a pair of dark denim jeans and a black hoodie. Creed is on the sofa, facing them in a black tracksuit that only seems to make his eyes darker, while Zane is sitting beside him in a pair of gray shorts and a matching sweatshirt.

We're all going to the same place, and how we dress for the situation is so different it's almost amusing. What matters more than anything is the fact that they're sitting here waiting for me, just like they said they would.

My chest clenches. Whenever they've said they'll show up, they've done so. Any promise they've made, they've kept it. Any emotion I've felt, no matter how deeply, they've validated it. Time and time again, they're speaking with actions and not just words, and as much as I like to put my walls up and hide from the world behind them, they've made it impossible for me to hide from them.

Clearing my throat, four sets of eyes spin my way. "I appreciate you guys. You know that, right?" I twiddle my thumbs nervously as their startled expressions shift to knitted brows and hints of confusion.

"Where's that coming from?" Eldon asks, scratching his jaw as he continues to stare me down.

I shrug. "I feel like I showed up here and flipped everything on its head with my drama, and you just seem to be rolling with the punches like it's no issue. I just wanted you to know that I see it, too, everything you're doing for me, and I appreciate it." I'm almost wishing I had kept my mouth shut as my cheeks heat under their attention.

"It's a good thing you're worth it then, isn't it?" Zane states with a smirk as he pushes up to his feet and saunters toward me. I roll my eyes but it falls flat as he envelops me in his arms and squeezes me tight.

My eyes drift closed as I hug him back just as tight before he slowly takes a step back.

"So, without Ari, how are we getting to the compound?" Creed asks as Zane grabs my hand and pulls me toward the sofas. He doesn't sit us down, though. He's just as eager to get out of here as the rest of us. But it's not going to be as easy as it was the last time I went to the compound since it was just me and Ari, and there's no way in hell all five of us would fit on the back of him.

"It will be easier if Brax makes a gateway for us," I state, and he instantly shakes his head before I can continue.

"I haven't been, so I wouldn't know where to go."

"I know, so I can either get Ari to take the both of us so you can create a gateway back this way or…" My words trail off, nerves getting the better of me.

"Or…" He cocks a brow at me as I turn my whole body his way, taking a deep breath before I blurt out the alternative.

"You can take the image from my thoughts."

Silence echoes around the room at my words, stretching into uncertain territory as his brows furrow, and I'm ready to retract the option.

"You want me to go into your mind?" he clarifies, and I offer a nervous smile.

"I trust you." The words warm my chest, confirming now more than ever that I mean every one of them. When I first arrived and he threatened to invade my thoughts without my permission, the mere thought left me feeling violated, but now, this is my choice, my offer. It feels entirely different.

It's funny what a little thing like consent can do to a situation to make it feel like a good idea.

"There will be nothing for you to trust," Brax advises as he stands, prowling toward me with slow, measured steps. "If you think of just that in your mind, I swear to leave everything else untouched."

A shiver runs down my spine as he comes to a stop in front of me. Wow. Could it really be so simple for him to delve deeper into my thoughts? I meant what I said, though. I trust him in my mind, and even more so to only see what he needs.

He steps closer and I can feel the eyes of the rest of my men watching our every move. He lifts his hand to stroke under my chin, a simple touch that calms me without even trying. From there, he trails his fingertips up my cheek before settling them at my temples.

My eyes close of their own accord and the vivid picture of the compound comes to mind. I see everything. The tree line, the imprisoned creatures, the shrubs, all of it. I can feel him in my mind, weirdly similar to a soft caress, and I bite back a groan. No one mentioned it was going to feel… good.

"What are you doing?" he mumbles as he presses his forehead against mine.

"I don't know what you mean."

"I'm supposed to find the image waiting, but it's like you're projecting it directly into *my* mind." He leans back and I blink open my eyes.

"I'm sorry?" It feels like a question because I don't really know what I did, but I also can't sense if he's mad or not. If I did something wrong, there was no intention to it.

"Don't be sorry, Shadow. That's just never happened before." Frown lines mar the skin between his eyes. One brown. One green. Both staring inquisitively at my soul through my own blue pools.

"You're still making me feel like I should apologize again," I mumble, and he shakes his head.

"I know exactly what I'm envisioning, so we got the task done, but could you see if you could give the image to Eldon as well?"

"Why?"

"It could be a magical ability, Raven." His voice softens as I meet his gaze and I nod. I'm so confused by every little thing that I didn't even consider that to be an option. Eldon steps up to my side a moment later, a gentle smile on his face as he approaches. "Place your hands on her temples like I did, Eldon," Brax orders, and he does just that.

Closing my eyes, I picture the compound in my mind, exactly like I did last time, but after a few minutes pass, Eldon drops his hands and takes a step back.

"I'm getting nothing," he admits, and I peer up at him, a hint of disappointment casting over me. Of course, finding another magical ability wouldn't be so easy.

"I'm sorry," I breathe, before hands squeeze my sides and lift me off the ground.

"Let's go before she apologizes us all to death," Zane says with a snicker, and the others laugh too. This time, I roll my eyes and mean it. Asshole. He places me down on my feet, tilting my head back to look into my eyes with a smirk plastered to his lips. "Shake your funk off, Dove. We've got this. Some things just take time."

I sigh, letting the stress I'm putting on myself melt away. I mouth my thanks to him and he winks before steering us toward the gateway Brax has now created.

Creed steps through first, followed by Eldon, and I sneak through next, Zane and Brax right behind me. My eyes widen in surprise when I realize Brax has brought us to the same spot I was standing in the last time. It's as if he's placed us exactly where my memory showed him I was.

The compound is as I left it and my familiar is where he said he would be. I can see him off to the left, close to the barrier.

"It doesn't look like a cage," Zane states as we head toward Ari, and I nod.

"I can't decide if that makes it better or worse, but it's a prison to them all the same. They're basically being kept as cattle for the students to slaughter," I grumble. I'm sure they're sick of me repeating myself, but it's hard not to when I can feel Ari's pain and heartache over the situation. Especially with Gia inside.

I run the remaining steps toward Ari, burying my face in his feathers as I stroke a hand down his chest without a single word passing between us first. His head dips down as usual and I take a deep breath, settling my heart rate with his.

"Anything new?" I ask, and he shakes his head as I take a step back. I can sense an almost awkwardness between the Bishops and my familiar, but I don't really know how to rectify it. Ari can't speak to them like he can to me, so the instant inability to communicate doesn't help.

"Who's that over there?" Creed asks, and I frown as I follow his line of sight to see two members of staff from the academy step through the barrier over by the forest.

"They're the staff that come to do checks on everyone every few days," Ari explains, and I reiterate the information to the others.

"Is it just those that can enter or people in general?" Eldon adds, looking at Ari for the answer.

"People can come and go as they wish." I relay the message again, and Brax frowns.

"How can the barrier tell the difference?" he queries, and Ari sighs.

"I'm not sure. I've always seen people come and go without pause."

When I repeat my familiar's words, Zane shakes his head. "I'm not sure I trust him on that. I'm worried if you go in there, you won't be able to get out, Raven."

"I trust him, Zane. I feel him in here," I explain, pressing my hand to my chest.

"I can go in first and check," Eldon offers, and before I can refuse, he does exactly as he says, stepping through into the compound without resistance.

"If you're going to have feelings for all of them, can I choose favorites?" Ari asks, making me chuckle, but I don't respond as I watch Eldon step back out of the compound with no issues. I sigh with relief. *"If so, he's definitely my number one right now."* I roll my eyes at Ari and Creed cocks a brow at me but I wave him off. We've

got more important things to focus on than Ari's favorite Bishop of the day.

"So we're going in there?" Zane asks, pointing at the compound, and I nod.

"Yeah, I want to see it for myself, see the conditions we're dealing with."

"When you get in there, touch Gia. She will know we are connected, as she and I are. She will help you," Ari explains, but my nose wrinkles with uncertainty. *"Trust me. You have an hour. If you're not out by then, I'll come find you myself."*

"You can't come and find us. If you do, you'll be trapped in the compound again," I state.

"What's he saying?" Brax glances between Ari and me.

"He's saying we have an hour to get in and out; otherwise, he'll come in looking for me, even though it will confine him to the compound." I give my griffin a pointed look but he simply blinks at me in response.

"Good. That's what a familiar is supposed to be. An extension of you, uncaring of the consequences to keep you safe, just as you are doing for his loved one and the rest of his pride." Brax has a point there, but I don't state it.

"Maybe I can have two favorites today."

I flip Ari off, not dealing with his smart mouth as I turn for the barrier.

"Let's go."

"Be safe."
"What else am I going to be?"
"I heard that."

I spin to face him, eyes wide and jaw slack as my heart races. I can feel my men watching me, but none of them interrupt the weird stare-off I've got going on with Ari. After a few moments, the tall and proud griffin nods at me and I do the same before stepping into the compound.

The magic tingles over me from head to toe, making me quake for a beat before it simmers down. The sun feels dimmer, the breeze gustier, and the grass damper beneath my boots.

"Where to?" Creed asks, glancing around at the trees and natural setting that surrounds us.

"I don't know. I don't want to piss anyone off, I just want to look around. Let's start that way."

Brax slips past me to take the lead as usual, and it's Zane who takes the tail position while Creed and Eldon flank my sides. I'm careful with every step I take. Branches, fallen tree trunks, and protruding roots create an obstacle course around us.

A growl in the distance makes us pause and I turn to the left to see three minotaurs gathered behind a fallen tree. They don't look happy to see us, but when they don't immediately charge our way, I continue on and they, thankfully, leave us be.

The sound of water falling in the distance pricks my ears, along with giggles, and I consider whether to head in that direction or not, but the memory of the sirens from the Gauntlet has me heading in the opposite direction.

"Can you hear that?" Creed asks, pausing, and we all stop with him.

"Hear what?"

"It sounds like tiny wings," Creed explains, and I squint, looking around us as I try to hear what he's talking about. Just before I tell him he's full of shit, I hear a small fluttering, barely audible over the breeze.

"Look up," Eldon whispers, and I tilt my head back and gape in surprise.

Another magical creature from folklore and fairytales. Pixies line the branches of the huge tree we're under. They're not paying us any attention as they go about their lives.

Wow. Just wow.

"Let's keep going before Ari comes to hunt Raven down, otherwise we'll never hear the end of it," Brax breathes, and I take an extra second to admire their little wings as they flutter so fast they're barely visible.

Continuing around the brambles, a thud halts us once more. Slowly turning to our right, my eyes widen at the sight of at least a dozen griffins.

"Holy shit," Zane mutters, and I look over each of

them in search of someone special.

I know it's her instantly. I may have been at a distance last time, but her eyes are locked on mine as she takes two steps toward us. I'm moving toward her in the next breath, not stopping until I'm a few feet away.

"Raven," Brax warns, worrying for me, but I know I'm safe.

"It's her," I explain, like that's enough, and before I can do anything else, I watch in awe as she extends a claw forward and bows her head. A beat passes before the remaining griffins do the same, and my heart starts to pound in my chest.

"What's happening?" Zane asks, but I don't have the answer. Instead, I take the remaining steps to Gia and stroke a hand between her eyes, resting my palm at the small dip just before her beak.

"Ari has told me much about you."

I gasp at her soft and sultry voice in my head before I find my voice.

"I dread to think." A chuckle echoes in my mind as she peers up at me.

"Help us, Raven. We believe in you," she says with a hum, leaving me breathless. There's pain in her eyes, sorrow in her heart, and a helplessness draped over her like I've never felt before.

"I will try my best," I promise.

"And we will try our best for you."

"For me? That's not necessary," I insist, and she shakes her head.

"It will be. The darkness is coming."

THIRTY ONE
Creed

A dull ache runs through my body from top to bottom and I turn over onto my back with a sigh. Another night, another training exercise. Last night, the weapon of choice was the staff. It's almost impressive, the damage you can do with a wooden stick. But I guess that's the whole point, using anything and everything we can get our hands on.

It's the reasoning behind it all that continues to elude us.

There's something in the air. I can sense it and it leaves me dreading the thought of what the future holds. I'm not the only student at the academy with a parent whose life was lost in a battle for the greater good, but that doesn't stop the thought from weighing heavily on my shoulders.

Whatever may come, I have a reason to fight. A reason

to not give up, no matter what.

Raven.

I've always believed that everything happens for a reason. Even at a young age, my brain twisted the loss of my father into a reason to be strong, determined, and now, I know everything in my life was meant to prepare me for this crazy ass woman who consumes me.

I'll do anything and everything in my power, including investigating a compound no one else on campus seems to care about. Raven does, though, and that's all that matters.

Laughter echoes from the lounge, the high-pitched melody from Raven has me shaking the covers off and rushing to get ready so I can join them. We've been passing on workouts some mornings if our nighttime activities with the Guild have been enough, but it's still not like me to be one of the last up.

Showering, I get my uniform and shoes on. I'm fixing my tie as I step out of my room into the lounge to find Raven and Zane at the dining table, chuckling amongst themselves. I have no idea what he said to make her smile like that, but the contentment on her face as he leans close and presses a soft kiss to the corner of her mouth warms my heart.

She's lowering her walls and letting us in a little deeper every day, and it only solidifies that this was all supposed to happen. We've all felt loss, hope, and now love. It will overcome everything.

Heading toward them, Eldon and Brax also appear from their bedrooms, but that doesn't stop Zane from claiming Raven all for himself, pulling her into his lap as the rest of us take our seats.

"Hey," Raven murmurs with a smile, glancing at the three of us, and I grin back.

"Good morning, Raven."

"Are you ready?" she asks, looking over her shoulder at Zane as if waiting for his approval, and when he nods, she focuses back on the table. A moment later, plates of food appear in front of Brax, Eldon, and me. Each is filled with eggs, bacon, and pancakes.

"You even got the plate this time. What a queen you are, Little Bird. Thank you," Eldon says with a snicker, and she sticks her tongue out at him.

"What has you in such a good mood?" Brax asks, digging into the food on his plate, and I follow suit.

"Nothing, I just actually slept for a change. I'm revitalized and ready for the day." She's practically bouncing in Zane's lap. Whatever she did, it's definitely given her the energy she's been lacking.

"Do you still want to go and find Lyra today? See if she can give us some information on the compound?" Zane asks, murmuring against her ear, and she eagerly nods.

"Please."

Fuck, she doesn't even have to say please. We'll follow her to the ends of the realm and let it burn if she asks.

All too quickly, the table is filled with empty plates and it's time to leave. Grabbing my backpack, we meet at the door and step outside into the gray and abysmal weather.

We make it to the end of our pathway before Raven pauses, tilting her head back to look at the sky. "Does the sky seem weird to you?"

I try to give it the same level of attention as she is. It's not raining, and the sky isn't completely filled with dark clouds... it's just really dark. To the point that I'm considering rechecking the time to make sure we're not early.

"I see what you mean," I murmur, but there's no real explanation for it. Raven's lips twist as she closes her eyes.

"My skin feels tingly, the air static-y, and it's almost like there's a strange taste on my tongue or something."

I frown, but it's Zane who speaks before I can.

"What does that mean, Dove?"

Her eyes blink open and she slowly lowers her head to glance at us. "I don't know, but my spine is stiff and the hairs on the back of my neck aren't happy," she explains, but it still doesn't make much sense. "Don't worry about it. Let's keep going before we're late."

Brax takes the lead and we join the students already on the main path heading to the academy building. It's deathly quiet. There's no murmuring among friends, no gossiping. Nothing. It really does feel like the weirdest and most solemn morning we've had for as long as I can remember.

As we near the double doors, there are three professors waiting for us and a heavy feeling settles in my gut. Since I'm holding position at the back of the group, I take an extra step closer to Raven as Professor Figgins speaks. "There's a gathering this morning. Everyone make your way to the courtyard, immediately," she declares, and Raven glances back over her shoulder to stare at me with wide eyes.

I have no answer for her, but a moment later, Leila appears inside the hallway, hollering Raven's name.

"What's going on?" Raven asks, falling into step with her somewhat friend.

"I don't know, my father mentioned there was an announcement but he didn't look happy. If anything, he was maybe a little… worried. I don't think I've ever seen him look so lost, not even when he was worried about me in the Gauntlet," she admits. Even I remember the sternness of his face and the tightness in his jaw as he worried for his daughter in the build-up to the third years taking to the pit. Nevermind when she was actually in there.

"Do you think the sky looks weird today?" Raven asks as we follow the crowd moving toward the courtyard, and Leila frowns.

"I mean, it does seem dark…" she admits, and Raven

nods reluctantly. Whatever she's sensing, I don't think the rest of us are feeling it.

Entering the courtyard, it's a surprise to see Burton there already waiting. It's not even a projection of him like it usually is. He's here in the flesh. "Why does that feel like a bad omen?" I mumble to Eldon as we come to a stop in the middle of the mass of students.

"I didn't think that was possible, but I know what you mean," he retorts.

Pursing my lips, I look over the group of men that seem to be standing with Burton , but they've all got their backs turned to us. One of them stands taller than the others, a fur cloak lining his shoulders drapes down to the floor, and it looks like there's a crown on his head, but I can't be sure. The others are dressed in black with brown satchels over their shoulders and scabbards at their waist. It's like they're dressed for battle, but if that was the case, they wouldn't be standing here so casually… would they?

They look completely out of place beside Burton in his usual pristine suit and slicked-back hair. The only noticeable thing different about him is how stiff his shoulders are. He turns to address us, a mask of calmness washing over his features from head to toe as he speaks.

"Good morning, students. We have an unexpected visitor today, but a fabulous one at that." The way the corner of his mouth twitches as he smiles tells me he's lying. "I would like to introduce you to Erikel. He's visiting from the Basilica Realm."

Nobody gasps, nobody startles, nobody panics. Because nobody but the fucking Guild knows what the Basilica Realm is. Why the hell is there a man from south of the wall here? The mere mention of the place has the memory of the flickering flames and burning lava flashing through my mind.

My gaze flickers to Brax, the only one of my brothers I can see without drawing attention to myself, and his facial expression looks as pissed off as ever. But when I spot Grave past him, I instantly spot the tension in his jaw.

Yep. I definitely heard Burton correctly. What the fuck is going on?

"Professor Burton, you humble me," the man states, his voice low and nasally as he spins to face us, sweeping his arms out wide in a grand gesture. "It's Erikel, King of the Basilica Realm. I'll also take the title of ruler as well, even Your Majesty, Your Eminence, Your Highness, whatever suits." A smile spreads across his face, mostly hidden by the facial hair covering his cheeks and chin. A scar mars the skin down his left eye. It looks angry from here, hot and rigid, yet it also looks older than time.

"I do not like this man," Raven whispers from her spot in front of me, and I place my hand on the small of her back, silently trying to comfort her.

"Of course, King Erikel," Burton corrects as he clasps his hands together. "Erikel arrived this morning with some students from their elite academy, Shadowgrim Institute. It is noted in our original guidelines from when Silvercrest Academy was first opened that we welcome one and all." The last part feels like it's being said through gritted teeth, but if Erikel notices it, he doesn't act as though he does. "With that in mind, Erikel and his students will be here for the remainder of the week, looking at how our academy operates and how our students achieve greatness."

At the mention of Shadowgrim Institute, the six men turn around in their black uniforms with sullen looks on their faces. I can feel the tension increase around me as they look out over the crowd, but again, it's only the Guild who seem to be having this kind of negative reaction. Everyone else simply seems intrigued by the new arrivals.

Were we this naïve and unaware a few weeks ago when we still didn't know the Guild existed?

Fuck.

"You may see some of the students in your classes. Please, ensure you aid them where necessary. We want them to feel as welcome as possible. Additionally, we have decided to host a farewell ball on Friday evening. As it's been so long since we've had visitors from another realm, it's only fitting that we mark the occasion. I hope you all agree, as all your families will be in attendance, along with

The Monarchy."

My teeth sink into my tongue, trying to keep my mouth shut before I call out this bullshit. I'm usually the quiet and observant one. If I'm struggling, I can't imagine how Zane and Raven are holding it together.

"Now, enjoy the rest of your day and follow the sun, destroy the shadows, and survive another dawn."

For the first time since I arrived at Silvercrest Academy, I repeat those exact words along with my brothers, Raven, and every other student in attendance.

"Follow the sun, destroy the shadows, and survive another dawn."

"I wasn't sure if the training would still go ahead," I admit as Grave greets us through the gateway. Today has been completely fucked up and I genuinely expected it to impact tonight's meet-up, but the way he shakes his head tells me I'm wrong.

"Are you serious? We need it now more than ever," he states, increasing the thrum of adrenaline coursing through me. He shakes my hand before moving down the line of my brothers and pausing at Raven. "Am I allowed to shake her hand, or will I wind up losing it?" He's peering at Brax more than anyone, making Raven chuckle as she takes his hand before any of us can respond.

"I'm standing right here, Grave. You can ask me yourself." She gives him a pointed look and he shrugs.

"I know, I'm just covering my back with these crazy fuckers. Especially since I've seen how this one handles a sword." He points at Zane, who grins with pride.

"What the fuck is this all about with Erikel?" Brax asks, redirecting the conversation, and a gloomy expression passes over Grave's face.

"We all have a lot of questions, and we're desperate for the answers, but the truth is, there's little anyone knows. I would give my left nut to know why we are just letting someone from the Basilica Realm into our academy. How did they even get here without being slaughtered for trespassing?"

I nod eagerly, completely in agreement with his line of thinking, but before I can respond, someone clears their throat from behind me. Peering over my shoulder, I find Professor Fitch with Leila at his side.

"As Burton mentioned, Erikel appeared with dated documents for the academy, forcing himself in with loopholes. If we knew his intentions, we would share them, but as it stands, we must remain vigilant and ready to act at any given moment." Fitch glares at every member of the Guild who has gathered around us to hear him speak. He seems to dismiss us, but before he can get two steps away, it's Leila who questions him further.

"Couldn't we have said no? Who did he first approach to be let in? None of this makes sense. Now we have to mingle with some guys from another academy, completely unaware if they are gifted or not." The moonlight reveals her reddening cheeks, clearly worried about questioning her father in front of everyone, but to my surprise, he doesn't raise his voice or get angry. He just shrugs.

"That's the thing, he was already in. Stepped through the fucking double doors of the academy like there's not a magical forcefield around the place." Fuck. How is that even possible? "Now, let's get on with what we came here to do, shall we?" This time when he turns to leave, no one stops him. "We'll be working on defensive magic tonight," he explains, turning back to us when he's a good distance away from the gateway. "You all know how to attack, but the ability to block and defend is just as paramount. It can be used as simply as mundane tasks can be done. Pair off with the fourth years; let's get you up to speed and fast."

The same fourth year, Dalton, who I worked with the other day, waves me over, and I accept his offer. He works quietly, my kind of guy. He doesn't fuck around either, getting right to it. "What you want to envision is almost like a bubble or a shield that you can change the size and shape of. Focus on protecting you or whatever else might be important to you and it should start to form. Let's get the basics of it knocked out first, then we can start trying to put it to use between us."

I hold my hands out in front of me, just as he does, envisioning a bubble-like structure as I think about protecting myself. It's frustrating at first, with very little showing, but I try to push through it.

"Are you thinking about what you would protect above all else in the realm?" Dalton asks, and I shake my head. "Maybe focus on that instead. That's what works for me."

I nod, shaking out my arms as I sigh, hoping to rid any tension from my limbs as I focus on what I would need to protect Raven. My eyelids fall closed and I instantly sense the magic between my palms. I peer through my lashes to find exactly what he had instructed me to envision.

"That's it. Now drop it and go again. We want you to be able to produce it on demand." I repeat the process over and over again until I'm almost doing it as quickly as him. "Perfect. Let's start trying it with each other. Actual attacks can always help increase your speed too."

He directs us out to a less crowded spot, but I make sure to check on Raven and the guys and I'm relieved to see them managing it too. Raven grins every time, pleased with herself, and it warms my little black heart.

Turning away from them, I focus on Dolby, preparing myself for the attack I know is coming. "I have ice magic. Do you have physical magic or do you need to use a weapon for this part?"

"I can summon my sword," I offer, not actually disclosing my magic to him, and he waves me off.

"Let's work on you blocking a few times first, then we can start alternating."

He warns me the first time that a blast of ice is coming and I just about manage to block him in time. The second time, he starts to count down from five, and by the fifth go, he hits me in the arm with ice because I couldn't get the magic to form quickly enough.

"Fuck," I grunt, irritated more than anything, as he looms above me with a hand out for me to take.

"You're not thinking about the important stuff again. Try not to focus on me. Focus on that," he offers as I roll my shoulder out, grunting in agreement.

Turning to face him head-on again, I pause, frowning when I can hear a commotion coming from across the field. Searching for the noise, I still when I see pink hair splayed out across the grass and realize that Raven is flat on her back.

"What the fuck?"

I'm moving before I even decide if I should intervene, but even if it was an accident, I'm about to lay someone the fuck out. As I near, I frown when I notice the fourth-year Raven had been working with is lying still on the floor.

As Raven rushes to her feet, it quickly becomes clear

that she's trapped between Sebastian and Genie. How the hell did that happen?

"Take the left, Creed, I'll take the right," Zane hollers, and I don't bother to look where he actually is. I can't take my gaze away from Raven. I just have to hope that means Brax and Eldon are coming at them, too, because these fuckers need to be stopped.

As I near Sebastian, he throws a huge gust of wind at Raven, knocking her straight back off her feet without pause, and I snarl. Focusing on him, I exhale, channeling my magic, and a beat later, he stills, hands dropping to his side as his chin slams against his chest.

It's one thing to prevent him from hurting her anymore. It's something else entirely to make sure he damn well pays for it. A gut-wrenching scream breaks from the fucker's lips as he drops to his knees, head in his hands, tugging at the strands of his hair as he writhes in pain.

"Creed," Brax hollers, and I almost consider ignoring him and finishing the fucker off, but if Raven needs me, I know that's more important. Leaving him in agony, I search for pink hair to find her hovering over Genie while Raven's fourth-year friend lays injured on the floor beside them.

"What did I miss?" I grumble, falling into step with Eldon as we hurry toward them. The entire practice has come to a halt as they watch the drama unfold. "Raven,"

I breathe when I'm within arms reach. I don't touch her, though. She's standing stock still, a wrinkle of confusion marking her forehead. "What happened?"

"I don't know. She used her magic to launch the rock at me," she explains, pointing down at the object beside Genie. "I touched it, Creed, and in the next breath, I was hurling it toward her." Her voice lowers with her admission so no one but me and Eldon can hear.

"What the hell is the meaning of all this? We shouldn't be attacking one another when there's a battle brewing on our fucking doorstep," Fitch snarls, looking from Genie to Raven and then the screaming ball of pain that is Sebastian. Reluctantly, I slip from his mind, and the noise stops, letting Fitch release a sigh of relief. "We're done for the night. Everyone go home," he grunts, stomping off without actually checking anyone. "Leila. Now."

Turning my full attention back to Raven, Brax and Zane step in closer to form a protective circle around our girl. "I don't know what any of this means," she murmurs, more focused on what she just did instead of why they attacked her. It's nothing new with them, I just didn't expect it to happen while we were training with the Guild.

Fuckers.

"So you touched her magic?" I ask, and she nods. "And when Brax tried to delve into your mind, you projected into his instead, right?"

"Yeah."

"That would explain why it didn't work with Eldon afterward," I surmise, thinking out loud.

"What would?" Raven asks, turning to me with furrowed eyebrows and concern flashing in her blue eyes.

"Mirror magic."

"Mirror magic?" Isn't that what Rhys mentioned…

"Yeah. I think you can replicate the magic of those around you."

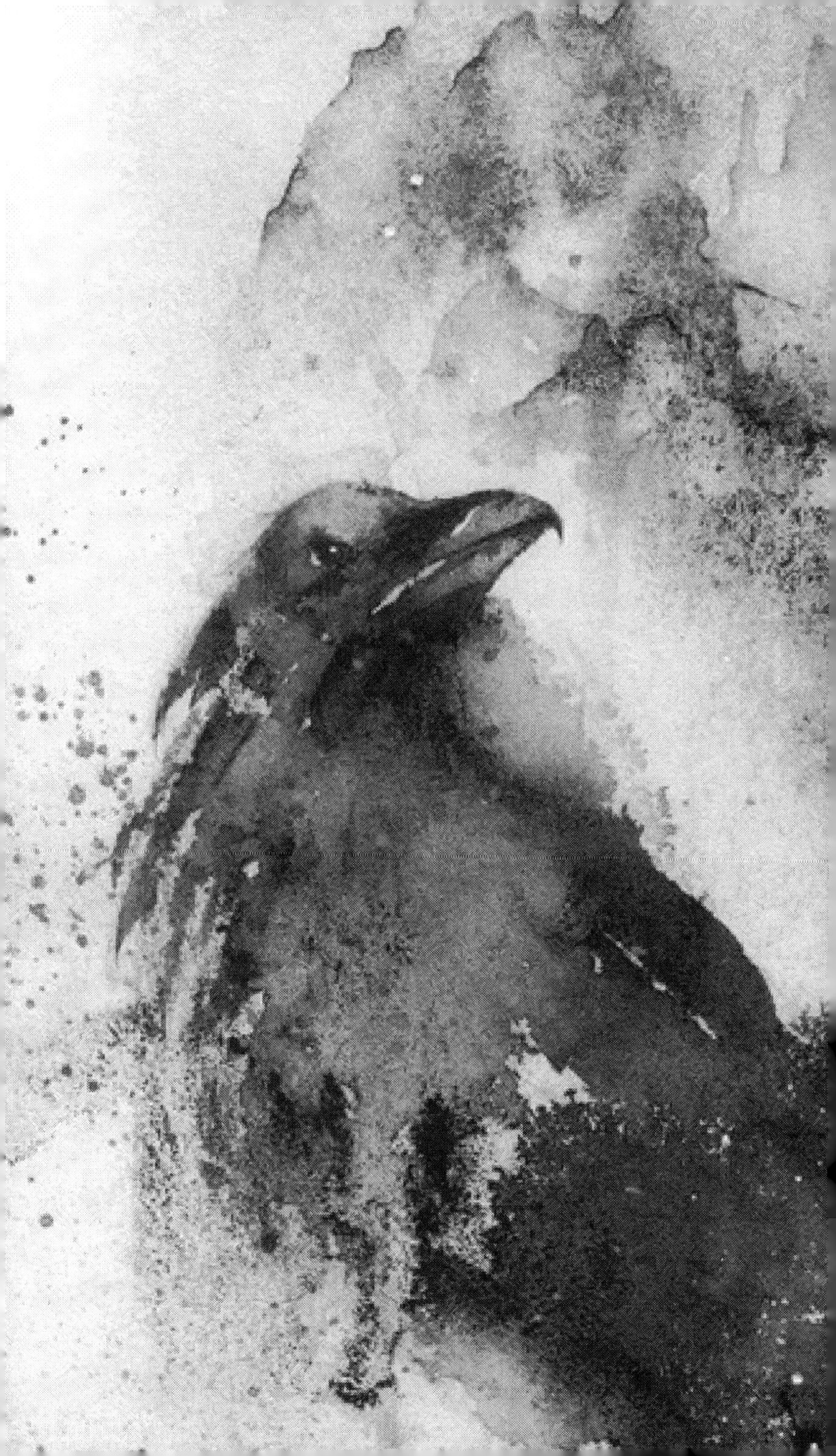

THIRTY TWO

Raven

Every morning, I wake up with something new on the agenda. Every morning, I wake up with a to-do list longer than the day before. Every morning, I wake up wondering what's next on the horizon. But above all else, I wake up every morning wanting my men more and more desperately than the day before.

After Creed mentioned mirror magic last night, we got home and I passed out in bed with Eldon. I don't even remember offering my lips for a goodnight kiss, I was just done. Lights out. But still, no shadows, so we're taking the wins where we can.

After classes are done today, the first thing on my to-do list is to play around with the idea of mirror magic to see if there's any truth to Creed's theory. Then we need to seek out Lyra to see if we can get any information about the compound, as well as going shopping for new freaking clothes for another ball I have no interest in attending for the departure of some guy I don't even care about. I just have to make it through classes first. Like that isn't exhausting all on its own. Then, I'll have the fantastic company that is my parents. The same parents who keep fucking me over.

Using my magic, I lazily put my uniform on before fixing my makeup and letting my hair fall in loose tendrils down my spine. No amount of magic can make the ache on your scalp go away from tying your hair too tight, so I'm going to have to deal with the irritation of it being around my face today.

I step into the lounge with my backpack slung over my shoulder to find my men patiently waiting. None of them are distracted, though. They're all leaning against the back of the sofa with their gazes fixed on where I'm standing. The way Zane's eyebrows have risen so high in surprise has me shuffling nervously from foot to foot.

"What's going on?" I blurt when I can't take it anymore.

"I don't know what you mean," Eldon states, rubbing at the back of his neck, and I roll my eyes.

"I *mean,* those looks on your faces." I wave my hands at them with a pointed glare and it's Creed who relents first.

"Well, we thought it might be a nice idea later, when

we go dress shopping, to get some food while we're out."

My eyes widen in surprise. Of all the things I thought he was going to say, that wasn't one of them. "Oh, okay."

"Like a date," Eldon clarifies, making my chest swell with a mixture of surprise and excitement.

"A date," I repeat like a damn fool as Brax pushes off the back of the sofa to take a step toward me.

"Yeah." He comes to a stop in front of me and I eagerly nod.

"Sounds good."

A smirk spreads across his face, replacing his usual scowl for a whole five seconds. "Perfect." He cups my chin, my next breath lodging in my throat. "Let's get these lessons over with for the day so we can get to the good stuff, yeah?" I fail to nod again as he presses his lips to mine in a deep kiss that has my toes curling in my academy-issued shoes.

All too quickly, he's gone, but the space he vacates is quickly replaced by Creed. He shakes his hair out of his eyes as he cups my opposite cheek, capturing my mouth in a sensual kiss that makes my temperature skyrocket. He pulls away far too soon, leaving me lightheaded as he smirks at me.

Eldon and Zane shove at each other to try and get to me next and I wind up sandwiched between them, Eldon at my front and Zane plastered to my back. Both of their lips pepper over my face and my hands clench the front of Eldon's blazer as a groan slips from my mouth.

"Okay, fuckers. Let's get going before we're late," Creed orders, but neither of them moves, making me pant between them. I'm ready to screw it all and stay here. I want to come apart in their grasp. Desperately.

"Soon, Dove," Zane whispers against my ear as if hearing my thoughts. His fingers flex at my waist, coiling the need inside of me even tighter before he disappears, Eldon too. Leaving me to helplessly and hopelessly gather myself, the promise of a date hanging in the air between us.

The sky is still dark outside, not a glimmer of sun peeking through the gloom, and it feels like a heavy weight pressing down on my shoulders. I can't shift the feeling it gives me and that just frustrates me more. Maybe I didn't realize how much I've come to rely on the sunshine to perk me up since I got here. The sky is a reminder of Shadowmoor and the thought of it twists my gut.

We've been lucky enough to avoid Erikel and his students all morning, but I know it's not going to last. I don't have good luck like that. I tend to get the, *yay, you're not dead yet* kind of luck. Awkward and uncomfortable situations follow me around like an omen or something.

"What are you thinking about?" Eldon nudges my shoulder with his as I take another bite of my lunch.

"Nothing specifically, just basking in the gloom," I admit, and he tuts.

"Nope, not on my watch. My little bird needs to keep her head clear. If we choose to let all of this shit weigh us down, we'll have no chance of surviving, nevermind succeeding." He cocks his brow and I roll my eyes at him.

I hate it when he's right. I hate it even more when he's smug about it. So, instead of responding, I stuff my mouth with the last forkful of risotto on my plate, but he already knows he's won.

"Are we going to see if we can catch Lyra now, before lunch ends?" Creed asks from across the table, and I nod, mentally ready to tick it off my list of shit to do today.

"Everything okay?" Leila asks, concern wrinkling her brows as she glances at me.

"Yeah, I just have some more questions about the compound and I'm hoping she might be able to offer some insight. Then, if not, the next person to speak to is Figgins. I just get the feeling she's going to be the hardest to speak to about it since she seems to run it."

"Good idea. Need me to come?" she offers, but before I can respond, her father calls her name with an air of urgency. Glancing around the room in a panic, I spot him by the double doors at the other end of the hall. I point him out to Leila and she quickly rises to her feet. "Nevermind, sorry," she murmurs, grabbing her backpack and racing toward him.

It's on the tip of my tongue to thank her for offering, but she's already gone.

"I wonder what that's about," Zane muses, turning back to face me, and I shrug.

"Since she didn't look worried, I'm going to leave her to it and not add anything else to my plate right now," I admit, and Zane nods in understanding.

"Good plan." I look at Brax, who is observing me over the rim of his glass, but he doesn't say anything else and neither do I. The second he places the glass on the table, the five of us stand without uttering a single word. Sometimes, it's weird how naturally in sync we are, but I think that's because I've never felt anything even remotely like this before.

Brax steps in front, marching through the dining hall like a man on a mission, and I rush to keep up with him, with Creed and Eldon at my side and Zane a step behind me. I scan the room, watching for Genie and any bullshit she may try to throw at me, but I don't see her. Or Sebastian, for that matter. Maybe they're off entertaining each other, but I quickly tamp down that thought as a sliver of bile threatens to fill my mouth.

The crowd of students in the hallway is small since most are still in the dining hall, and by the time we reach the main entrance, there's no one around at all. Let's hope that means Lyra isn't too busy.

I frown as I approach the door to her office, noting that it's sitting slightly ajar. I don't think I've ever seen it like that. It's always closed. I still raise my hand to knock, not wanting to show up to ask for a favor, only to piss her off before I even get started. But before my knuckles hit the wood, Brax catches my wrist. Turning my scowl his way, he shakes his head and taps his ear with his free hand.

Listen, he mouths, and I strain my ears to hear over my thundering heart as he slowly releases my hand.

"Excellent. This is exactly what we needed."

"Of course."

Two people are talking on the other side, two familiar voices, but neither of them belonging to Lyra. I think... is that...

"Sebastian," Creed whispers in my ear, adrenaline coursing through my veins. It is, but who is he speaking to?

"Everything is in place. The plan is foolproof. Now we must all play our parts, son, and the rest will fall exactly as it should." Son? But that doesn't sound like my father.

Glancing over my shoulder, I come face to face with Zane, who mouths the one word I was really hoping he wouldn't.

Erikel.

I should have fucking known my brother was up to no good. My hands clench at my sides and my nostrils flare with anger.

"And the other thing we discussed?" Sebastian asks, making me strain even more as I lean closer to the door.

"All set. I told you; get me in here and there will be endless power at your feet. I'm a man of my word."

My jaw goes slack with horror as the realization hits me hard. Sebastian. He let them in? How? And, more importantly, why? What is this all about?

"Good, but remember, my father mustn't know," Sebastian insists, eradicating the next question on my tongue. If Sebastian is involved with this man, then I was sure Abel would be too, but he can't be.

What the hell is Sebastian up to?

I'm ready to barge through the door and demand answers, but hands suddenly grab my waist and lift me off the floor. "Not now, Shadow. Not yet," Brax breathes, taking a step back from the door, then another, and another.

I want to fight him, kick and scream, demand he put me the fuck down, but deep down, I know he's right. Even if I don't want him to be.

Fuck.

He doesn't release me until we're around the corner, the presence of other students acting as a buffer for him as my feet touch the floor.

"Don't be mad at him, Dove." I glance at Zane and exhale heavily.

"I'm not mad at any of you guys, and I know Brax did the right thing." I swipe a hand down my face. "I'm mad that Sebastian would have the fucking audacity to do that. I'm mad that I don't have any answers for what he's doing or why, but most of all, I'm mad that I'm related to him. His blood runs through my veins, too, and it infuriates me." My chest harshly rises with every breath and I can't contain it.

Instead of going to Lyra to hopefully get some answers, I've ended up with more questions. This is the story of my fucking life.

A bell chimes in the distance and everyone starts moving around us, heading to their next class, and I reluctantly fall into step with them. I'm done with today.

Trudging to Fitch's class, I'm ready to be in my fitness clothes and training so I can burn off some of this excess energy, but to my surprise, when we get there, he's directing everyone into a classroom.

Leila is already in her spot and I take the seat beside her, dropping my bag to the floor with a thud.

"Any luck with Lyra?" she asks, and I shake my head.

"She wasn't there," I explain before pointing at the door. "How come we're in here today?"

She grimaces. "That's why my father called for me. He didn't want them to get a view of our training, so it's class work." She nods to the far left of the classroom and I turn with a frown, which deepens when Erikel and his students come into view.

Fuck. My. Life.

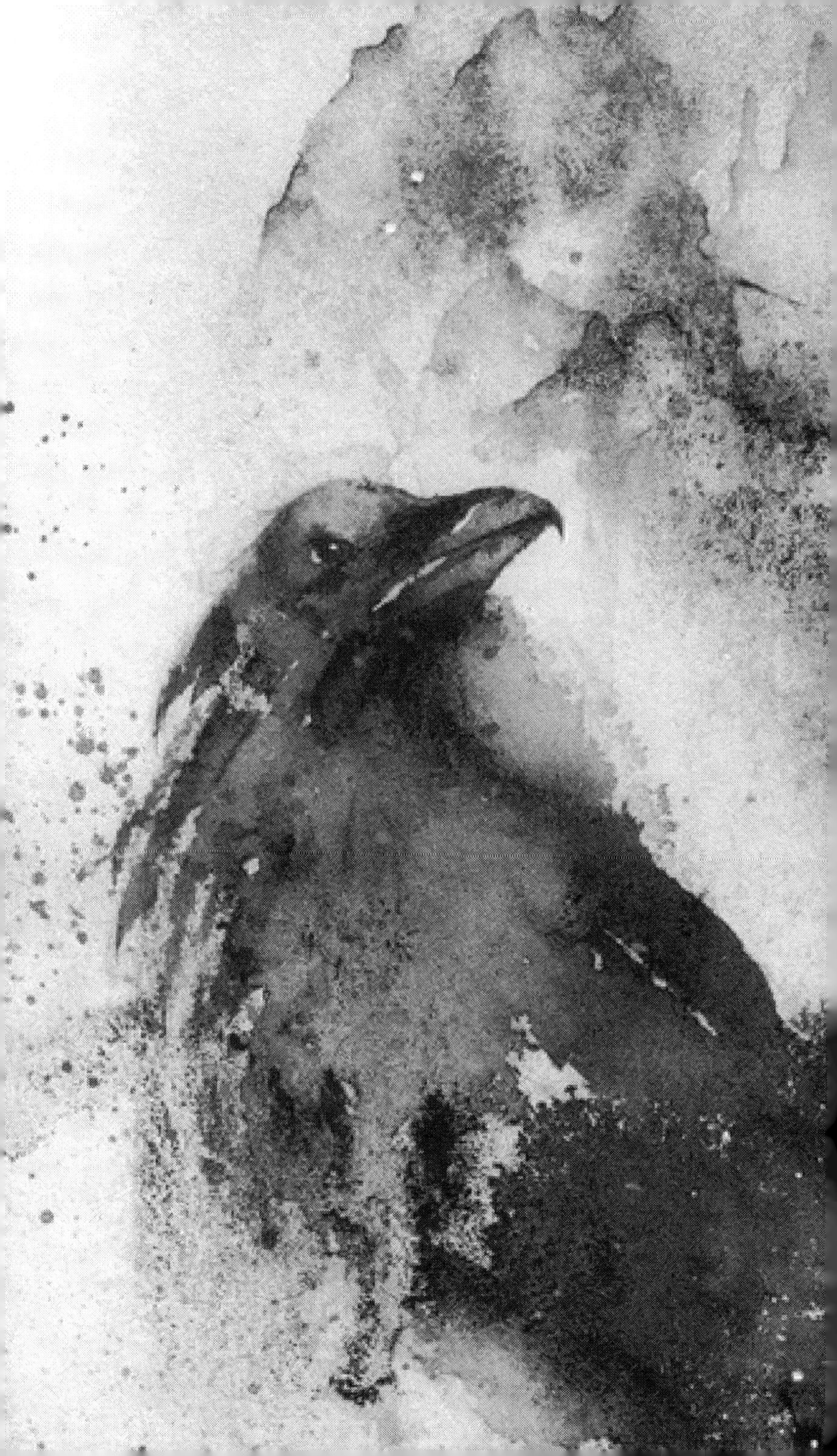

THIRTY THREE

Raven

I don't know why I didn't mention anything to Leila about Sebastian. I want to blame it on being completely distracted by the new attendees in our class, but deep down, I know I'm more wary of her than I want to admit.

Another attempt at crossing paths with Lyra comes up empty, and searching out Burton to talk about the Sebastian situation is even harder. Apparently, neither of them are on site, and that leaves a heavy weight on my chest. I don't really know what I'm supposed to do with this information or who I'm supposed to go to, but I can't handle it alone. It's bigger than me, than us, and I'm not going to pretend it isn't.

"I sent a message to my father so I can keep him in the loop about everything before he gets here for the ball. We've got this, Dove. Try not to let it weigh you down.

Let's take a timeout from all of the crazy, do some dress shopping, and eat some awesome food."

I sigh, leaning into his side as he drapes an arm around my shoulders. It really does sound like a good plan. We deserve a minute to just be us, and if that involves shopping for a dress for an event that I don't care about, then so be it.

"I never thought Zane would have such words of wisdom," Eldon muses with a snicker, but instead of reacting to his friend's words, Zane just holds me tighter.

It's quiet on the way to the store. We literally threw our backpacks in the house and headed straight out, staying in our uniforms to hopefully miss the crowds. The idea of a real date together leaves an extra bounce in my step, lifting my mood with little effort, despite the gloomy sky above.

"It was a good idea for Professor Fitch to move us inside to a classroom lesson while the Basilicas were watching," Eldon states, and I nod in agreement. Basilicas seems to be the name traveling around the academy and it's annoying to say it's actually sticking. Not that I care. It just makes them feel more... permanent.

"Agreed. Especially if they're only observing and not actually participating or showing their own abilities," Creed adds.

"Although, the fact that *we* also had to do book work was annoying as hell. I thought the class was never going to end," I grumble, and Zane hums in agreement. I'd rather be bored the entire time than give the Basilicas an advantage. In what, I don't know, but my gut clenches at the thought of it.

The silver and white sign of the dress shop catches my attention and pulls me from my thoughts. A shiver runs through me at the memory of the last time I was here with Creed and how he got me all worked up, only to leave me hanging.

The bell chimes above the door as we step inside and I'm instantly overwhelmed by the number of dresses on display. I don't think I recognize a single one from the last time I was here. I was planning on just grabbing one of the others I had tried on, but things must have been moved around because they're not where they were.

"Hi, how can I help you?" I recognize the assistant instantly and watch as her eyes widen as she looks from one Bishop to the next. Her cheeks are pink by the time she reaches Brax, and I'm long forgotten.

"Don't worry. We've got it from here," Zane insists, reaching for my hand and pulling me further into the store.

"Yeah, of course," she rambles, but I don't turn back to check on her as Zane starts pulling out dresses, waiting for me to accept or decline.

I laugh and roll my eyes at some of the ones he pulls out, some way more revealing than necessary, while others look like the kind of frilly things that even your grandma wouldn't be seen dead in.

Creed, Eldon, and Brax watch with amusement, happy to let Zane take control until we've got a solid four options to look at. Two black, one white, and the last a vivid pink one that I'm really not sure about but Zane insists I try.

"Let's try these babies on, shall we?" Zane says with a wink, placing his palm on the small of my back as he guides me toward the back of the store.

"Are we ready to—"

"We've got it from here. Maybe go take a break or something." Eldon states, interrupting the store assistant. If I weren't so turned on by the confidence in his tone, I would probably be embarrassed.

She offers nothing more than a nod in response, her cheeks as pink as they were earlier as she scurries off. Sometimes, I forget the attention the Bishops bring, the presence they have, and the confidence they ooze. I think I must be getting acclimated to them.

Zane walks me to the center of the same dressing room that I was in the last time I came with Creed and hangs the four dresses on the clothing rack. The second a few more chairs appear, matching the large one already in the corner of the room, I gulp.

Nope. Definitely not acclimated. Not one bit.

Nerves dance through me as they each get comfortable in their seats, eyes fixed on me as I stand frozen in place.

"Let's see which is your favorite, Little Bird." I shiver at Eldon's nickname for me as I nod, at a complete loss for words.

Taking a deep breath, I run my hands down the lapels of my blazer before taking it off and draping it over the clothing rack. I kick off my shoes and socks next before removing my skirt and blouse, leaving me in my bra and panties.

I can feel their eyes on me, penetrating every inch of exposed skin. Wetting my dry lips, I reach for the first dress, the white one, and as I organize the material on the floor so it's easy for me to step into, I feel hands at my waist, making me still.

"Let me help you, Dove."

Fuck.

Zane's hands graze over my thighs, leaving goosebumps in their wake, and I have to stifle a groan. When he offers to help, he doesn't mean with the fabric of the dress; he simply means holding my hips while I do it. I can feel the warmth from his body, but he doesn't stand close enough for the feel of his pants to brush against my skin.

He's teasing me, I know it, and I'm a fucking sucker for it.

Stepping into the dress, I rise back up to my full height, pulling the material along with me before slipping my arms into the straps. Zane's hands stay where they are, his thumb skimming over my skin as he leans in close to whisper in my ear.

"Let me zip you up."

They're not sexy words, not one bit, so why the hell do they heat the blood in my veins and leave me dizzy for him?

I'm screwed. This is going to be worse than when I came here with just Creed. He drove me insane as it was, and now, with all four of them here, I know I'm going to be a puddle of need by the time we're done.

He releases his hold on me and the only sound in the room is that of the zipper as he secures it in place. "Beautiful," he breathes, and I lift my gaze to look in the floor-length mirror. He's already watching me, his hands settling back on my waist as he finally steps in close enough for me to feel the thickness of his dick. "What do you guys think?" He tilts his head to look at the others, but I can't bring myself to move.

"Hot."

"Stunning."

"Ridiculously beautiful."

Damn. I wasn't prepared for the show of appreciation and compliments. I definitely don't know how to handle that.

"What do you think, Dove?"

"I think it's nice, and the loose straps are cute, but I

want to try that black one on," I murmur, barely able to hear my own words over the thunder of my heart in my ears.

It's a black, sheer material, with tiny rhinestones and crystals scattered across the chest, waist, and hips, covering the important parts, with a sweetheart neckline and no straps. It's probably more daring than I'm used to, but it looks gorgeous.

"Let's do it," he agrees, undoing the zipper for me before dragging the straps down my arms, his fingertips caressing my skin as he does, and a shiver runs down my spine.

When the material pools at my feet, he offers me a hand to step out before using his magic to place the white dress back on the rack. The black one is in his hands a moment later, and this time, he does the honor of laying the material out for me.

With my hand in his, I step into the material, but he grips my hips before I can dip down to get the fabric. Slowly, his fingers trail down my thighs, over my calves, and down to the black dress before he gathers it up and retraces his steps in the opposite direction, sweeping his fingers over my skin and up my body. There are tingles left in his wake and a new level of desperation thrumming through me, but I manage to restrain myself somehow. For now.

I hold the neckline in place once he's got it fully lifted so he can secure the zipper, and when I glance in the mirror, a thrill of excitement rushes through me. I already know I love this. Zane has the zipper halfway up when he pauses, glancing at me in the mirror with a thoughtful look on his face.

"What?"

"Take your bra off. See it without the straps." It's not a question, or even an order, but a beat later, he flicks the clasp and the straps of my bra fall loose on my shoulders.

"You just wanted to see my boobs," I mumble, pulling the material down my arms and tossing my bra aside while Zane grins at me.

"Guilty." He winks. It's playful, fun, but devilishly sexy and hits straight at my core. He pulls up the last of the zipper before taking a small step back to admire me in person instead of just my reflection. "Fuck, Dove. Just fuck."

I nibble my bottom lip as I spin slightly, trying to catch a glimpse of the dress from all angles. The rhinestones and crystals stop perfectly mid thigh, and the sweetheart neckline sits just right. It's a winner.

"That's got to be the one, Shadow."

My gaze cuts to Brax, who sits with his elbows braced on his knees and a deep frown on his face. If anyone else were to look at me like that I would worry they were mad, but not him. That's almost his happy face.

I softly nod, glancing at Eldon and Creed too, who are also eagerly nodding along.

"Yeah, this is the one I want." I gently run my fingers over the material as I look at myself in the mirror again and Zane steps closer, pressing himself to my back as his hands come around to my front, his fingers splaying across my stomach.

I can't take the building desire inside of me anymore. "What is it with you guys getting me hot and bothered in a dressing room? If this is some ploy to leave me wanton and desperate, then I'm not for it." My chest heaves with every breath, the rhinestones dancing under the light as Zane catches my eyes in the mirror. "The tension is too much. I can't do it again. You're going have to go and let me do this alone. I won't be long."

Zane shakes his head, but it's Eldon I hear.

"No, no, no, Little Bird." I turn back to him when he doesn't continue, and once our eyes meet, he smirks. "That's the whole idea."

"What?" I ask, still just as breathless, even though I got everything off my chest.

"I want you right now, Dove," Zane whispers against my ear. "We all do."

"But the assistant," I ramble, pointing to the curtained archway that leads back out to the main area.

"Wasn't an issue when you came here with Creed. Was she?" Brax retorts, a guttural rumble to his tone as my breath lodges in my throat. I glance at the man in question, a dark, predatory look flashing in his onyx eyes, and I know he lured them all here with a simple murmur of how insanely turned on he had me last time.

How do four men I haven't known for very long know what I need before I do?

He's got me there. They all have.

"Let's get this dress back on the hanger before we ruin it," Zane whispers against my skin, pressing gentle kisses over my shoulder blades, adding fuel to an already fiery inferno.

He uses his magic to place the dress back on its hanger, leaving me in only my panties as his palms run over my skin, up the valley between my breasts, and back down to tease at the waistline of the only fabric between us.

"It would be rude to be the only one naked," I murmur, arching my back as I reach my hands over my head to find his hair, tugging at the ends eagerly, and he nips at my skin.

"You're right, it would be," Eldon agrees, striding toward me without a single item of clothing on, and my jaw drops. He swipes a hand through his hair as he rakes his eyes over me. Combined with Zane's touch, I feel electric.

A second later, I feel the nudge of Zane's cock between my ass cheeks, but this time, there's not even his pants between us and I realize my panties are gone too.

This is happening. It's really fucking happening.

Eldon grabs my chin and crushes his lips to mine, making my eyelashes flutter closed as he consumes my mouth and my whole damn soul. My pulse pounds in my ears as I panic, trying to listen for the assistant. As much as a bit of voyeurism is my thing, there's a *real* chance she's going to come back here.

My nipples pebble, exhilaration rippling through me as a hand trails up my thigh. It can't be Zane; he's cupping the swell of my breasts, and it can't be Eldon either, because I'm wearing his hand as a necklace right now.

I blink open my eyes, but I can't see anything past the sight of Eldon and his mouth on mine. He breaks apart a moment later so I can look down just in time to see Creed swipe the tip of his tongue over my clit.

Holy. Fucking. Shit.

I sag in Zane's hold and his lips trail down my throat, kissing in between where Eldon's fingers are splayed out. I'm already about to explode, and their slow, sensual touches tell me they're far from done.

"Spread her legs for me, Zane," Creed murmurs, his lips brushing against my lips as he speaks, and the only warning I get is a snicker in my ear before I'm completely lifted off the ground. My hands drop from Zane's hair as I try to stop myself from falling, but it was never going to happen, not with Eldon right in front of me.

Zane's fingers dig into my thighs, holding me in the air, legs wide for Creed, and I catch a glimpse of myself in the mirror. Fuck. I'm mostly obscured by Eldon's back, but the desperate look of need on my face says it all. With Creed on his knees before me, that only leaves one of my men not close enough.

Brax.

Tilting my head to where he sat earlier, I find him exactly where I left him. Only now, he's as naked as the rest of us, lazily pumping at his cock as he watches us.

Damn.

As if sensing my gaze, he looks up from my breasts to meet my eyes. "I want you to come all over Creed's fingers. *Then*, I'll come play."

I hum in approval, completely bewildered by just how much I enjoy taking his order as Creed follows his demand, too, plunging two fingers deep into my core at the same time he sucks at my clit. I cry out, unable to mute the noise before it bursts from my lips, but I wouldn't take it back even if I could.

Clutching Eldon's shoulders, my next cries of ecstasy are captured as he takes my mouth again while Zane sucks at my neck.

I'm writhing between them so fast I'm burning up, sure I'm going to die when the orgasm swarming inside of me crescendos, shattering me into a million pieces. I can't breathe, I can't see, I can't hear. All I can do is feel the onslaught of my climax as Creed continues to feast on me until there's nothing left for me to give.

"Holy fuck," I rasp when Eldon releases my lips, a pleased grin on his face. One that is mirrored on Creed's and Brax's, too, as I look at them, and I manage to spot Zane's smirk in the mirror before he slowly lowers me to the floor on wobbly legs.

"Good little Shadow," Brax purrs as he saunters toward me. Without a word, Creed and Eldon move to the side just enough so there's a direct path for him to get to me. The second he's within arm's reach, he extends his hand out and cups my pussy.

"Fuck," I gasp, leaning back on Zane for support as my grumpy gargoyle grins down at me.

"Now this is mine." With his palm flat against my clit, he teases three fingers at my entrance, feeling just how wet I still am. The burning look in his eyes reveals just how pleased he is.

Zane's hands slip to the globes of my ass as he murmurs against my ear. "This is mine."

My eyes go wide, a spark of wild pleasure fluttering through me, but I shake my head as I brace my palms on Brax's chest. "Not here," I breathe, hating the words as I say them, but there is nowhere for us to fucking clean up.

It's going to be bad enough as it is.

"Don't worry, Shadow. You're forgetting we can take care of it all." I blink up at Brax, my jaw slack as I try to find another obstacle in our way, but the reality is, there isn't one.

I nod. One little signal and the four of them are moving all at once. My feet are swept from under me and a second later, I find myself kneeling over Brax with my knees braced on either side of his waist. There's no time to prepare as he thrusts his cock deep into my core and I scream out with pleasure.

My body heats, likely leaving my skin covered in an array of pinks and reds from the pleasure as I watch both Creed and Eldon tug on their dicks in front of me. Brax's hands grip my waist while Zane spreads my ass wide and swipes his tongue along the hole he's been so eager to claim.

"Taste them, Shadow," Brax grinds out, his jaw tense and his eyes dilated.

Desperate to do just that, I brace my hands on his chest and roll out my tongue with my eyes flickering between them. Eldon moves first, nudging his cock against my lips, and I suck on his tip at the same time Zane teases a finger at my ass, stretching me. I feel so full already, and I know it's only going to get even more consuming when he's really inside me.

Relaxing my body between Brax and Zane, I focus my energy on sucking between Creed and Eldon, propping myself up on Brax's chest with one hand so I can grip whoever I'm not sucking as I interchange back and forth.

I freeze when Zane uses two fingers to scissor me wider, which makes Brax buck up into me instead of waiting for me to grind down on him, and I see stars. I need to feel all of them. I want them to fucking paint me with their climax. I want to stain their lips with my own, and I want everyone to know they're mine.

"Are you ready, Dove?" Zane asks, his lips moving across my neck and shoulders as I nod. Brax manages to pause his thrusts for a moment as Zane lines himself up, and I choose to distract myself and the anticipation building inside of me with a cock in my mouth. Creed is the lucky winner and I swallow him to the back of my throat as I groan, a mixture of pain and pleasure rippling through me as Zane slowly breaches my tight hole with his length.

My eyelids close, my mind filled with nothing but sex as the world slips away, leaving nothing but the different touches against my skin. The bite of Brax's fingers at my ribcage. The fullness at my core and the tantalizing feel of both cocks inside of me rubbing against my sensitive walls. The heat on my tongue from Creed's needy cock. The drop of pre-cum spilling from Eldon's cock in my hand.

When Zane is fully seated inside of me, his cock as

deep as possible, I take a second to catch my breath. Then the need to move overwhelms me.

"Use me," I plead before sucking Creed back down, and my wish is their command.

Brax fucks me relentlessly and Zane quickly falls into tandem with him, ensuring I'm filled at every moment. Creed's fingers tangle in my hair as he begins to fuck my mouth, hitting the back of my throat with every thrust while Eldon pulls his cock from my hand, tugging at his length himself before he comes all over my face. Warm ropes coat me, a drop landing on Creed's dick, and I get just a hint of his climax before I'm chasing my own.

Every muscle in my body coils tight, squeezing around each of the men consuming me. The world tips sideways, everything unraveling in slow motion as wave after wave of pleasure consumes me. My nerves are frazzled, my body thrumming with euphoria.

Creed is the first to fill me, his cum coating my tongue as I swallow every drop of him, his groans encouraging me every step of the way. The second he moves back, I fall onto Brax's chest, unable to hold myself up any longer, and he bands his arm around me, holding me in place with my head on his shoulder as he plows into me again and again.

My pussy still milks him for all he's worth, finding an extra few waves of my climax to chase as he whispers in my ear. "That's it, Shadow. Make me come." The last word is all but a snarl as he does just that, and Zane starts to chant from behind me.

Completely spent, I can barely keep control of my breathing. I'm sure I'm about to pass out as they both retreat from my body, leaving me a quivering mess. I feel more delirious than I have ever been in my whole life until Creed brushes a tendril of hair back off my face.

"So, about food—"

I interrupt before he can say anything else, my eyes pinging wide as I become more alert.

"Clean me up first. Then you can feed me."

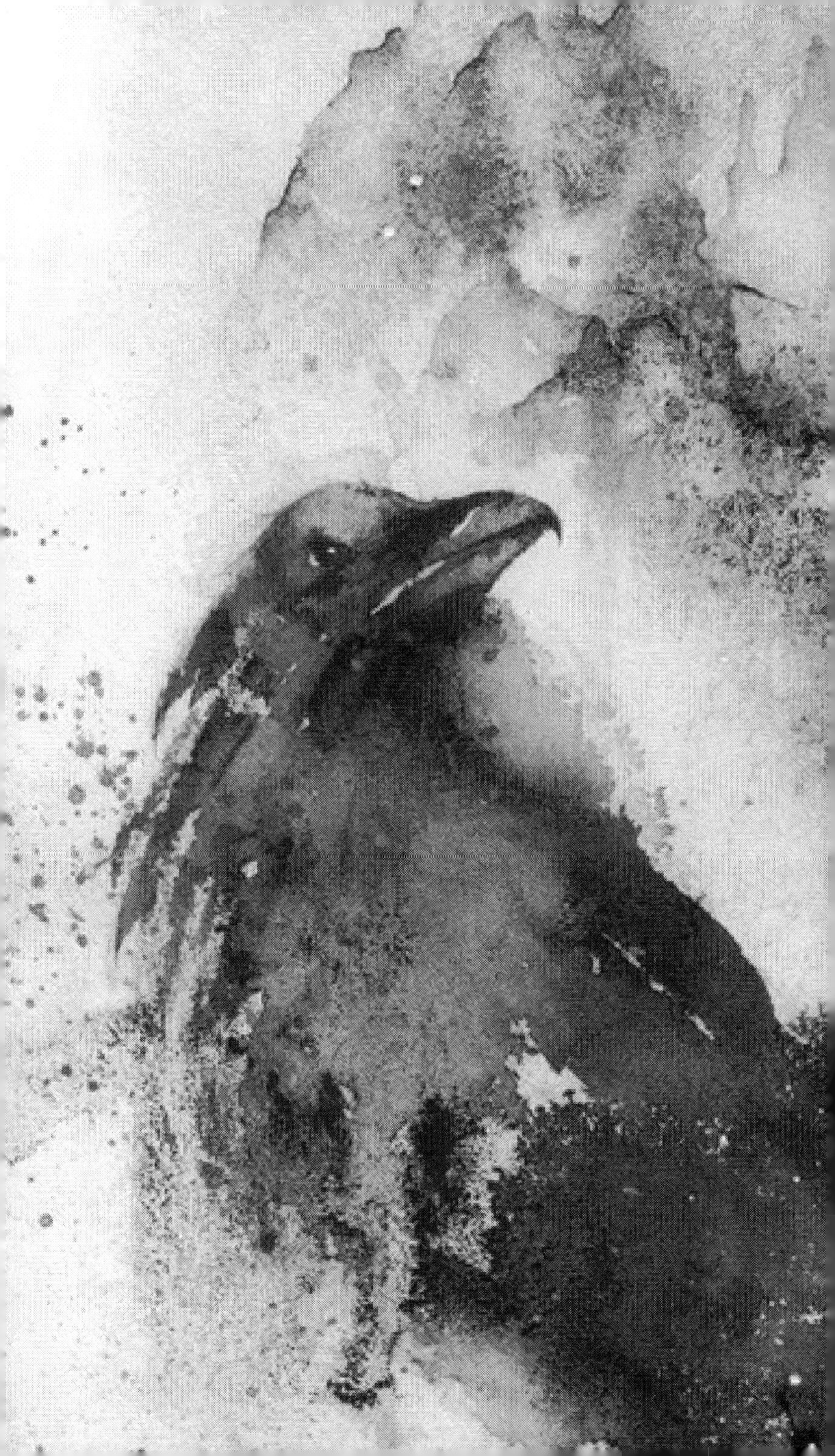

THIRTY FOUR
Raven

My fingers glide over the black, shimmering rhinestones and crystals that cover my dress. A shiver runs down my spine and my core clenches at the memory of the last time I wore it. Does it really count as wearing it if I tried it on for a brief moment before my men shattered my body and wrung me dry?

This time, at least, I'll be wearing the ensemble for a little while longer. I've opted to wear a pair of black peep-toe heels, smokey eye makeup with a deep red lipstick, and my hair braided back into a chignon with a few loose tendrils framing my face.

The store also had a matching black rhinestone purse, which I snatched up. Not that I made eye contact with the girl as she recommended it; I was too busy riding the afterglow wave and I didn't want to spoil my fun by worrying if she heard or not.

A knock sounds from my bedroom door, and before I can answer, it swings open and Zane peeks his head around the frame. His hazel eyes pierce mine and his tongue slips out as he takes me in.

"Fuck, Raven."

Slowly walking toward him, I smile. "If you're offering for us to stay here and do that instead, I'm all in."

"I wish," he mutters, opening the door further as I approach. "But my father already reached out through the shell to make sure I was on my way."

"Shell?"

"Yeah, the emergency communication," he explains, pointing over his shoulder like that explains it all. "Weren't you given one too?"

I frown, thinking back to when I got here, but I definitely don't recall being given one. Is Abel a member of The Monarchy? Technically, but he's not a Monarch. All I got was a spoonful of my father's bullshit followed by an envelope from Lyra with my new life inside it. But I remember tipping the contents of that out too and there was nothing there.

"Um, no. I don't think so." I wave him off at the same time Eldon hollers my name from the lounge.

"Ready?" he asks when I come into view, and I shake my head.

"No, do you want to stay here with me instead?" I pout, hoping it will work, but the second he shakes his head at me, I know I'm not getting out of this.

"Come on. Let's go. The quicker we get there—"

"The quicker we can leave. I know," I interrupt with an eye roll, and he reaches for my hand, halting me in place before I can make it to the door.

"What I was going to say was the quicker we get there, the quicker we can say goodbye to these unwanted guests and come home so I can fuck you straight into next week. Sound good?" His thumb runs over my knuckles, sending a jolt of electricity through me.

"Yeah."

"Good. Now, get that hot ass in the carriage. I want every fucker there tonight to know that you're ours. Well, *mine* at least," he adjusts with a grin as he grips my hand tighter and leads me to the waiting carriage.

Brax is already outside, his strong, wide frame outlined by the limited moonlight. Creed rushes out a step behind us, along with Zane, and it's not until we're all seated in the carriage that I realize they're all wearing the exact same outfit: black suits with crisp white shirts, black ties, and black shoes.

It's crazy how they can all wear the same thing yet look completely different. Brax still looks like he's about to unalive someone. He'll just look delicious as he does it. Zane looks like he's about to address a damn nation, while Eldon looks one smirk away from dropping every girl's panties in all his playboy glory. Creed, on the other hand, looks deep in thought, like the words to a fairytale or folklore song are being crafted in his beautiful mind.

I'm lost in my appreciation for my men as we travel, arriving at the main academy building all too soon, and I instantly regret not pep-talking myself on the way here instead of ogling the goodies on display.

Brax exits the carriage first, offering me his hand as he steps out, which I take with a murmured thanks.

"I'm nervous about my parents being here," I add without prompt, but I feel like if I don't say it, it will be left building inside of my chest before I eventually explode.

"They are," Zane responds before Brax can even turn to look at me. A stone hits hard in my gut and my nerves turn to all-out anxiety.

"How do you know?"

"When my father called, he mentioned that he ensured we've all been put at an extended table. Together."

"We?"

"All of us," Brax clarifies, his hand still clutching mine as we follow the trail of other guests into the venue. I think this is the most public display of affection he's shown me that doesn't involve beating someone. I don't want to spook him, so I keep my lips shut as I look up at him, waiting for him to explain. "And our parents. It will be one big happy time." His amusement at the situation is at a zero and I'm right there with him. But if Rhys is there, I'll feel a little safer, I'm sure.

The crowd proceeds inside until we appear at the same double doors that lead to the ballroom where the last event was held. I'm still undecided on whether the events here are a good idea. The last time I was inside these four walls, I was definitely overwhelmed by my parents and brother, but once we got out of here… that ended up being a night of a lot of firsts between me and my men.

If that's the same selection on the menu tonight, then maybe an hour or so with unwanted family members might be bearable.

"Did your father know if Burton will be here?" I ask, and Zane shakes his head. We should assume he'll be here, but since he's been completely absent the past few days, we can't be certain.

"We can only assume, but there hasn't been anything mentioned."

After hearing Sebastian's conversation with Erikel, or the little we did, at least, we've been searching for Burton ever since. I haven't heard or seen Lyra either, which has me even more concerned. I've even spoken to Fitch, but still, there's been nothing. I just couldn't bring myself to give the details to him. I don't know why. I want to see

Burton. No one else will do unless he doesn't show up today, then we're going to need options. Like Rhys, he'll help us.

I hope.

Speaking of the man, it's like he heard his name in my thoughts and summoned himself. He's waiting by the doors, talking with two men and a woman I haven't seen before, but they look to be hanging from his every word. I have to remember this man is very high up within The Monarchy, highly regarded, and a big influence. It's weird that he's all of those things while also being Zane's father and my most recent savior when my parents were being… themselves.

Maybe tonight might work out well for me to have a moment alone with my mother to understand her side of things. She clearly wasn't happy with what Abel was doing, but why wasn't she openly stopping it? What don't I know? What can't I see?

"Raven… are you okay?" Rhys's voice pulls me from my thoughts. I hadn't realized I'd zoned out. I hadn't even paid attention to the fact that we stopped.

"I'm fine, sorry. I'm all up in here when I should be more alert," I admit, tapping my temple, and an understanding smile spreads across his face.

"It's understandable. Do you all want to follow me?" He takes off, side by side with Zane, without another word, and I squeeze Brax's hand tighter for support. Creed steps up to my free side, placing his hand on the small of my back while I feel Eldon's presence right behind me.

I spot the table from a mile away and internally cringe. It looks huge and obnoxious in the center of the room, right between the podium that's been set up and the entry doors. It's like everyone else's seats have been placed around it. It's commandeering the whole room and it's all my fault with my batshit crazy parents and their drama forcing Rhys to take these measures.

My mother notices me first, her smile spreading from cheek to cheek when she sees me. She's up from her seat and darting the remaining steps between us in the blink of an eye, enveloping me in her arms a moment later.

Her hold is so tight, I'm short of breath, and I find myself hugging her back just as strongly as a weight is lifted from my shoulders.

"My darling girl," she breathes against the side of my head, rocking me slightly from side to side.

"Mama," I whisper, hating that I still lean on her despite everything she's kept from me, all the secrets she's been hiding. But no matter what, her arms are always comforting, and that must mean something, I'm sure.

Leaning back, she glances from Brax to Creed then over my shoulder to Eldon with a smile. "I've been hearing a lot about everything going on. Even Professor Burton came by. He mentioned you have a familiar, Raven. A familiar! That's amazing, and a griffin no less. Unbelievable. How are they?"

"He's great, thank you." As much as he's not all that great, I don't want to get sidetracked with another one of my issues when she holds the secrets to another. "We must talk, Mama. There's so much I don't understand."

She cups my cheek, a sadness darkening her eyes as she nods softly. "Soon, my love. For now, let's be the fake-ass chirpy Hendrixes, agreed?"

My eyes widen in surprise. "Did you just say fake-ass, because that's… are you even my mother?" Her chuckle wraps around me, warming my heart. By soon, I hope she means tonight because I can't keep waiting. I try to clarify that fact with her, but she's already dragging me toward the table.

Glancing over my shoulder, I find Brax, Creed, and Eldon all staring at me with concern etched into their features. I force a smile, but it does nothing to their stance as they reluctantly follow after us, greeting their own families.

I startle when my mother pulls out the seat between her and Abel, nudging me to take it. My nostrils flare with annoyance as I do, my father's presence on my left stiffening my spine, but if he notices, he doesn't seem to care.

"Raven, how are you?" I turn to him with a stone face, which makes his smile spread wider. "Professor Burton was talking about how you have a familiar now. A—"

"Griffin, yeah, I'm aware. What should I expect from you with regard to that? Are you going to steal him? Hurt him? Use him as a weapon?" I cock my brow, not wanting to deal with his bullshit, and for once, the smile on his face slips.

"Raven, that's not what—"

"That's not what, *Papa?*" I bite, not caring that I'm cutting him off after everything.

He sighs heavily, leaning back in his seat with a hint of defeat slumping his shoulders forward, and that's when I remember Sebastian is sitting on the other side of him. My pointed stare turns into a glare that he returns. Good. The feeling's mutual.

"Raven, dear, how are you? I told Rhys that we wanted to be close to you so we could chat, but it seems men don't really listen," Eldon's mother says with a chuckle as the chatter around us gets louder. "We really must plan a ladies' day. The three of us. Me, you, and Evangeline. It's been too long."

That... actually sounds like a good idea. My mother alone with no interruptions or unwanted listeners? Yes, please.

"Count me in," I reply, smiling wide as servers approach

the table offering out drinks. Glancing around the room, I try to see if I can spot Burton. Both of my parents have mentioned him and I would really like to discuss the fact that Sebastian was meeting with Erikel in secret.

"Have you had much interaction with the leader from the Basilica Realm?" my father asks, his voice lower than usual, and I whip around to face him, expecting him to be deep in conversation with Sebastian, but to my surprise, it's me he's looking at.

My eyebrows pinch in confusion, but as much as I don't want anything to do with this man, intrigue forbids me from stopping the conversation. "Erikel?" I clarify, just to be sure, and he nods.

"Very little. He was in one of my classes the other day, but otherwise, only at the gathering announcing his arrival." I let the fact sink in, and I'm sure I'm seeing things when I see him sigh in what looks like relief. Surely not. "Why?"

"Why what?" he asks. The shutters quickly fall back into place on his face and I sense Sebastian looking between us.

"Why would you ask that?"

"No reason," he murmurs, reaching for the glass in front of him. It's a murky brown color and strong if the grimace on his face is anything to go by.

If he's going to try and leave me in the dark, I can direct

the conversation elsewhere if necessary. "What about you, Sebastian? Any interactions with the Basilica guests?"

The corner of his mouth lifts in a sneer, like he would love nothing more than to set me on fire, but instead, he attempts to be civil. "None. Why would I waste my time with lowlifes like that?"

"Sebastian, you mustn't say that," Mama interjects, and he glares.

"You lost the right to tell me what must and mustn't be said a long time ago," he grunts, snatching the glass from Papa's hands and downing the rest himself.

Well, this is going to be an eventful night. I'm sure of it.

Glancing around the table with wide eyes, I send silent, pleading looks to each of the Bishops sitting around the obnoxious space, watching my family drama unfold. I might be asking for whatever was in my father's glass at this rate.

"Good evening, everyone." My head spins to the podium where Professor Burton stands. "Before the food is served, I wanted to say a few words." The room goes quiet, all of the chatter around us coming to a stop as he holds everyone's attention. "As I'm sure you're all aware, we are gathered this evening to celebrate our surprise guests from the Basilica Realm. Erikel, Ruler of the Basilica Realm, and a select few of his students from Shadowgrim

Institute." He continues on about how fabulous it's been to entertain them all week and I start to drown him out when my focus shifts to my father, who seems to be leaning incredibly close to me.

"Raven," he mumbles under his breath, making me freeze. Of course, he chooses this moment to throw something at me, I should have fucking known. "Raven," he repeats when I don't give him attention quick enough or acknowledge his existence.

Desperate to get him to shut up, I glare at him out of the corner of my eye, enough for him to see the deathly stare. "What?" I hiss, my body locked and ready for whatever crap he's going to throw at me.

He leans in closer, pausing a beat before he speaks. "Just know that for every ounce you hate me, I love you ten times more."

Just... what?

I frown, my pulse ringing in my ears as I turn to face him head-on, but he's focused on the podium. My mother taps my thigh, trying to get my attention, but I'm stuck in place.

Why did he say that?

What the fuck does that mean?

My breath comes in short, sharp bursts as I begrudgingly turn back to the podium in time to see Erikel approach Burton. "Please, a few words from our guest of honor,"

Burton insists, taking a step back to give him all of the spotlight.

"Thank you so much for having us," Erikel says with a rasp, like the words taste wrong on his tongue as he spits them out. "Coming to Silvercrest Academy has been a dream for far too long, but I'm pleased that after all this time, I'm here." His gaze scans the room, committing each and every person to memory. "But, it's with mournful news that I have to announce the gem that is Silvercrest Academy, and its surrounding city, will no longer stand so tall and bright among the darkness."

I sit straight and stiff in my seat, hanging off of his every word. Each of my men glance my way from across the table, uncertainty and confusion flickering in their eyes as it does in mine.

"I'm sorry, Erikel. Whatever do you mean?" Burton asks, politely stepping forward with a light chuckle. A glint of silver flashes between him and Erikel and a moment later, Burton screams in agony.

We watch in horror as Professor Burton's blood runs crimson down the blade as he falls forward, the sword slicing through him even more as gasps and screams ring throughout the room.

I'm on my feet before I even realize it, kicking my heels off without a passing thought, but when I get both feet on the ground, I'm suddenly locked in place, unable to move.

Panic kicks in as I stare at a manic Erikel, laughing down at his victim before turning his attention to his audience.

"Friendly visits are for friends. I am not, nor will I ever be, a friend, companion, or ally of the Elevin Realm." I try to take a deep breath as his words unravel. Whatever lies he's twisted up in are rushing to fill the room now, to his delight. "The only reason we're here is for control and power. A war, if necessary." His cloak drops to the floor, spilling over Burton with complete disregard, to reveal the same outfit underneath that his students are also wearing.

Arms out wide, he takes a deep breath and hollers at the top of his lungs; at the same time, the magic holding me in place is lifted. "Bring in the Battalions!"

Doors crash open with a boom from behind as hysteria echoes around us. Soldiers storm the room, led by a giant of a man dressed in golden armor with copper and crimson stains. Black eyes consume the room, instilling fear into every person present. Every person but one.

I know those eyes. I know them without a doubt. Gasping over my shoulder, I seek out my quiet and observant love as one word passes his lips.

"Father?"

AFTERWORDS

Wow, I don't even know where to begin. Since I started writing this book, so much in my life has happened and changed. A very close family member is now a stroke survivor. I know more about strokes now than I thought was possible, but our gal is strong, and her strength allowed me to find the words to continue writing this book.

Lord help you all with book three because my fierce Nan, the Linda who does all of the Linda-ing in the Emerson U Series, is currently very ill, and again her strength is MAKING me keep writing.

All I can say is, surround yourself with strong women who believe in building each other up, it changes your world. I hope that one day people will say this about me.

I want to be a cheerleader for everyone, I want to rev you up, even on my worst days. I want to see the world smile.

I'm not going to lie, this ending... wasn't the ending outlined for this book, it wasn't even meant to be a part of this series haha but my fingers just started moving and I had no control over any of it. I blame Creed and those dreamy onyx eyes. Or maybe I blame Brax, because... well, it's Brax haha

Truly, from the bottom of my heart, thank you for

being here, and thank you for the silent strength you give me every day to give you the best version of myself, even when the world would rather I didn't.

My heart is full.

Here's to Cursed Shadows, coming January 2024

THANK YOU

Thank yous from me always go like, thank you Michael, thank you kids, thank you alphas, thank you betas, thank you Kirsty, thank you covers, thank you interiors. I'm spreading all of the thank yous in all of the places lol because I'm grateful for every single person that graces me with their presence, talents, and shoulder to lean on. I love you all and you know it, and if you don't hit me up and I'll remind you.

But, for this one book, my biggest, wholehearted thank you is to the man I get to call my husband every day.

Michael.

The world was stacked against us, and yet we rose up. We're a team, we always have been. Whether that was operating as passing ships in the night, supporting our family, and putting our time on hold to raise two beautiful children, or trying to piece together a flatpack box from Ikea.

It's you and me.

But nothing has shown me that more than the past few months.

After a phenomenal two weeks in Florida, your mum had a stroke. Wordlessly, I filled your shoes wherever necessary, making sure that between us we reached 100%

as parents, family, friends, and spouse.

A calm before the storm blew over us for a week or two, and now my nan is in Critical Care. Wordlessly once more, as a team we're reaching 100% as you squeeze your size 10's into my little size 5's.

I can face any storm when I'm with you.

But one day, we'll get to enjoy the sea breeze and sunsets with a cocktail in hand as we smile at the world.

Keep smiling, handsome.

Thank you

xx

ABOUT KC KEAN

KC Kean began her writing journey in 2020 amidst the pandemic and homeschooling… yay! After reading all of the steam, from fade to black, to steamy reads, MM, and reverse harem, she decided to immerse herself in her own worlds too.

When KC isn't hiding away in the writing cave, she is playing Dreamlight Valley, enjoying the limited UK sunshine with her husband, children, and furbabies, or collecting vinyls like it's a competition.

Come and join me over at my [Aceholes Reader Group](), follow my author's Facebook page, and enjoy Instagram with me on the links below.

ALSO BY KC KEAN

Ruthless Brothers MC
(Reverse Harem MC Romance)
Ruthless Rage
Ruthless Rebel
Ruthless Riot

Featherstone Academy
(Reverse Harem Contemporary Romance)
My Bloodline
Your Bloodline
Our Bloodline
Red
Freedom
Redemption

All-Star Series
(Reverse Harem Contemporary Romance)
Toxic Creek
Tainted Creek
Twisted Creek

(Standalone MF)
Burn to Ash

Emerson U Series

(Reverse Harem Contemporary Romance)

Watch Me Fall

Watch Me Rise

Watch Me Reign

Saints Academy

(Reverse Harem Paranormal Romance)

Reckless Souls

Damaged Souls

Vicious Souls

Fearless Souls

Heartless Souls

Silvercrest Academy

(Reverse Harem Paranormal Romance)

Falling Shadows

Destined Shadows

Cursed Shadows

Unchained Shadows

Printed in Poland
by Amazon Fulfillment
Poland Sp. z o.o., Wrocław